GOLDEN QUEST

Order this book online at www.trafford.com
or email orders@trafford.com

Most Trafford titles are also available at major online book retailers.

Second printing
May 2009

Printed in Victoria, BC, Canada.

ISBN: 978-1-4251-0468-9 (Soft)

Our mission is to efficiently provide the world's finest, most comprehensive book publishing service, enabling every author to experience success. To find out how to publish your book, your way, and have it available worldwide, visit us online at www.trafford.com

Trafford rev. 12/23/2009

www.trafford.com

North America & international
toll-free: 1 888 232 4444 (USA & Canada)
phone: 250 383 6864 • fax: 812 355 4082

This novel is dedicated to my dear friend Esther Hirabayashi and my grandson, Kai Ihara. One of you chose a multi-cultural life and the other was born to it. You are both so blessed!

The inclusion and victimization of New York City in this story was written before the terrible events of 11th September 2001. There is a natural coincidence between my choice and that of the real-life terrorists because New York is the ultimate symbol of the American way of life. Thus, any assault on New York is, symbolically, an attack on America itself.

JW

Thanks to Nadien Cole of Nadien Cole Advertising for technical assistance and jacket design.

n.cole@shaw.ca

0930 hrs. 21st June 1990. West Germany.

According to the attending coroner's assistant, the corpse found on the banks of the River Weser downstream from Bremen had been deceased for several days and the man had likely been dead before he went in the water. This initial pronouncement at the scene was received by Kriminalpolizei Inspector Helmut Neinscheer with a grunt of displeasure. "Fifty thousand marks a year we pay that asshole just so he can tell us a man covered with cigarette burns, pulled fingernails and broken toes, bruised all over and with his throat cut, did not die in the water. What have we come to, Baumgarten?" The tall gangly figure in the rubberized raincoat looked at his assistant, Sergeant Baumgarten, as if he should have some divine answer to the mysteries of bureaucracy.

Baumgarten, a dedicated and successful evader of blame, turned his dark, sleekly-combed head back and forth with the dejected innocence of the outsider, who, excluded from membership, forever peers inward through a fogged window. He vouchsafed no word. Neinscheer had given up trying to bait Baumgarten months ago, but once in a while the devil still rose within him.

They stood in the drizzle, watching the van taking away the bagged corpse, wanting to go home, yet unwilling somehow to climb into the relative comfort and dry haven of their police car. "Interesting, though, the SS number tattoo. Shall I put in a request with Bonn to get a name?" Baumgarten finally broke his silence.

"Some of the scheisskopf skinheads have taken to getting themselves tattooed like that, but this one looked old enough to be genuine. Yes, someone there can go through the old records and give us an identity. Perhaps we'll request dental records too, if any, to be sure. Pity though."

Despite his reticent nature, Baumgarten could not help himself. "Pity what?"

"Pity the river wasn't full of ex-Schutzstaffel corpses."

"This sinister individual will lead our country into the abyss and our nation into an unprecedented catastrophe." Extract of letter from General Erich von Ludendorff, prominent Wehrmacht General of 1914-1918 War, to President Hindenberg of Germany, commenting on Adolf Hitler's appointment as Reichkanzler in 1933.

8th April 1945. Berlin, Germany.

Reichminister of Propaganda Dr. Josef Goebbels beat his fists with rage on his desk. "One could tear one's hair when one thinks that the Reichsbahn is having an Easter holiday while the enemy is looting our entire stocks of gold," he yelled at his staff.

His frustration was justified. As a consequence of a February third bombing raid on Berlin, which had severely damaged the Reichsbank, he had opposed the decision of Reichsbank President Dr. Walter Funk to move all the gold reserves of the Third Reich to a better place for safekeeping. Goebbels had not wanted the gold to leave Berlin. Funk had been partially correct, however, in that the enormous treasures deposited in the Reichsbank vaults were no longer secure. Heavy bombing and the growing threat from the Eastern and Western fronts made looting or capture almost inevitable. The Third Reich was assailed from all sides and soon Germany might be overrun.

By February eighteenth, the transfer had been effected. One thousand million paper Reichsmarks, a considerable amount of jewellery, gold coins and valuable artifacts, along with one hundred tons of gold worth two hundred million dollars American had been shipped and stored in the Kaiseroda potassium mine near Merkers in Thuringia.

Now, only a little over a month later, American forces under command of General George S. Patton had crossed the Rhine and threatened capture of Merkers. Fearing losing the treasures stored there, Reichsbank officials frantically tried to fetch them back to Berlin. They were thwarted primarily by the lack of available rolling stock to effect rail transportation because the German railway system, the Reichsbahn, was having an Easter holiday.

In light of the priority of the task, it being wartime, the totalitarian nature of Nazi Germany and the urgency made implicit by the nation's impending collapse, it was incredible that people should be taking holidays. Goebbels was rightly upset because on this day he had been advised that only ten percent of the stored bullion had been safely removed, the rest had fallen into American hands.

Turning to his diary, he entered his displeasure, darkly ending with the comment, directed at Funk and his Reichsbank staff, that *"...by criminal dereliction of duty they have allowed the German people's most treasured possessions to fall into enemy hands. If I were the Führer I should know what now has to be done,"* he wrote.

However, Goebbels was wrong on several counts. Where Hitler might have initiated, or approved deadly retaliation in previous years, he was now a defeated, worn-out shell, contemplating suicide and taking the German people with him. Demented, still preaching victory, he lived in a surrealistic world, trapped in his Berlin bunker as the Allied armies closed in on him.

Far from being arrested or worse, within days, Reichsbank President Funk, Chancellor Secretary Hans-Heinrich Lammers and others were back in the Reich Chancellery bunker, persuading Hitler to authorize a further ex-Berlin shipping of the just-retrieved reserves plus others distributed throughout Germany. The intent was to transport the treasure to Bavaria for safekeeping. Hitler, worn out, finally gave reluctant agreement after tough argument.

Goebbels was also morally wrong in assigning ownership of the gold to the German people. It was in their possession, but rightfully belonged to others, namely raped nations and people exterminated in the concentration camps who had fallen in thrall to the Nazis. Additionally, Funk and his adherents were merely following the example of the Schutzstaffel and others who had been shipping Nazi gold out of Germany for months. The Nazi beast was dying and the jackals were stripping away the tasty morsels and running off with them, often for personal use.

10th April 1945. Kinder Schlossen Akademie, ApfelStrecht, Berlin.

Gottlieb Demsch stamped his cold feet and sticking a thumb under the sling, re-shouldered his Mauser rifle. He was cold and damp because a fine drizzle had been falling since about midnight. Sentry duty, he had found, was the same whether in France, Poland, Russia or Germany. It was invariably cold, often wet, and thoroughly depressing. The early hours were the worst and the faintest light of dawn creeping through the Berlin sky did little to cheer him. The old shrapnel wound in his left shoulder ached, as it always seemed to do now when it was cold. A mug of brown liquid passing for coffee had been a welcome break two hours ago but now it was just a dim memory, lurking fitfully in his bladder.

He had a square, boyish face beneath his cap, but close scrutiny revealed aging lines and minor scars etched by the experience of an infantryman who had seen much action. Webs of fine care lines spread from the corners of his pale blue eyes. A broad nose hovered over a straight mouth, which could deceptively twitch with good humour at any time. Now, however, his morale at low ebb, he fell to depressing thoughts. On all fronts, the Wehrmacht was in full retreat. The Americans were over the Rhine and the Russians were only fifty kilometres away. He wished he could desert and surrender to the Americans, but members of the fanatical S.S. were everywhere. Already lampposts and trees, even in the Unter den Linden, were decorated with the hung corpses of soldiers executed for desertion. To be caught without iron-clad papers away from your unit was to risk summary judgment and instant execution.

That thought took him to Ilse. He had been wounded first in France, in nineteen forty, and then, after taking a bullet which broke his left arm in Russia, expected repatriation. It was a false hope since manpower was so scarce and he had been reassigned to garrison duty in Berlin with the Ninety Second Reserve regiment. Ilse was older than Gottlieb, with two children; widow and orphans to a Luftwaffe officer. She had become his mistress because he could provide rations from his allotment to keep the family alive. He had known she did not care for him the way he cared for her, but he too needed someone to hold in the dark hours, some relief from the horrors and night phantoms of war. She had endured the growing demands of his young sexual awakening on a filthy mattress in the cellar of a bombed-out house, knowing the children listened to her humiliation. Yet he could not help himself, any more than could she.

Now, Ilse was dead. Several cans of food, blasted into the gutter from a store by bombing had been too much temptation and she had been shot on the spot for looting. The children, in the midst of the lost-war mayhem, and the unquestionable demise of organized government, had been sent for *"adoption into a suitable National Socialist home"*. Thus the farcical bureaucratic wheels, the Nazi fantasy of continuum ground on inexorably, dominating everyone's lives.

That had left him really alone. His parents had been dead for a year, killed in an air raid on Essen. Gottlieb had little regard for the Third Reich. As a child, membership in the Hitler Youth had only left him feeling threatened. The early successes of the war had not enthralled him for he remembered the scorn of his father directed at *'Corporal'* Hitler. Varti had been a captain on the staff of von Ludendorff himself in the last war and he, along with his old General, had predicted the calamity which was now befalling the German people. Perhaps it was as well the old man was dead; he would have found no satisfaction in being right. Gottlieb felt no loyalty to Hitler's Germany. It had cost him not only good comrades' lives, but also his parents, his lover and his brother. He himself seemed fated to suffer the enduring physical effects of his wounds. These he would otherwise not have suffered had the Nazis avoided taking the German people into this mess.

Gottlieb was plucked from his reverie by the sound of diesel engines outside the high wall of the schoolyard where he stood guard and suddenly, two trucks turned into the gate. From the first one, a figure in the black uniform of the S.S. emerged and marched resolutely up the steps. It was a Standartenführer and he paused in front of Gottlieb with the bored arrogance of the invincible.

"Ist hier das Gefechtsstand des zweiundneunzigsten Regimentes?"

It was a puzzle why such an important officer would be seeking the field office of his humble Ninety Second Regiment, but Gottlieb knew better than to give even a sniff of imagined insult to a Colonel of the Schutzstaffel. Going rigidly to attention, he peered over the officer's shoulder so as not to cause offence.

"Jahwol, Herr Standartenführer!"

Without another glance, the man thrust past Gottlieb. Moments later, a Kubelwagen drove into the yard and parked at the foot of the steps. The driver and his companion were both S.S. and they lit cigarettes and sat waiting with nonchalance. Gottlieb was glad for this for if they came up the steps, he would have to challenge them. As an Unterscharführer, he had risen to Hitler's rank of the last war, but he knew he did not want to have to challenge these men.

Behind him inside, he could hear the Standartenführer talking loudly to Feldwebel Schwenke, his section leader. The drivers from the trucks got down from their vehicles and clustered around, handing out cigarettes to each other. From one of the vehicles came a hacking cough and Gottlieb began to panic. There were obviously more men out there than he could identify or cope with and it made him nervous.

Moments later, the S.S. Colonel came out and without any acknowledgement of Gottlieb's parade ground salute, climbed into the Kubelwagen which promptly pulled out of the yard and disappeared.

At eight o'clock, Gottlieb was relieved and he went inside to report to Schwenke. "So what did the Totenkopf straight-back want, Otto?" The fat warrant officer, his arse hanging over the sides of the chair looked up at him in distaste. Whether it was the insubordinate reference to the S.S., or the lack of respect for Schwenke's own rank made little difference to Gottlieb.

"He wants *you*, Demsch!" The Feldwebel saw a flicker of fear in Gottlieb's eyes and it gave him an idea of how to get rid of this scheisskopf. "Yes, Demsch, he has a purpose for you. God knows, somebody must have one." The podgy fingers grabbed a huge rubber stamp and pounded it into an inkpad. He punctuated his next words by banging the stamp onto documents in front of him. "Here you are"...Thud..."Papers for you and"...Thud... "Three men I have selected"... Thud..."To go on"...Thud..."Special assignment."

He gathered a sheaf of papers. "Here, orders signed by an exalted member of the Reichssicherheithauptamt, assigning you and your three arschloch friends Streicher and Stowaski and Beckmann, to Standartenführer Mannheimer for special service. Pack your kit, you're leaving Berlin." Schwenke's piggy eyes gleamed in satisfaction as he proffered the papers. In a flash of inspiration, he had rid himself of four troublemakers.

Gottlieb, for his part, looked at the Feldwebel in disgust. The man was a disgrace, taking favours and payments from his men to spare them duties they wanted to avoid. His billet was full of contraband cigarettes, crumpled marks and brandy that he used to trade in the black market. With these riches, any woman within twenty kilometres would spread for him and the fat greasy bastard knew it.

"The trucks outside, Demsch. They will be staying for the day. Find a place in this rat hole for the drivers to sleep today and place a guard on the truck, which has twelve prisoners in it. They will not be allowed out of the vehicle by order of the Standartenführer!" He added the order just as Gottlieb opened his mouth to protest. "You will be leaving tonight with them."

"Where are we going?"

"Straight to the Russian front, I should hope. Get your sorry arse shot off. Why don't you ask the Standartenführer?"

Gottlieb turned and left. Somehow straight to the Russian front leading a unit comprising three ordinary Wehrmacht infantrymen and a corporal from a reserve unit did not seem like the game plan of an S.S. Colonel. The possibilities worried him. Still, it sounded like they would probably be leaving this death trap which was some kind of plus, so he hustled off to break the news to the only other three real soldiers in Schwenke's unit.

Berlin was still clouded over as the day wore on and only a few American planes arrived to drop bombs. He slept fitfully through the day, stressed like everyone else in Berlin by the bombing, but also by the unknown nature of the coming assignment. By nine o'clock in the evening Gottlieb had his men ready. He was worried about taking orders directly from an S.S. Standartenführer. Usually, orders from such an exalted rank were filtered down through several others. He need not have worried. When Mannheimer arrived, he was almost considerate, although remaining aloof and distracted.

"You will place two men in each truck and we will be going to pick up a special consignment and then driving to Berlin-Michendorf station to load a train."

"Where...?"

"You have no need to know. Now, get ready."

Quickly Gottlieb organized his men. The prisoners of war, Russian and Polish army men, had not been out of the truck all day and the vehicle reeked of the sanitary bucket he had ordered placed onboard. Within minutes, they were out of the courtyard, the sounds of their engines fading in the darkness.

The streets were deserted. These days, the British air force rarely missed a night, bombing blind if they had to, into the wreckage which was Berlin. This night was no different. Barely were they on their way and the sirens began to wail. Flak batteries opened up and searchlights probed the sky. Bombs began to fall and the patter of shell fragments from the anti-aircraft gun bursts became as much a hazard as the enemy's efforts. Falling from three or four miles up, the metal shards were deadly to anyone they hit.

They were frequently held up and diverted, but Mannheimer was up front in the Kubelwagen, blustering his way through. The scene was horrific. Buildings left and right were gutted and roofless, walls standing like ragged dominoes with their incendiary-bombed interiors burned out. The blank windows stared out like dead eye sockets mutely appealing their fate. Bomb-blasted walls had collapsed like waves on a beach, ramps of broken masonry slumping from them. In the light of flames, sitting in the cab of the first truck, Gottlieb could see the wreckage in great detail. A floral patterned wall on the third floor of an apartment house hung over a precipitous drop while nearby, a bathtub, supported by its plumbing, teetered centimetres from its inevitable fate. In the next room, floor joists only a half-metre long supported a wardrobe, which seemed to clutch the wall behind it. Its doors were open, revealing clothing hanging inside as if the owner would return to make a selection at any moment.

The streets were filled with rubble. Glass, charred timbers and roof slates littered their route and blackened flakes of debris floated down through the smoke. A fine mist of masonry dust penetrated the cabs of the trucks, tickling the backs of their throats and irritating their sinuses. Frequently there were the accompanying acrid smells of charred debris and the faint whiff of the dead, rotting in their collapsed houses, without rescue and abandoned. Gottlieb also discerned the familiar residual smell of high explosive.

Eventually they stopped and Gottlieb suddenly realized they were at the end of the Unter den Linden. They were drawn up at what had been the Reichsbank, now a mound of stone rubble after taking numerous direct hits by aerial bombs. Mannheimer was at the truck door, banging on it imperiously.

"Get your men up to the red board up there. Start loading the trucks."

A cluster of men stood atop the rubble near a red board, holding shielded lights. Gottlieb rolled his eyes at the thought these men were trying not to provide an aiming point for the British bombers. Massive fires visible for a hundred kilometres surrounded them and they were worried about their flash-lights. Beside the men they found a hole going deep into the bowels of the bank's vaults. In minutes, a procession of men was staggering under the weight of boxes, sacks and trunks. The bombs were still raining down and Gottlieb reflected how crazy this was, like some Wagnerian operatic Gotterdamerung in real life. At any moment he expected a fur-draped and statuesque Brunhilde to appear through the smoke, brandishing a spear and trilling damnation at the top of her contralto lungs.

For almost an hour the men laboured, stumbling and falling over the uneven debris, hauling loads a fit man might manage but under which the starving prisoners could barely cope. Eventually, Mannheimer came up and ordered everyone back into the trucks.

"We are hauling away gold?" The question burst from Gottlieb, despite his determination to say nothing.

"You do your duty and hold your tongue!" There was no mistaking the Standartenführer's stern warning.

With sighs of relief, they all piled back into their respective trucks and started off again through the ruins of Berlin. It took them forty minutes before they reached a siding by the Berlin-Michendorff railway station. In the light of burning buildings, the chain of men laboured, backs bent, to offload the trucks onto the waiting railway cars. A section of soldiers guarded the area, terrified at their exposure and venting their fears by yelling at and abusing any prisoner who did not work fast enough. There were four wagons and three rail coaches, coupled to a locomotive, steamed up, ready to go.

The prisoners laboured frantically. They needed no urging for the sooner they were done, the sooner they could escape the hell of the bombing. Nobody needed a second reminder of their danger as shell splinters had pierced the canvas roof of the prisoners' truck on the way over and killed two of them. The remaining ten had been offloaded, slipping on the bloody interior of the vehicle. Nearby, an old bomb crater fifteen metres across told of the awesome power of the bombs. The hulking wreckage of a locomotive lay tipped over on the crater rim, testimony to the explosive force.

Eventually, with their bowels puckered, they piled into the train. A group of civilians, Reichsbank personnel, Gottlieb assumed, appeared from nowhere and jumped into the first passenger carriage while the prisoners were locked in a freight wagon. Gottlieb and his men took the last passenger carriage while Mannheimer took the middle one for himself and his two men.

The locomotive crew frantically jerked levers and the giant wheels spun and grabbed, spun and grabbed at the tracks. With nerve-wracking slowness, the train pulled them to relative safety out of the station yard. A stick of bombs burst behind them almost like a farewell shot and then the darkness of the countryside fell around them.

The Nazi hierarchy had developed an almost comic-opera disregard for the state of affairs within Germany and the pronouncement that the planned trip would only take two days was made a mockery by the status of the railways. It was a given in strategy that the destruction of the railway's ability to function would cripple the German war effort. The Allies had forcefully executed this plan with interdiction bombing of junctions, bridges and every building, tower and support structure. During the day, cannon and rocket firing Typhoon fighters gleefully strafed anything that moved on the rails. The result was a catastrophic breakdown in the functioning of the Reichsbahn system.

It took five days for them to travel a bare two hundred kilometres. The sojourn in the train was one of sheer boredom, the wooden seats turning their buttocks into nerveless jelly at the hours spent on them. It was getting warm and the close confines produced the usual smells of dirty clothing, sweat and leather. Gottlieb and his men spent hours walking along the tracks, sometimes walking ahead and swinging up onto the carriages as the train slowly chuffed past them. The stops and starts were endless and for most of the days they laid up, avoiding the fighters. Once they were strafed, a nerve-wracking experience until the Typhoon broke off its attack after a short pass, probably out of ammunition.

They foraged at farms along the track because their rations gave out in no time. Seeing them approach, the inhabitants fled, happy to have them ransack their homes as long as their hoarded food supplies, buried safely, were left intact. Gottlieb reflected how it was a sad state of affairs when the once-glorious Wehrmacht stole from Germany's own hapless population. What little they did find they used, passing the scraps to the prisoners who were in dreadful straits, incarcerated in their wagon. When the wind blew the wrong way, the stench was incredible and already, at two stops, bloated corpses had been rolled out beside the tracks to rot where they landed.

12th April 1945. Underground, Kaiseroda Salt Mine, Merkers, Thuringia.

"Jesus Christ!" Although softly spoken, the expletive burst from the rigidly at-attention and saluting soldier. Wildly, his eyes swivelled left and right as he sought desperately to accept the scene before his eyes. Exiting from the rickety freight elevator were no less than five Generals and a couple of Colonels. The glint of stars on collars and helmets in the dimly lit passageway was like a galaxy of celestial lights to him.

He gulped as he recognized Supreme Commander Allied Expeditionary Forces General Dwight D. Eisenhower, then, General Omar N. Bradley of Twelfth Army Group, next to him the unmistakable General George S. Patton of Third US Army, then, Divisional Generals Eddy and Weyland. Every one of the officers clearly heard the soldier's words.

"At ease, soldier."

The Private First Class exhaled for the first time, blood thumping in his ears as the group of Generals made off down the passageway of the mine. He knew why they were here. They had come to see the treasure. He was half a mile down below the Thuringian plain in Germany, in a rock salt mine near Merkers. In the thirty kilometres of subterranean passageways, one of the caverns was of special significance. He knew, because despite the tightest secrecy, he had seen for himself its contents.

Entering the cavern known as Room Number Eight, the visiting dignitaries entered what could only be described as an Aladdin's Cave. Almost twelve thousand square feet in area, the cavern was covered half a metre deep with seven thousand bags in twenty rows, stacked three high. The bags, they were assured by their guide, contained gold bars and coins weighing two hundred and fifty tons and worth two hundred and thirty eight million dollars American. There were suitcases, trunks and boxes bulging with gold teeth fillings, gems, rings, cigarette cases and other personal wealth, looted from death camp victims.

A billion in paper Reichsmarks lay in sacks. Rembrandts, Van Dycks, Raphaels and other masters were stacked along with other priceless artworks in almost careless abandonment. Nearby caves would yield four hundred tons of documents, many of them patents for inventions worth another fortune.

Even before the awesome sight of such wealth had been brought fully home to him, General Eisenhower ordered its removal for safekeeping to the Reichsbank building in Allied-occupied Frankfurt. He also issued urgent priority orders to units known as the Gold Rush teams who were assigned the task of seeking out and recovering the financial assets of Nazi Germany as defeat overwhelmed it.

15th April 1945. Somewhere.

"We will be stopping soon and will be met by two trucks bearing loads to be put on the train. One of the trucks will then be loaded with items I shall identify, from the train. Then, you, two of your men and seven of the prisoners will board the truck to travel with me," Mannheimer stared at Gottlieb. Gottlieb could not see the point of leaving only one surviving prisoner on the train, but shrugged. The Standartenführer probably did not know or care how many of the wretches had died. He wanted seven. He would get seven.

An hour later, the train shunted onto a siding and stopped, quietly huffing steam and settling into the dull routine of waiting. They had no idea where they were. It was rumoured they were in Czechoslovakia but the last two stations they had passed had been bombed so badly that not even a sign gave a clue to their whereabouts. They remained there through the night, bored and restless.

0530 hrs. 16th April 1945.

Just at dawn, two loaded trucks arrived and the prisoners were let out of the train to transfer their cargo. The civilians on the train gathered around, enthusiastically enumerating the various boxes, sacks and trunks of contents. When both truckloads were put on the train, Mannheimer ordered the civilians to an area on the other side of the train and Gottlieb and his crew swung into action. In a short time, they took from the train twenty wooden boxes, twenty sacks and three steel boxes, the latter which Mannheimer had been keeping in his railway carriage.

From the way in which the Standartenführer hovered around the steel boxes, Gottlieb deduced they were more valuable than the other containers, which by now, he was fully convinced contained gold. The metal boxes were over a half-metre long and about thirty centimetres square. They were painted black and double padlocked. Each had a white number stencilled on the side.

Streicher and Stowaski loaded seven of the prisoners into the back of the truck and climbed in with their machine pistols at the ready to guard them. Maltreated, starving and exhausted, the prisoners presented no threat. The effort of labour seemed to them a fair exchange for being released from the confines of their terrible railcar and getting some fresh air. Gottlieb squeezed into the cab of the truck with Mannheimer, his three steel boxes, and the S.S. driver, Manfred Dorffman.

"May I be permitted to know where we are, Herr Standartenführer?"

"We are near the village of Grosskirschenhäller."

Gottlieb was grateful for the information, but received it with a little dubiousness. This business of offloading what were obviously items of great value made him nervous. Something was afoot of which he had no knowledge. Whether Mannheimer had sanction to do this or if he was committing grand theft was open to question - and threat to Gottlieb by association.

Dorffman moved smoothly through the gears of the big truck and soon they were rumbling down narrow unpaved roads through the countryside. Mannheimer was consulting a sheet of paper on his lap and giving directions. They drove for twenty minutes before turning off onto a narrower road, which took them down to a ford in a small river. There were low hills around them, heavily wooded, and the lane they followed dragged branches and foliage along the sides of the truck as they went down it. Right after the ford, they climbed a steep slope that sent Dorffman down through the gears to low. At the top of the slope, still between hills, he turned left into a field, stopping the truck just inside the high hedgerow.

Everyone dismounted and walked over to an old barn that sat about twenty metres away. Shovels were produced and inside, under Mannheimer's orders, five of the prisoners began an excavation close to a wall. The truck backed up to the door and the two remaining prisoners began to offload it.

Mannheimer insisted that a volume of earth equivalent to that of the cargo be shovelled into the back of the truck. Gottlieb could only admire the organizational capabilities of the man. The top layer of earth, with dried manure and old straw, was put aside to be replaced over the cache when it was put in place. When the truck was offloaded, Mannheimer took the two remaining prisoners round the back of the barn with shovels.

After a while, bored, Gottlieb strolled up to the entrance to the meadow where the barn stood. It was a beautiful morning, with mist just finally evaporating off the grassy open space they were in. Hills around them were heavily treed and the spot was very private. He thought how tranquil it was, no signs of war and a perfect day in the country. He unbuttoned his fly and groping for himself, began to urinate over some blackberry bushes, which grew in profusion along the side of the lane. It was almost as if as his bladder was voided, there was space within him to absorb the tranquillity of the countryside. For the first time in months, he felt at peace. Shrugging himself together again, he strolled back into the field and walked to the barn.

In the gloomy interior, the cargo had been buried. Tramped down by busy feet, the back-filled dirt floor of the barn looked like nothing was buried there. He looked around, impressed. He had spied the prisoners on his way back, assembling around the outside rear of the barn, guarded by Streicher and Beckmann. Dorffman drove past him, parking the truck in the entry to the field.

Suddenly, his reverie was shattered by the ripping fire of a Schmeisser submachine gun on full automatic. With the seasoned reaction of an experienced infantryman, Gottlieb bolted a round into his Mauser, flipped off the safety catch, and ran out the door and around the building. Despite readying the weapon, he did not expect trouble, so carried the weapon at high port as he rounded the side of the barn. He was not entirely surprised to see Standartenführer Mannheimer coming the other way, a still smoking Schmeisser dangling loosely in one hand.

"We had no further need of the Slavic Untermenschen."

The flat dismissal sat ill with Gottlieb. He had never personally witnessed it before, but here was the ruthlessness of the S.S., as he had heard.

Mannheimer released the empty magazine from the weapon and paused as if suddenly realizing he carried no replacement.

"Where are Streicher and Stowaski?"

"They are filling in the excavation back there. Go to the truck, we have to get going!"

For a moment, the two men glared at each other. Gottlieb did not like or accept what had happened and there was a suggestion here that Streicher and Stowaski were to be left behind. He found it odd, but a senior S.S. officer was hard to argue with. Shrugging, he turned and began to walk back the way he had come.

There was a thud behind him as the sub-machine gun was dropped to the ground. Then, there came the snick of metal on leather, followed by the deliberate metallic staccato of a weapon being cocked. Without even thinking, Gottlieb turned and fired. The round took Mannheimer through the breastbone, and he hung in the air for a moment before dropping the automatic pistol he had drawn. He grunted once and then pitched backwards to lie spread-eagled like a black spider on the ground.

Walking back, Gottlieb reached down and picked up the Luger. Mannheimer had meant to shoot him! He stuck the weapon into the rear waistband of his trousers, hitching up his tunic to get it in. Anxiously, he trotted to the rear of the barn to see what had happened there. He was shocked. A deep trench had been dug and slumped in it, around it, and hanging over its edge, were nine men. The seven prisoners were dead.

It was obvious that Streicher and Stowaski had been standing to one side, and that the machine pistol had been turned on them first. Streicher had taken a bullet through the throat and was quite obviously dead. Stowaski had taken two rounds, one through the chest and one through the stomach. Putting his rifle aside, Gottlieb sank to his knees and thought he felt a faint pulse. This was horrible, horrible. He remembered that Stowaski had smoked and without any sense of sacrilege, fished into the breast pocket of the soldier's uniform and took out a packet. He struck a match and lit the cigarette he had selected, but the cardboard tube drew with what tasted like goat shit, making him choke. He threw it in the hole and tried for the pulse again, but there was none.

"Very good, Herr Untershärführer. Now perhaps you can assist me, no?"

Damn! He had forgotten about the driver, Dorffman! Turning, Gottlieb stared into the muzzle of another machine pistol.

"Where is the Standartenführer?"

Gottlieb merely jerked his head to the left.

"Ah, you have disposed of him. Very good, Demsch! Now I want you to bury all these bodies, so get started! Soon I will be a very rich man, yes?"

Gottlieb stared at the S.S. private, knowing he was in a real fix. Sooner or later, Dorffman would make him go and drag the Standartenführer's body to the pit. With the Luger sticking out of the back of his trousers and the butt holding up his tunic, Dorffman was bound to see it as he followed him and either kill him immediately, or disarm him. The Luger was now his only chance. It was intended that he should be shot anyway, but not until he had acted as gravedigger.

Deliberately, he slowed the scene down. Moving steadily but slowly, turning to keep the Luger out of Dorffman's view, he dragged some of the wretched Poles and Russians to the lip of the pit and rolled them in. He knew he had to make his move before it was the turn of Mannheimer's corpse as it meant turning his back on Dorffman to go retrieve it. The Luger dug in his back ribs every time he bent over.

Too soon, it was time for Streicher and Stowaski. He had to try it with one of them, if conditions were at least favourable; otherwise it had to be the last no matter what poor opportunity it might present. Facing Dorffman, he selected Stowaski and grabbing him under his armpits, dragged him towards the hole. He faked a stumble and fell backwards, the heavy weight of the dead man falling atop him. Dorffman rolled his eyes with impatience and took his hand off the forward grip of the Schmeisser, allowing it to hang muzzle down from his right hand.

Putting his right arm behind him as if to raise himself, Gottlieb grabbed the butt of the Luger then let himself fall back. He knew the weapon was already cocked, and shielded by the body, drew it from his waistband. Thrusting the weapon out over Stowaski's lolling shoulder, he pumped off three rounds at Dorffman.

The first one took the S.S. driver through the stomach, the second through the chest as he jack-knifed, and the third went high. The machine pistol went off under the death grip and Gottlieb cringed beneath the inert corpse of Stowaski. The rounds went high and wide and suddenly stopped.

For a moment, Gottlieb lay, as he was, just thankful to be alive. He knew now he was the last surviving person in the field. After a minute, he rolled out from under the weight of Stowaski and got to his feet. He went over to Dorffman and kicked him in the ribs. The body moved but there was no response to the abuse.

The gunfire might attract attention from the locals, but Gottlieb doubted it. Somebody was having a war, but this was a secluded part of the world that wanted nothing to do with such nonsense. There was a fortune in gold buried in the barn, and eleven dead men nearby. He knew he could not go back to the train alone, even if he could find the way. He could succumb to the temptation of digging up some gold, but he could not risk the chance of being seen. There was the truck to get away in, but it could be a liability should he run into any kind of Wehrmacht, S.S., or enemy combat units. In that event, it was better he not be carrying any valuables. He could, at some future date, return in his own good time and retrieve some gold for himself. The base, opportunistic greed instinct was not in his nature but he had spent four years foraging for a living, so the thought came as no surprise.

Walking back to the hole, he rolled those prisoners who were not already in it down into the moist earth. When he got to his own men, he retrieved their identity documents, wallets and cigarettes. He did the same with Dorffman before going around and stripping Mannheimer's body of any useful items in the pockets. After dragging the Standartenführer to the edge of the pit, he took great satisfaction in kicking him into the ground. The bastard had been going to do the same to him. Fucking S.S.!

A mound of old manure was piled behind the barn and it was sprouting a profusion of nettles. Once this was spread over the backfill, the new growth would quickly disguise the grave. After mounding the dirt slightly to allow for subsidence, Gottlieb was done. All of a sudden, he felt his stomach turn over and he fell to his knees, retching bile into the dirt. The adrenaline was gone, the suppressive influence of intense activity over. Now the mind shock set in. Even in Russia, he had never come so close to being killed. That it had happened at the hands of people he should have been able to trust shocked him. These people had murdered his friends after betraying simple trust.

For a few minutes he stayed on his knees, feeling wretched. Still nobody had shown up to investigate the gunfire. He fell to thinking about his plight. As a prisoner of war, with Germany finished, he supposed he should surrender to someone, preferably the Americans. He remembered the slogan on a Berlin wall: *"Enjoy the War, the Peace is going to be terrible."*

Gottlieb had seen first-hand the deprivation of the defeated. The German people were about to take their turn to suffer. He needed an edge, a nest egg to sustain him. Only metres away lay more wealth than he could ever earn in a lifetime. He might never get back here before the site was discovered. He knew from handling the boxes that some of them must contain gold ingots and impossible to carry and disguise on his person. Others however had rattled and clinked and might contain gold coins or jewellery which would be more readily transportable, not to mention more easily converted into cash without question.

Going back around the barn, he retrieved all the shovels. Now he was thinking more rationally, he realized they were a dead give-away lying there. Throwing all but one in the truck, he went into the barn and began to dig. It took a while but after broaching one sack with the shovel blade, he filled two pockets with gold coins. As an afterthought, he sought another sack, which contained jewellery. In the aftermath of war, he knew the black market would proliferate and selling *family* jewellery to get by would be less suspicious than having gold coins. He took a handful and then carefully replaced Mannheimer's back filling.

After one more look at the inside of the barn, he went to the truck and climbed in. Wrapping the gold in some rags, he stuffed it under the seat, feeling safer without it on his person. He was not used to driving but after grating the gears some, he managed to turn into the lane outside the field. As the sound of his engine faded, the country returned to its peace and serenity. A lark sang and several fat pigeons flew down from a nearby copse to seek worms in the freshly turned earth.

1300 hrs. 13th February 1990. Shin Bet (Israeli intelligence offices) Tel Aviv, Israel.

It was a warm day in Tel Aviv. As Mordecai Bar-Havalah entered the air-conditioned relief of his office building, he was met by an excited Rebekka Cassovilich. A Sabra of Russian immigrant parents, Rebekka was a gorgeous woman with dark-flowing curly hair, magnificent beauty and a figure that made men drool. Were it not for his devotion and love for his wife, Mordecai reflected, he would, on the instant seize Rebekka and carry her away. She looked positively ravishing now; flushed and vibrant, totally unaware of the effect she was having on him.

"It's starting! *'Operation Exodus Two'*!"

"Come!" He seized her arm, alarmed at her lack of security. They worked in a sub-Directorate of the Israeli Mossad intelligence service and their duties were highly classified.

In his office, Rebekka repeated, "Exodus Two is happening!"

"Rebekka, calm down! We have been up for it and then been disappointed before. What makes you think this time is any different?"

"They have just announced a unification agreement! Free elections are coming!" she spoke triumphantly, as if he deserved his opinion quashed on the spot.

For years they had studied East Germany's Deutschland Democratic Republic, seeking its flaws, its weaknesses. They had carefully monitored the past months as the power of the government there had failed. Communist satellites of the Soviets had been collapsing like a house of cards recently. Rising protest against the Communists had strengthened but Mordecai knew that the leaders of the East German government were not only rabid Communists, but also willing to savagely preserve their form of order on the country. Accordingly, they had expected a backlash, a show of force such as Budapest in the nineteen-fifties, but none had come. In August last year, the Hungarians had opened their border to Austria and East Germans *on holiday* had fled to the West in their thousands via that route.

There had been massive demonstrations on the fortieth anniversary of the Republic on October seventh. Communist party chief Erich Honecker had been replaced by a hard liner, Egon Krenz, and Mordecai had waited for the boot to stomp. But in early November, the government had toppled and an enormous street party had taken place at Berlin's Brandenburg Gate. As a result, millions of East Germans could then freely visit the West as the Berlin Wall had been torn down. Mordecai himself had visited Berlin to witness this phenomenon with a view to possibly furthering Israeli interests in the events. Rebekka was now telling him that Communist domination of East Germany was going to be over.

Taking her notes, Mordecai settled down to draw his own assessment of events in Europe. Israel had many reasons to be interested in East German events. The collapse of Communism gave more freedom for Jews to emigrate from Europe to Eretz Israel. There were many present and future political considerations and consequences, but there was also a darker, more demanding need. War criminals and information on their whereabouts lurked protected behind the Iron Curtain. Such particular considerations were the foundations of Mordecai's section and the reason for his visit to Berlin. Exodus Two was so code-named because the collapse of the Communist Bloc would result in a second Exodus to match the nineteen forty-nine immigration into Israel which had founded the state.

Now, Mordecai's duty was to the secondary reason for elation if the German borders did indeed open. Special teams would have to be dispatched clandestinely, as soon as access was available, to retrieve any available evidence relating to Nazi war criminals. The last great triumph of the Shin Bet had been the apprehension and abduction of Adolf Eichmann. If Rebekka was right, then a new era of success was promised in Nazi-hunting, since many of them had taken refuge in East Germany. Yet Mordecai paused in his contemplation. He shared Rebekka's joy but as senior officer of the department, he kept a secret she was not privy to - yet.

The thought of it took his breath away and he excused himself, getting her to leave, before going to his safe and opening it. Inside, a slim file, old and much thumbed, came to hand. His long-deceased predecessor had placed it in the safe twenty-five years ago. Inside were three sheets of paper. The first was a handwritten letter from an American, Saul Greenspan, who had been a Captain in an infantry unit of the Third Army in the Second World War. The letter was so old it was getting flimsy:

"Dear Sirs,

As an American Jew, I fought in the Third Army under General Patton to liberate Europe. The word 'liberate' sounds grandiose unless a person visits one of the Nazi death camps and then it becomes totally inadequate. I was shocked to my very being by the sights of Dachau, which was not (reportedly!) as bad as others. I have had life-long nightmares about what I may have seen at the other places.

I know that distant relatives died in these places. They were distant enough to insulate me from their deaths, yet as a human being, let alone being a relative and a Jew, I cannot find words to describe my horror. After returning to the States, I became a successful lawyer and worked with the B'nai Brith and other organizations to try to avert a repeat of this human tragedy. I have applauded the success achieved in bringing some of these monsters to justice but weep to think of those who escaped.

My advancing years and experiences with my law practice have, I think, taught me restraint. Now that I have been stricken with cancer and do not expect to live much longer, a new perspective has overcome me how-

ever. While I was in Germany, I met a German soldier named Beckmann who may have held the key to tracking down more Nazi monsters.

Just before the war ended, he was detailed to escort a shipment from the Berlin Reichsbank to southern Germany. He believed the shipment was mostly gold and the officer in charge was a fanatical S.S. Colonel. At some point, the train they were on stopped and this Colonel, some of his comrades, and a prisoner work detail unloaded some of the shipment and made off in a truck. They were supposed to return within hours, but never did.

The soldier was left behind on the train with an S.S. soldier named Kranzler who told him that there was indeed gold taken off the train, but there were also boxes containing documentation of bullion shipments, their routings and consignees. In effect, these documents traced the escape routes, fake identities and destinations of senior Nazi officials at the highest level. I believe therefore, that retrieval of these documents will provide a great stride in bringing more Nazi war criminals to justice.

In the discussion, which followed the non-return of Colonel Mannhouser, (I think that was his name), Kranzler showed the briefcase Mannhouser had left behind, arguing that the briefcase proved he intended to return to the train and it should wait for him. Beckmann claimed he searched the briefcase while Kranzler was absent and stole a map and co-ordinates from the briefcase without Kranzler knowing. He later lost this information to an American army patrol.

I always had my doubts about this information, and besides, it probably belonged to the American military to which I owed my first allegiance. Beckmann was captured by one of my platoons and tried to bargain his way to better treatment by trading this information. I always suspected he was scamming us, but I can't be sure. He had abandoned the train shortly before it was taken over by a Soviet army unit. I am enclosing a copy of the orders under which he and his comrades were operating when these events took place.

This all may mean nothing, but in this final chapter of my life, I offer it as a legacy to my Jewish heritage.

Sincerely,"

The signature was illegible. Mordecai, for the thousandth time, put the letter down and scrutinized the next few pages which were more ancient than the letter. The first was a list of possible locations for burying a shipment transferred out of Berlin. One of the site options appeared to be placed in the cleared area of the Iron Curtain, although the exact spot was vague. So, it seemed very likely that, buried very securely in one of the most patrolled areas of the world, protected by barbed wire, minefields and automatic machine guns, there was a fortune in gold, and the documented whereabouts of important Nazi war criminals Mossad would love to get their hands on.

Agents had visited all of the listed sites, surreptitiously seeking the cache, but come up empty handed. They had even been to a place high on the plateau of the Vogtwold, trying to confirm its whereabouts. Undaunted by the Frontier fences, they had penetrated the wire, trading their safety for the prize of Nazi mass-murderers. It was however impossible to countenance retrieving the information in such an area, especially without a precise location. It would not be safer in Fort Knox. The other document in Mordecai's hand was flimsy and disintegrating, a Wehrmacht transfer order, placing four soldiers, Demsch, Streicher, Stowaski and Beckmann under the command of an S.S. officer, Mann.... A fold in the paper erased the name. A purple ink stamp with the scrawled name *Schwenke* smothered half the orders.

Mordecai nodded. His predecessor, Colonel Jakob Stapouski had sent men to talk to this Schwenke more than twenty years ago. Yes, Schwenke admitted to sending those men off. Standartenführer Mannheimer's orders (it was Mannheimer, not Mannhouser) had been authorized by Ernst Kaltenbrunner himself and could not be questioned. Despite earnest interrogation, augmented by drugs, ex-Feldwebel Schwenke, then a fat one hundred and twenty-kilo black marketeer, pawnshop owner and brothel-keeper, knew nothing more. Since the mere asking of these questions would arouse thoughts in his avaricious soul, he was considered expendable. His remains had been disposed of.

Now, with the prospect of an open border and possible reunification of Germany, the cache, if it even existed, might become accessible again. Taking the prospect further, Mordecai realized with a start that clearing of the minefield would become a priority. Minesweeping devices would be utilized to make the area safe and at the same time would reveal any metal buried beneath the soil. If Saul Greenspan was right and the truck's contents had been buried there, engineers of the East German army had laid mines all around the burial site, without detecting it. Sweeping for those mines would now reveal its presence, the detection devices going crazy over the density of the gold buried there.

As a young man, Mordecai had fought as a tank commander in the Six-Day War. He even had a flesh wound as a badge of valour, not that he saw it that way. They had been heady times, the proximity of death ignored by the indestructibility of youth. A lifetime of more mature contemplation had relived the real terror of combat and infused him with more realism. Now, he felt the gut feeling of imminent action and the heavy weight of national responsibility and the lives of his people came upon him. With the glazed eye of a man with no answers to the forthcoming questions he would spark, Colonel Bar-Havalah reached for the telephone and demanded a secure line to his superior.

16th April 1945. Vogtland, Germany.

Gottlieb Demsch drove for an hour after leaving the barn. The truck was running low on gas and he had no means of getting any fuel. He was terrified of being found by an S.S. unit. Without written orders, he would be strung up on the nearest tree if they caught him. He was worried about the gold too. If anyone apprehended him and searched the truck, he would have some serious questions to answer. In such an event, he had already determined he would shoot first. Yielding and dying was not an option anyway, but now he had all that gold back there to live for.

Reaching a quiet road junction with a group of large trees on the corner, he stopped the truck and taking a shovel, buried the gold coins between the exposed roots of a huge beech tree. There was some oilskin wrapping in the truck and he carefully wrapped and buried the documents and identities he had taken from the bodies. He added the pistol, reasoning that an infantryman would not be expected to carry an officer's weapon and it may cause him problems. It was time he disappeared. He could return later to this cache.

He drove the truck another ten kilometres until the steeple of a church announced a village ahead; and then he abandoned it. Shouldering his rifle and a packsack containing some black bread, würst and canned meat, he turned into the next field and began a cautious march westward, headed for the American line of advance. Two days later, slipping by the token action of a German infantry unit confronted by American tanks and mechanized infantry, he emerged from a ditch with his hands raised and became a prisoner of war. Relieved of his rifle, he joined thousands of fellow Wehrmacht personnel in a huge camp near Coburg.

**1530 hrs. 23rd June 1990. Upper reaches,
Rio Pilcomayo, Gran Chaco, Paraguay.**

The white-walled rambling stucco ranch house was screened on the south side by palomanto and quebrachos trees. Beyond that, a long slope of pampas gave a view of cattle dotted about for miles. Inside, the air was cool and pleasant. In a huge multilevel lounge with a brick tiled floor, a massive fireplace stood cold. A few feet to the right of the stone hearth, double doors of metal-studded dark oak barred entry to another room, supervised by a blonde man dressed in blue jeans and cowboy boots, a loose Tyrolean sweater hanging over the automatic pistol stuck in his waistband.

From behind the doors the muted mumble of a voice came faintly. The speaker was either on the telephone or his guest talked much more quietly. It was not the business of the guard to know and he did not care. Inside, two men sat, one either side of a huge, ornately carved wooden desk. The older man sat in the large high-backed chair, which matched the desk, while the other sat in a Spanish lounging chair. The room was an expensive study-library with books lining two of the walls. Behind the desk, drawn window blinds shut out the view over the grasslands outside. The third wall was covered, floor to ceiling, by a glass display case in which lay artifacts of inestimable value to the owner.

Pinned to the rear of the cream-coloured wall of the case was the complete black formal uniform of a Nazi Schutzstaffel Obergrüppenführer. A series of Nazi medals were pinned to the chest and gleaming black jackboots stood beneath while the high-peaked cap with the Totenkopf badge hung next to it. The silver double lightning flashes on the collar were in counterpoint to the golden glint of several Hakenkreuz, the Nazi swastika. The uniform and its regalia looked immaculate, like it had been worn yesterday.

Just along the wall from the uniform was a large portrait of Adolf Hitler, personally signed. An S.S. ceremonial dagger, elaborately engraved with the S.S. motto '*Meine Ehre Heisst Treue*', also hung there. Other photos and mementoes of the Third Reich filled the case, many displaying the presence of a tall lean man with blond hair in the presence of most of the leaders of the Nationalsozialistische Deutsche Arbeitpartei. The man behind the desk had the same haughty handsome features as the figure in the pictures; he was but older, with a more lined face and now totally white hair.

He fumbled with a handkerchief in his grasp, twisting it with the white-knuckled fury of a man too infirm to throw a major physical tantrum. "So, Fegelin was unable to get any more information than that?" The German words were made harsher by the barely controlled anger of the man.

The younger man, in his mid-fifties with dark hair salted with grey and a square, open face, leaned forward, anxious to please, "No, Señor, the only information he obtained was that the items were removed from the train at a siding some distance beyond Chemnitz. He said it was several hours journey beyond Chemnitz, but the train spent much of its time stationary because of the Allied bombing, so what we have is an approximate area only. Kranzler was told by Mannheimer to stay on the train. When Mannheimer did not return the next day, the train left without him and Kranzler has always assumed since that day that Mannheimer either stole the gold, or else his plan was changed. As a private soldier, he had no authority to detain the train any longer. It is reasonably certain that if the boxes were hidden, it would have to have been in the Vogtland," he referred to an area of Saxony, close to the Czechoslovakian border, south west of the Erzgeberge Mountains.

"And the briefcase?"

"It was left by Standartenführer Mannheimer on the train. That coupled with an assignment he was given had convinced Kranzler that Mannheimer proposed to return as stated, in several hours. Why would he leave it if he did not intend to return? This also supports my theory that Mannheimer came to harm. Kranzler waited until the next day to look inside the briefcase. It contained a number of written instructions to Mannheimer, giving him suitable options where to bury the metal boxes with the sacks of bullion. Route instructions along with the various coordinates were included for his assistance in completing this task. Kranzler insists there were also copies of receipts to the Reichsbank for the gold, and one to Ernst Kaltenbrunner for the metal boxes."

"Kranzler did not have this information to pass to Fegelin?"

"No, Señor. As I have explained, Kranzler left the train before it reached Bavaria. Removing the paperwork from the S.S. briefcase, he threw the briefcase away, reasoning it would be suspicious for him to have such a thing. When he was later captured by the Red Army, he discovered that the paper relating to the burial sites had disappeared, making his proposed bargaining position useless. It was ten years before he was repatriated to Germany."

"He thinks the other soldier, the Wehrmacht one, may have taken this paper?"

"Yes."

"Did Fegelin get a name, a description?"

"It must have been Reinhold Beckmann. Kranzler said the man had been eyeballing the bullion and trying to incite his friends into stealing it for days. He is a tall man, well built, with sandy hair and blue-grey eyes. His home was in Hamburg."

"All of these men must be traced and vigorously interrogated."

"We think we can find them."

The man behind the desk broke out in a fit of coughing. Racking spasmodic explosions of unrelieved exhalations came from him, the handkerchief over his mouth receiving a spray of bloodied sputum. His guest looked away, partly out of compassion, mostly out of fear. As his master's health became more tenuous, so his resolve to see his mission accomplished became more determined. The man knew the total ruthlessness and single-minded determination, which could be brought to bear to achieve results. Thousands had died at a word from the man opposite and old age had not mellowed his disposition.

"*Think* you can find them? Is that the best you can do?" the voice was even raspier now and a mouthful of water followed by a sip of brandy from a glass at hand eased the laboured speech.

"Señor, we have to assume that Mannheimer was not committing treachery and making off with the gold and the steel boxes. If he was, as we have already agreed, the whole matter is lost," the speaker paused, seeking the slight nod of agreement before proceeding. The question of S.S. officers committing treachery had, in the past, brought screeching fits of acrimony from the older man. Despite his clinging to the glory days of the S.S., and their vow of personal allegiance to Hitler, one mention of Heinrich Himmler, former Reichsführer and leader of the Schutzstaffel, could bring the old man to apoplexy. At the very end of the War, with Hitler holed up impotently in the Reichsbunker in Berlin, Himmler had sought to seek a peace with the Allies, causing Hitler himself to throw a fit, so betrayed did he feel by Himmler's treachery. Hitler had, in the old man's estimation, done the right thing and deprived Himmler of all his rank and privileges. By then it meant nothing, but the principle was preserved.

Seeing that no frenzy was imminent, the younger man continued more comfortably, "Kranzler gave us some names. In addition to seven Slavic Untermenschen, three Wehrmacht soldiers accompanied Mannheimer, plus his driver. That is twelve men total. I think it is reasonable to believe the Slavs are not part of this. Mannheimer undoubtedly intended to liquidate them anyway. Our focus should therefore be on the other four men and Mannheimer. One of them must know where the gold was buried. Since no sign of Mannheimer has been detected by our network of dedicated watchers, either he is dead, or in hiding and unable to get to the gold. Through the Swiss, we have traced almost every unaccountable source of gold deposits so there is no solid reason to believe he took any amount of gold. It is my belief that Mannheimer is dead and we should therefore concentrate on the three Wehrmacht men."

The old man nodded, encouraging further comment.

"The train was to be met by three separate shipments from regional Reichsbanks on its way south to Bavaria, thus augmenting its load. Someone, anticipating problems, had carefully planned several places along the way as possible caches. I believe information reaching Mannheimer compelled him to hide the boxes at one particular location. Perhaps he received new orders by way of the trucks that met him that morning. It is hard to say because he may have made the cache almost anywhere."

The older man nodded. "You have the Wehrmacht names?"

"Yes, Kranzler remembered - with a little persuasion," the visitor passed over a sheet of paper with four names on it.

"Hmm. Unterscharführer Gottlieb Demsch, Sturmann-Mann Wilhelm Streicher, Anwater Georg Stowaski, Anwater Reinhold Beckmann. And my original question, the area?"

"Señor, it must be close by. The repository site must be close to the tip of the Czechoslovakian border, where it sticks out into Germany," the speaker winced as his choice of words brought a grimace from the man opposite. "There is one hitch though."

"Hitch?"

"Yes. There is a huge tract of land, five hundred metres wide and hundreds of kilometres long which we cannot get access to."

"The border."

"Yes, Señor. We have barbed wire, mines, automatic and manned machine guns, armed guard patrols and watchtowers. If the site lies within its boundaries, it would explain why it has never been found. Even if someone knew the exact spot, they would not be able to get access to it. We are similarly helpless."

"Not necessarily! There are still Kameraderen living in positions of influence in East Germany. Besides, the promised free elections in the East zone have been eclipsed by Bonn calling for reunification." The idea of Germany being one again brought tears to the old man's eyes and he took a sip of brandy to hide his emotions.

"Could we risk it? Will the frontier fortifications be removed?"

The old man shrugged. "If they are, we will have access. At the same time, such action will unearth the cache. If it is there, we must be first to find it! The key lies in your finding the person or persons who know exactly where it lies. Someone knows it! Someone knows where it lies! Go out and find them! And include every person on that train in your search. Report to me as soon as possible!"

Dismissed, the guest made for the door. He had his hand on the doorknob when the voice behind him rasped again. "Joachim. I understand that Fegelin dumped the body in the River Weser and it was found."

Joachim Wesler turned slowly. "Yes Señor."

"Dead bodies attract attention. All attention is unwelcome. Why did he not dispose of it where it would not be found?" There was a depth of menace in the chill words which gripped the bowels of the listener.

"Fegelin is a psychotic, Señor. Such men like to display their work. They think they are artists."

"You tell him that if he fails me again in this way, he will be put on display himself. I will have him spread all over a salon in the Louvre. He will still be alive but unable to communicate."

"Yes Señor," the visitor shuddered, knowing the threat was entirely possible.

The private airstrip on the ranch was only a quarter mile from the house and Joachim Wesler had flown the Navajo in himself. A King Air sat in a small hangar, fuelled and ready for an immediate departure in the event the Señor's security was breached. Two of the guards were qualified on the aircraft and one of them was always on hand for such an emergency. As he walked to the airstrip, Wesler wondered how the old man had known about the disposal of the body. Although shocked, he was not surprised. The old man had lines of information unknown to others. It was a fact guaranteed to prevent disloyal thoughts.

Through all the years he had served him, Wesler had been in total awe and terror of *El Jefe*, as he was locally known. There was no *Herr Obergrüppenfuhrer*, *Heil Hitler*, Nazi salutes or heel-clicking, but you always knew it was there: the power, the ultimate authority, the iron backbone of total righteousness. It was always there, just as he remembered it as a small boy, accompanying his father who had served El Jefe both before and after they left Germany, until his death ten years ago. Joachim Wesler had taken over from his father, secure in his right of inheritance by a lifetime of indoctrination and rewards for faithful service. He knew the terrible cost which would be exacted upon him and his family if he betrayed the cause. Not that this was possible, however. Steeped in the tradition and folklore, he was almost as fanatical as the old man. Indeed, he hoped to be his heir.

He remembered now the long weeks shut up in the steel coffin of a U-Boat, crossing the Atlantic to land under cover of darkness on a South American shore, the whisper of his father in his ear. "Landfall, Joachim. And now, we start anew." That had been forty-five years ago and they were still working behind the scenes, to what end he did not fully know, but he still had faith.

Firing up the Navajo, he let the engines warm up for several minutes and then took off into the light wind from the west. Turning southeastward, he looked down on the ranch and the buildings. The grasslands seemed to stretch forever, cattle dotted around and the occasional cluster of dwellings belonging to the estancierios who tended them. Behind him, he knew the indistinct smudge of the Andes ramparts marked the western limit of the pampas. It was a wonderful setting, its remoteness in the Gran Chaco of Paraguay making an ideal hideaway for Höher Zwech, while the aircraft gave them mobility. They had been protected by the coup of General Alfredo Stroessner who had seized power and served as Presidente of Paraguay from nineteen fifty-four until a year ago. The repressive, autocratic regime had been a perfect hiding place for Höher Zwech. Now, with Stroessner in exile, external scrutiny of Paraguayan civil rights violations made tenure of their security more fragile and Wesler was very concerned. It was an hour and a half flight to Asunción and turning on the autopilot, he mused on the past few years.

El Jefe had influence in many things. Since any Communist government was anathema to a National Socialist, he had become uncomfortable with the Chilean Socialist government of Salvador Allende just behind his back and over the Andes. So, he had secretly plotted his overthrow, using the military as his tool. In the early seventies, the American CIA was working to the same end, but never discovered the deep-cover help they got. When Allende shot himself at the end of the military siege of the government buildings in nineteen seventy-three, General Augusto Pinochet became dictator.

A seventeen-year era of terror and oppression followed for the luckless Chilean people. Tens of thousands of them, '*los Desaparecidos*' were arrested, brutalized, tortured and killed, purely for political and paranoid reasons. El Jefe had revelled in it. Only a short distance away, he had helped history repeat the *Nacht und Knebel* terror of Hitler's Europe. The formula still worked.

The side benefit was the supply of disposable young women made available. The grateful Pinochet had been happy to have his Dirección de Inteligencia Nacional thugs hand over the more attractive female prisoners to Wesler, who flew over the Andes to a remote military airstrip. Bound and drugged, the women were flown back to the Chaco, usually a half dozen at a time. The hacienda had cells in the basement where they were kept pending El Jefe's personal pleasure. Obviously, they could not be released to talk about him afterward, so they were handed over to Karl-Heinz, one of the bodyguards. By the time he was finished with them, most begged to be put out of their misery.

Occasionally, a real prize, a blonde would arrive. The Arayan instincts of El Jefe would be aroused and days would be spent carefully arranging the evening when she would be brought to him over dinner and finally, to his room. Wesler could not bear the screams that usually followed and generally withdrew, leaving Karl-Heinz outside the door, the guard, ear to the door, feeding his sadistic instincts.

Now that events in Chile were working towards democracy, Wesler supposed his supply of women would dry up. There would be no satisfaction from kidnapping Indian women from neighbouring Brazil or Bolivia. They would not appeal. Besides, it was a security threat so close to home. Still, as his condition worsened, El Jefe's appetite had declined. Perhaps soon he may die. The thought had mixed feelings for Wesler. He knew only that the current search for the gold and boxes in Germany held the key to what was being planned. Droning through the sky, he sank into a reverie about the future.

1800 hrs. June 24th 1990. Cologne, Germany.

Reinhold Beckmann settled down with his newspaper. It had been a busy day at the garage where he worked as an auto mechanic. Hildegard, his wife, had prepared a nice stew and he had downed a couple of Pilsners with it. Before his favourite television show came on, he would catch up on the news.

He had finished reading and was about to dump the newspaper to the floor when a small paragraph on page eight caught his eye. A body, identified as one Rudi Kranzler, an ex-S.S. soldier, had been fished out of the River Weser. He had been tortured and the journalist had taken some license in speculating that Nazi gold was involved.

The story was several days old, the body being found three days earlier, but Beckmann froze. Rudi Kranzler, S.S. and gold only added up to one thing in his mind. Suddenly, he saw himself again, on that train from Berlin. Gottlieb, the corporal, had left with the Standartenführer and not come back. Kranzler had shown him the briefcase and he had stolen the documents when that scheisskopf was not around. Although those bastard Americans had then stolen it from him, he still had an idea roughly where it all took place. He had friends with murky backgrounds and contacts who might pay for such information. He reached for the phone.

25th June 1990. Germany.

The reclusive owner of the ranch in Paraguay had been right, as usual. The torture and brutal murder of an ex-S.S. soldier was indeed news. The Kripos saw no need to withhold details from the press. Indeed, stymied for lack of evidence, they welcomed the opportunity to appeal for public input on the crime. None came, but Inspector Neinscheer had acted as soon as he had positive identification of the victim as one Rudi Kranzler. It was next day before the death was brought to the attention of the Bundesnachtrichtendienst, the West German security service. The murder of any ex-S.S. personnel carried an automatic flag in the computers but Kranzler's name was flagged to a higher level and his death became a cause for immediate scrutiny.

The press speculated wildly on the torture and death of an ex-S.S. man, swinging from Israeli reprisal to Nazi treasure. When investigative reporters discovered no sinister history clinging to Kranzler, they focussed on the treasure aspect. This was also more politically correct as nobody wanted to dwell on the Holocaust thing. Lacking some further event revealing a trail, the story began to fade and within a few days, Rudi Kranzler was consigned to history and a slim file at the Kripo headquarters.

The media speculations, stressing torture, were transmitted worldwide in newsprint and television, ensuring that it reached the notice of anybody who cared. And there were many who cared. The Bundesnachtrichtendienst was not the only agency with flags on the files of ex-S.S. soldiers. Now, a stagnant chessboard, set up by history and draped with cobwebs by the passing years had suffered the taking of a pawn - Kranzler. His removal sent vibrations through the cobwebs to shadowy entities waiting to send the board into motion again.

The Gold Rush teams of the British and American post-war occupation forces had amassed a ton of paperwork relating to undiscovered Nazi gold. In their files there were unsubstantiated stories and firm leads which had petered out in the turmoil of post-war Europe. There was little doubt that millions of dollars worth of gold from the Berlin Reichsbank alone had gone missing by one means or another. As the years went by, this pile of paperwork became more and more compressed in the archives as it settled, undisturbed.

From time to time, share certificates, patents and the odd gold coin traceable to the Nazi hoard had surfaced but nothing of sustained interest happened to promote a general hue and cry. Still, the records contained prompts, or cues for action in the event certain information came to light. Kranzler was a prompt. Kranzler was a cue. Kranzler, as a pawn, was not entirely insignificant.

Early hours. 26th June, 1990. Gran Chaco, Paraguay.

At three in the morning, the waning embers of the fireplace matched El Jefe's state of mind. His mood was somber and reactionary, a book in his lap temporarily forgotten as his mind now drifted. He went horse riding each day and was still a competitive fencer, a sport which he had competed in at the nineteen thirty-six Olympics. He considered it kept his mind sharp also. Unfortunately, at seventy-five years, his lungs appeared to be giving out on him. The doctors he had seen had been useless and he dared not show himself at the kind of internationally renowned clinics that might be of any help at all.

His mind drifted further as he reached for his ever-present snifter of brandy. What proud days had been his! He often thought of Reinhard Heydrich at such times. What great friends they had been! What things they had accomplished together - until those Slavic murderers in Prague had killed Reinie. What a loss to the world! Reinie's murder had led to his own promotion and with pride he had tried to model his actions on what he thought Heydrich would have wanted him to do.

One of the direct results of Heydrich's demise in Czechoslovakia was that he himself had been drawn into the Höher Zwech, the *Higher Purpose* organization. This group had been set up by Himmler to ensure that, whatever the outcome of the war, the Nazi creed would be preserved, backed by funds, so that it could rise again. To this end, a totally secret and highly placed group of men became privy to Höher Zwech and worked as shadowy figures to achieve its ends. They were an elite within the S.S. elite. Even Hitler himself was unaware of the organization. It had been reasoned with great cynicism that if the Third Reich collapsed, Adolf Hitler would die by some means and could remain only a figurehead, a martyr, or deity, of the organization. It thus made sense that he not be included.

All kinds of smoke screens had been used to hide the Höher Zwech organization. The fabled Bavarian redoubt, an impenetrable fortress with werewolf partisans fighting to the death had been a convenient smoke screen near the end of the war. Eisenhower had fallen for that one. When S.S. Oberführer Josef Spacil had robbed the Reichsbank at gunpoint and fled Berlin with one of the last airplanes to depart the city, he had passed on a lot of the money to Otto Skorzeny, the famous Nazi Commando. Skorzeny had later used these funds in the nineteen-fifties in an organization called *Der Spinne. The Spider* had rescued ex-S.S. men and shipped them off to destinations such as South America where they could escape prosecution. That too had diverted attention to the wrong place, away from Höher Zwech.

The biggest smoke screen had been the repeated reference to *Odessa,* in all kinds of publications, including novels and even movies. It was obvious that an organization as fanatical as the S.S. would not just allow itself to dissolve, but would want to perpetuate itself. People expected to see such manifestations as Odessa and El Jefe had actively encouraged this shell organization's reputation, reasoning that while investigators focussed their energies on such nebulous entities, Höher Zwech was left to function without detection. He had referred to this strategy as *hiding out in the open.*

In nineteen forty-four, he had been appointed overall guardian of the Höher Zwech organization. The responsibility was awesome, but so was the power. He had at his command one of the most fanatical, influential and capable groups of people who had ever lived. Many of them had stayed behind in Germany after the war. Their job had been to act as communication points, feeding information to and from Paraguay. Many had been recruited into the security organizations of the West German Bundesnachtrichtendienst and Kriminalpolizei civil police. Others had become ostensible enemies by joining the East German Staatssicherheit and Volkspolitzei but in reality they maintained their first loyalty to Höher Zwech.

It was these men who had given El Jefe his incisive and familiar insight into Germany for the past forty-odd years. Privy to secrets from both sides of the Iron Curtain all this time, he could have made a fortune selling them to either side. He had disdained such action however since he had indeed a higher purpose. El Jefe's greatest wish had been the ultimate subversion of the entire world to S.S. principles but the opportune time had not yet arrived. His first duty however had always been to preserve the secrecy of Höher Zwech.

In the book on his lap, he had compiled a list of people who knew about the shipment. To this he now added the Wehrmacht and S.S. men who had been with Mannheimer. Carefully, he ruled through the names with a yellow pencil, indicating they were missing, but not proven dead.

Through Kranzler's name, a red line now showed he was dead. Ernst Kaltenbrunner also wore a red line. The Allies had executed him in nineteen forty-six, following the Nürnberg trials. Because the shipment had been a secret operation of Höher Zwech, there was no reason other than suspicion to include the name of Martin Bormann, that pig-faced, scheming and opportunistic secretary to Hitler. Bormann had sources of information, which could possibly have penetrated Höher Zwech's secrecy, and he sported a green line, even though a West German court had officially declared him dead in nineteen seventy-three.

Joachim Wesler was there, with no line through his name. There were a lot of red-ruled names, people whom El Jefe personally knew were dead, or he had liquidated. Several agencies, including the Allied Gold Rush teams were included as possible sharers of the secret, even by remote intelligence. He had made the list as comprehensive and exhaustive as possible over the years. The last name on the list was his own, appended with the kind of thoroughness El Jefe had directed towards all affairs in his life.

He thought he might now be only one of two people alive who knew the contents of the steel boxes which Standartenführer Mannheimer had hidden. The gold with them was important, but paled into insignificance against the contents of those boxes.

Carefully recorded within were names, S.S. numbers, histories, new identities and escape route information of every member of Höher Zwech, including himself. Not only that, but details of all the gold shipments in amounts, destinations, and methods of transfer were attached. If the contents of the two boxes were to fall into wrong hands, the repercussions would be catastrophic. All members would be revealed and hunted down. The death of the organization would result, an event unthinkable to him. The assets and riches derived from the initial gold shipments, now worth billions of dollars, would be forfeit. Governments would topple and history would be rewritten. It could not be allowed to happen and El Jefe had long ago done what had been necessary to safeguard the two boxes and ensure that any lucky gold-seekers would not stumble on the greater treasure.

Now there was little doubt Mannheimer's cache would soon be found. Joachim was surely correct; it had to be in the frontier zone. When mine detectors were used to sweep the ground and clear the area, how could they not detect the gold? He would have to send a message to his superior, inform him of the situation. This he dreaded for this man held the ultimate power and direction of Höher Zwech. The thought of this man brought a scowl to his face. Only the previous year, the senior committee had relieved him from leadership of Höher Zwech, over his protests.

They had claimed he was becoming too frail! He had raged and pleaded but there had obviously been some kind of plot against him. The committee had met in Asunción six months ago, one of the very rare occasions when he had ventured forth from the security of the ranch. It was Kirschener who had led the charge against him, that stupid innkeeper who had somehow wormed his way into power. The committee accused him of being too old, infirm and incompetent to continue as the true leader of Höher Zwech. Raving at them, he now realized, had just lent credence to their accusations and he had been unable to dissuade them. Obviously, the decision had been made in his absence and there was no way to surmount it.

The new man had been voted in, staying in the background through the arguments, only coming forward when he knew his position was firm. Bastard! Now he, El Jefe to his assistants, had to be subservient! Well, he would show them! He still had the fire in him to continue the crusade. They would learn that he alone had the dedication, the power to strike where a strike was needed. He could succeed without them and now, here at this moment, the enlightenment came upon him. He realized it was the current of re-dedication flowing through his veins that brought the solution to him, the perfect way to show them all.

After all these years, they had ousted him, but still could not take from him the day to day functioning because none of those *scheisskopfs* knew how to do it. He had been careful all those years to garner to himself all the little secrets and knowledge. Still, although he had to fear this new leader, he had kept his own little plan to himself and he had the means of carrying it out now, whether the others approved or not. Better they did not learn of it! The plan was his and his alone. Even Joachim Wesler did not know of it but would act with total loyalty to his orders.

Regarding the gold and other items, El Jefe knew he could not be seen to fail in the least way. Contemplating this exposure, he twisted his handkerchief, his bony fingers turning whiter as the linen strangled the blood vessels. He felt the cough coming, rising from deep within, irresistible as the revenge of the Jews in his nightmares, implacable as his own will.

His vision blurred behind the tears and he loathed the weakness. It came more often now, despite his resolve. He was the only one left with the dedication and duty to preserve the calling. He saw dear, sweet, Reinie again, resplendent in his uniform, saluting Hitler and Himmler on the steps of the Berlin Sportpalast. How splendid they were! Such Gods! They had known the way the world should be and had the courage and conviction to act upon it! He had been present at the Wannsee Conference in January nineteen forty-two when Hitler had revealed *Endlösung,* the *Final Solution* to the Jewish problem. Now, the filthy Jews controlled the world through their infernal banks! But he knew how to deal with that!

He paused, the roll of reckless retribution halted by realities. His course of action was limited, controlled by men who had usurped the power laid down by the indomitable founders of the Nationalsozialistische Deutsche Arbeitpartei. They would forever be locked in their lust for power, yet timid in action, afraid to move and afraid not to.

He counted himself a realist and knew his time was coming. He had read all the history books about the Third Reich. He saw the flaws and the opportunities missed. Still, it had been a close-run thing. The entry of the Americans, with their unassailable industrial might and millions of soldiers had helped swing the balance. And who had led the Americans into the War? A Jew! The infernal Roosevelt had risked impeachment to wage war on the Nationalsozialistische Deutsche Arbeitpartei.

He could not die without striking back. Those fools in control never would. But he knew how to deal with it! Except, they watched him. He knew this with the preservation instincts honed by years of suspicion. They would liquidate him if they learned of his intent. Still, he had a resource the world had not yet fully recognized. He had a resource to wreak havoc upon the Jews, an iron fist of retribution, which he could unleash. He could claim credit for having empowered this band of warriors in a gesture of solidarity against the Jews. This resource he could refute and ignore if they failed in implementing his plan, a total denial of association. They were equally as implacable in their hatred of the Jews as he himself. He could isolate any failure from himself so his new masters would never know. He would thus win either way! The old man shuddered, feeling the power so close to his hands. The day of reckoning was almost here! Gotterdammerung was close. He reached for the brandy and, as always when his emotions were high, it scalded on the way down, burning into his stomach. It brought the fire back and his eyes cleared. Resolve sprang into his face and his jaw set. He would not, could not, fail!

Any thought of destruction of the Jews immediately brought Israel to mind. The means were almost to his hand. Only he knew about the biological agent, which had been preserved with the gold. He had arranged it and knew the full details and efficacy of it. It was one of Hitler's *Vergeltungswaffe*, a secret terror weapon. Now, with the buried treasure almost in his hands, he would soon have the means of destroying the Jews. He only needed to recover the third steel box! With the wisdom of age and research, he knew that the honour coming from valour and dedicated purpose was secondary. Everything always came down to one thing. Money!

While preservation of Höher Zwech was important (even though the charged responsibility had been taken from him) and recovery of the gold was necessary, these were eclipsed by the power of the biological weapon. It alone provided the means for him to revenge the Third Reich before his time was over. There was only one drawback and that was the quantity available. It would probably be insufficient to wipe out the Israelis. To have the agent analyzed, copied and produced in sufficient quantity would require secure facilities beyond his means. The cost and possible security breaches were prohibitive. Besides, he personally did not have the time left to him to wait.

It thus boiled down to how he could use the current stockpile with a one-time maximum effectiveness. His imminent possession of the biological weapon had crystallized the rambling thoughts of forty years into a plan, which could not fail. While Tel Aviv as a target would remain a backup plan, his course now seemed clear. He would deploy the biological weapon in a place other than Israel where the Jews were concentrated and influencing the world with their filthy methods. He had just such a place earmarked. Not only that, the effects of the weapon would merely be a diversion from his ultimate aim, which would achieve world domination.

With the Americans neutralized, his allies could then pick off Israel at their leisure. He would telephone soon, taking into account the time zone change. The call would be secure he knew, because of the encoded links. For almost fifty years he had talked to these stalwart and deadly allies of the Third Reich. The time had come to use them again.

The white claw of his hand grasped the brandy glass, shaking with the intent of his purpose. He raised the glass, sipping and spilling as he nodded his head fervently. He swallowed awkwardly, some of the brandy trickling down his chin. He coughed; a tiny dry hack, which brought no relief, only becoming more intense as it lured a major eruption from his lungs. Brandy sprayed as he hacked and coughed without relief, seizing a nearby handkerchief to catch the efflux.

1000 hrs. Wednesday, 27th June 1990.
Wadi al Kebec el-Zendre, Libya.

Hassan Abdul el-Saaed sat back on the cushions of his tent. The woman beside him stowed the phone in its latch. Bounced five times through the ionosphere via satellites, the chances of intercept had been remote, but the man he had communicated with had been careful in his choice of words. His credentials had been authenticated by the name: *Herr Blücher.*

For years the man had been a legend amongst el-Saaed's people. In a lost cause, almost a half a century before, he had supported and encouraged el-Saaed's grandfather in the war against the Allies. Undeterred by the bad choice of his grandfather, el-Saaed and his father had maintained contact with this amazing man. Advice, armaments and intelligence had flowed their way from Blücher. It was hard to figure how his hatred of the Jews eclipsed even their own. In the late forties, el-Saaed had watched as the Israelis had driven his father from their ancestral lands. He had watched from child eyes as faithful fighters had died in the cause, struck down by the advance of the Infidels. Long had he listened to the stories of the old men, crouched around smoldering dung fires in the Palestinian refugee camps while infants and elders died in the unsanitary conditions. How he had yearned for redemption! Now perhaps it was here. He raised his bloodshot eyes, the thick dryness of a Scotch whisky hangover droning in his head. "Go! Send for Abu!"

The woman climbed from her seat, conditioned to her peremptory dismissal. She knew she had little but sexual value to el-Saaed and he could have her throat cut at any time. More likely, do it himself. She paused momentarily, feeling his wet deposit flow from within her onto her thighs. The sourness of his whisky breath and the thoughtless chaffing of his whiskered face lingered on her body, emphasizing his careless use of her.

Outside, the blazing desert sun was almost at its zenith and the Wadi al Kebec el-Zendre was baking. The tent was set only yards from a curved cliff about two hundred feet high which threw blessed shadow in the afternoons. From one of the cracks in the cliff seeped the precious clear water, which was the only reason this place was occasioned with a name. Yards beyond a small pool, the overflow evaporated into the dry air. Nearby, overhangs of rock left shelves on which slept the men who currently dwelt here. The rocks protected them from the prying eyes of American spy satellites.

The camp was a place of training: in indoctrination, weapons, language and other skills important to a branch of terrorism known as Tewfik. The Tewfiks knew no allies and even killed people of Islam, if it suited their purpose. Two dozen men currently dwelt here, training and awaiting their treasured opportunity to strike a blow, fight in the Jihad and give themselves, if necessary, to Allah and live in eternal paradise as a reward.

One such man, now strolling to el-Saaed's tent, was Abu el-Cetti. A Yemeni, he had left his family four years before at the age of nineteen. Slim and medium height, his skin was fairly pale, making him a primary recruit for people who sometimes needed to disguise their race. His eyes were dark and deep-set, his nose straight and Aryan. Although his face now sported a wispy beard, it could be shaved and his long hair trimmed so he could pass for a European, perhaps a Spaniard or an Italian.

Entering the dark tent, he whispered the traditional greeting, "Alahu akhba."

The gray bearded and tousled el-Saaed grunted in reply and gazed at him keenly.

El-Cetti returned the gaze, reflecting inwardly that el-Saaed had obviously been drinking again. Probably, almost certainly, he had been keeping company through the night with the whore he kept. The other recruits whispered about this, out of earshot, awed by the reputation of the man, but puzzled by his flaunting such behaviour in the face of Islamic law. They kept silent out of fear of his wrath.

The hawk-nosed man before him had been el-Cetti's mentor for the past three years. Virtually unknown to the Israeli's and their allies, el-Saaed had been instrumental in the deaths of dozens of Israelis. He had personally taken part in and plotted numerous bombings and direct killings. For hours each day, el-Cetti had listened to the stories, listened to the doctrine of his teacher as he expounded a never-ending diatribe of hatred against the Jews. The other man, the Imam, was subtler, training him in the more devious and irrational perversions of the faith. El-Cetti did not know it was wrong to kill according to the Koran. Fully indoctrinated, he only knew it was a blessed mission for every Arab to destroy anything and anyone not faithful to Islam.

He himself had made his bones, crept silently up to kibbutzim in the dead of night, dispensing death to men, women and children and blowing up the carefully nurtured farms, carved with love and devotion out of the desert's sterility. The thrill of it raised a sexual excitement he was loath to acknowledge. His existence was a sterile one, pure to the tenets of his faith. The stern neutrality of his life was altered only by the death and destruction he had sworn to wreak. Yet it left him confused, disturbed, and his only solace was to draw further into the monk-like state in which he endured. Each act of cruelty he committed brought a faint relief, soon eclipsed by a greater torment.

"The German has called."

The statement jerked el-Cetti back to the present.

El-Saaed was looking at him intently. "I have not spoken of him before, so you know nothing of him." Briefly, he outlined the man's history with himself and his family. "He is a man beloved of our people, a great executioner of the Jews. He tells me he has a use for us, one which will cause great harm to our enemies."

"And *he* will make use of *us*?"

The older Arab scowled. "Only as it suits the will of Allah! He has a weapon to use against them, one of terrible consequences. Yet, he lacks the means of delivery and has asked me to assist. I believe we shall do this. There are other additional crippling effects we can cause if we plan carefully, Inch Allah!"

"What is it we have to do?"

"I do not know the whole plan. It is too dangerous to discuss such matters over a telephone. You will go to Greece next week. There you will be told what is required of you. Hassan Ali Ben-Ahwed will go with you. He will be your controller. After the plan is made clear, he will return and report to me and I will authorize your action by code."

When the briefing was completed, el-Cetti left a little confused. He was to proceed on a mission so far unrevealed. He was to fulfill some plan, yet he saw no glory for him, certainly felt a gut feeling that there would be no sacrifice worthy of Allah.

Six days later, shaved and hair trimmed, he entered the Athens airport. His passport listed him as Juan Pedro Antonio, a civil engineer from Malaga, Spain. He was fluent in Spanish and conversant enough in engineering matters to pass cursory inspection. Ben-Ahwed had traveled the day before and picked him up in a rented car. They drove to a nondescript hotel a few blocks from the Acropolis and awaited their contact.

0800 hrs.Wednesday, 4th July 1990. London, England.

Raymond Barton reached out playfully to fondle a breast as Mandy sought to entrap it in the cup of her bra. It was a gesture of levity, an intimacy to break the mood, but the sheer chauvinism, on top of the row they had been having caused her to step back with a hiss. "Don't *touch* me!"

"PMS!" He had previously sniffed; rankled at her snippy attitude, but it had been too much. Mandy was furious. Finishing dressing, she stalked from the tiny bathroom, her long black hair flowing behind her like a flourished banner of war. Taunted and tempted by the tight roundness of her buttocks and the swaying of those hips on the high heels, he followed, perversely determined to rejoin battle.

"I think I'll take that German assignment Willie McIvor offered me!" It was a threat she would not rise to right now, but with the unerring aim of a lover's ability to hurt, he planted the dart. She stalked on through the flat, grabbing her ridiculously pink plastic raincoat from the peg on the hallway wall. Without a backward look, she closed the door in his face, leaving him looking at generations of thickly accumulated paint. After a moment, he went to the stove and poured himself another cup of tea. He spilled milk from the container over the edge of the cup and tipping the saucer into the sink, left it and walked to the window.

Looking out into the London drizzle from the upstairs window, it seemed the world was as grey as his mood. He didn't know why they fought so. Sometimes it happened late at night and there would be joint forgiveness, sealed by a tempestuous and sweaty encounter in the tight confines of the miserably small bedroom. At other times, like this, morning fights led to hours of sulky and determined separation until by evening, firm lines had been drawn and it might take days to achieve reconciliation.

He didn't even remember what the bloody argument was about! Something to do with him: his job, his impecunious ways, and messiness, leaving the lavatory seat up - whatever. The familiar red London double-decker bus arrived below and he saw Mandy step on, never a backward or upward look. Maybe tonight he wouldn't come home. The tight confines of the place made it an unsuitable battleground for a man to try to deal with the ire of a sullen woman.

In the bathroom, he finished shaving. He had earlier only done one half of his face when war broke out. Slapping more shaving foam on, he picked up the razor again. As he scraped away, he enlarged his threat to Mandy in his mind. His boss, Willie, had offered him the opportunity to cover some stories resulting in the tearing down of the Berlin Wall. It would be interesting to see events, to see the physical and sociological changes in the German people. And he remembered clearly that three-metre high concrete monstrosity which had cut Berlin in two.

He had spent three years in Germany in the British Army Intelligence Corps. It had been mundane analysis and enumeration of Warsaw Pact military formations and equipment, not very esoteric stuff, really, but mildly interesting. He had taken the military commission to help pay his way through university and taking German had given him a leg into the job. His grammar school had been mildly upper crust and his father had been in the Foreign Office, or some such thing, so he had the necessary social background.

What had really been interesting in Germany was Astrid. The blonde, beautiful daughter of an affluent West German surgeon, she and Ray had spent two wonderful years of loving together in Bonn, sharing an apartment. When his army commitment was over and he was sent home, she had been pressured by her parents to break it off and not go back to Britain with him. They had both been devastated but had several passionate reunions when his new civilian job as a reporter had taken him back to Germany.

That had caused a row or two with Mandy. Two months after they began dating, he had gone back to Germany for a week. Two days were reserved for Astrid and Mandy had spotted the scratches on his back when he returned. She had called him many nasty names, followed by a passionate reunion, which sparked their moving in together into his dingy Bayswater flat. Only two weeks after, a letter arrived from Astrid announcing her forthcoming marriage to a German industrialist, Rolf Klemerer. She apologized for not telling him to his face, but had lacked the courage. With a fine turn of descriptive words, Astrid had lamented the passing of their affair, hinting that in the distant future, maybe they may meet again.

Unable to resist opening the letter, from a female hand in Germany, Mandy had gone on the rampage, searching the flat and unearthing photographs, other letters and sundry evidence of a love affair only in repose. Returning home, Raymond had been met at the door to the flat with this evidence of infidelity. It had taken three days, heavy florist and jeweller's bills, and a proposal of marriage to resolve their differences. Then, an article only days later in a German social magazine extolling the great love between Astrid and her husband, plus their plans to live in America, helped quell Mandy's suspicions.

Still, in Mandy's mind, a trip to Germany for Raymond meant Astrid, not work, even though she thought Astrid was in America. That was the dart he had planted. Women!

Now, Raymond looked in the mirror. He had never regarded himself as handsome, really, rather ordinary. His face was square, with slightly puffy cheeks and a fleshy nose with a pair of bushy pelmets for eyebrows, topping grave grey eyes. He was six feet tall, built a little heavier than he wished, although little exercise and a liking for his pint of bitter negated any prospects in that regard. A shock of fine sandy hair fell to one side of his head, giving him the kind of public schoolboy look that shouted his nationality.

Now, the barb he had sent at Mandy really did involve Astrid for she was already back in Germany again with her husband. After almost a year in the United States, a death in the family electronics and construction business had resulted in his promotion to CEO of Klemerer Elektro-und Baubetried AG and he had been transferred back. With the guilt of after-anger, Raymond realized how much he might have hurt Mandy.

He had no intent of ever starting another fight by mentioning Astrid's name in any context. Still, perhaps going to Germany for a few days for Willie might allow things to cool off here. He had no intention of seeing Astrid, their affair was over and he knew he loved Mandy too much to even think about meeting Astrid. Besides, being the wife of the president of KEB probably filled all of Astrid's days.

It was ten o'clock when, fresh off the Circle Line of the London Tube, he entered the offices of *Current Events Magazine*. Willie McIvor was in his office, frowning at a video monitor.

"Hey, Willie!"

"Hey, you bum, where've you been? How's Mandy? Is there fresh coffee in the machine?" Willie always asked questions in batches, never singly and the respondent merely answered the one most appealing.

"Pissed off with me again. I thought I might duck out of town. Is that German feature story still open for coverage?"

"Yeah," the tight little man with the yellowed fingers of the inveterate smoker stubbed out the butt he held and looked up, "Things are happening fast. By October, this unification agreement shit should be a fact of life.

I want to get some material together so that when unification happens, we can run an article and reflect on some of the background stuff. What we are looking for is not the mainstream Berlin shit. I'd like some good, solid anecdotal stuff from the rural areas of Germany...What was it like when the Red Army arrived? Did you get separated from relatives? Anybody you know got killed? Do you know people who escaped from East Germany? That kind of thing.

Did you hear the story about Grossburschla and Altenburschla, Ray? The Red Army rolled too far in nineteen forty-five, through Grossburschla into Altenburschla and the locals turned out and persuaded them to go back eight hundred metres to where they belonged. Pretty gutsy! A few thousand people like that and maybe the Russians could have been persuaded back to eastern Poland!"

Raymond grunted. The story was beginning to sound like a lot of work. He would have preferred something more newsworthy, flashier for the times, yet he heard himself agreeing to go.

"That's super, Ray. Gladys will have the tickets for you this afternoon and you can be in Germany tonight."

1835 hrs. Wednesday, 4th July 1990.
El Shazar Hotel Restaurant. Tunis, North Africa.

El-Saeed sat back, contemplating his friend, Yussef Bin-Yussef. They had concluded a very interesting talk and he was happy his companion had come on side with the plan. After all, had he not, Yussef seemed cheerily unaware his life would have been forfeit. El-Saeed had not risked travelling here just to have security broken by some blabbermouth who was not a fully committed partner.

1900 hrs. Wednesday, 4th July 1990. Germany.

Peering down at the dirty-looking stratus cloud covering most of Germany, Raymond Barton thought it would be nice to see the country again. Astrid apart, he had enjoyed his time here. He had been a shoo-in for a permanent Germany correspondent when his Army term was up in nineteen eighty-eight but he had not been able to bear being so close to Astrid. If she was unable to live her own life without her parents interfering, then it was time for a break. He had instead settled for the magazine job in London and been called upon for frequent assignments to Berlin and other major German cities.

The hiss of engine noise fell off and he felt the nose of the aircraft dip. The flight was starting down for Frankfurt. The local representative, Al Shapiro, a loud New Yorker whom he had grown to really like and appreciate, was to brief him on latest events. When the plane landed, he took his time getting off, preferring to avoid the stampede mentality of the uninitiated travellers. He arrived at the baggage carousel at the same time as his single suitcase and shouldering his portable computer, headed for the taxi ranks outside.

He phoned Shapiro on his cell phone on the way into town and arranged for Al to pick him up later. Alice Shapiro would be pissed off with him again. Almost a year ago, he and Al had gone out on the town and the stupid bastard had picked up a girl in one of the tawdry bars they always seemed to gravitate to. The blame for the dose of clap Al got had been shifted somehow onto Raymond, who had never seemed capable of redeeming himself in Alice's eyes.

The cell phone was definitely an instrument of the new age. He was available twenty-four hours of the day to pursue stories and in turn be pursued. Mandy knew the number, so if she wanted to call and make peace, so much the better. If not, fuck her! My, it was wonderful to be a male of freedom, footloose on the Continent! But God, how he missed her! The high cheekbones of her face swam into his mind, the thin but sensuous lips, the nostrils flared in passion. Her dark eyes, pools of mystery, looked out from her brilliant mind through a model's face. The quick-tempered flashes of anger, profanity, tempered by a yielding slender body blessed with long thighs and up-tilted breasts spoke to him. A *Siren*, that was it!

He checked into the Hotel Excelsior, opposite the south entrance of the Hauptbahnhof, flashing his company plastic. Willie had long since succumbed to his expense claims being mostly meager. Such a tight fisted attitude on the part of a reporter was uncommon and bred suspicion in a manager's heart. The room was functional, clean, but little more. It suited him; he had no need of luxury. Luxury bred sloth on the trail of stories. He showered to freshen up and then it was time to meet Al. Taking the time zone into account, it was after eight, so time for an evening meal.

Within minutes, Shapiro, a punctuality freak, phoned from the lobby and Raymond headed downstairs.

"How's Alice?"

"Who the fuck knows, or cares, even?" Al spitefully kicked his BMW out into the traffic on Baseler, headed for the Friedenbrücke. "We'll go to the Textor over in Sachsenhausen, it is reasonably quiet in there and if we can get one of the corner tables, we can talk." Al was dressed in a lightweight grey suit, no tie and sporting flamboyant shirt wings.

Grudgingly, Ray had to admit he looked good, with a hint of carefree. "You folks split up?"

"Yeah. She ran off with some goddamned Kraut restaurant owner."

"And you are broken up, hurt, and want her back."

"Fuckin' -A man. How's randy Mandy?"

"Alone tonight...or she'd better be!"

"Still fighting?"

"Oooh yes!"

"Women! - Well, let's have a party, you poor benighted Limey bastard!"

The Friedenbrücke took them over the smooth surface of the Main River into the nightlife area of Sachsenhausen. Al quickly found a parking spot and entering the restaurant, they did indeed manage to find one of the quiet corners behind an old wooden table and settled into the benched alcove. Within minutes, a blue and grey stone Bembel filled with Apfelwein was set between them, with two of the local diamond-patterned Schobbeglassen. Al, of course, had ordered Rauscher, the fieriest of the apple wines, for which the district was famous. About to protest, Raymond then bit his tongue. With their women troubles, maybe it was appropriate to get pissed tonight and worry about tomorrow's horrible hangover later.

"Well, here's to the Fourth of July!" Al raised his glass.

"Yes, freedom from colonialism."

"There's everything and nothing going on, Ray." Al picked at the homemade pasta he had ordered. "The whole re-unification thing is totally out of hand, nobody knows what is going on any longer. With the frontier down, East Germans are flocking this way by the thousands and the social implications are enormous. The government, police and security organizations are swamped. Already, with the initial euphoria wearing off, more level heads are pointing to the unemployment, job-creation and other social welfare costs placing new tax burdens on the working people."

"Is that where the stories are, social issues?"

"It's not what Willie wants, I know. My best suggestion is that you head down to Nürnberg by train and then connect through on the Leipzig line. If you rent a car this side of the old border, you can work your way pretty much along the course of the border, and see what you pick up. You can cross freely both ways now, although the minefields and barbed wire have not been cleared yet."

"A sort of travel-guide-ramble with anecdotes?"

"Yeah, it sounds trite, but I guess you have to get out there and talk to people to unearth the human interest."

"Sounds like a colossal bore."

"Yeah, I know you'd rather be snuggled up with that sexy piece of baggage, the randy Mandy, but if you'll get your head out from between her legs and into this story, maybe you'll get something."

Raymond grunted and took another swig of his Apfelwein. The Rauscher burned on the way down and he dreaded to think what it was doing to his organs. By morning, only partially converted by a liver bent on revenge for his actions, it would have migrated to his brain cells, which would die by the millions, the pain supposedly acting as a deterrent to ever doing this again. Twice he had pulled out the cell phone to phone Mandy but stubbornness won out. Besides, he knew how Mandy treated surrendered prisoners. Abject apology and remorse over the telephone did not reap the physical rewards.

It was midnight when a taxi dropped Raymond back at the Excelsior. There were no messages, so he stumbled upstairs to bed and before he could stabilize the spinning room, passed out.

0900 hrs. Thursday, 5th July 1990.

Prompted by a distressed bladder, Raymond wakened. The faint light through the blinds only mildly impacted on his eyes, but it was the rolling over and out of bed that unleashed a monstrous clamour of torment in his head. By the time he reached the bathroom, he could feel each pulse of his heart as a capillary-stretching bombardment of pain. Clasping his hands around his skull to prevent it bursting, he went back into the room and ordered a pot of coffee from room service.

The courageous act of calling the Hauptbahnhof revealed a suitable train departure at noon, so he had almost three hours to get going. Thank goodness he did not have to drive right now. He cursed Al for not only creating his predicament, but also having the cunning to plan his mode of travel accordingly. Back in the bathroom, he stripped and turned on the shower. For two minutes, he leaned against the wall, letting the hot water stream all over his body. Then he brutally turned the water to cold. It was an old Army trick. It didn't sober you up, but it confused the mind, rather like stopping after banging your head repeatedly against a brick wall.

Wrapped only in a towel, he retrieved the coffee tray left outside his door and bent down to his bag to get the extra-strength Tylenol he always carried. Bending down pooled blood amongst the packed ranks of dying cells in his head and unleashed another pinnacle of suffering.

1130 hrs. Thursday, 5th July 1990. Hauptbahnhof, Frankfurt.

Distressed as he was and with no reason to suspect it, Raymond missed the surveillance put on him in Frankfurt. Folding his newspaper, the man in the lobby casually strolled behind the toiling Englishman as he went to the Hauptbahnhof and lining up behind him, took note of his destination.

It was a low-grade identification of an ex-British Military Intelligence personage, now masquerading as a journalist but in all likelihood, an operative of the British Secret Service, taking orders from Century House in London. After phoning the information in, the man went home. If it were considered important, somebody else would pick the Englander up in Nürnberg. It was not his concern.

On the train, Raymond drank three bottled waters in the buffet before tackling a late breakfast. The countryside was slipping by in a blur as the electric-powered express train sped along on smooth, welded track. He would have to rent a car on the west side of the old border due to the chaotic and inefficient habits instilled in the East by nearly fifty years of Communism. Similarly, he would not choose to stay in the east since the hotels were of poor quality and service. He spread a travel map of Thuringia and Saxony on the table and squinted against the painful light reflected from the pages.

The Czechoslovakian border was close by, the old Iron Curtain frontier wending eastward to meet it close to the town of Plauen. *'Liebensraum'*, the excuse for Nazi expansion into the Sudetenland came to mind and Raymond supposed there might be some stories there running a thread through that Nazi invasion and the later Soviet invasion. Good, so he would rent a car in Nürnberg as planned and drive from there, head willing.

1500 hrs. Thursday, 5th July 1990.

"You bastard! You low-down scummy piece of dog shit! You rotten fucking septic arsehole!"

Raymond held the phone away from his ear and regarded it with quizzical alarm. He could still hear Mandy's raging loud and clear from the earpiece of the cell phone. It had rung, he'd answered, and this is what he'd got. She seemed to be slowing down now, after a magnificent display of non-repetitive invective. He had known British Army sergeant majors that couldn't swear as well as Mandy.

"What the hell are you talking about?"

"You slimy cock-sucker, don't play coy with me!"

This was really out of hand! "Mandy, would you calm down! I don't have a clue what you are on about!"

"The flat, you childish goddamned black-enameled vandal!" (She still hadn't repeated herself.)

"What about the fucking flat?" Raymond was now arousing.

"You wrecked it, you rotten, fucking arsehole!" With the repetition came the collapse and he could hear her frustrated wail as tears came.

"Mandy, the flat was perfect when I left. I even put the lavatory seat down!"

"Everything is wrecked. Oh, my God!"

"What?"

"Even *your* stuff is wrecked! We've been ransacked, burglarized!"

"What's missing?"

"Nothing! What do we have to steal? Everything is just pulled apart. Oh, darling, I'm sorry! I thought it was you because you were gone. I'm sorry, darling, I..."

"Mandy! Call the police. Don't touch anything!"

"Yes, very well."

He envisaged her delicious lips quivering and she had apologized to him! If only he were there! His salacious thoughts were rudely terminated by the resurrection of his headache and the plundered feeling of a homeowner who has had an intruder. He pulled the rental car off the highway and sat in mild alarm. Why would anyone vandalize his flat? "Get the police there and call me as soon as you know a little more."

"Very good Raymond. I'm sorry," she broke the connection and was gone.

1540 hrs. Thursday, 5th July 1990.
Office of the Deputy Prime Minister, Tel Aviv, Israel.

Mordecai Bar-Havalah sat with his spine tingling. Across the desk, Yakob Morgenstern leaned forward with intensity. The ex-General of the Israeli army, famous for his actions in the Six-Day War and the Golan Heights was not a man to be taken lightly. In his new political position of Deputy Prime Minister, Mordecai knew Morgenstern handled, for the Prime Minister himself, the more unsavoury and politically untouchable tasks. The words he was about to hear came directly from the top.

"Mordecai, this matter is of the gravest urgency! We have sworn never to give up on the hunt for Nazis. If we can get this information out of Germany, it will be untainted, the original, unexpurgated key to the whereabouts of some of them who got away after the war."

Bar-Havalah knew what was being said. If the Israelis waited long enough and patiently enough, the German authorities *might, eventually,* choose to share the information, or they might not. However, anything received would not likely be unexpurgated. There were too many skeletons in German closets to allow the Israelis free access to everything. They would have to go after it themselves.

A further grim factor was the post-war alteration of documents and disinformation perpetrated by all the Allies who had spirited away *valuable* Nazis by the dozens to serve their own ends, whether technological or financial. Werner von Braun, of the American space program was probably the best known, although not a recognized Nazi, or Israeli target. After the war, Reihhold Gehlen had headed the West German intelligence agency, the Bundesnachtrichtendienst. The ultimate fate of bigger Nazi fish was still unknown and the Israelis would not likely terminate hunts for such individuals until the centenary of the end of the war. Until then, the Western powers had sealed the records, hiding their amoral acts, which they could not afford to have the light of history shine upon.

"So, you have authorization to take whatever steps necessary to recover the information intact. I don't need to remind you how vital this mission is, but I do need to tell you to be as discreet as possible. You not only have to recover this stuff, but do it in such secrecy that we can snare those animals before they can be forewarned. There must be no hint from their spies, none in the press, and diplomatic incidents must be avoided absolutely.

Four teams of *David* are hereby assigned to your group and you have full authority to proceed with *Operation Harvest*. Do you have any questions?"

"Do I report to you?"

"No, there is a need for deniability. Brigadier Ogradoffchik will be your contact. A specialist communications team will handle methods of contact and you will be briefed accordingly tomorrow."

Since the Munich Olympics massacre of Israeli athletes in nineteen seventy-two, the Mossad had kept an active but deep-cover unit in West Germany to follow activities of any group which might provide a threat to the state of Israel. The Baaden-Meinhoffer's, the Red Brigades, numerous Neo-Nazis and Arab-sympathizers were scrutinized and penetrated where possible. Occasionally, information to disrupt threatening activities was fed to the West German security people. Although such acts risked compromising the unit's existence, it was deemed better to have the Germans deal with these activities where possible. Where such feeds were deemed inappropriate, hard action had been taken and people had died. The West Germans were left with their strong suspicions but no hard evidence of the unit's existence.

The four David units comprised twenty of the toughest, most deadly troops available in the world. Technologically capable and utterly ruthless, they would willingly give their lives to serve his commands.

2030 hrs. Thursday, 5th July 1990. Plauen, Germany.

Raymond had hit pay dirt. Driving into Hof, a place he previously marked as an overnight point, he fell into conversation with the manager of a restaurant who had recommended he go to Plauen, in the old Eastern zone. So, he changed his plans. It felt strange to drive across the frontier without stopping, as the highways were now open. The wire fences and the signs warning about mines, guns and death were still in place either side of the road, yet there were no longer wooden barriers, nor concrete chicanes providing death zones and spiked steel claws in the road to stop vehicles.

On arrival, he checked into a quiet pension on one of the side streets and went out walking to get the feel of the place. Like many Germany towns, especially on railways, Plauen had suffered heavy bombing in the war. Much of its centre had been rebuilt with the typically tasteless concrete structures favoured by the Communists, but there was still some old-world charm to sections of the town.

Walking down Nobelstrasse, he had come to the Vogtland Museum, which was situated in three old houses dating back to the late seventeenth century. Within, exhibits celebrated the craftwork for which the region was famous, mainly lace and hand-made musical instruments of almost every variety. He never got beyond the door, being waylaid by an elderly lady behind the lobby desk.

She proceeded to bend his ear for five minutes, extolling the attractions of the area. It was then that Raymond had the idea. It was old folk who liked to talk, liked to recount their past to anyone who would listen. Excitedly interrupting the lady, he explained what he wanted.

"Ach, you should go to Walderen's Bierstube on Alte Pausauerstrasse. All the old men gather there to play checkers and tell tales. You will probably find my husband, Rudi Stemmer there, as usual. For a beer and providing a willing audience, they will spin you some tales."

Walderen's had a concrete patio out front which overlooked the valley beyond the town. Several wooden tables with benches were interspersed by small leafy trees in tubs. It made for a shady spot from the hot July evening. Rudi Stemmer was immediately recognizable with his completely bald head and giant luxuriant moustache and mutton-chop whiskers. He was revelling in the victory of a just-finished checkers game when Raymond arrived.

"Entschuldigung, bitte, but Frau Stemmer sent me to see you. I am a reporter and have been sent to seek out some human-interest stories concerning the Border. Also, events which have taken place in the past here, now it is coming down. Can you help me?"

"You are from Berlin?" Rudi Stemmer's Saxon accent differed so much from Raymond's, explaining the question. He was a skinny little man, with the deeply wrinkled brown skin of a worker who had spent lots of time outdoors. He was a retired carpenter, the fact reflected by sinewy arms and large, work-worn hands.

"No, actually, I am from Britain," Raymond was confident in his fluency, but to get caught out by these men would not inspire trust. "I would be willing to buy a round of beer for some stories."

"Ah, Englander!"

"Yes."

The game was over and with the natural urge of old folk to talk, encouraged by a voluntary and captive audience buying beer, the men at the table made room for him.

"Do you mind?" Raymond produced the tiny Sony recorder he always carried and set it in the middle of the table.

Now, back in his room, he played back the tape. He was regaled again with inconsequential life histories and daring-do of the war, but threaded through it were some useful leads. There had been quite a few attempts to penetrate the border fortifications since the Communists sealed off East Germany. Determined people trying to flee Communism had thought this remote and sleepy part of the world would offer less vigilance, with tragic results. One exciting lead was of *Nazi Gold*, with gunfire and intrigue in the last few days of the war. Another was an exchange of gunfire between the East German border guards and an armed party caught in the open death zone in the autumn of nineteen forty-seven. The Vopos (Volkpolizei) had been tight-lipped over that event.

One of the men had told him to go interview Franz Verhstassen who lived only a kilometre away from the fence. Franz had more to do with the border than anyone else in Plauen. There was no telephone listing for the man, but Raymond had directions and after a quick lunch, headed out in his car.

Turning off the paved road as instructed and onto a twisting dirt road, Raymond found himself wondering at the scenery. The rolling and picturesque woodland should have been delightful, yet large areas of the trees seemed to be diseased, dying and stripped of leaves. This must be the *Valdsterben*, the destruction of Germany's forests from Eastern industrial pollution that Raymond had read about.

Verhstassen's house was up a sidetrack, soon after a river ford, which Raymond had been assured, was safe to cross, and near the top of the plateau, which the border followed. The house was old and picturesque and from an adjacent workshop, the sound of a power saw screeched through the clearing. Approaching the work area carefully, Raymond alerted an elderly man of his presence and explained his visit. The old man seemed happy to take a break from his work.

Running a hand through his long wispy white hair to remove sawdust, the old fellow only succeeded in making the effect more unruly. His head was narrow, the pink of his scalp showing through the strands. His face was a patchwork of wrinkles, interspersed by exploded capillaries. He looked about eighty years old, perhaps less, with stringy but muscular arms, splotched with age spots and prominent veins. For all that, a bright pair of forget-me-not eyes abutted a nose once broken badly and sporting a nasty scar. He saw Raymond's gaze and touched the spot with a finger. "Brownshirts. Nineteen thirty seven."

He went inside and came back out with a jug of home-brew beer and two large steins. Sitting on the porch, his hair still sprinkled with sawdust, he produced a large curved pipe and tamped it with tobacco. He talked for an hour and a half, placing on the tape enough information to give Raymond an article. He told of abortive attempts where fleeing people never made it through the barrier to the West. Some had stopped, asking shelter, putting him at grave risk, but he had never refused them. He was a kind old man, eloquently troubled by the iniquity of the frontier.

Still, he saved the best until last. Yes, there had been a mysterious heavy truck nearby in the late days of the war. There had been gunfire, which locals had assumed was part of the American offensive, as the Amis arrived only a day or so later. With troops bivouacked all around and a curfew on the population, free access into the area had been impossible. By the time the Americans had pulled out, the Russians had arrived and sealed the frontier.

Two locals had been shot at, one wounded, when they went snooping and this had provided a deterrent to others. Over the next few years, there were the odd outbursts of gunfire, most notably the firefight of nineteen forty-seven. After the mid-fifties, when mines were laid and multiple barbed wire fences and machine guns guarded exodus from East Germany, fewer attempts had been made. When the Berlin Wall went up in nineteen sixty-one, the frontier had also been upgraded to seal it completely.

Raymond thanked the old man and after taking some pictures of his house, took a short walk uphill to the actual frontier. It was a strange experience to approach the formidable frontier zone from the east, as many would-be escapees had. First, there was a clear zone of fifty metres, denuded of vegetation. Between it and the first high wire fence, a track ran parallel which had been patrolled at erratic times with vehicles manned by Border Guards. Signs warning intruders for the last time that they were entering a death zone were spaced at frequent intervals. A short distance away, an abandoned guard tower on high wooden stilts brooded over the sterile area of the death zone. Farm tractors had once frequently raked the area immediately before the fence, ready to betray footprints left by would-be escapees. Already grasses and dandelions had sprung up, mute testimony to the fragility of Man's doctrines in the face of Nature.

Inside the fence were the old familiar signs lettered *Achtung Minen*! With the skull and crossbones signifying death, the meaning was clear in any language. Running off a roll of film, Raymond thought he had captured the essence of the Frontier's menace and ultimate futility. Willie could use them to illuminate the article he had now firmly developed in his mind. He climbed the abandoned watchtower to take the last few frames and gazed out over the minefield between its two fences. While not as outwardly menacing as the Checkpoint Charlie border crossing in Berlin which he knew intimately, the death lurking under the bucolic surroundings brought a shiver to his body. Unconsciously, his writing talents arranged words in his head to describe the scene. Walking back through the woods, he went to his car. The saw was shrieking again. Herr Verhstassen was back at work.

Around nine that night, Verhstassen was still ripping pine stock when he was interrupted again. At first he thought it was the Englishman, back again, but this time it was two men. He thought how popular he was becoming. Shutting down the radial arm saw, he turned but didn't like what he saw. He had seen men like this before, men with a cold callousness.

They were polite at first, asking him if he had received an English visitor. Verhstassen responded in kind but the atmosphere chilled when he asked them their business.

"What did the Englishman want?"

"Merely stories to write for his magazine."

"What did he *really* want?"

"I have told you! What business is it of yours?"

Before he knew what was happening, one of the men had grabbed him, wrenching his arm behind his back. The other had whipped out a pistol and stuck it in his face.

"You have three seconds to tell us what the Englishman wanted!"

"I...have...told you..." The pain in his shoulder was agonizing, exacerbated by his arthritis.

Suddenly, he was whipped around and bent over the bench, his right arm stretched out beneath the saw. One of the men pushed the switch and the blade turned, beginning its ascending pitch whine.

"No, I swear, I have told you everything!" He struggled uselessly as the blade was guided only millimetres from his sleeve. With a sudden swift movement, the blade was drawn right through his forearm. He screamed shrilly as there was a spurt of red and the buzz of bone being cut and then everything was suddenly splattered with blood. The severed arm twitched and his artery was pumping out his lifeblood.

"There is still time to save yourself!"

"But there...is...nothing!" Oddly there was not the amount of pain he'd expected, but he felt light-headed. He tried to say something else but a hammer smashed down on his head, fracturing his skull and driving bone fragments into his brain. He was dead before his body slumped to the floor, his arm still pumping blood as his heart went into one last spasm.

2300 hrs. Thursday, 5th July 1990. Frankfurt.

Al Shapiro whistled as he stepped off the elevator on the tenth floor of his apartment building. Alice had called. All was forgiven and she would be home tomorrow. He'd bought a bottle of champagne and some flowers and would order Chinese food delivery, which she loved. Tomorrow night would be a celebration. Just went to show, those old German wieners couldn't match a strong Jewish-American prick, trained in the Bronx!

There was a pair of skinheads coming down the hallway and he tried to avoid eye contact with them. They were usually aggressive if bothered and tonight was supposed to be a night to contemplate love. He had to put the champagne and flowers down at his door in order to fish out his key. Suddenly, there was an explosion of pain in his head as he was driven into his door, the resounding bang of his forehead meeting the wood soundless to him. His knees turned to water and he slumped to the floor, dropping the key.

There was the rattle of the lock above him and then two pairs of arms grabbed him under the armpits and dragged him inside. Almost as an afterthought, a head and arm appeared from his doorway, scanned for observers, and then hooked the champagne and flowers inside.

When Shapiro began to recover from his daze, he found himself staring into the muzzle of a pistol. He was flabbergasted by what had happened, overloaded and shocked by the event. "Wallet in my jacket." He thought it was a robbery, but the mirthless smile on the bigger of the two shit-heads told him there was something more sinister. Friends of the Kraut restaurant owner? A bad loser?

"You had a visitor the other day." Shapiro gaped at the man. This was getting more weird by the moment! "I believe his name is Raymond Barton." There was a long pause while Shapiro waited for enlightenment.

Suddenly, out of nowhere, the other man hit him in the side of the jaw. "Answer!"

"Ye..yeah!" He had felt the bony grate of his jawbone as it almost became unhinged. There was a salty metal taste in his mouth and he spat blood from his bitten tongue. The white rug was splattered and he wondered how he could take the stains out.

"What did he want?"

"Information."

"Ja, but on what?"

"Stories for an article. He's a journalist, like me. He was sent to do some investigation on the tearing down of the Wall and the Frontier."

"Very good, Herr Jew Shapiro, but what *investigation*?"

"What? He was just working on human interest stories!"

Al felt himself grabbed by the chin and a hand closed over his mouth and nose. A sudden punch to the right kidney turned him twisting and vulnerably to one side. His arm was grabbed and something, the butt of the pistol, was pounding on his fingers. He tried to scream through the hand but the sound just filled his head, compounding the agony.

"Make a sound and you die!" The muzzle of the gun was grinding into his eyeball. He had seen it had a silencer mounted and knew he would die long before any help could come. He sucked in air and held it tight against the pain, terrified.

There was relief from punishment but an ascending level of agony from his injuries as the smaller man began to systematically but quietly ransack the apartment. The larger man kept the pistol firmly to his head while the search went on.

"What are you looking for?"

"You tell *us*, Herr Jew Shapiro!"

He had nothing to offer; their visit was a mystery to him. Vaguely, he began to wonder what Ray Barton might have stumbled into. His thoughts were arrested by the return of the smaller skinhead, shaking his head. With a horrible finality, the gun came around right between his eyes.

"We know about the gold, Jew. Tell us what Herr Barton knows."

Shapiro gaped. "Gold? What the hell are you talking about?" His evident lack of knowledge signed his fate. He watched horrified as the finger tightened on the trigger. His last thought was of Alice.

Anna Grueben discovered her Father's mutilated body the next day. She visited him regularly, now that Mutti was dead. She thought he had had an accident with his saw and did not appreciate the extent of his head injury. There were brown stains everywhere from the blood which had whirled around the saw blade and been flung in a pattern from it. When the ambulance and police arrived, they saw a different picture and Anna was at first mystified by their reactions.

Next day, Alice Shapiro was under no such illusion concerning the means of her husband's death. One look at his shattered head and she ran shrieking into the hallway, barely assimilating the fact that the apartment was torn apart.

14th October 1945. Germany.

When he was processed out of the Wehrmacht, the soldier made his way to Hamburg. As a native of Dresden, he had been offered a travel warrant to take him back there. Like almost every other German soldier, he had no wish to be sent into the Russian zone and since all his family were dead, he settled for a ticket to Hof where he claimed to have an aunt. He had been given a few marks as survival money and spent two days in the area before travelling on to Hanover.

He left Hanover driving a car, with a tank full of gas, and a wallet stuffed with American dollar bills. Three of the gold coins had been sold, albeit cheaply, but he was solvent. He arrived in Hamburg two days later and bought himself an apartment house that was only lightly damaged by bombing.

0800 hrs. Friday, 6th July 1990.

The Kripos got off to a fast start. Al Shapiro had told Alice about Raymond Barton's visit and where he had gone. Alice's scowl at the mention of Raymond's name had contradicted her statement that they were friends. They sent off a routine enquiry concerning Raymond, asking any police unit who could locate him to take him in for questioning. The investigating officers got a rude awakening only hours later when the police in Plauen faxed back a response, which intensified the hunt for the Englishman.

Two dead and obviously tortured bodies in his tracks was too much of a coincidence and an all-points, arrest-on-sight warrant was issued. This in turn flagged the Bundesnachrichtendienst, which had a low priority surveillance on the man. Credit card use and the car rental agency's information on the Toyota's plates pinned down Raymond's location. A massive manhunt commenced in Plauen.

0200 hrs. 12th September 1946. Vogtland, Germany.

The man crawled carefully over the uneven ground. He had passed under the wire marking the frontier on the West German side and he was about fifteen metres out into the area beyond. The night was black as pitch as he had deliberately chosen a moonless one. Low clouds blocked out any other kind of light and he had spent two hours in the woods beforehand, letting his night vision come to its peak. Even so, he could just barely see his hand before his face and only the faint outline of some higher trees on the far side of the meadow guided him to his goal.

He had studied all the maps but there was no village of Grosskirchenhälle. He was not surprised that Mannheimer had made the name up, just to lull him. An old local map showing roads had enabled him to trace a narrow track from a nearby ford on the other side of the border. Coupled with backtracking from memory, he had managed to find the place again.

He had carefully blazed two trees, on their west side, at the very edge of the open area and used them as a starting point. He was dressed totally in black woollen clothing, which would not rustle as he moved. In a holster on his back he carried a Luger pistol he had bought from a needy ex-Wehrmacht officer. A small flashlight dug into him as he moved and the American Army entrenching tool and wire cutters also strapped to his back hampered his careful movements.

Dimly, a darker shape swam before him; a shape he knew could only be the barn. Once inside, he could shine the flashlight and start digging for the treasure he had dreamed about for the past sixteen months. The barn was still about forty metres away and it was at least another forty, he had estimated through the binoculars earlier, to the first line of wire on the Russian side.

He could feel his heartbeat in his eardrums and it reminded him of the night he was wounded in France. Thousands of East Germans had fled the new Communist regime and many had been killed trying to cross the frontier which had been closed since the Russians took their post-war occupation zone under control. Signs made it clear that trespassers in this zone would be shot on sight, but his mission transcended any apprehensions he might have about being shot at.

Carefully, he eased forward again, totally unaware of the trip wire suspended only a few centimetres above the ground. His hands and trunk passed over it, but his left knee caught it as he pushed forward. There was a wild clanking of alarms off to his left and suddenly voices were raised.

"Achtung! Achtung!" A couple of rifles were fired his direction, but the man knew they could not have seen him and were firing blind. They were trying to panic him into betraying his position, and it worked. He stumbled to his feet and fled back the way he had come as fast as he could run. A tuft of grass caught his feet and he went down, just as there was another deeper report and he saw the expected climbing trail of a flare pistol round going into the sky. There was a small depression before him and he rolled into it, put his face into the soil and screwed his eyes shut as tight as he could.

When the flare popped, the glow penetrated his eyelids and it seemed like the sun had come to earth. There was some spasmodic shooting, but obviously, the Border Guards could not see him and were still trying to scare him enough to break cover now they had some light to see him by. After ten seconds, the flare drifted down and began to dim. Once it went out, the intruder knew the guards would be blind and not recover night vision for several minutes.

As the flare went out, he counted to five and then leapt to his feet again, fear lending extra power to his driving legs. In seconds he was back at the wire, the cutters in his hand. Thirty seconds later, he was flat on his back in the cover of the woods, chest heaving while he cursed and cursed his luck. He would need a better plan, a diversion or something, to gain access to the frontier zone with enough time to get even some of the gold out.

0900 hrs. Friday, 6th July 1990. Plauen.

Raymond came out of his pension. His Toyota was parked invisible behind the hedge of the house's garden that the owner had converted into a car park. Today he was going to take a drive across the border to visit the spas of Bad Elster and Bad Brambach, about thirty kilometres away. Last night he had structured his first article and after fleshing it out with the flavour of any discoveries today, he could fax it off to Willie in London.

It was going to be another beautiful day and he was looking forward to seeing the famous Erzgebirge mountain range. He stopped at a stop sign, about to take the road south out of town, waiting for a police car to drive by. Just as he was about to pull forward in expectation of its passage, the vehicle slammed on its brakes and swerved towards him. Rocking on its springs, the vehicle came to rest only inches from his bumper, blocking his way.

A policeman was scrambling out on the far side of the vehicle when Raymond, in the angered flash of a near miss, threw open his door. Behind him there came a screech of tires and he threw a glance over his shoulder to see another police vehicle hem him in from behind while still another skidded sideways to point itself forty-five degrees to the road and headed right for him. In seconds, he found himself hemmed in by five pistol-wielding Polizei.

They searched him roughly, handcuffing him and shoving him into one of the patrol cars with two policemen. One officer jumped into the Toyota and in seconds they were speeding off, sirens blaring. Despite his enraged questioning of their actions, none of the officers spoke to him, a fact that unnerved Raymond. In minutes, they pulled up at the Polizeipräsidium where he was marched into a bare room with a wooden table and two chairs, kept watch over by the stern, unyielding stare of a single officer.

Another man entered the room. "You are Herr Raymond Barton?"

"Yes, what is this all about?"

The detective, a tall thin man with pockmarked face and sparse black hair raised a palm. "Please, you will respond only to my questions!" To the side, a second detective now entered the room and stood, arms folded, against the wall, watching Raymond's profile. "You have a friend, Alvin Shapiro, who lives in Frankfurt?"

"Yes, I visited him a couple of nights ago and we had dinner together in Sachsenhausen." The two officers were staring at each other, a blank exchange that conveyed nothing to Raymond. "Look...!"

"And you also visited Herr Franz Verhstassen locally?"

"Yes, I saw him last night. Very nice, helpful man," Raymond stopped, riveted. "What has happened?"

"They have both been found dead, Herr Barton," the officer said it in an *as-if-you-didn't-know* tone of voice.

"But I didn't...They were *murdered*?"

"Yes, Herr Barton," the cop stretched out the 'yes', emphasizing his disbelief in Raymond's ignorance of the matter.

There was a long stunned silence. "Something's going on! My girlfriend phoned from England yesterday to say our flat had been broken into and ransacked," Raymond fumbled in his jacket for his cell-phone but the arresting officers had taken it. "Look, phone her. Phone the police in London. She will have reported it by now. They can tell you! Phone my boss in London, Willie McIvor at *Current Events Magazine*."

"Yes, we will do all these things, Herr Barton, while you sit in your cell and decide when you are going to explain yourself to us."

Raymond would have retorted but he was, he realized, operating without the full facts. It might prove better in the long run to say nothing until Willie in London sorted this mess out. He felt numb at the thought that Al Shapiro had been murdered. Taking him by an arm, the uniformed officer took him downstairs and locked him up in a cell by himself.

Enquiries from Bonn concerning a certain Mr. Raymond Barton brought the same response from London as the Frankfurt Kripos had received from Plauen. Scotland Yard wanted to talk to Mr. Barton. *Immediately.*

After receiving a complaint from his fiancée, Miss Mandy Smythe, concerning a break-in at the flat they shared in London, the Metropolitan police had investigated but could not find Ms. Smythe when they tried to pursue the enquiry. She had not been seen at her workplace where she was a computer analyst, nor had her parents heard from her, even though she had told them, the day of the break-in, that she wanted to stay with them until the break-in matter was resolved. She was presently presumed to be missing.

With Federal capital crimes to investigate and the Bundesnachtrichtendienst also on his back, the senior investigating officer in Bonn, Chief Inspector Mattias Schultze, got on the phone to Plauen immediately and instructed the police there to ship Herr Barton to Bonn as soon as possible, under escort.

1000 hrs. Saturday 7th July 1990. Plauen.

When the police officers came for Raymond they first sent him to the bathroom and then handcuffed him for the journey. A raincoat thrown over his shoulders hid the fact that he was manacled and they went out to a waiting car that would take them to the airport at Nürnberg.

It was only about seventy kilometres on the A9 Autobahn to Nürnberg and at the speed they were travelling, it would take about thirty or forty minutes to do the trip. Raymond had settled down to a dull state of incomprehension. The Kripos had told him about Mandy being missing and he had to agree, it only made him look guiltier of something, although what exactly he didn't know. He had hardly slept in the night and the added worry about Mandy had knotted his stomach into a clutch of concern.

They were halfway along when the radio crackled to life. The tinny voice of a dispatcher instructed the driver to pull over in the next autobahn rest area and wait for a car following them. Police and prisoner alike wondered what else could be happening. Carefully changing lanes, the driver brought them to the right and slipped into the exit road. It was a little-used stop, with no services, other than some public lavatories.

The car stopped and they sat and waited. One of the two officers got out and strolled up and down, smoking a cigarette. Done, he stepped on the butt and climbed back in with a sigh. "Here they come."

The driver saw the other car pull off the freeway and come up behind them. Two men got out and walked towards them, one on either side of the car. Raymond was sitting diagonally behind the driver and he turned his head to the left as the driver wound his window down, as did the officer next to him. The man on the driver side marched by almost as if he was going to go right by then suddenly swivelled as he reached the line of the windshield. His left arm came up wielding a pistol and there was a muffled cough as he shot the driver in the face.

The man next to Raymond exclaimed and grabbed for his shoulder holster. The side passenger window starred and imploded glass fragments and then the man in the back seat leaped back, taken in the chest by a bullet. A second cough came and his face suddenly sported a hole, red splatters staining the rear window behind him.

It had all happened so fast and Raymond just froze. The man on the right side of the car threw open the rear door and waggled his silenced gun to indicate he should get out. Raymond knew the other man now had a gun pointed at his back and had absolutely no other choice than to shuffle across the seat and put his feet on the ground. Ducking his head, he left the car and moved away from it. He was shaking so badly he could barely walk. They both grabbed him and thrust him into the rear of the other car, face down. One of the men climbed in the back with him and pushed his gun into Raymond's back. In moments they were speeding away down the autobahn.

Still handcuffed and helpless, Raymond harangued the two men, trying to get something out of them. He needed a clue as to what was going on and nothing was forthcoming. According to the police, Al and Herr Verhstassen had both been murdered and after reporting their flat trashed, Mandy had disappeared. The man in the back seat with him, finally exasperated, moved the muzzle up to his neck and pushed hard. No word was spoken; the message was to stay quiet.

In a very short time they were in Nürnberg. The man next to him told him to get down on the floor, a prod of the pistol encouraging him to comply. It was a tight uncomfortable squeeze and the man placed his feet on top of Raymond's, his pistol held loosely against Raymond's crotch. For some reason, he found this more disconcerting than when the weapon had been held to his head. They stopped a couple of times and then turned at a road junction. Not knowing the town, Raymond had no idea which way they were going. They stopped again and he heard the faint sound of people crossing the street. The driver pressed the accelerator and they pulled away.

"Scheisse!" The yell from the driver was followed by a terrific crash from the left side and Raymond's head was driven against the rear right door. The door burst open and he half-fell out into the roadway. There was another crash from nearby and he flinched, waiting to be run over by some other vehicle. Rolling onto his back, he could see that their car had been rammed side-on by a big Mercedes which must have run the traffic light. His escort in the back seat was slumped over, blood running from a head wound. He could not see the driver, but sensed he was out of commission also.

He gathered his knees under him, dizzy from the blow to the head, and somehow straightened them, staggering sideways and falling against the rear side of the trunk. Bouncing off, he reeled away, staggering to the sidewalk. There was a shout behind him and something like a loud bee sang past his ear. There was a coffee shop on the corner and he lurched through the doorway. A counter with an attractive blonde lady behind it blocked his path and he swung towards an opening next to some cold drink coolers.

The blonde yelled something at him but he was in the kitchen, dodging a cook and headed for the back door. The alley smelled like freedom and he dashed up it, turning right, away from the corner of the street where the car had been hit. A few yards up was a department store side entrance and keeping his arms folded to hide the manacles on his wrists, he turned in there, taking an escalator to the second floor. A washroom sign urged him on and he burst into the tiled retreat, finding it empty. He went into one of the stalls, locked the door and sat on the toilet, breath heaving in his chest.

It was hard to analyze what was happening. In the last twenty-four hours, four men who had come in contact with him had been killed. His flat in London had been turned over, Mandy had disappeared and it was inescapable that someone believed he knew something of which he was unaware. Raymond searched desperately through his mind, trying to make connections to the men he had met, but there was nothing. It could only have something to do with a situation he had stumbled upon blindly. For that, some gang was willing to murder two police officers, out in the open, in broad daylight. That gave him pause.

The police had obviously been searching for him in Plauen. Now they would be searching frantically, believing he was part of the double murder of their comrades. There was nothing more determined on earth than cops searching for cop-killers. It was time to leave Germany. But how? His wallet, cell-phone and passport were in the hands of the police. He had, literally, nothing in his pockets that might help.

With the adrenaline rush subsiding and his heartbeat coming under control, Raymond tried to concentrate. He would need help. He needed to shed the handcuffs. He needed money. He needed a way out of Germany. From a phone he could use his memorized credit card number to call someone, but whom? Willie McIvor was too far away to help and for all he knew, might turn him in for Al's murder. Astrid! She was the only person he could trust and she would help him, he knew.

Leaving the washroom, he went through the department store, keeping his arms folded, trying to hide the manacles in his sleeves and shambling along like he was a carefree shopper killing time. As he'd suspected, there was a row of telephones at one of the ground floor entrances and he went up to one on the end. A woman went up to the one next to it and she was close enough not to miss a word he might say. Since most Germans knew English, he would not be safe even talking to Astrid in that language.

He turned away, shambling over to the opposite wall of the lobby, stomach churning, and mind in an uproar. The woman was haranguing someone, probably her poor husband because the credit card payment had not been made and she couldn't charge some inconsequential thing she craved. Raymond wondered how much the poor bastard would pay him right now to stroll over and strangle the damned bitch.

His head kept swivelling back and forth, wondering when the next person might appear who could need the phone. He stopped himself, catching up with the thought that he was making himself obvious as a person of suspicion or distress - a loiterer. It was not a moment too soon as a uniformed security guard strolled out, circled the lobby and, after giving Raymond a knowing scrutiny, went back inside. With a massive application of self-control, Raymond eased his breathing and tried to look casual. The woman was winding up her conversation and he had to get on the phone and look normal before the guard came back. Fortunately, the police had left a few coins in his pocket to pay for the call. Awkwardly, he wrestled the necessary change out of his pocket into the phone pay slot.

The phone rang. It was eleven o'clock. Would Astrid be home? He willed her to answer the phone. On the fourth ring, as he began to panic and lose it, the phone was picked up.

"Klemerer residenz," it was a man's voice, reeking of service.

"Frau Klemerer, bitte."

"Whom shall I say is calling, sir?"

"Herr Barton."

"Thank you." The wait seemed interminable. Even though being on the phone was legitimate, Raymond dreaded the security guard's return. The man's glance had been obvious; act normally, or else! One sight of the handcuffs and he was in real trouble.

"Raymond!" It was Astrid. "Where are you, what are you..."

"Astrid, shut up and listen!" Raymond paused, her silent acquiescence his clue to go on. "I am in the deepest shit you ever saw! I need your help. I need it now. I need it unreservedly and with commitment!"

"Of course, darling, you know you can count on me!"

"I am in Nürnberg. Get here as soon as you can, bring your passport and lots of money."

"Raymond, what is going on?"

"Astrid, just trust me, I desperately need your help!"

" Very well, but how shall I find you?"

"Oh shit!"

"Are you not in a hotel?"

"No. I have no wallet, no money, and no credit cards."

"Very well, I shall phone for a hotel reservation. Let me see, hmm, the er, Atrium!... Ja, the Atrium Hotel in Münchenerstrasse. Can you get there?" Astrid sounded triumphant at her ability to pick a place.

"Yeah, I'll find it. When can you get here?"

"About four hours, I guess."

"Oh, shit!"

"What?"

"I am being pursued. I don't know whether I can stay hidden that long."

"Hidden?...Raymond, what the...?" Astrid dropped the thought, caught up in his anxiety. "I will call ahead, make a reservation and tell them to let you into my room. Meet me there."

"Very good. Tell them to expect Herr Stoltzer."

"I'm on my way, Liebschen!"

It was difficult with the handcuffs, especially trying to keep them concealed from passers-by, but Raymond managed to consult the telephone directory for the Atrium address and looked up the name of the department store, read from the glass doors. He found a convenient city map in the back of the book. The Atrium turned out to be two kilometres away, in the Luitpoldhain Park. Since he had no money, Raymond was forced to walk but it gave him time to think and killed off some time until Astrid's arrival. He walked the whole distance with his arms folded to disguise the handcuffs. The hotel was a ritzy-looking place, all glass and concrete. Knowing he had no resources, the police would hardly look for him in such an expensive place.

The desk clerk gave him a quick, knowing look at the mention of Astrid's phoned-in reservation. He stepped to his computer keyboard and communicated with it interminably before sliding a key onto the counter between the raised front portion. "Room five ten, Herr Stoltzer. Have a pleasant stay."

Raymond had been terrified the man would ask him to sign something. It would be impossible to do so without revealing the handcuffs and he had been madly searching for an excuse to suddenly disappear in that event. Now he had to pick up the key while the man scrutinized him. The man's eyebrows were gradually going up as Raymond hesitated to pick up the key.

"Oh, is there a message for me, or Frau Klemerer?" The man turned to scan the rows of room pigeonholes and Raymond seized his opportunity to raise both hands and snatch the key, shielded from side view by the raised counter frontage.

"No, sir, there is nothing."

"Thank you." Raymond headed for the elevators, using his body to conceal his two-handed button push from the clerk's gaze. He found himself shaking and took a long, deep breath.

"Raymond!" Hours later, Astrid stood in the doorway of the hotel room, beaming her pleasure. She was still as beautiful as ever, long-flowing white-blonde hair, tight black toreador pants over her gorgeous long legs and ample hips. A white cut-away vest under a fawn coloured open jacket gave equal and tantalizing glimpses of a bare midriff and substantial cleavage. Her grey eyes sparkled her pleasure at seeing him and he melted to the sight of the pale pink lip-gloss, which touched off desire for her like a fuse on a stick of dynamite. He remembered the pleasures those narrow lips and tongue had offered him in the past and despite his plight, he felt a stirring in his groin. Astrid stepped forward, dumped her shoulder bag and embraced him. The uplifted firmness of her large breasts reinforced the body chemistry he was suffering.

Her eyebrows went up when she saw the handcuffs, but with the lasciviousness of familiarity, her hand crept up his thigh and the flat of her palm pressed against his growing erection. "You are pleased to see me then?"

"Astrid! Stop that! You are a married woman and I'm engaged now."

She pouted for the sake of form, confident in her small victory that she could arouse and tempt him at any time. Stepping forward again, she kissed him gently on the cheek. "Why don't I open the honour bar and pour us a couple of drinks while you tell me what this is all about," she was being remarkably calm under the circumstances.

"What have you told your husband?"

"Rolf is in Paris for a few days, he has my cell number, so he can call me if he needs to. He will not be concerned. He spends all his time working at KEB and neglects me," she was proffering Raymond a scotch but her free hand went to his face and stroked his cheek. "He's not as good as you, Raymond, and I think you are at my mercy," she tugged playfully at the handcuffs.

"Astrid! Knock it off! Mandy is missing and people have died. I need your help and I have nowhere else to turn."

"I should be angry if you turned anywhere else first, Raymond. Now, tell me!"

Quickly, Raymond outlined the story to her. It struck him again that it was all a little James Bond-esque, with the good guy marching into the bad guys' game, escaping by a hair, and then meeting a beautiful woman in a hotel room.

For all she liked to play the blonde bimbo, Astrid was as smart as she was beautiful and grasped the situation immediately. "So, you came looking for a story which was promising to be a real yawner and people you have met with have been systematically murdered. It is understandable, I think, that the police should want you in custody but there is another party at work, namely the men who killed the two cops in the rest area. Do you have *any* clue what this is about?"

Raymond shook his head. "This whole thing got started after I arrived in Germany. I'm only guessing, but buried Nazi gold is the only story I've blundered across which could trigger these events."

"If someone has kidnapped Mandy, then they expect to use her as leverage for some purpose. To make you talk?"

"About what? I don't know anything!"

"Perhaps Nazi gold, Raymond. *Do* you know where it is?"

"No, of course not! *Jesus,* Astrid!"

"So, what is your plan now?"

"I have to get these manacles off my wrists and figure out some kind of disguise. Then I have to get out of Germany, go back to London and try to find Mandy. Maybe you can buy me some clothes, hair dye and glasses. You had better get some plain clothes and stop looking so gorgeous. There is not a man in Europe who could forget seeing you looking like that. You certainly will arouse suspicion walking into a hardware store and buying cutters and a hacksaw."

Astrid smiled and began to purr at his compliment.

"And get yourself a room, we cannot stay together."

"But Raymond!"

"Don't *but* me, Astrid. If any of those people, cops or bad guys find me, you are in deep shit too. They have not hesitated to ruthlessly murder people I have met with. I will not have you at risk!"

"Raymond, the room is in my name. If I rent two rooms now, it will be suspicious. If you rent one, you will have to surrender your passport, which you told me you don't have. British national. No passport? No room! Even if you had the passport, the police will know where you are in a matter of hours. I think you are stuck with sharing a room with me," Astrid smiled smugly.

"Oh, very well! Go and get the stuff."

Astrid left. While she was gone, Raymond phoned Willie McIvor. Willie already knew about Al as a matter of course, but the other murders caused him to whistle down the phone. "You've obviously stumbled across something really big, laddie."

"Yes, Willie, but how the hell am I going to get out of this? I have to find Mandy! All the ferries, airports and railways will be watched. I'm a marked man and Interpol will be on this now, so the Bobbies will be looking for me too if I get back there."

"Listen; let me see what I can find out from this end. Meantime, I think you should move on. Use Manny Kruppe in Hamburg as a contact, and here - use this authorization for calls so they can't be traced," Willie rattled off a bunch of numbers. "Phone me tomorrow."

Raymond signed off more concerned and confused than ever. Astrid was back in an hour and a half, toting a large bag. She had bought and changed into clothes while out, returning in blue jeans and a dark coat with a headscarf covering her mane of blonde hair. She dumped cutting tools, changes of clothes and toiletries for both of them, plus a bottle of scotch and items for Raymond's disguise onto the floor. It took almost an hour, but the manacles were removed and they discussed their plan further while Astrid scrubbed the Clairol dye into Raymond's hair. She had bought scissors and an electric trimmer and would shorten his hair when it was dry.

Astrid had been doing some more clear-headed thinking. "The best way to get you to England is on a car ferry. We can use my car and you can hide in the trunk when we board and also when I drive through customs at the far end. They rarely search too many vehicles, so the odds are good. Have you considered that if people are really holding Mandy, you must let them know where you are? If you continue to hide, how can they contact you?"

"I have a nasty feeling they can, without any help from me. Someone is plugged into the authorities, how else could they have intercepted that car on the way here to Nürnberg?"

"Odessa? CIA? KGB? Bundesnachtrichtendienst?"

"Yeah, or something very much like them. I just wish I could figure this out!" Raymond clenched his fists in frustration, gazing at his new image in the mirror. Astrid had shortened and darkened his hair and the clear glasses gave him a studious air.

1400 hrs. Saturday, 7th July 1990. Polizeipraesidium, Frankfurt.

Chief Inspector Matthias Schultze looked up from the pathologist's report. "So, this tells us Shapiro was killed after Herr Barton left Frankfurt but it does not clear him of complicity."

Across the room, Inspector Mark Stumpfl nodded. "There is more to this than we presently know, sir. Two civilians murdered, perhaps by the same group, in different places, only hours apart. Then we have the two officers killed and Herr Barton escaping. The evidence at the scene does not suggest he escaped by himself, but had accomplices.

I have ordered details on all murders in Germany for the past two weeks and my men are sorting through them. There is a report of gunshots coming from the scene of a car accident in Nürnberg but before the local police got to the scene, the two men in the car had vanished. They were both reported as injured, but disappeared in the melée following the collision."

"That is certainly odd. Descriptions?"

"The usual contradictions, but one witness insists that a third man left the car right after it was hit. It struck him as strange that he did not stick around to help the other men he was travelling with. The offending vehicle in the crash was driven by some woman who has been charged with impaired driving, so it was an accident, not a set-up collision. Why shots were fired is unknown."

"I think you are right, Mark, it must have been Herr Barton. Nürnberg is the obvious place his vehicle would have gone. Yet we still need him to explain what has been going on. Has Interpol been brought in?"

"Yes, I am sure he will try to get back to Britain somehow to investigate the disappearance of his fiancée. It seems he was maybe telling the truth about that, which only muddies the water further."

"And the interrogating officer says his anger was real, so he may not be responsible for her disappearance. Well, put out a priority on him and alert all travel facilities. See what other clues there may be in Nürnberg."

1500 hrs. Saturday, 7th July 1990. Athens, Greece.

The man el-Cetti and Ben-Ahwed met in a dingy cafe spoke Spanish fluently and they conversed in that language, el-Cetti translating for his associate. El-Cetti was to proceed to New York per arrangements already made. There, he would be contacted and given a weapon so powerful it would kill thousands of people. It was to be a strike against the Americans.

El-Cetti, quickly seeing that any weapon of mass destruction should be better directed against Israel, suggested it be released in Tel Aviv, but the man would have none of it. "You must obey the plan," the man became quite authoritarian. "Smarter men than you have conceived this method and it is part of a greater plan to destroy Israel. This is merely the beginning of a master plan to rid the world of them. By the end of the year, Israel will cease to exist."

It did el-Cetti no harm to listen to the rest of the briefing, but his mind was whirling with the possibilities. Already, he entertained the idea of reneging and carrying the weapon to Israel. He would send Ben-Ahwed back to el-Saeed, suggesting such. What would some South American Spaniard know about the fight against world Jewry? He had deduced from the accent that is where this man was from.

The man gave him a briefcase with money, airline tickets and a new identity to enter the United States. Hotel reservations were made to ensure his contact there would know where to find him. The man handed them a large sealed envelope that contained the detailed plan, warning them it was encoded, meant for el-Saeed's eyes only, and any effort by them to view it would be fatal. Since their training made them conscious of the need to compartmentalize any operation by need-to-know, the two men readily agreed. Next day, Ben-Ahwed left, carrying the plan, along with el-Cetti's suggestion.

Two days later, the phone rang. It was el-Saeed. "How is your mother?" It was the code authorizing the mission.

"She is well, but sad of heart. She pines to hear my brother's voice."

"Your brother has erred in judgment. His father has rejected his words. He must come back to Allah to receive forgiveness. Allah watches his every action. Allah akhbar!"

"Allah akhbar." El-Cetti hung up the phone, heavy of heart. El-Saeed had rejected his plan and made it clear his life was forfeit if he did not carry out his orders. Without the secret weapon, he could do nothing. If, when he did have it, he tried to change the plan by journeying to Israel with it, watchers would kill him. Besides, airline security would probably ensure he could not smuggle such an object onto an aircraft. He went to a local mosque the next day and prayed to Allah for guidance. There was no response. He had hoped that he could die on this mission, but the plan did not call for that. Now, he learned he would have to cool his heels in Athens for nearly a week before leaving.

1500 hrs. Saturday, 7th July 1990.
Secret Intelligence Service, London.

"Is he one of ours?" Sir Ralph Ponsonby leaned way back in his chair at Century House in London and regarded the man opposite. His fat, three hundred pound body overflowed the seat, but seemed to cause him no discomfort. His bespectacled moon face made its habitual squint as the question was posed and he gazed out over the substantial mound of his belly at his companion. An old school tie lay limp across his shirt, as if it had over-feasted on the gravy stains it sported.

"No, sir. He was a low-grade military intelligence analyst on a term commission until nineteen eighty-eight, paying his way through university. He is a journalist now and has no direct connection with us."

"...Direct?"

"He is on the *possible list*, people we would approach if they were going into sensitive areas and we could make use of them."

"In other words, he might still be considered, by outsiders, as one of ours."

"Yes sir. Incidentally, his father was a Lieutenant-Colonel during the second war, commanding officer of an Allied *Gold Rush* team, the units that had the responsibility of tracking down Nazi gold."

"And the decrypt puts him right in the middle of this?" The conversation was taking place because GCHQ, the British electronic snooping agency had, from all the telephone conversations taking place, picked out the one between Willie McIvor and Raymond Barton. The intercept request had been made at the highest level of the Secret Intelligence Service, by Ponsonby himself. The computers, monitoring literally millions of conversations simultaneously, had been clued to search for certain key words in a conversation and had picked them out and recorded its content. "Where was he?"

"Traced back to Nürnberg, sir, at the Atrium hotel, room five ten."

"Get some people on it. I don't like the kidnapping here at this end. Put a team on him and get him out of Germany, if you can."

"Yes sir." The assistant walked from the room, closing the door behind him. Stencilled in gold letters on the outside of the door were the words: *Director, European Counter-Intelligence.*

1700 hrs. Saturday, 7th July 1990. Atrium Hotel, Nürnburg.

When the phone rang, Raymond and Astrid froze. "Your husband?" Astrid shook her head. Raymond picked up the phone like he would a poisonous snake. The sound on the line suggested it was long distance.

"Hello?" The voice was British. Raymond's foreboding grew. Why would someone place a call in Germany and initiate the conversation in English? "Hello, are you there, Mr. Barton?" Raymond felt his bowels turn to water. Covering the mouthpiece he whipped around to Astrid.

"Pack everything. Now!"

Without a word, she leapt to obey.

"Mr. Barton, are you there, sir? This is James Grier from the Embassy in Bonn. Do I have Mr. Barton?"

Raymond listened, silent.

"Sir, *'Arthur'* wishes to be remembered to you."

Raymond was electrified. *Arthur* was a classified operation he had worked on in the Army. The man was establishing his credentials.

"What do you want?"

"You are in a spot of bother, I understand. *'Uncle'* wants you to get out of there *immediately*. Phone in to your old office number as soon as you can." There was a click and Raymond was left with a dial tone.

"What is it, Raymond?"

"We're blown! Somehow, people know where we are. Phone for a porter, we have to get out of here. Order a taxi also."

"But I have my car!"

"We'll come back for it. There's no time to carry the bags out to the parking lot!" Frantically they threw their stuff together. The porter was quickly at their door and Astrid gave him ten marks to take the bags down and load them into a taxi. Raymond was kicking himself for not paying heed to Willie's warning on the phone. He had wasted time.

On the way down in the elevator, they planned their departure. They would walk close together, yet far enough apart so they could pretend to be together, or apart, as circumstances dictated. If the police were already watching the place, the disguise, plus the fact he was not alone might help them get by.

The elevator doors opened and Astrid walked out, Raymond slightly behind and to her right. They were halfway across the lobby when they saw two police cars brake to a rapid stop outside. They had arrived without sirens. Four uniformed and three plainclothes men leapt out, ignoring the protests of the doorman at their infringement on his territory as they hurried to the main doors.

Grabbing Astrid's arm, Raymond engaged her in conversation while steering her towards the gift shop. He held his arm out, indicating which way she should go, trying to act naturally, and conscious that a sudden dash to one side would alert the police. They had split into three groups, the uniforms taking the stairs and one plainclothes officer staying in the lobby. The rest went to the elevators.

There was a side entrance to the hotel on the other side of the gift shop and Raymond and Astrid slipped into the passageway leading to it. Doors for salons lined each side and numerous people were passing to and fro. Looking over his shoulder, Raymond saw only a young couple following in their path; the man carrying a tourist bag slung over one shoulder. At Raymond's whisper, Astrid moved away from him, slowing her pace to give them some separation again.

The doors to the street were along another short passageway, around a blind corner. As Raymond turned the corner, two men jumped him, one faking blundering into him as the other jammed a gun into his ribs. "Come carefully, Herr Barton." The words were spoken with determination and he knew he was helpless. "You will walk..."

The man's words were cut off as a purse slammed into his face, knocking him off balance. Wielding her heavy bag like a hammer thrower, Astrid prepared to hit him again, but was tackled from behind by a third man. Raymond had thrown an elbow at the man who had initially bumped into him, receiving a grunt of pain as encouragement. His recovery was swift however and he launched a powerful kick that caught Raymond in the back of the knees, bringing him down.

Before Raymond knew it, a pistol was coming to bear on him. The man had fury in his face and there seemed no hope. Suddenly, there was a muted cough and the man's expression turned to one of surprise. He froze and then slowly crumpled, shot through the chest. Trying to climb to his feet, Raymond caught a whiff of perfume and then the muzzle of yet another gun was shoved into his side.

"This way, Mr. Barton." It was the young woman tourist he had seen walking behind them moments before. She was pretty at close range but there was no doubt of her determination and the heat from the muzzle against his shirt told him it was she who had shot his assailant. Glancing over at Astrid, Raymond saw the male companion close to her, so she was probably covered with a gun too. Unconscious, or dead beside them, lay the other thug who had jumped him.

"Carefully now, you are with friends." The statement did not reassure Raymond in the slightest but he had no choice. With a gun on each of them, they were helpless. Outside in the street, a delivery van miraculously appeared at curbside and they were urged quickly into it.

1200 hrs. Saturday, 7th July 1990.
Office of the Director, European Counter-Intelligence,
Secret Intelligence Service, London.

"One dead, sir, the other unconscious and suffering possible permanent neck injuries."

Ponsonby leaned back precariously in his chair, his considerable bulk causing it to creak alarmingly. He seemed unperturbed but his assistant winced, expecting a momentary upset. "Burton and this woman - this - er, Astrid Klemerer, they got away?"

"Yes sir, they were seen climbing into a van at the side entrance of the hotel in company with two others. We believe they saw the police arriving, went out the side door, and ran into the two casualties. By the time the police got their act together, they were long gone, the two men were down and Barton's bags were still sitting in a taxi out front, with an impatient driver."

"So, they changed their plan at the sight of the police, ran into the two - what did you call them, Jenkins, *casual help*?"

"Yes sir, they were freelancers."

"And then, they either overpowered the freelancers or had help from these other people."

"Quite right, sir. We now have three parties chasing Barton: the Kriminalpolizei, the *freelancers* employers, and the people who got in the car with Barton."

"You are sure they are not part of his group, or whatever?"

"Possible, I suppose."

"If not, there are four parties. We have to include ourselves."

"Yes, of course."

"The embassy got in touch with Barton?"

"Indeed. The timing of the whole thing would suggest he fled right after the call, but the hotel was already under surveillance by the three parties I have indicated."

"Do you think Barton will call Berlin, as we asked?"

"Hard to say, sir. He *should*, but again, we do not know whether he went voluntarily with these people. He could be captive again."

"Him and the woman," Ponsonby mused, leaning further back, bringing the chair to near-terminal cant. "I wonder why everyone is so interested in our Mr. Barton?" The question was rhetorical. Ponsonby had suspected from the start what was going on and as soon as Jenkins was gone, he would be opening his safe to review some briefing information.

"I have a nasty feeling there will be more, sir. At a time when German re-unification is taking place and Communist states are succumbing to common sense, one might expect nothing quite so deep as this strange business."

Ponsonby looked at Jenkins with new respect. Old hands developed a sense, a hair prickling, an antenna tuned to the slightest zephyr of circumstance. Jenkins was maturing.

"Very well," Ponsonby sat forward decisively, the front legs of the chair groaning at the impact. "I want a *'Search One'* initiated on Raymond Barton."

Jenkins looked alarmed. "A *Search One*? Would you confirm that, sir?" A Search One authorized armed conflict, trespass across international boundaries and airlift support to secure the person or persons identified. It could only be authorized after consultation with Ten Downing Street.

"Yes George, Search One. I don't want to tie your hands, but you must receive my authorization before resorting to the ultimate sanctions of such an order. Go find Raymond Barton!"

Jenkins left, mind in turmoil. He disdained use of the creaky old lifts in Century House, preferring to nimbly steer his feet down the concrete stairs. Normally it was an uplifting experience, like a complex dance step as his quick feet took him down, the tempo raising the level of adrenaline, boosting his sense of power. Now, he went down unconsciously. Ponsonby, once again, was several steps ahead of him. The old bastard had already sought and received authorization to escalate the situation. Something was going on to which he was not privy and even toasting his feet before a roaring fire this evening, nursing a couple of shots of Dalwhinny single malt was not going to ease his concerns.

Had he known Jenkins' thoughts, Ponsonby would have been proud, but Jenkins was already far from his mind. With a fat paw, he pulled a file from his safe, spun the combination and returned to his chair. The first week of his appointment to Head of European Counter-Intelligence, ten years before, had been an eye-opener. Secrets previously denied him were placed in his care with the attendant responsibilities, risks and stomach-acid consequences. His vision of the British Empire, its democratic process, cricket and fair play had been shaken to the core.

To preserve placement as the quintessential fountain of democracy and freedom, several British governments, through the services of various secret manipulators, had engaged in the basest activities and subterfuges imaginable. Having attended a public school, Ponsonby knew the clichés that attended the image of such bulwarks of the Empire. Yet it was these very highly regarded, honourable individuals who, with a determination born of patriotic duty, saw fit to suborn their avowed principles to satisfy patriotic ends. One of Ponsonby's heroes was Winston Churchill, whom he believed had stated that in order to defend democracy, it may be necessary at times to stoop to the same kind of devious behaviour that the enemy engaged in.

The file was code-named *'Sandbag'* and Ponsonby shuddered at the revealing words the British often chose to name their secrets. He preferred the American computer-generated method that would spit out a totally sterile and disassociated name instead of one which suffered from human association weaknesses.

The Sandbag file was intended to achieve one purpose; protect the British government from embarrassment. Indeed, it called for any scrutiny to be sandbagged at any cost. Amongst a catalogue of possible embarrassments, the extraction and relocation of certain high-ranking Nazis from Germany in the closing days of the Second World War was listed. His office had permanent and deadly authority to accomplish this responsibility. If Ponsonby had reason to believe that Raymond Barton had stumbled across such information, he was pre-authorized to have him eliminated if it was the only way to preserve secrecy.

Ponsonby sighed. He would have to pass on the bad news to higher levels of government and a special committee would have to be convened to determine and sanction any action necessary. Despite his authority, it was shared responsibility, democracy at work, relieving him of postmortem inquiry. At the same time, he reflected wryly, preservation of the 'Sandbag' secret would automatically be compromised by the mere appointment and briefing of any committee members. Shaking his head at the contradictory pressures of his business, he dialled a secret number from the file, punched in a code reference and hung up. Pushing back, he rocked his chair towards terminal imbalance again, and waited for the phone call to be returned.

July 1947. Vogtland.

It had become an annual pilgrimage. He was back again, walking the woods of the Vogtland. Ostensibly, he was writing a book on bird watching and this was a prime area of woodlands to catch sight of owls, woodpeckers and other deep-forest birds.

Staying in the shadows of the woods, he focussed his binoculars, not on the sleeping owl twenty metres away, but out into the open sunlight illuminating the frontier zone. What he saw, or rather did not see, froze him to the spot. He had expected the heavier wire and more secure barriers, but the barn was gone. Obviously, the Vopos had seen it as a focal point for escapees and it blocked their field of fire, so they had demolished it. The land had been ploughed and there was now no trace of where it had been.

Now, even with the line of sight on the trees he had blazed last year, and the higher foliage of the tall trees opposite, the line he was able to draw was, at best, a one dimensional fix on the burial site. He could go out there all day and dig around and would still not strike the exact spot. He had foreseen himself, sneaking out under cover of darkness and hidden inside the barn structure, digging uninterrupted. Suddenly, the gold had taken a giant leap away from his reach. Unless he could come up with some scheme, he might never retrieve the gold now. Throwing himself to the ground, he pounded his fists against it, cursing and cursing with rage.

2100 hrs. Saturday, 7th July 1990. Nürnburg.

In the van, Raymond and Astrid were blindfolded and made to lie face down on the floor where a tarpaulin was pulled over them. A stern warning to keep their faces to the floor and not to talk was issued as the van accelerated away. Both of them were fearfully conscious of the two weapons trained on them. Astrid was shaking and Raymond took her hand and squeezed it with as much reassurance as he could muster.

He was hopelessly confused. Besides the police, two other groups seemed to have shown unwelcome interest in him and for what reason he did not know. Perhaps he would soon find out. Within minutes, he was totally confused about their whereabouts in Nürnberg, a city he did not know anyway.

After about ten minutes driving, the van pulled into a quiet parking area and stopped. Raymond and Astrid were led inside a house, guided to seats and made to sit. After a couple of minutes, their blindfolds were removed.

"Mr. Barton, I want you to tell me everything you know," the speaker was a lean sun-tanned man with an easy air, dressed in grey slacks and a white golf shirt. The German speech had a very slight accent which Raymond could not place.

Raymond regarded the man for a long moment. How he opened this conversation may be important. "You are not the first person to ask me that question. There seems to be a growing opinion I know something of value. However, I am unaware of it. Perhaps if you could give me a clue...Like who you are and what your interest is?"

The man took his turn to regard Raymond. His jaw set as he reached a decision. "I am empowered by my employers to take any action necessary to secure information of which I believe you have knowledge. Unlike the people who murdered your friend Alvin Shapiro, I am not a wanton killer. I *will* complete my task, however, be assured."

"Do you have Mandy?"

"Mandy?"

"Don't fuck with me! She's missing. Since you have me, I suppose you have her too!"

"Are you saying this lady has been abducted?"

"Yes, my fiancée in London."

A look of concern crossed the man's face. "I can assure you, Mr. Barton, I know nothing about your Mandy. If she has been taken by the people we rescued you from, she is in grave danger."

The empathy was plain and Raymond suddenly felt on safer ground with these people. "Who are they, these other *people*?"

"I will explain later, but first you must tell me what you were doing around Plauen and admit your relationship with the British Secret Intelligence Service."

"What?" Raymond was stunned. "I don't work for them! I'm just a journalist on an assignment! I work for *Current Events Magazine*!" The outburst was spontaneous, the shock obvious on his face.

"But you served in British Army Intelligence and being a journalist is a very good cover, is it not?"

Things began to make sense to Raymond now. "Look! If I was on some kind of Intelligence mission, which I am absolutely not, what am I doing using Astrid as an asset? She is just an old girlfriend, married now, and I phoned her when the police took my wallet, cell phone, passport, clothes and left me with nothing to get by on. Surely, if I was working for Intelligence, I could expect some expert back up! The police are hunting me for murders I did not commit!"

"Murders? More than one?"

"Yes, an old man I interviewed near Plauen was brutally murdered the same day as Al. The police think I killed them both, but I didn't and furthermore, I couldn't be in two places at the same time, so I obviously didn't do one of them and by extension, I didn't do either! On top of that, two officers escorting me to Bonn were brutally shot to death on the way to Nürnberg by some party or parties unknown who then abducted me. I only escaped from them by a fluke when there was a car crash."

"Excuse me." The man rose and left, his politeness countered by the attentive and armed guard who remained in the room. Astrid was in another room, being questioned by another of their abductors. It was half an hour before the man returned. "I have just received authorization to release you and Frau Klemerer, Mr. Barton," the man raised a palm to arrest Raymond getting to his feet. "First, however, I require your word that you will pursue this matter no further. In return for that, we will get you back to Britain, if you wish."

"I am a journalist. There is a story here and you are asking me to walk away from it?" Raymond felt the need to pressure. He needed information.

"Yes, in addition to helping you, I have been authorized to also promise you an exclusive on this story, when my principals are ready to release it. Until then, you must remain out of the matter entirely. My other, still viable options, are to keep you captive, or even dispose of you and Frau Klemerer."

The options seemed nasty to Raymond. "What about these other people who are hunting me? Do I go to the authorities in Britain for protection?"

"If by the *authorities* you mean the government, I would strongly advise against it. You must trust nobody. Forces are at work of which you are unaware and certain parties will kill you if they think you are close to secrets they are sworn to protect. You are lucky that I believe your story and have some corroborative information."

"But this is preposterous! You are telling me now I cannot even trust the authorities in Britain! Where can we possibly hide until your *Principals* are *ready?*"

"That is not my concern. What is your answer to our offer?"

"Well, yes, of course! Do we have any choice?"

"And do you want to go to Britain?"

"I shall have to make a phone call first to my editor."

Astrid still had her cell phone in her purse and one of the men brought it in for him. Raymond dialled the number for Manny Kruppe in Hamburg. Manny put him on hold while he punched buttons to initiate a conference call to London. In a minute, Willie McIvor was on the line.

"Tom! Great news, your grandmother called; she's O.K. and didn't go where we thought. She actually went on holiday and wants to meet you in Frankfurt. Manny has the number!"

Raymond was stunned. Willie was calling him *Tom*, and his grandmother had died six months before. He had asked for special leave for the funeral, so Willie *knew* that she was dead. Then it hit him! Mandy was in Frankfurt! She had not been abducted but had followed him there somehow! Willie was double-talking because he suspected the line was tapped.

He could barely keep the excitement out of his voice, the news had hit him like a punch in the stomach and he could not find his breath. "Tell Granny I'll be there as soon as I can. By the way, this story is on hold, it may amount to nothing," Raymond looked at the man as he told the lie to Willie.

"Talk to Manny. Anything else?"

"No, bye. Manny are you there still?"

"Yes, Raymond," the heavy voice of Kruppe came down the line.

"Give me Granny's number."

After scribbling it down, Raymond pressed the end button and looked up at the man, who appeared not to have picked up on anything untoward. "Well, are you satisfied?"

"That is good, Mr. Barton. Can I have your assurance that you will now return to Britain and stay out of this matter?"

"Yes, I just learned my fiancée is safe. Evidently, she followed me to Frankfurt and is waiting for me there. I would like to get back to her. When will the story be ready to break?"

"About three weeks."

"Three weeks?...How the hell are we going to stay alive?"

"That is your problem, Mr. Barton, but I promise you, it is a huge story. You will be famous."

Raymond nodded his head, accepting their release as a first step to getting free.

"Good! Now, where can we drop you?"

"How about back at the Atrium hotel? If Astrid's car is still there, we can disappear."

"Very well. As a gesture of our good faith, I would like to return these to you," the man proffered a manila envelope.

Opening it, Raymond was stunned to find his wallet and his passport. Last time he had seen them, the police in Plauen were taking them away from him. He tried to speak, but the man was leaving the room. Pocketing his belongings, Raymond scowled. Whatever was going on was pretty serious. Seemingly, this man was tied to the cop-killers, or was a cop himself. Shaking his head, he looked up as Astrid appeared in the doorway, escorted by two men. One of them beckoned, and he left the room.

The journey back to the hotel was done in reverse, the pair of them under the tarpaulin again, ignorant of where they had been taken. It was almost midnight when the van pulled away from the curb, leaving them a block from the Atrium. There was no point in trying to retrieve any of the baggage, which had been loaded into the taxi earlier. Raymond crossed the street to watch the car park while Astrid went to retrieve her Mercedes. She was going to drive around two blocks, in a figure of eight, while Raymond watched to see if she was tailed.

A few minutes later, clean, she pulled into the curb to pick Raymond up. Climbing into the car, he held out his hand. "Give me the phone again, I must call Mandy." Raymond had explained to Astrid that Mandy had not been kidnapped at all, but for some reason had travelled to Frankfurt.

"Maybe she is coming to scratch my eyes out!" Astrid had smiled at Raymond and he felt a strange twisting in his gut as he realized just how accurate that might be. Mandy was pretty ferocious when roused and if she thought he had come to Germany to screw around with Astrid, following him to Frankfurt was something she just might well do. Had she been abducted or had she faked her disappearance and was she now a lioness on the prowl? And what about the wrecked flat? Had she lied about that? It was not logical.

He dialled the Frankfurt number, adding the room extension Manny had given him. It rang three times before Mandy came on. "Mandy, darling! Thank God you are all right!"

"Raymond? Oh, Raymond! It's so good to hear your voice!"

"What are you doing here?"

"Where are you?"

"Nürnberg, we'll be there first thing in the morning."

"We?"

Shit!... He had already let the cat out of the bag! "I have help, but there are people searching for me and I had lost my wallet, passport, the whole lot!"

"So, are you with Astrid?"

Raymond felt like a little boy again. His mother had told him once that he could never do anything but what she would automatically know; mothers had the power. Mandy could read him like a book. "She was the only person I could turn to, Mandy."

"You couldn't ask your own office?"

"Mandy, please! This is a very, very serious situation I am in. People have died! Now, why did you come here?"

"I got suspicious."

"Mandy, please stop this thing about Astrid, I..."

"No, Raymond, I am your fiancée and I have rights. I tried your cell phone, but there was no answer, so then I phoned Larry McIvor at the newspaper and he told me you had come to Frankfurt. So, here I am and as I guessed, you are with Astrid. Not only that, but you say you can't get here until morning. Need another night with that bitch, do you?" Mandy sounded tearful and stressed, like she really needed Raymond.

"Can you meet us somewhere other than the hotel?"

"No, I..." Mandy's voice broke off and then she came back on the line again. "I am expecting a call from Larry. Please hurry, Raymond. I am at the Sheraton Congress at forty-four forty-eight Lyoner Strasse, room ten twelve." The line went dead.

"Shit!" Raymond dumped the cell phone savagely back into Astrid's purse.

"What's the matter?"

"Mandy *is* being held prisoner."

"How do you know?"

"She called Willie McIvor '*Larry*'. Twice!"

"Could she not be mistaken?"

"No, she has met him several times, we even dined together with him. It was no mistake. She deliberately promoted the dispute over you to hide the fact she was using the wrong name. Besides, she says she can't leave the hotel to meet us and it sounded like somebody prompted her with the excuse she used. She also referred to the magazine as the *newspaper*. Somebody is holding her, Astrid! Not only that but she gave me the *exact* address of the hotel."

"And so?"

"Despite the exactitude of Mandy's profession, she could not give directions to save her life. Normally, she could easily arrange to meet me at a McDonald's without giving me any other clue, like what city it was in. No, either somebody told her what to say, or she is telling me things are not normal!"

"Why did you bait her about being there in the morning? We can be there in just over two hours driving."

"Because I am dog-tired and arriving in the middle of the night without a plan and any necessary equipment would be foolish."

"Well, that was quick thinking, but I think maybe you do want to spend the night with me."

"Astrid! Stop being so tiresome. This is not some kind of comic opera being played out here!"

"Sorry, Raymond. I'm just trying to lighten the mood. So, what do we do now?"

"Well, let's go get a meal and hatch a scheme to get her free. We also need more clothes, another cell phone and I think it's time I armed myself. Then you should go home, this is getting too dangerous."

"What! Leave you now? Raymond you can't do without me!"

"Yes I can. You will get hurt, or else Rolf will get dragged into this and he is not expecting trouble."

"Rolf will be fine. I don't think these guys even know who I am right now and besides, you are going to need help to rescue Mandy. Besides, I certainly want to meet this woman whom you have chosen over me."

Raymond groaned. Astrid was right, he needed all the help he could get, but the idea of the two women coming face to face was a situation he dreaded. There was bound to be an almighty catfight. And he would be in the middle!

"What did the Israelis want?"

"Israelis? Is that what they were?"

"Yeah, one of them dropped a few words of Hebrew when he thought I wasn't listening."

"You speak Hebrew?"

"No, but I know *'zai gezunt'* means *'good-bye'*."

"So now we have Mossad, the British Secret Service, the Kriminalpolizei and a bunch of murdering thugs looking for me. I wonder which group has Mandy?"

"Don't know, but I want you too, Raymond." A slender hand fell tenderly onto his thigh.

"Astrid, you are incorrigible."

In view of the growing mistrust they felt for authority, Raymond and Astrid decided to attempt rescuing Mandy themselves. Although he had promised the Israelis he would return to London and lay low, it was obvious he could not do that without retrieving Mandy first, and taking her along. It was a daunting task for a pair of amateurs. The warning the Israeli had given Raymond about the British involvement was brought home when he phoned his old military unit number from a street pay phone, as they had instructed. An unknown voice had asked him whether he could make it to Bonn himself or should a team be sent to collect him for his own safety?

Raymond couldn't quite decide why, but it sounded phony and after telling the man he would get to Bonn himself, he hung up and went back to the all-night restaurant they were eating at across the street. Not ten minutes later, a car screeched into the street and after inspecting the pay phone he had used, four men launched what they obviously thought was a covert search of the street, taking down car registrations. Astrid's Mercedes was a block over, so they had no worry. They quickly finished their meal however and set out.

"How are you going to manage this, Raymond?" Astrid was at the wheel and they were now hurtling along the E-42 autobahn towards Frankfurt at a hundred and fifty kilometres per hour.

"First we have to sleep. How we get her free I don't know, but it isn't going to be easy. Just going up to the room and knocking on the door is not the way to do it. Obviously, whoever it is wants me and Mandy is the bait. They just don't know that I know she is being held."

"Could Mandy be the key? Could she have knowledge these people think you have shared? After all, your flat was searched and she lives there too."

"God no, Astrid." Raymond groaned. "Please don't make this any more complicated. Mandy is a computer programmer and doesn't speak a word of German. Neither one of us can possibly have information to trigger this situation!"

"The room is their home ground then and we need to get her out. It may be easier if we can get them to leave the room."

"I agree, but she has already been prompted to refuse to leave and if I keep pushing that point they'll get suspicious and we will lose the element of surprise. We need weapons."

"No problem, I am licensed and we can buy what we need."

"Hopefully, they want me in the room and they aren't planning on taking me as I enter the hotel, although there are bound to be lookouts. The trick is to get to the room without them realizing it is me."

"Us!"

"Well, one of us, if not both. My other concern is that if Mandy realizes it is me knocking on the door, she may do something desperate to protect me. So, unless we can talk to her again, and pass the word, she has to be kept in the dark too."

"So, we arrive incognito; do you mean like room service, maid service or the like?"

"Yes. I was thinking, what if we took the room above them, poured water all over the floor and then claimed to be plumbers when they complained about the water leaking from above?"

"Most of the floors are concrete and it probably wouldn't leak. Besides, as soon as they call the front desk, there will be people all over the place, so they would probably not complain. Still, I think you are onto something. What if they are watching the hotel security cameras?"

"Then we are fucked every which way, Astrid."

"What about a fire? We could pull the alarm on their floor, maybe generate some smoke. There would be enough confusion to disrupt any watchers."

"What if they don't leave the room?"

"We call them on the house phone, pretend to be the front desk and tell them it is a genuine fire and order them out. The only way they will be able to control Mandy is by escorting her out, same as they must have got in. They couldn't afford to have a couple of fire-fighters confront them in her room, she'd be quick to reveal them and by then the place will be crawling with cops too."

"Astrid, you're brilliant!"

0300 hrs. Sunday, 8th July 1990. Frankfurt.

They stopped on the way into Frankfurt and checked into a small hotel. If the people holding Mandy at the Sheraton had watchers out, they would recognize Raymond if they tried to check in there, so they decided to stay away until they had a firm plan.

Raymond slept fitfully, his mind oscillating between fear for Mandy and plans for her rescue. Black coffee gulped down at eight o'clock did little to erase his fatigue. Astrid first went to a bank and withdrew five thousand marks. Going to a gun shop, she produced her licence and purchased a Smith and Wesson Model 39 automatic pistol for Raymond. For herself, she bought the more compact Model 469 that was smaller and built to U.S. Air Force specifications for aircrew. She also bought a smart dark blue conservative suit and blouse so she could, if necessary, imitate a hotel assistant manager. Raymond purchased some coveralls and then they both restocked on their day-to-day clothes, toiletries and all the other things, which had gone missing in Nürnberg. They signed up for an additional cell phone so they could communicate while apart.

While waiting for the phone to be programmed, Astrid took them to a stationery store where she had a couple of plastic nameplates made to provide authenticity. That led her to a further idea and she had fake security identity cards made with their pictures, which they could clip to their lapels. Raymond realized that without some kind of smoke, there would be no urgency for anyone to vacate the premises. He went to a store that sold horticultural supplies and bought a smoke bomb, intended for destroying wasps' nests. Placed in a room they would rent on the same floor as Mandy's, with a purchased electric fan to drive the smoke into the hallway, it would provide enough physical evidence of a fire.

They packed their stuff in a couple of suitcases and put them in the rear of the Mercedes. Taking to the streets, they headed for Mandy's hotel. They knew they had to effect their plan as soon as possible because Raymond had to play the role of the distressed fiancé and show up quickly. Any further delay would create suspicion.

"Astrid, these fellows know about you."

"What do you mean?"

"They must have listened in when I talked to Mandy before, so they know you are with me, so they *expect* two of us to show up. We know Mandy is jealous of you, but she is not totally off the wall. I think she perpetrated that near row about you deliberately so they could not control what she said and allow herself to drop the clues to me. Also, she defused any suspicions they may have about my delaying getting here as my infidelity and so, out of her control."

"Smart lady."

"Yes, she is. But she has also given us a clue how to get back at them. What if I call her again five minutes before we are ready to make our move and surreptitiously give her a clue that I am coming for her, like really coming to rescue her, confirm I got her warning?"

"That would certainly get her working on our side and increase our surprise factor. It should also prevent her from taking any chances she might otherwise take if she thought she was protecting you. Also, Raymond, if we tell her our arrival time is an hour away, it will throw off the timing of her captors. They will relax, thinking they have a sure arrival time and then we can spring our fire drill. If they think we are still an hour's drive away, they cannot logically suspect we pulled the alarms!"

The plan was beginning to gel. As Astrid drove, Raymond cleaned and loaded the pair of Smith and Wesson's.

"So, where do we take them? At the room or in an elevator?"

"Elevators should not be used in event of a fire. That is standard. The stairs will be too public with many guests going down them. I think we should take them in the room, where they think they are in control, and try to figure a back-up plan in case it does not pan out."

"We could tell them when we make the Front desk call to take a certain elevator, making sure it is held on their floor, tell them it is reserved for them."

"Yes, that should work, but only as a back-up. We need the privacy of the hotel room if there is any resistance to us."

Raymond noted Astrid had avoided the word *shooting*.

"Can you do this, Astrid, can you shoot someone?"

"Yes, Raymond. I have been with firearms all my life and am really quite adept. As far as determination is concerned, these people are fucking with someone I love, so they are nothing to me. Certainly, I expect them to be armed, and in light of events so far, they may shoot us if we don't get them first."

1000 hrs. Sunday, 8th July 1990. Sheraton Hotel, Frankfurt.

As they had arranged, Astrid first went for a little cruise around the hotel. While she picked nobody up as an obvious watcher, she felt sure they were there. She took the elevator to the eleventh floor, pinning on her fake security pass and nameplate on the way up. Walking to the fire door, she opened it and went down the stairs to the tenth floor. There was nobody on the floor, but she felt like eyes were upon her. Ten twelve was only about ten metres from the block of elevators. Pushing the down button, she waited for the elevator, her scalp crawling with anticipation.

She removed the identity plates on the way down and then strolled over to the counter in the lobby. The clerk had no problem with her request for a room on the tenth floor. She told him she was meeting her husband and wanted to surprise him as they had first made love here, somewhere on the tenth floor.

When a woman as gorgeous as Astrid admits to clandestine sex and intimates it is about to happen again, the testosterone count of the average male eclipses his IQ many times over. The clerk on duty had no problem finding a vacant room on the tenth floor for Madame and she headed for the main entrance.

Five minutes later, a Mercedes pulled in and she was escorted through the lobby by a scholarly-looking man in blue jeans and a Cardin sweater. The clerk jealously thought how inadequate the man looked alongside the woman. A bellboy followed them, his barrow laden with two suitcases. They all disappeared into an elevator.

Raymond made the call to Mandy, on the cell phone, from their room, ten seventeen. It was further down the hallway from the elevators than ten twelve, on the opposite side. She picked up on the second ring. "Mandy, sorry to be so long but there was an accident on the autobahn. I'll be with you in about an hour. I am only a hundred kilometres away now. Astrid has gone home and I have a rental car." He added the bit about Astrid at the last moment, receiving a thumbs-up from her at the deception. Now the abductors should only be expecting one person instead of two.

"That's great, Raymond. I can't wait to see you. Did you talk to Larry at the newspaper?"

"Yes, I understand your concern. Larry says not to worry, everything has been worked out and we can go home as soon as we want. In fact, I think you have had such a rough time, I should treat you to a holiday in Puerto Vallarta!"

"Darling, I look forward to *that*!"

"See you in an hour! Love you!" Raymond broke the connection.

"Did she get the message?"

"Oh yes! Not only did she repeat the fake identity of McIvor, she told me immediately she knew our plan."

"How?"

"We both read a book recently by James St.John where the heroine is rescued by the hero and they take off for a randy stay in Puerto Vallarta."

"Can I come along? Threesomes can be fun!"

"Astrid!"

Five minutes after they had called Mandy, Raymond and Astrid went into action. Checking the hallway was empty, they started the electric fan and popped the smoke bomb. In moments, a thick cloud of acrid fumes was pouring into the hallway. Raymond devised a wedge and leaving the door ajar, reached around it to jam the opening so no one could see the source of the smoke. He then went down the hallway, pulling fire alarms as he passed them, then started back, systematically knocking on doors. In moments, bells rang hotel-wide. Astrid phoned room ten twelve and, insisting she was the front desk, ordered them to evacuate immediately. Doors banged open up and down the corridor as people poked their heads out, caught the fumes in the air, and began to comply with the evacuation order in good Teutonic fashion.

Astrid had dashed to the far end of the corridor from Raymond and they systematically worked their way towards ten twelve, trying to pace themselves. They knocked on doors and called out the need for the occupants to leave via the stairs. They were each about ten metres from the door of the room when a man with black curly hair and mean features opened it and peered out. He turned to say something to the interior and then stepped out, his hand inside his jacket at the ready.

Astrid called to him as Raymond rapidly approached from the other side and, being engaged in conversation, he naturally turned to her first. He was nothing if not alert however and ignoring Astrid's urgent orders to leave the building, he turned to Raymond who was closing fast. Suspicion, and even recognition, lit up his face and then suddenly, Astrid had hit him with the flat of her pistol and he went to his knees.

Raymond didn't hesitate, but kicked the semiconscious man in the face, snapping back his head and projecting him sideways into the door opening. Without a pause, he leapt over the slumping body and adopted a two-handed grip on his pistol inside the door. A large man with greasy blonde hair stood close to the wall to his immediate right and Raymond felt the hot rush of a bullet by his chest as the silenced pistol spat at him.

He jumped forward, rolling to the floor and the pistol spat again. It was followed by the thunderous roar of another gun as Astrid followed him inside and fired. The round took the man in his left shoulder and he staggered, trying to raise his gun arm to bear on her. Raymond was coming up, aiming his weapon when a flash of movement came at his left peripheral and Mandy slugged the man with a table lamp. Without another sound, he slumped to the floor, blood from his shoulder spreading over the pale grey carpet.

"Shit!" The world stopped completely.

"Quick, Raymond, help me!" Astrid went to the entry and they dragged in the man who had come to the door.

"Raymond, I..."

"No time, Mandy, we have to get out of here!" Raymond grabbed her by the arm. She was in blue jeans and a blouse. He dragged her to the door.

"Wait!"

"What?"

"I need this!" Shaking him off, she went to a table by the window and snatched a portable computer. "The brief-case! Over there! Take it!"

"Come on!" Astrid was waving wildly from the doorway.

They fled down the hallway to the stairs, joining a throng of people pouring down from the upper storeys. There was a faint wail of sirens coming from outside, growing in intensity. The smoke was wonderful. It created just the right sense of urgency and made everyone cough and splutter, without destroying their vision.

At the foot of the stairs, a couple of policemen who had been nearby, along with hotel staff, were herding guests through the main doors while fire appliances were already pulling up outside. A dozen fire-fighters, impersonal behind their breathing apparatus, were rushing to the doors, ready to initiate any rescues. In the milling stampede of people, they made it outside and rushed to the car park.

In one minute, they were inside the Mercedes and Astrid pulled away. With great aplomb, she ignored the tearful reunion taking place between the front and the back passenger seats.

"What the fuck is going on, Raymond?"

"We don't really know yet, but there appears to be several groups of people interested in finding me to get information I apparently have but don't know about. People have been killed. What do you need this stuff for?" Raymond pointed to the computer and briefcase Mandy had insisted on taking from the hotel.

"This baby," Mandy opened the lid of the computer, revealing the keyboard and screen, "is a very advanced prototype unit not out on the market yet. It is a Toshiba four eighty-six PXT. It contains the fastest processor to date, the eight oh four eight six. It incorporates one point two million transistors, runs at twenty-five megahertz and has one hundred megabytes of RAM and a huge disk memory. Somebody must have serious pull to have one of these before it is actually out on the market."

"Does she make this up?"

"University of London, degree in computer science and post graduate studies in advanced programming. Astrid, meet Mandy."

"Hello." Astrid took a hand from the steering wheel and offered it.

"Pleased to meet you, Astrid." Raymond did not miss the frosty politeness as Mandy turned back to him. "The men we took this from were communicating on this advanced system through a telephone modem. I'm sure they were getting instructions and information while reporting back. There is a five digit code to gain access into their program."

"How do you know?"

"I counted the key taps when the man entered the program."

"You think you can hack your way into it?"

"Sure, but it will take time and some equipment. I need to write a program to interrogate the software and then I have to connect to a pretty sophisticated computer, probably a mainframe, to break in."

"Can you not just guess?" Astrid's eyes swept the rear view mirror.

"Yes, Astrid, but it might take years to do it. The permutations of possible characters making up a five digit code, even using only numbers and letters, is astronomical," Mandy's voice was condescending.

Raymond's nervousness at the inevitable meeting of the two women escalated. He could see Astrid's neck was flushed and he expected the catfight to start at any moment, despite the plight they were in.

"So you need a big computer, ja?"

"Yes."

"Then why don't we ask Rolf, Raymond?" Astrid turned briefly and regarded Raymond who was working on opening the locked briefcase.

"Could we?"

"Of course, I'll phone him now and see if we can get into one of KEB's facilities. I think they have one in Cologne."

"I'll get busy writing the program," Mandy looked busy already.

For all the danger she had been in and the recent adrenaline rush of the rescue, Mandy was awfully composed, Astrid thought.

After a long conversation with her husband, Astrid finally slipped in her request. On top of her vagueness of what she was up to, this unusual demand roused his suspicions and she had to do some fast-talking, augmented by some pillow-talk to get his permission. "One a.m. until four. It is the only time there is any freedom of access. He will make the reservation, whatever that means, and one of his staff will meet us."

"That's great, Astrid, I should be able to manage in that time."

"Jesus Christ!" Raymond started aghast at a handful of pages taken from the now-open briefcase.

"What is it?"

"These printouts. Those people intended to question me, there is an order against my name telling them to kidnap me and ship me off for interrogation," Raymond turned, staring concerned at Mandy. "You were indeed the bait, Mandy, and they probably intended to kill us both!"

"But why?"

"I don't know, but maybe the computer will tell us when you crack it."

The open expanse of the E-35 autobahn stretched ahead of them as Astrid left the limits of Frankfurt. She eased her foot down, headed for Cologne. Along the way, Mandy described how she had been kidnapped in London, literally picked up on the street and drugged. Her story did little to enlighten them on who had done it and for what purpose.

0100 hrs. Monday, 9th July 1990. Cologne.

It was just a few minutes after one in the morning when they pulled into the car park of the Cologne office of Klemerer Elektro-und Baubetrieb AG. There was parking for several hundred vehicles but only about half a dozen of the reserved spaces had vehicles in them. The building was a fanciful modern structure three storeys high with stone facing, interspersed by steel and glass towers, pinnacles and triangles. It gave the effect of a company disinterested in budget or functionality. It spoke of corporate power.

Walking up the wide terrace of steps through the floodlights, they were greeted at the door by a fussy little man who locked the door immediately after they entered and then ushered them to a reception desk manned by a security guard. He paused only long enough in his subservient gush of German to Astrid to make them sign in and introduce himself as Werner Kallembach, and then led them upstairs. A security door at the first corridor was opened remotely by the guard downstairs who had them on video camera. Werner opened a second door with a magnetic card.

Entering, they found themselves in the outer office of a computer complex. The air conditioning hissed with the typical excess of an environmental system trying to nurture its electronic charges. Temperature, humidity and pollutants were zealously controlled. A semicircle of consoles faced them before a glass wall and when Werner threw a switch, a row of cabinets were highlighted behind it like icons in a museum of rare antiquities.

"Honeywell supercomputer!" Mandy's words were uttered with reverence, as if Werner had unveiled Jesus on the cross, stirring back to life.

"Yes." Werner resumed his attention to Astrid, sloughing off the rude interruption of the Englander Frau.

"I will need a couple of two and three-quarter high density floppies for this portable computer and access to a program which can give me phone link traces."

Werner ignored Mandy, favouring Frau Klemerer, who suddenly put both her hands on his shoulders and thrust her face in front of his. "Herr Kallembach. My husband's company, KEB, has already hired you. They must have been impressed. You need not bother to try to impress me. You must however impress the lady who has made her request. If you do not impress this lady, give her all your co-operation, I promise you, you will be seeking employment elsewhere tomorrow morning."

In the next two hours, Werner Kallembach, a very clever and accomplished practitioner of the computer arts went from a skeptic to a believer, from a believer to a worshipper, from a worshipper to a disciple. With a few careful questions, he plunged his intellect and skills into partnership with Mandy as they tackled the problem of breaking the codes and protocols of the portable computer's software. Astrid and Raymond merely looked on or provided coffee from a machine in an adjoining room. They had to do a little translating at first, as Werner's English was not that strong. However, the more complex the computer jargon became the more literate the computer pair became with each other.

Mandy had explained carefully to the two of them what they were up against in breaking into the computer. Firstly, since it was a portable, it could only exchange electronic information by fax or a modem when hooked up through another medium, namely the telephone. Because of the high-speed baud bandwidth, a cell phone had an especially limited application and was also probably more susceptible to security breaching as it radiated energy for miles. Thus, a hard line was required and the keyboard operator could only communicate when plugged into a telephone system. The significance of this was that the other end of the line could only communicate when the computer went on line. In short, it was logical that the portable would always initiate a contact.

When signing on, the operator would probably get a screen prompt saying a message was waiting. This must be accessed and retrieved by a secret code, which would also be required to give an adequate receipt for the message. Additionally, it was highly likely that fixed-time schedules for contact were in force. Should there be an unexpected delay between contacts, security measures would be escalated to ensure the system was not breached. Since they had indeed breached the system by stealing the computer, they may be faced with such problems on contact. They just had to hope that so far, neither of the men they had rescued Mandy from had alerted their masters to the situation, or all was lost. Likely, they were in police custody and temporarily incommunicado.

With this in mind, Mandy had pointed out that they must get on-line as soon as possible for the highest potential for maintaining contact. Any doubts at the other end would probably terminate the link. Hence, they were in the computer facility, communing with the mainframe. Firstly, they had to switch on the portable computer and plug it into the mainframe so the bigger computer could interrogate the security numbers on the little one.

"Well, let's see what it is all about," Mandy opened the lid of the computer and reached for the power-on button.

"Just a minute!" Raymond reached out and grabbed her wrist. "What if this thing is booby-trapped?"

"You mean like a pound of plastic explosive? Raymond, this thing is packed too tight to squeeze anything else inside."

"Yeah, but I've heard they can combine the stuff into regular plastic."

"And we all just got blown up, right?" The sarcasm was unmistakable.

"Mandy, these bastards have been trying to kill us. You said yourself this is probably an item not on the market yet. Don't you think they would protect it?"

"Hmm - There is more than one way to do that without blowing it up. You men are so *violent,* Raymond."

"And being more *deviant,* you women would do it another way."

"Absolutely, like totally erasing the memory at power-up and rendering the whole thing useless." They looked at each other, sudden disbelief on Mandy's face.

"Let's see now," Raymond picked up the computer and turned it in his hands. There was an external power receptacle, one for connection to a telephone, one for a headset and some multi-pin sockets. The power button had a locking slide to prevent inadvertently turning the device off. Setting it back on the table, he studied the keyboard and pop-up screen. There was a raised *TOSHIBA* emblem above the keyboard and he ran his fingers over it. "Give me a knife or nail file or something."

Carefully, he moved the point of the proffered nail file under the *T* where some faint scratches appeared in the case. It popped out in his hand, having been held in place by two tiny prongs plugged into female receptacles. "I'd say this is a mod the manufacturer did not incorporate."

"It must complete a circuit of some kind. I suppose we can only trust it was a security device and we have disarmed it," Mandy reached for the power switch again and turned it on while Astrid, ever the joker, pantomimed her fingers in her ears.

There was a momentary pause and then they heard a whirring sound and a few clicks as the computer began to boot itself. "Clever bastards!"

"But not as clever as you, my darling!"

The screen on the computer began to light up and a Windows-style prompt page appeared. Mandy went to work.

It was almost two thirty before the first break in decoding the password came. The rolling screens of number and letter permutations began to stop like the mad symbols of a slot machine slowly falling into place. After the first, the second came quicker, then the third, followed rapidly by the fourth. The fifth arrived only seconds later.

"*Alpha, One, Seven, Bravo, Eight*," Mandy carefully wrote the symbols on a sheet of paper. Turning, she inserted a disk in the portable and booted it. At the prompt, she typed in the five symbols and watched. Another Windows screen coalesced on the monitor. Five automatic dialling options were detailed, listed only as one through number five.

Rolling the mouse, Mandy went into memory and tried to display the five telephone numbers stored in the dialling menu. A flashing icon told her that a password protected access. Anticipating this, she already had Werner setting up a solution. Like most modern companies, KMB maintained a program that interrogated and recorded every contact made through modem. It was a security tool to prevent industrial espionage and control virus inputs. Werner had plugged them into the output of this software. One by one, she dialled the numbers one through five, using the mouse to highlight them. As the screen icons showed connection, she hung up and only a second later, the numbers showed up on Werner's monitor.

Numbers four and five were un-programmed and free. The first three connections had given them three lines of digits, varying from ten to twelve numbers.

"Get me a telephone book."

"No need!" Werner's fingers sprang to life and a directory of overseas calling codes appeared. "*Three three* is France. The *One* is Paris. *Three four* is Spain. The *One* is Madrid. *Four nine* is Germany and the routing code of *two two eight* is Bonn."

"Germany, France and Spain," Raymond mouthed the countries ruminatively.

"What's your guess?" Astrid turned to Raymond.

"I don't think Germany. In fact, I don't think any of the three. I believe there will be some kind of call forward function to isolate this end from the true location of the correspondent."

"I agree, but how do we figure which one," Mandy pitched in.

"We dial and see what happens," Astrid, always impetuous.

"Yes, but if there is a further security password, we will be stymied and they must monitor time on line," Mandy was looking ahead.

Raymond demurred. "True, but have you ever heard of a wrong number? Surely, they must be prepared for someone, somewhere, to dial by accident and then hang up when they realize they have the wrong party. I'm sure they would not want to go on full security alert every time there is a wrong number and anyway, what if the wrong number dialler gets inquisitive as to why there is a security password? No, I think it will be a simple call forward arrangement and any security will be found at the ultimate end. By then, the software we have will have given us the destination, surely."

"It can do that?"

"Oh, ja!" Werner's pride showed.

Astrid urged them on. "Which one first, then?"

"Spain!" Raymond was adamant.

Taking a deep breath, Mandy dialled the number on the computer keyboard and pushed *Enter.* After the briefest of pauses, the number dialled rang once and then they heard a click. There were a series of other clicks and then the computer screen came to life, displaying a file directory.

"Now that we are in, let's see what is stored," Mandy rolled the mouse again, bringing up a directory of files stored in memory. There were ten in all and she immediately tasked the computer with printing them out. They were in code, but yielded to the mainframe in minutes.

There were four transmittals and six messages received. All were in German. Raymond and Astrid seized the sheets as they scrolled out of the printer, scanning them for content.

The fourth message had been already read ten days before and was referred to by an earlier transmittal. It contained the names and addresses of several men. Raymond was startled to see those of Al Shapiro and himself. They were obviously onto something. The remaining names seemed to be Wehrmacht soldiers for they had ranks, service numbers and units beside them. An addendum sheet identified the soldiers as members of an army unit that had picked up a gold shipment from the Reichsbank in April nineteen forty-five and left Berlin with it.

Werner seized on these with delight and went to another computer terminal. In minutes he had accessed old Wehrmacht records. "These men are dead," he pointed to half the numbers, which he had crossed off. "This man was found dead two weeks ago, floating in the River Weser. Tortured and killed!"

"Oh, I don't like the sound of that but it rings familiar to recent events that have happened to me. That leaves these seven names," Raymond looked back at Werner. "Can you get descriptions, or even their service records?"

"Easy!" Werner went back to the computer and moments later reported. "All of the men went missing in the last few weeks of the war, their fate unknown." Werner went back to work. Cross-referencing their names and birth dates, he deduced that five of the men were never heard of again since they were in none of the computer bank data forty years later. He worked through employment records, retirement pensions and driving licence information. There were no certificates of death filed with the statistics bureau. Now they were left with two possible names:

Reinhold Beckmann and Wilhelm Streicher.

Further research showed Reinhold Beckmann to be a middle-income mechanic, close to retirement. Wilhelm Streicher was president of a freight-shipping company in Hamburg.

"That's our man," Raymond tapped the page with a finger. "Anyone who had access to gold would not be an auto mechanic. Let's go to Hamburg."

"Do you want to try getting through to the other end?" Mandy asked Raymond.

"What do you think?"

"Well, we may not be ready, but with all this technology available, now might be as good a time as any," Mandy was on a roll.

"Go for it!"

Mandy took a deep breath and then dialled through the computer keyboard. There was the same delay and clicks before the call proceeded to a new line. Werner was manning another terminal and trying to track the routing. From Madrid, there was a satellite link.

"Buenos Aires!"

"Wait! It is going onward." A series of digits came up on Werner's screen. "*Five, nine, five*. That is Paraguay!"

They looked at each other. "Why would someone in *Paraguay* be involved in this?"

"Is that really the end of the line?" asked Raymond.

"Oh, yes!" Werner was adamant. "I have done this before. Last year we had someone in the Congo trying to access our database and we tracked him down the same way." He made to say more about the story, but realized his visitors were not listening.

"On to Hamburg?"

"Yes." In minutes they had packed up their stuff, thanked Werner, and drove out of the main gate, the guard waving to them. Later today, they would be in Hamburg. They would be on a fishing expedition. Whether Streicher could help them or not would only be determined by his reaction to the questions that they posed him.

During the balance of the night, soon after they left, three men crossed the parking lot of the KEB complex. They were experts in their field. Crossing the outer security fence, they had already rolled into the guard's shack and overpowered him. The gross threat of a knife across his genitals had persuaded him to divulge entry codes for the building. His reward from the black-clad intruders was a blow to the head, which rendered him unconscious. They entered the main building and silently moved into the computer area. Before Werner Kallembach knew it, the masked men were upon him.

It took twenty minutes to break him. He had fallen madly in love with the black-haired English beauty who knew more about computers than he and his loyalty was total. Missing several fingers, he finally broke and told them all they wanted to know. Someone's security had been breached and now they went to control the damage. Aided by Werner's confession, one of them sat at the main console and copied to a floppy disk all the information Mandy had collected. With a few expert keystrokes he erased all record of their activities.

Inserting another floppy, he fed the computer evidence of an abortive attempt to access details of a new process KEB was close to completing. To investigators, it would appear that industrial espionage had been attempted. Poor Herr Kallembach had suffered the ultimate price for being unfortunate enough to be there at the time. Nodding to one of the others, the man pulled the floppy and stood up.

Before he could know, Werner felt a terrible pain in his throat. He tried to speak, but it was impossible. He fell to the floor; face down, watching in horrible fascination as a spurting red pool spread around him across the rubberized tile.

0900 hrs. Monday, 9th July 1990. Hamburg.

There were two telephone numbers for Herr Streicher in the Hamburg telephone directory. One was obviously a business number as alongside was the company name, Spedition Streicher GmbH. Astrid got busy and determined this office was in a building off the Binnenalster, on Neuer Jungfernstieg. The home number was on the nearby Alster Lake and she whistled with admiration.

"This man has one of the best business addresses in Hamburg, and lives only a few blocks away at one of the most prestigious addresses overlooking the lake. He must be loaded. I wonder if he is good-looking?"

"Astrid!"

Raymond phoned the business number and found himself talking to a receptionist. "Herr Streicher, bitte."

"I am sorry, sir, but Herr Streicher is out this afternoon. May I take a message?"

"Is he in town?"

"I am sorry sir, I cannot tell you that."

Raymond had a flash of inspiration. "Please phone him and tell him it is one of his very old friends from the Vogtland calling. I will stay on the line as I know he will speak with me." There was a short pause and then some clicks as the call was transferred.

"Ja?" The voice was cautious.

"Herr Streicher, we have a common interest in matters of the past which I do not want to discuss over the telephone. Could we meet?"

"Do you have a name?"

"It is not important. I am interested in certain events concerning shipments at the end of the war."

There was a long, pregnant pause. "Come to a warehouse on the Saint Pauli-Landungsbrücken. It is right across from the sailing ship on Pier One. Look for a red sign with a lobster on it. Are you alone?"

"There will be two of us."

"Someone will meet you." The phone clicked off.

"Well, that was easy. I wonder what we are in for?" Raymond stared into the phone's earpiece as if he might discern something there.

1000 hrs. Monday, 9th July 1990. Dockland, Elbe River, Hamburg.

It was decided that Astrid would go in with Raymond while Mandy stayed in the car with the pistols in case there were any problems. Mandy's lack of German could cause problems and would be something of a give-away as to who they were. Raymond would establish a cell phone link to Mandy and leave the phone on so she would be warned if trouble started.

The street was along the north shore of the Elbe, which was lined with docks and shipping terminals. The high masts of the old windjammer tied up at Pier One showed them the way and they were lucky to find a parking spot in the car park. The place was swarming with tourists visiting the old green-hulled ship. A large sign announced it was the *'Rickmer Rickmers'* and souvenir booths lined the edge of the car park. A three-story warehouse with old hoists overhanging the street was opposite and a red sign with a large white lobster marked their destination.

Crossing the busy street, Raymond and Astrid walked up to the door. An athletic-looking young man saw them coming and rolled his shoulders and shuffled his feet, affording them the body language of willing yet cautious recognition. After giving Raymond the once-over and casting an appreciative eye over Astrid, he opened the door behind him and they ascended some wooden stairs. The place smelled of tar, hemp and lamp oil.

After three flights of stairs, they came into an open area and the young man knocked on a door. A voice called from within and their escort held open the door, allowing them entrance. The room within was about fifty feet long and twenty wide, the windows fronting the river. Heavy pillars of timber broke up the expanse, creating naturally secluded areas. A full size billiard table and a scattering of easy chairs and tables filled part of the room. Exercise equipment and an office area with desks and computer stations were counterpoints to an exotic and well-stocked bar with an old fashioned mirror. In a corner opposite was a large hot tub and in it were a man and a woman.

The man was florid and elderly, his thinning dark hair pasted to his scalp as if he had submerged his head. He had a strong face and looked like a stolid character. The woman was a much younger blonde, her large naked breasts floating on the surface of the water. She seemed indifferent to being so exposed and casually raised a glass of white wine to her lips as they approached.

"Herr Streicher?"

"Yes, and you are...?"

"You can call me Reinhold Mannheimer."

The man's eyes narrowed at the name and suddenly behind them, there was the mechanical rattle of a weapon being cocked. Raymond turned. The young man behind them had found a machine pistol from somewhere since entering the room and now moved towards the windows, bringing the weapon to bear on them such that his employer was out of the line of fire.

"Is that necessary?"

"That depends. I work in several businesses, which mandate tight security, Herr Mannheimer. Now tell me why you are here," Streicher reached out for a stein and took a mouthful of beer. Raymond saw an automatic pistol lying close to his hand.

"Your name was obtained for us through an associate. We are journalists and investigating a story concerning a cache of gold which was supposed to have been buried by the Nazis at the end of the war."

"*Supposed* is a good word, Herr Mannheimer, I know nothing about such a cache."

"Were you not on a military detail which left Berlin in April nineteen forty-five on a train to Bavaria which carried gold bullion and other valuables?"

"Oh, yes, I was on a train, but there was never any evidence to any of us that we were carrying gold."

"Even though you picked up your load at the Reichsbank?"

Streicher shrugged. "Nobody showed me gold. I think you are chasing a phantom."

"My information is that you were actually one of the men who took gold off the train and buried it in the Vogtland."

"Well, your information is wrong. What exactly is your interest in this?"

"A story, naturally."

"Then, if you cannot make it up yourself, I certainly cannot do it for you."

Raymond regarded the man closely. He was obviously wary, but unless there was some way of levering more out of him, they had gone as far as they could. "Well, I thank you for your time, Herr Streicher. If you should think of anything we could use, please call this number." Raymond put down one of the generic *Current Events Magazine* business cards which had remained in his pocket.

Crossing the street outside again, they headed for the car.

"Huh!"

"What Astrid?"

"Silicone!"

"Silicone?"

"Yes, those two floating grapefruits you couldn't take your eyes off up there! Silicone!"

"Astrid!"

"Well, it's true! It's a wonder they did not sink, or, float off up to the ceiling, they were so chemically enhanced."

"He seemed all right, although it was hard to tell if he really knew anything."

"Yeah, he was so relaxed about the interview he needed a gun on us at the mention of the name *Mannheimer.* I wonder where he picked up the scars, I thought they made him very rugged and experienced looking."

"Scars?" Raymond replayed the scene in the hot tub. Streicher, he remembered, had a red face and a thick, fairly hairy body, yet there *were* a couple of scars, one on the left shoulder, the other on the left arm. They had looked like bullet wounds. "Oh God!" Reaching the sidewalk, Raymond stopped dead. "Astrid, the army records showed Streicher as having no distinguishing features. Wounds would have been mentioned. It would be part of his history as a soldier, with possible decorations for being wounded."

"Gottlieb Demsch's records showed him with wounds: Two separate campaigns, both injuries to the left arm."

"Do you suppose?"

"Gottlieb Demsch!" They turned as one, involuntarily and shocked, staring open mouthed at the blank windows above the lobster sign.

"Let's go back!"

"But why, Raymond?"

"Because he is the only lead we have. I have a feeling he is trustworthy and if we can tell him his secret is safe with us, then we can work with him. If it truly is Demsch up there, then he must know something; why else would he have changed his identity to one of the missing men?"

They climbed the stairs again and knocked on the door. The young man answered. "Herr Streicher will not see you." His face was firm.

"Tell him we wish to save the life of Gottlieb Demsch." The door was closed in their faces, to reopen moments later.

"You had better be brief, Herr Mannheimer-journalist-Englander!" Streicher had left the tub and sat at a desk in a terrycloth robe, busy lighting a cigar.

"What we have to tell you is for your ears only." There was a long pause and Raymond sensed the tenseness from the bodyguard.

"Otto!" Streicher inclined his head towards the door. After a moment, the bodyguard reluctantly headed for the door. "Berta!" The blonde scowled before rising and stepping from the tub. She showed no inhibition, flaunting her long-flanked nudity to Raymond who could feel Astrid bridling beside him. "Now then," Streicher handled the pistol Raymond saw earlier with a casual menace, the butt resting on the desktop. "State your business!"

"Firstly, you are not Wilhelm Streicher, you are Gottlieb Demsch."

"How can you imagine such a thing?"

"Streicher's Wehrmacht records show no physical marks, such as wounds.

Gottlieb Demsch's show two wounds, both to the left arm and shoulder."

The wary eyes moved briefly to the hot tub. "How do *you* get access to Wehrmacht records?"

"We stole them from some people who intend us harm. Your name is on a list of people to be forcibly interrogated regarding the whereabouts of the gold we mentioned earlier."

"Who are these people?"

"We don't know, but I can tell you that at the present time, at least two policemen are dead and we are being pursued by British Intelligence. Also, at least two unidentified groups of violent people, as well as the Kriminalpolizei who think we were involved in the deaths are involved. We have also talked to a group of Israelis."

"Mossad?"

It took fifteen minutes for Raymond and Astrid to outline the facts from their viewpoint, by which time, Streicher-Demsch had poured them each a drink although he had not admitted his identity. At the end, he silently regarded them, saying nothing. Finally, he asked for the cell phone number, promising to call the next day. Seeing they had no option, they agreed.

Descending the stairs again, Astrid and Raymond felt they had been more successful. They moved towards the street crossing and Raymond quickly told Mandy they were on their way back before disconnecting the link. A van coming towards them began to slow in the curb lane and out of the corner of his eye, Raymond saw the side door unaccountably opening while it moved. Suddenly, he realized the man in the darkened interior was holding a weapon. Just as the van drew level, he extended the gun and aiming at them, pulled the trigger.

At the same moment, because of its slowing, the van was passed on the inside by a student riding a bicycle. The rider received the initial impact of the full-automatic gunfire, which almost cut him in half. The bicycle swerved into a lamp standard, the bloody remains of the cyclist sliding to the ground in a tangle of entrails and metal.

In the brief moment they were shielded, Raymond seized Astrid and threw her to the ground behind a newspaper vending machine, just as the last few rounds spattered along the wall of the warehouse. Two pedestrians went down, wounded by the bullets. A shotgun now roared from the van and the top of the metal newspaper vendor was decimated by buckshot. The flat rapid crack of an automatic pistol came from behind them as Streicher's bodyguard opened up with ten quick rounds which dimpled the back of the van.

The van driver had floored the accelerator and the roar of its engine almost eclipsed another automatic weapon opening up from another direction. This sounded like an assault rifle and peering up, Raymond saw the back of the van disintegrating, chunks of it being blown off by the seven point six-two millimetre rounds. A winking light came from the side of the van and Streicher's gunman went down, his back blossoming red as he was shot through the chest. People were screaming and panicking as another vehicle went roaring by in pursuit of the van.

"The S-Bahn! Quick, we have to get out of here."

"No Raymond, I have a better idea." Grabbing his hand, Astrid led him across the street, diagonally westward towards a row of warehouses lining the dockside. Gunfire still rattled along the street from the direction the vehicles had taken and the sound of police sirens began to rise. They had travelled maybe a hundred metres when suddenly, something zinged off the concrete wall of the building beside them.

Turning, they spotted two men, obviously in pursuit of them and closing fast. Astrid pulled Raymond into a narrow alley between two buildings and they ran as fast as they could towards the river. Around a corner, they came to a solid-looking square building with a green domed roof. Inside, four elevators descended underground, connecting to a pedestrian tunnel that went under the Elbe to the south.

One elevator door was about to close and they desperately stuck their hands in, stopping the door. Four people inside looked exasperated with them as they charged in and jabbed the door-close button. Just before the door finally closed, Raymond saw the two men were only metres from the building. With a lurch, the car started down, rumbling and clanging into the dank shaft like a tumbrel of the doomed. Both of them were breathing hard and Raymond could feel the blood pounding in his head.

"How far to the other side?"

"A couple of hundred metres." Raymond returned her look of chagrin. In a narrow subterranean tunnel, they were virtually trapped and their only hope was to outrun their pursuers. If they had to wait for an elevator at the far end, they were finished.

The indicator glowed, showing they were at the bottom of the shaft and the elevator lurched and groaned once before stopping. They increased their unpopularity with their fellow travellers by shouldering their way past them and darting out into the white-painted concrete hallway beyond. Seeing the passageway sloping away to the left, Raymond headed for it but Astrid seized his arm and swung him around.

The next elevator stood empty, ready to depart. "Quick! Double back!" Within moments, they were in and stabbing the door-close button. With total mechanical stubbornness, the elevator ignored them. From their right, they could hear the clanking and whirring of the adjacent car, settling into the last few metres of its descent, undoubtedly bearing the two gunmen.

With a tightening in his guts, Raymond stabbed the button again. They had played a gamble but if the gunmen saw them in here, there would be no place to flee. Feeling like a rat in a trap, he thumbed the button one more time and was rewarded by the blink of a light and the door jerked. With agonizing slowness, the door began to slide closed. An elderly man and his wife walking towards them began to accelerate their pace, extending their arms in a mute appeal for the elevator car to wait for them. The rumbling of an opening door grew louder next to them and there came the slap of hurrying feet on the concrete.

Almost with his hand in the door, the elderly man reached out, disdain on his face for their lack of courtesy in not holding the car for him. Raymond and Astrid had shrunk back, huddling into the front corner away from the door, trying desperately to stay out of sight. Suddenly, the old man was knocked spinning, hit from the side by a man running from the adjacent elevator. He cried out, the sound inaudible to them as the door slid the final few centimetres closed and they were alone. A few seconds of further play on their nerves and then the car lurched, the cables groaning as it clanked upwards.

"Astrid, you are brilliant!" Raymond spoke with the first breath he had taken in over a minute.

She smiled weakly and then looked serious. "Just hope there is not another one waiting for us up top!" The apprehension crawled over them as the elevator car ascended. Raymond felt like the myriad legs of a horde of poisonous spiders whispered over his skin, each ready to inject deadly poison at his slightest movement. A clammy sweat broke out over him and Astrid's hand felt no better as she slipped it into his and squeezed.

The elevator stopped and paused, tormenting them like a melodramatic executioner. A dozen people waited patiently for them to step out and Raymond went first, still holding Astrid's hand. He felt like he was on eggshells and the first one that cracked and broke would signal death. The glass doors to the outside revealed nobody loitering and they walked out with a confident air neither of them felt. Off ahead of them, they could still hear the sounds of gunfire.

"It's the Hafenstrasse!" Astrid was referring to a row of large houses, garishly mural-painted and sporting smashed windows and barricaded doors. The squatters who lived there had been in pitched battles with the police for years when attempts were made to evict them. The place was an armed camp and now the inhabitants were exchanging pot shots with the police who had arrived in large numbers. In the middle of the street, burning furiously was the van that had attacked them in the first place. No attempt was being made to extinguish the blaze since it was too risky to be out in the open.

Raymond pulled out the cell phone and dialled for Mandy.

"Raymond! Are you okay? Is Astrid okay?"

"Yes, listen, we need to rendezvous...Hold on...Where, Astrid?"

"Tell her to take a right out of the car park and follow the street all the way to the Hauptbahnhof, the railway station. Get her to park the car and wait for us near the ticket counter."

Raymond passed along the instructions and hung up the phone. They set off back along the docks, looking to flag a taxi. At the train station, they spotted Mandy wearing the packsack containing the computer, trying to look like a tourist. She had already been propositioned three times by men before they got there and was getting thoroughly nervous. Raymond walked by near her, caught her eye, and she followed him out at a safe distance.

Five minutes later they were a block away, checking into a fifty deutschmarks-a-night hotel. It was something of a sleazy area and the two girls were amused by Raymond's embarrassment to find half the hotel operated as a brothel. Still, it gave them the perfect cover for one man to be staying with two women.

Raymond was concerned. "It is only a matter of time before somebody catches up with us. Even if we lay low until this is all over, we will be found, so I think we have to bring this matter to a conclusion as soon as we can. We can't outrun everyone. We need money to get by and a place to operate from."

"Well, this is as good as any. We fit right in and Mandy and I can make a few hundred deutschmarks a day right next door."

"Astrid!"

Mandy was grinning. "More action than in this place, right, Astrid?" For the past ten minutes a bed headboard had been beating a steady tattoo against their wall from next door and the faint moans of feigned purchased pleasure penetrated the room.

"I have to go shopping again and get some supplies and disguises." Astrid picked up her coat and started to wind her long blonde hair up under a leather cap. Raymond thought the hair upswept to expose her slender neck was just as alluring as before and she certainly did not look any less noticeable. In a minute, she was gone.

When he turned around after locking the door behind Astrid, Raymond found Mandy close behind him. She slid into his arms and for a moment they stood holding each other close. Then she arched her back, grinding her pubic bone against his crotch. Moving, she crushed her breasts against his chest and her tongue slid into his ear while delicate fingers worked the back of his neck. In moments he felt himself responding, a heat of passion rising up between them like the swelling magma of a volcanic eruption.

Raymond's hands slid over Mandy's buttocks as their tongues met, pulling them closer in a frantic friction of rotating hips. Her breath exploded harshly and he knew how wet she was going to be. Backing her to the large bed, he pushed her down, roughly pulling the slacks and undergarments down her legs. He buried his face in her, wanting it all, but she was tugging at him, wanting him inside her. Frenzied fingers working with common purpose but no co-ordination, they stripped naked and coupled with an urgency they had never experienced before.

The totally overwhelming experience was so great, it was soon over, but the orgasmic heights they reached transcended anything that had gone before. In the aftermath, they felt like suicidal beings that had rushed to their own erotic destruction only to find life and peace on the other side. Raymond wondered if it was the stress release, the erotic influence of being in a brothel, or Astrid's presence, but something different had just happened. His whole groin and thighs were soaked and Mandy felt like a warm wet and luxurious haven which he never wanted to leave.

"I like her, Raymond."

His head was still swimming from the height he'd reached. Was that what this was then, a stamp of possession? No, that would have been accomplished in other ways, more personally crafted to bond him to Mandy. Lust between two knowing people. What the hell, you couldn't analyze it!

Astrid returned a little over an hour later from what she now boasted was one of her *famous little shopping expeditions.* She carried two bags and the packsack was also full. She sniffed the air delicately, savouring it. "This place smells like a brothel!" She looked at the discomforted Raymond and then slipped a hidden wink to Mandy.

"We are going to be skinhead punks." Quickly she displayed the clothes, hair dyes, earrings and make-up equipment she had purchased. "Those guys are walking disguises, so we should fit right in by standing right out." It was a shrewd remark. The lurid personal appearance of many of the young Germans had reached the point where people would rather turn their heads than try to accept them as a normal view.

Clustering in the bathroom, the girls stripped to their underwear and began to cut and dye their hair. Both of them cut off half their gorgeous hair and Astrid dyed hers green while Mandy's became purple. Teasing, tweaking, spraying and combing, they styled their hair into impossible spikes and curls. Harsh purple and black makeup applied to eyes, rouged cheeks with nose rings and studs in the ears changed their appearances immeasurably. When they presented themselves to Raymond, he gasped at the sight.

Compared to their natural beauty, they had made themselves unattractive and as character-less as real skinheads. Yet there was a raw edge of sensuality to their appearance. "Which one of you can I have first?"

"Forget it, buster!" Oddly, it was Astrid who reacted. "Now, your turn!"

The girls dragged him into the bathroom and sat him on the toilet seat while they began to cut his hair even shorter. When they produced shaving cream and a safety razor each, Raymond protested but they were adamant. He felt like some ancient emperor, being ministered to by two scantily clad slave women. The closeness of breasts, thighs and hips in undergarments became too much and his shorts began to bulge.

"Look at this, Astrid, Sir Galahad's lance is coming to the ready!"

"Again?" there was a disapproving sound from the green-headed lovely and the next Raymond knew, a mug of cold water was poured over his crotch. At first he was mad, but both girls broke out in peals of laughter and fell to the floor, helpless at his discomfiture. He started to get up, but they pushed him back. "Hang on, we're not finished yet."

While Raymond sat trying to figure out why they teased him instead of fighting with each other, the girls took more cosmetic pencils and drew designs on his naked white scalp. They attached earrings to him and slid a gold ring into his nostril before allowing him to stand and look in the mirror. He would not have recognized himself.

On the bed were half a dozen wigs they could later wear and several sets of clothing each. While the girls had been doing their hair, Raymond had gotten in contact with Manny Kruppe and arranged for a drop off of ten thousand deutschmarks. He knew that Willie McIvor would put up the money; events had proven he was onto something huge as a news story.

Astrid had bought a couple of light nightdresses for herself and Mandy. Since there was only the king-size bed in the room, she began to pile clothing and cushions on the floor to sleep. "Come to bed, Astrid," Mandy held the sheets up invitingly on the other side of Raymond and he looked like he was going to have a seizure. Without an argument, Astrid stepped over and slid into the bed beside Raymond.

He lay awake for a while, too conscious of what lay next to him on either side. Then fatigue caught up and he drifted off into a deep sleep. He dreamed he was making love to a beautiful woman who was being very vocal and awoke to hear the sound for real. Somewhere above them a woman was either having or giving an impression of a massive earthquake of an orgasm. A street sign outside flashed on and off, illuminating the room with a reddish glow. Mandy was pressed against him, tight and warm while Astrid had kicked off most of her share of the sheets.

She lay on her back and he could hear her well-remembered deep steady breathing. Turning his head, he could see her profile, the green hair reflecting the red light as a puce haze. Her nightdress had no shoulder straps and it had slipped down. He could see her naked breasts rising and falling, the large nipples pools of darkness in the pink glow. Suddenly, Mandy stirred and he felt her head come up alongside his, her gaze following his. Her hand crept down his body and squeezed his hardness. "Naughty boy." In moments, she was asleep again, her breath soft against his shoulder.

Raymond placed his arm around her and she snuggled further down with a small moan of satisfaction.

1000 hrs. Tuesday, 10th July 1990.
Hotel Grüben, Hamburg.

Just after they returned from breakfast, Raymond's cell phone rang. "Herr Mannheimer?" Raymond waved at the girls to turn the television down. "Bring the papers to number fifty two, Ernst Dobrünnenstrasse, two blocks east from you. Bring your two friends also. I would invite you to a restaurant but their colourful appearance may insult the maitre d'. In half an hour." The caller clicked off.

"That was Streicher. He wants a meeting in half an hour. He knows where we are, knows about Mandy and that we have changed our appearance."

"How?" Mandy was shocked.

Raymond just shrugged. "If he knows, who else does?"

"Yeah, I think it is time we moved on and I also think we have to trust him. What shall we take with us?" Astrid was already rummaging, looking for Raymond's answer.

"Put everything in the trunk of the car. We'll come back later for it. Just keep the weapons, the money and a light bag with the wigs."

While Astrid paid the bill, Raymond and Mandy carried the bags out to the car where she had left it. Opening the trunk, they slid the three bags inside. Turning east along the street, they walked to Dobrünnenstrasse. Raymond felt self-conscious at first because of his appearance. Several pedestrians gave him a wide berth, which at first amused him and then he fell into the role, scowling at one couple and causing them to quicken their pace. Astrid and Mandy were way ahead of him, enjoying the attention immensely, like a pair of fashion models on a photo-shoot.

The address turned out to be a dingy doorway sandwiched between a pawnshop and a grubby quick-food cafe. They paused, disturbed by the exposed situation they were in, until a door opened behind them at the curb. Streicher himself sat at the wheel of a nondescript car and beckoned them to get in. In moments they headed off down the street but not before Raymond saw another car following them.

Streicher saw his glance. "It's okay, they are mine. Cannot be too careful, the place you visited yesterday was bombed and two of my men were killed. Whoever did it obviously thought I was inside."

"Where are we going now?"

"To a little place I have outside the city."

"We need the stuff out of our car."

"Give me the key and I'll have one of my men pick it up. Do you have those papers?"

"Photocopies of them."

"And the originals hidden away to hold me for ransom, is that it? Don't worry Herr Mannheimer; it is time for co-operation, I think. Without your warning, I may now be dead. Incidentally, you were wrong about the number of people after you. There are actually about seven different groups anxious to either make your acquaintance or else eliminate you."

"I'm truly flattered."

"In case you are wondering, yesterday's shooting was staged by a party unknown. The second vehicle was manned by men in my employ. I had to be on guard after you made yourself known to me. One man died in the van that attacked you but was burned beyond recognition. Otto was considered a bystander victim after we removed his gun before the police got there. The police do not know you had been visiting me, but the opposition obviously did. You were being watched. The Hafenstrasse people joined in the gunfire and the blame for the whole thing has been placed on their shoulders. The police suspect drugs, extortion, prostitution, gang-rivalry and their investigation *is continuing*."

1207 hrs. Tuesday, 10th July 1990.
Near the Hauptbannhof, Hamburg.

Helmut Wollfarthen was a small-time crook and drug pusher who worked the Hamburg dockside. On the side, he had a couple of young girls who kept him in pocket money, working the street near a couple of live sex shows. Although tough in appearance, with long sideburns and oily backcombed black hair, Helmut was a poseur who avoided physical confrontation like the plague.

From behind dark glasses, he surveyed the cars parked on the street near the Hauptbahnhof. The particular one he was interested in had an overdue parking ticket stuck under the wipers. This was of no concern to Helmut as he never paid them anyway. He was here to retrieve the vehicle, hired by Manny Schlegel for whom he often did small jobs.

Unfortunately, the instructions to Helmut Wollfarthen were not totally explicit. With more urgent matters to discuss, Streicher failed to stress that the sole task was to remove the baggage from Raymond's car. He had not meant for the car to be driven since it could be followed and some sort of cut-out would be required to foil any surveillance.

By the time Wollfarthen got the order from Schlegel, through a couple of intermediaries over the phone, he mistakenly understood he was to take the vehicle. It had crossed his mind that the vehicle could be hot or loaded with drugs but since his trusted instincts detected no surveillance on the street, he strolled up to it. This was easy money and after unlocking it, he climbed in. Turning the ignition key was his last earthly act for the car exploded in an enormous fireball, killing him instantly.

1330 hrs. Tuesday, 10th July 1990. Outside Hamburg.

"We are safe here," Streicher finished with his cell phone. "My men report no followers and they are watching the last couple of intersections on the road into this place. Now, let me see the papers."

Raymond spread them on the table and sat back. They were sitting in the kitchen of a small farmhouse about fifteen kilometres out of Hamburg. It was a cozy place and well appointed, like a rich man's secret retreat should probably look.

Streicher looked carefully at each one, making non-committal grunts. He studied the list of names last. Taking out a pen, he carefully lined through *Mannheimer, Dorffman, Streicher* and *Stowaski*. "You see, Herr Mannheimer? You, and I, Streicher, are both dead."

"How do you know all these men are dead?"

"I buried them."

"You mean you killed them?" Astrid was horrified and felt the sudden confinement they were in.

"No, I only killed Mannheimer and Dorffman. Had I not, they would have killed me. Their guns were still smoking from killing soldiers - two of them my friends. I was to be next. They wanted the site to be kept secret and we were all expendable."

Now, after proper introductions, Streicher, for he had still not admitted to being Gottlieb Demsch, and seemingly, wished to retain the identity, described that morning back in April, nineteen forty-five.

When he had brought them up to date, he moved quickly on to the present situation. "My people have identified a number of groups interested in you. First, the Kriminalpolizei want you for murder. Scotland Yard wants you for kidnapping. The Mossad are on to you. What their interest is, who can say? The British Secret Service want you and I suspect by extension, the CIA will be involved. The group you stole the papers from is still out there, looking. I can only speculate, but I doubt Reinhold Beckmann, if he is still alive, has forgotten about the gold. There was an incursion into the frontier area in nineteen forty-seven which resulted in some shooting, as you have already discovered. This incursion came from the east side and nobody came out to the west, so we have to assume an interested party from behind the Iron Curtain is also involved. Lastly, I have to include anyone who finds out about the prize. With that much money at stake, we are safe from nobody."

"So, what next?"

"In view of the way everything is coming to a head, get the gold and disappear."

"You do know where it is then?" Raymond felt the question necessary.

"Yes."

The Three Musketeers, as Raymond and the girls had come to know themselves, exchanged glances. "What about us?"

"I feel, since you warned me, that I owe you in this matter and you have demonstrated trustworthiness. A partnership?"

"Fifty-fifty?" Astrid was quick with money concerns.

Streicher smiled. "I think not. How about seventy-thirty - the thirty split between the three of you?"

"Just how much is there?"

"I cannot calculate it as I never saw inside the boxes. As I told you, I took some gold coins to get me started and they fetched a good price. I believe there will be at least thirty million marks, depending on how it is sold. Some bullion dealers have expensive scruples, others don't."

Mandy said, "And then what are you going to do?"

"I shall disappear under a new identity and take up residence at a vineyard I have purchased. My interest in the gold is as much a lifelong ambition as a need for more wealth, you understand. Its recovery has been paramount throughout my life.

Now you have shown me I must disappear with or without it as soon as possible and I want to try to disappear with it rather than without it."

Streicher's cell phone rang again. He listened, turned quickly to Raymond and then hung up. "The man I sent to get your baggage is dead. He climbed into your car and tried to start it. It blew up."

"Booby trapped?"

Streicher nodded. "It is a good job you only opened the trunk to put your stuff in there. Now, it is time we got as far away from here as we can. I shall charter an aircraft to take us down to the Vogtland. I have property there, close to the area of the border in question."

0930 hrs. Wednesday, 11th July 1990.
Rio Pilcomayo, Gran Chaco, Paraguay.

El Jefe sat in contemplation, a printed sheet in his lap. Herr Barton was fast becoming a nuisance, popping up in all kinds of places where he did not belong. Because his father was ex-Lieutenant Colonel Alexander George Barton MM, DSC and an important officer in the British Gold Rush team and ex-Foreign Office dignitary, the younger Barton's presence was taking on the appearance of involvement. The old man knew the temptations which gold meant to the average person. After all, had not some of the staunchest Nazi party members succumbed and smuggled gold out of the Third Reich before it fell?

To accord the same greed to Colonel Barton was only one small step of logic. Even though he was dead, his son might easily be privy to the whereabouts of gold and the recent turmoil in both Germanys was an obvious trigger for him to follow possible instructions of how to retrieve bullion. It was too much of a coincidence to ignore.

Then there was this German girl, Astrid Klemerer. He knew her lineage, and also, her family connections. It was too much of a coincidence to see her involved. There were obviously forces at work beyond his control. Well, El Jefe knew exactly how to deal with such situations. These people needed to be interrogated and information extracted from them. It was of such vital importance that he could not entrust the job to anyone but himself. His course was clear. They would have to be brought here to the ranch.

1000 hrs. Wednesday, 11th July 1990. Vogtland.

They had flown down the night before on a chartered aircraft, been picked up by some of Streicher's people, and brought to the house nestled in the woodland. The mixed woods carpeting the rolling hills made a pleasant scene and it felt peaceful and safe after the ordeals they had been through in the past few days. An elderly lady from the village had arrived early, bringing breakfast supplies, which she served in the picturesque kitchen. She had since left and they were all clustered around the table, sharing another pot of coffee.

"How do you propose to get to the site if it is between the wire, in a minefield?" Raymond asked.

"I have been thinking about that problem for forty-five years, especially since the fortified frontier and minefields went in during the early sixties. Now, since unification, I believe I have the answer."

"Can you just use minesweepers?" Astrid waved the coffee carafe at Streicher's empty mug but he shook his head.

"Yes, but the problem is not as easy as that. The frontier was built to keep people getting from the East to the West. Most of the mines are the anti-personnel type. Over the fields of Northern Germany, they had to guard against large vehicles crashing their way through the Border, so there was a salting of larger mines to disable such attempts. Because the woods are so thick in the Vogtland, discouraging vehicles, I believe all the mines will be anti-personnel. These in turn fall into types: Blast, the type you step on and get blown up. Fragmentation, the type hung on stakes above ground, which can be triggered by trip-wires or remotely. Finally, bounding, the type which leap out of the ground when triggered and spray the area up to twenty metres around with shrapnel and steel balls."

"Sounds hideous."

"It is. There are over three hundred different types of mines made today. Most likely, ones in the area may be old types, from the War, swept and reused, or made in the USSR or East Germany. These would include the PPM Two type, or, SM Seventy and POMS-Two, POMZ-Two , PMD-Six, PMD-Seven, along with anything else they could lay their hands on. Many of these mines could be made of wood or plastic, which is difficult to sweep. They are all nasty.

Through the years, I had two main options to get into the minefield. One was to crash in with heavy equipment but the time required in the area to locate, excavate, load and retreat was too long and such a method would have guaranteed a fire fight with the Border Guards and their reinforcements. Military dogma tells us that an eighty per cent clearance is acceptable by this method, known as *breaching,* but think of the risk posed by the other twenty percent of mines undisturbed! The other method was pure stealth. You have all seen movies of men poking their bayonets into the ground to locate mines and this is still the best, though most laborious and time-consuming method.

This could not be accomplished in one night and, of course, returning nightly was not an option. The slightest hint of encroachment to the guards would also have resulted in a firefight. I know. I have been there.

One other method was to dig a tunnel and in view of the permanence of the frontier, we actually did start one since it was the only alternative. We knew listening devices would have discovered that, especially as we would have had to mole around trying to locate the exact burial spot. However it was the only positive course I could find to mollify my frustration. We had to stop when we found bedrock too close to the surface. It would have been too noisy to continue and any seismic activity to find a route would have alerted the Border Guards.

Now reunification has removed the Border Guards, so people are free to go into the minefield if they so wish without any kind of alarms or shooting taking place. The answer to obtaining access proved simple. What I have done is contracted with the Government to clear the mines in that area."

"Brilliant!"

"Yes. I have equipment already out there including a reinforced plough, bulldozer and large front-end loader with wide bucket. Once the above ground fragmentation mines such as the POMZ-Twos are removed, we scrape the ground to a depth of a half metre out to the site, clearing or exploding any mines in the way."

"What about the bounding mines?"

"Hopefully there are not too many of those, but the cabs of the equipment have steel plates welded over them. The fragments cannot penetrate them."

"The authorities have approved this?"

"Yes, but they want a bond of ten million marks as indemnity that no person going in later steps on an undetected mine and sues."

"You have paid that?"

Streicher laughed. "Of course not. It is peanuts against what is buried there, but I never give the government money anyway. I asked them for permission to conduct secret trials of a patented method to remove mines of all types. If it succeeds, I promised them a share of the patent. You see, apart from the military application of good minesweeping, it is big business. There are an estimated one hundred million mines in the world now, many dating from the Second World War. Millions of hectares of land are useless and thousands of people are being killed and maimed annually, in countries such as Vietnam, Cambodia, the Sahara and other African areas. It can cost up to a thousand dollars a mine to remove them, so, as I say, it is big business."

"And once you retrieve the gold, the trial is dropped?"

"You guessed it!"

"What about the others," Astrid spoke for the first time.

"What others?"

"You know. The people who have been pursuing us."

"They will not know."

"But someone *does* know. Someone told the S.S. Standartenführer where to find the barn. He did not just stumble upon it, did he? They also told him what to bury there. They will be watching. There is also good reason to believe the word got spread a little further. The surviving S.S. man on the train and your friend Beckmann know *roughly*, where to go looking."

"Yes, but they did not accompany us, they have no idea where the gold went after we left the train!"

"You have been visiting and watching this area for forty-five years. What's to say they haven't done the same? Do you think the sounds of exploding mines will go unnoticed?" Astrid had made her point.

Streicher looked up suddenly. "The word will have to be spread locally that we are doing this work. People will be warned off and a screen of security men will keep the area clear. Still, you may be right, Astrid. Back in nineteen forty-seven there was a gun battle up in that area. As I told you, I bought my 'retirement' acreage here and visit every year. The locals told me about what happened but were quite vague since it all seemed to happen on the Oster side. Perhaps someone did go in there after I reconnoitered it and managed to disturb the site."

"You think they may have removed the gold?"

"Not likely they could walk away with several hundred kilograms of boxes and sacks while being shot at. Supposedly, the fence was not breached on the West side, so they could hardly have made off into the East, right into the arms of the guards."

"Suppose the East Germans were part of it."

"I cannot accept that. Word is there were heavy casualties and several guards were killed."

"But some of the party escaped," Raymond pressed.

"Not according to the Vopos' propaganda, but we may never know."

"Unless the cache is empty," Mandy's words caused them pause.

"*Several hundred kilograms*?" Astrid had picked up on Streicher's statement.

"It might not all have been gold, Astrid. I did not inspect the contents."

Streicher's cottage was only a half-kilometre away from the frontier, down the slope. On his instructions, men in the advance party had cut trees up to the wire, preparing access to the open area. The cottage was small and reminded Raymond of Franz Verhstassen's home on the other side of the old border.

A large shop nearby contained the heavy equipment Streicher had mentioned, along with welding and heavy-duty mechanical tools. On one side of the shop, a ravine fell away and was partially filled by excavated dirt from the abandoned tunnel. They all walked up to the frontier and gazed at the wide death zone before them. Streicher had brought a huge gun case with him. Some of the wire had been cut already and a taped-off area with signs warned trespassers of the danger they courted should they enter.

"So, that's what a minefield looks like?" Astrid had not seen one before up so close.

"It looks like a quiet meadow," Mandy looked contemplative.

Streicher nodded. "Yes, but one person, one animal, even a bird out there can precipitate a hail of death."

"Where is it?" Raymond was more direct.

Streicher stepped forward. "Right about there," he pointed, "two thirds of the way to the other fence, there is a small bush, just to the left of that leaning tree. That gives us the line to approach. Once we get there, we will need to thoroughly clear an area to make it safe to dig."

"How deep?"

"About a metre. The bodies are a little more shallow. The electronic sweepers will detect metal helmets and rifles buried with them but they are about ten metres east of the gold and we do not need to disturb them."

"Yeah, I suppose if we unearthed some dead bodies, the authorities would want to investigate."

Streicher began to unzip the rifle case and extracted a large hunting rifle. Fitting a scope, he aimed the weapon into the minefield.

"What is that for?" Mandy was out of sorts with guns.

"It is a Steyr-Mannlicher Model ST," Astrid answered for Streicher, "what calibre?"

"It takes a four fifty-eight Winchester Magnum. You are a hunter then?"

"I have been around weapons all my life. My stepfather is a great enthusiast. Is that a laser sight?"

"Yes, an Aimpoint Two. It has magnification as well," Streicher turned to Mandy. "To answer your question, and demonstrate the deadliness of the minefield, Mandy, I am going to shoot one of the stake-mounted POMS-Two mines. This rifle fires a five hundred grain slug with a full metal jacket at a velocity of nearly seven hundred metres per second and the impact should set the mine off. Please, everyone, get down low."

Carefully, Streicher loaded the three-cartridge magazine, worked the bolt to chamber a round and took aim. He seemed to take an interminable time but suddenly the rifle roared and kicked back into his shoulder. Almost instantly, there was a flash in the middle of the area and with a loud crack, his target exploded. They barely had time to jump when two more mines went off. In the aftermath they could hear metal scything through the vegetation and something pinged off a post nearby.

"Good heavens!"

"Yes. The bullet knocked the mine away from under its trigger pin that was attached to a trip wire. When it got tugged, it set off the other mines. They are usually connected in groups of four, so one did not go off. Here, Astrid, give it a try."

Astrid took the rifle and inspected it carefully before raising it to her shoulder. In seconds she had blown another mine, and its partners.

"Well done! Perhaps we can make this your job tomorrow!"

They returned to the cottage and sat out on the veranda, sipping on drinks. Nobody was crass enough to open any discussion on how they would spend the money to be recovered tomorrow. Streicher exuded a grim jubilation that he was at last within reach of his lifelong dream. Astrid was withdrawn when not engaged in small talk and Mandy stayed close to Raymond, keeping body contact like she was afraid of losing him.

0600 hrs. Thursday, 12th July 1990. Vogtland Frontier minefield.

Thirty men showed up on a bus. Twenty of them were security guards, dressed in military-style camouflage uniforms, carrying portable radios. The remainder wore dark blue coveralls and they were the actual work crew. The drivers wore body armour under the coveralls and carried military tank crew helmets. All the vehicles were radio equipped.

In ten minutes, the first vehicle, the bulldozer, was at the fence. The driver closed the plate steel door over his observation slit and guided himself into the fence using the television camera mounted on the front of the cab. There was a camera front and rear, joystick controlled, and a quick release plug would allow him to quickly replace any camera that got hit by shrapnel. There were half a dozen replacement cameras under his seat.

Ten metres to his right, Astrid leaned the hunting rifle on a sturdy low tree branch, ready to snipe any mines he identified for her. Streicher was on the other side, radio-equipped and spotting with a pair of binoculars.

"Sniper, this is Dozer. How do you read?"

"Five by five, Dozer," Astrid spoke into the boom mike attached to her headset.

"Okay, I'm going in. There is one target about ten metres, one o'clock."

Astrid turned on the laser and swung the Mannlicher, every blade of grass springing into clear focus. "Got it!" The pineapple shell of the mine, attached atop a stick twenty-five centimetres high almost filled the sights of the scope. The red dot of the laser was centred on the shape. Breathing out, she steadied the rifle and squeezed the trigger. The rifle barked and kicked back, the shot immediately followed by two explosions ahead of the bulldozer. The metallic rattling of fragments off the bulldozer came to her ears. With a roar of its engine, the machine clattered through the severed strands of barbed wire, entering the field.

"Seven metres at ten o'clock, can you see it?"

"No! Back up a bit. Hold it! There it is!" Again the rifle went off, accompanied this time by four detonations.

The blade of the bulldozer came down, digging into the ground and the engine revved up as the driver put it into forward motion. Earth and vegetation curled up before it, piling a metre high before the driver turned on one track, pushed the earth to the side and then backed up. Down came the blade again and the bulldozer moved on past the abandoned mound, going deeper into the field. A muffled thump came from beneath the chassis and white smoke poured out from an anti-personnel pressure mine detonation.

"Fifteen metres, one o'clock."

"Got it!" Only one explosion this time as the rifle spoke. Astrid was now four for four on shots.

Forwards, turn and back, forwards, turn and back, the bulldozer was now fifty metres into the minefield, piling up echelons of earth mounds either side of its path. Astrid missed with her sixth shot and had to get the driver to stop while she took out the mine with a seventh shot. Only yards further on, there was a heavier explosion and a massive clang echoed along the cleared forest walls of the frontier space. White smoke billowed up from the front of the bulldozer. It had hit a heavier mine, intended to disable vehicles.

"Dozer from Control One. Dozer, are you OK, Heinrich?" Streicher was anxious.

There was a long and pregnant pause. "Yeah, wow, that was an experience, the dozer was singing like a violin. Looks like it blew a chunk out of the blade!"

"Be careful!"

"How much did you say you were paying me for this?" The question was obviously rhetorical for the engine roared again and the lumbering machine curled up another section of ground.

In thirty minutes, the bulldozer had reached the target zone. Here the driver employed another device, a three-metre long pole boom lowered to the horizontal with a vertical bar welded on the end. Within a minute, this rig had snagged a trip-wire and blown two more mines. Backwards and forwards went the bulldozer, building a rectangle of ploughed ground, surrounded by a two-metre high bank of earth. Once the driver had to stop, getting Astrid to hold fire while he opened his door, went out, and replaced the front camera which had been destroyed by a steel ball.

By noon the loader was able to come on-site and began to scoop a further few centimetres off the area cleared by the bulldozer. It was a little more vulnerable with huge rubber tires, but its wide bucket would probably scoop up any remaining mines. Quickly, the skilled driver scooped and dumped his way out to the area they were interested in. Twice the dumping of material triggered pressure mines but they were buried under earth the same instant they exploded and proved harmless.

By two o'clock, the job was done and the site was ready for a manual sweep using a metal detector. As part of his plan, Streicher had dismissed the workers for the day and proposed to go out alone to do the job. Raymond then volunteered to go with him.

They drove out in a light truck, the detection gear in the back along with some shovels, survey tape, pegs and a mallet. Getting out of the truck was an eerie feeling. Knowing he was out in a former killing zone, with deadly mines all around and maybe some remaining, made Raymond's scalp crawl and he couldn't figure out why he had volunteered.

Streicher quickly strapped on the harness of the metal detector, attached it to the carrying snap and turned it on. They walked to the far side of the cleared area and he moved along, sweeping the detector left and right. Stripped of the meager topsoil, the clay beneath was damp and brownish-ochre. Raymond marked the swathes that had been swept with chunks of dirt. They were covering about a metre per pass and on the fourth one, the detector gave a brief audible yelp. They both froze as Streicher re-swept, pinpointing the spot.

Carefully, Raymond went down on one knee and slid a special mine prodder into the earth. This tool was a pointed metal rod about two feet long with a spade handle on one end. On the third careful insertion, the rod met resistance. Streicher passed him a trowel and Raymond carefully excavated next to the object. The dirt was loose; a long narrow strip turned over but not removed by the bucket. Sure enough, a rounded metal shape was revealed. They had decided not to remove any mines they might find. More modern ones had mercury switch triggers to thwart their removal. Although they did not expect anything that new, the old ones might be unstable enough to be best left undisturbed.

Taking a stake and some red tape, Raymond marked the position of the mine. After that, he stopped walking alongside Streicher, staying in the safer zone behind him instead but they found no more mines before a strengthening squeal from the device warned of a concentration of metal. Quickly Streicher delineated the zone and Raymond placed more lumps of clay to mark it.

"Tonight." In the one word lay forty-five years of waiting and Raymond saw the look of almost sexual expectation on Streicher's face.

Despite the amount of help he had needed to position himself for this moment throughout the years, Streicher had never lost sight of one main fact - there was nobody he could trust. As a consequence, he had most carefully insulated others from knowledge, or even suspicion, that the gold might exist. While he might provide the means and cost of extracting the gold, there was always the fear that he could be double-crossed at the last moment by someone imbued with the greed of gold. He freely admitted the corollary. After living with it for so many years, he knew.

The plan now became that he and Raymond would drive into the cleared area between the frontier wire and remove the gold, taking it back to the house and loading it on a larger truck parked there for the purpose.

1600 hrs. Thursday, 12th July 1990.
John F. Kennedy Airport, New York City.

El-Cetti cleared U.S. Immigration at the airport without any kind of problem. He was automatically videotaped several times while passing through the Customs hall, but his was a face amongst thousands, a grain of sand in the desert.

He had seen the spread of New York from the Olympic Airways Boeing 747. His feeling of hatred towards this careless display of opulence grew as he crossed the Hudson River, bound for the New Jersey side. The towering ramparts of Manhattan gave him the greatest offence. It was a monument to American domination, American support of Israel and concurrent oppression of his people.

2300 hrs. Thursday, 12th July 1990 Vogtland. Frontier minefield.

Streicher fired up a Mercedes truck with a low, open bed. Raymond climbed in beside him. On the back of the truck behind the cab was a wooden box containing two machine guns and eight magazines.

Astrid climbed onto the back cradling the Mannlicher, a night star-scope attached. She would be their watching guard from the trees. Mandy stayed at the house, since the road to it was the only way in. She was to act as an advance guard. Four roving security men, two on the fence and two in the woods were assigned to patrolling the vicinity. Everyone else had been sent home and the area was deserted.

Pausing only to let Astrid off, Streicher drove straight into the cleared area. The ground was rough, but it only took a few minutes. The night was dark but clear, stars building in intensity overhead as the final flush of sunset disappeared. The woods were a black wall, deep and silent as a poised beast. A faint light pricked the trees as a guard picked his way along.

Raymond felt his skin prickle as they moved through the fence. There was still deadly menace out here, still the risk of an un-swept mine blowing up under them. Streicher stopped the truck, pointing it at the five metre wide marked area and leaving the headlights on. They unloaded picks and shovels, along with a pair of battery lanterns and a metal detector.

In minutes, they had swept the detector over a massive return from underground, the instrument warbling as if it were going to explode. They both felt the tension mount. Only inches below the dirt was a fortune in gold. Having had so long to study all aspects of the excavation site, Streicher had come up with the idea of driving in a steel rod to test the subsurface. It only took minutes, guided by the detector, to outline the area to be excavated. Quickly, they seized the shovels and set to work. It felt strange at first, plunging shovels into the earth in the middle of a minefield. Astrid checked in on the radio and after exchanging signals, they set to with a will. Because the bulldozer had stripped off half a metre of the topsoil, they did not have to dig very far before Streicher's shovel clanked on something hard.

Since the boxes were buried side by side, once they were able to unearth one, the rest could be levered out once the covering soil was removed. The boxes were made from oak so they had not rotted over the years although the hemp rope handles originally attached had turned to useless strands.

Streicher turned whenever he took a break, looking into the darkness where Mannheimer and his own friends were buried. He felt like he wanted to exhume them, see how they were. He had no regrets for the men he had killed, it had been self-defence and their motives had been evil. For the others, the Russians, the Poles and his own Wehrmacht friends, he felt only a lingering loss. They had all had family who had never known their fate, never laughed, loved or even argued with them again. And one of them, poor orphaned Streicher, he had impersonated for all these years.

In two hours they had unearthed twelve boxes and ten sacks, which had rotted so badly that they left them temporarily. There were also the three metal boxes Streicher remembered Mannheimer being so proprietary about. All went on the truck.

From time to time, they heard Astrid checking in with the lookouts. As part of Streicher's long planning, she had two radios, one for the patrols on one frequency, the other for Mandy, Raymond and Streicher. She wore two microphones, one clipped to each lapel for ready communication. Every short while she would call the lookouts by number and to verify security, their correct answer was to reply by a name chosen in an alphabetic progression. Raymond was monitoring the guards' channel with an earplug, the microphone strapped to his lapel. Streicher had the other. The guards had progressed from *Adolph* through *Bernhardt* and *Charles* to *Sigmund* when there was no response from the wire patrol to the east.

"Ein," Astrid's soft second call came into Raymond's ear and he held out a hand to Streicher to arrest his efforts with the shovel. He had to admire the calm in her voice. The woman was amazing. He tapped his ear which had the speaker in it to alert his companion. There was a long pause and then Streicher came alert as Astrid's voice came into his ear on the other channel. "Streicher. There is no reply from number One."

"Very well, we are coming out."

Without a sound, the two men nodded at each other and, abandoning their tools and climbing into the truck, closed the doors as silently as they could. Each had grabbed a machine gun on the way past the truck bed.

"Four men. Coming from the east along the wire. Dressed for action and armed. They are a hundred and fifty metres away."

"If they open fire, Astrid, shoot to kill."

"Very well. *Three* and *Four* plus Mandy are still with us but *One* and *Two* are out of touch."

Quickly Streicher motioned to Raymond who got back out and climbed onto the truck bed where the higher elevation would enable better directed fire than from inside the cab.

Beside her tree, Astrid watched the four men approaching. Through the night scope, she saw they moved with the economic lope of professional soldiers, carrying their weapons at the ready and shouldering light packs. She wondered what they had done to the two guards who had been out there. She checked again that the magazine was properly set in the rifle.

"Mandy."

"*Teresa*."

"Four armed men coming from the east along the wire. Prepare for a quick departure." She turned her head, lips to the other channel microphone. "Three."

"*Thomas*."

"Head back to the road. Watch for us to pick you up... Four."

"*Theodore*."

"Same for you, see you on the road."

"This is *One...Tadeusz!... Two* is with me. It is us, coming in from the east!"

Nice try! Thought Astrid. She had seen one of the men turn his head to speak into the radio microphone lifted from one of her guards. These guys were smart! She turned her head to the left and spoke into the channel for Streicher. "They have the other radio. Get out! Now!"

She knew she had to reply on the guards' channel, pretending she was fooled, otherwise the men would know they were truly discovered. There was a dip in the ground and now Astrid could only see the upper torsos and heads of the approaching men. Just as she was keying the mike for the intruders, the truck starter whined. In the clear night air, it sounded very loud. She saw them hesitate momentarily as the truck fired up and then they rushed forward, about a hundred metres away.

With a roar of the engine, Streicher hit the accelerator and the truck bounced forward. Raymond was only half-ready for the wild ride over the rough ground and clinging on desperately, wondered how he could possibly aim his weapon. There was a winking in the darkness off to their left and suddenly the air was filled with a swarm of angry bees. Because the intruders were slightly lower and the piles of topsoil gave cover, most of the rounds went high, but a few hit the upper cab of the truck with sharp metallic plinking noises. Cursing, Raymond wedged himself behind a box and extending his arms as high as he could, emptied a magazine in the general direction of the gunfire.

In the meantime, Astrid got off one round, knocking over one of the middlemen. She hit him in the chest before she realized that his bulky appearance meant he was probably wearing body armour. Levering another round into the breech, she drew a bead on the next man in line and shot him through the head. Her third round was hurried and she cursed the miss as the men went to earth and she jammed another three rounds into the rifle.

The truck was almost up to the wire now, Streicher desperately fighting the wheel as it bucked over the rough ground. He was driving purely on night vision and with the headlights off, the deep darkness of the forest hid one bank of earth and the left fender slammed into a mound of clay. The vehicle rocked and tilted, shedding two boxes of gold and almost losing Raymond.

Finally straightened, Streicher gunned the engine and they shot through the wire as a second burst of gunfire came out of the darkness. Raymond heard the loud crack of Astrid's return fire before he yelled at her. Sheltered momentarily between the trees on the track to his house, Streicher stood on the brakes. Astrid appeared like a ghost, grabbing Raymond's extended arm and then she was beside him. He pummelled the roof of the cab and turning on the lights, Streicher shot off down the hill.

They had only gone fifty metres when figures appeared in the headlights and a burst of gunfire took out one headlight and the radiator. Cursing, Streicher stopped and baled out of the door, directing a full magazine at the men below. The three of them sheltered at the rear of the vehicle, taking pot shots down the trail. The hot smell of radiator fluid filled the air.

"Quick, Raymond, grab a box!"

"Streicher, now is not the time to worry about the gold!"

"No, you don't understand! Quickly now before those others trap us from behind!"

"But Mandy..."

"If she is okay, this is the best way to help her. Trust me!"

Grabbing Streicher's proffered weapon, Astrid jammed in a new magazine and laid down a stream of fire as they each grabbed a box from the back of the truck and shouldering it, staggered into the trees to their right. There was a thicket covering a small gully and Streicher threw his box, indicated Raymond should do the same and then returned to the truck to repeat the process.

Raymond thought it madness to be doing this under fire, but Streicher was a man possessed and would not be denied. Incredibly, the sole headlight still shone, blinding their attackers to their movements. Grabbing two last boxes, the three of them were into the trees before a crash of gunfire totally wrecked the front of the truck and darkness suddenly fell, accompanied by a total silence.

They seemed to be on an old game trail and Raymond followed Streicher, wincing as branches whipped across his face. The box was already becoming incredibly heavy and the weapon in his hand was getting no lighter either. After only twenty metres, they turned left into another thicket, blindly staggering through the brush. Raymond actually fell over Streicher, who had stopped and seconds later, Astrid was blundering into them.

"Here! There is an air shaft for the old tunnel!" Streicher stooped to a pair of rotting tree boughs and cast them aside. Attached to them was a plastic camouflage sheet, covered with forest detritus. Beneath was a wooden cover, which they quickly slid aside. Streicher shone his lantern down the vertical shaft that was revealed. A galvanized culvert with a metal ladder bolted to it went down three metres into the ground.

"The gold!" Streicher shinned down the ladder until his shoulders were level with the ground and Raymond placed the first box on his shoulder. Nimbly, driven by his life-long urge, Streicher went down the ladder and quickly reappeared, ready for the second box. "This tunnel will take us to Mandy," Streicher's word coaxed Raymond to new efforts.

"Quickly! I hear them!" Astrid's hiss came from the darkness and Raymond grabbed her arm and pushed her towards the hole. Their pursuers were taking a terrible risk, rushing through the dark woods against armed opponents.

The camouflage sheet was still attached to the rotten bough and Raymond dragged it over his head like he was bedding down. Light flickered and flashed up at him from below and he could feel he was treading on Astrid in his urgency to get down. He found a handhold on the underside of the wooden cover and slid it back into place under the sheet. Suddenly, he was isolated from outside in a narrow, closed environment. Heavy exhalations of exertion resounded in the shaft and he feared they were so loud the men above would hear them. Then, from above, he heard a rip of automatic fire, close by, instantly responded to from another direction. A third firearm opened up and he felt a momentary satisfaction at the thought those bastards up there were now firing at each other.

There was a dank smell of undisturbed sub-earth and he was panting too much to escape it by breathing shallowly. He passed through a tangle of cobwebs, which explained Astrid's low cry of disgust moments before. Finally, he backed into an open space, pushing Astrid behind him. Streicher's backside was in his face, pushing some old boards over the spot where he had dumped the gold boxes. The flashlight briefly revealed the Nazi Reichsbank emblems before the last board fell over them.

The tunnel was low, only about a metre high and barely as wide with sections of metal sheets bolted in an arch to shore it up. A very narrow gauge of rusted railway track ran along the floor, which sloped away. The damp earth was gritty to Raymond's touch and already his knees felt wet.

"The tunnel only goes another ten metres to where we had to stop. If it has not caved in, we can get out the other end. I don't think they will discover the entrance," Streicher waved to indicate he should go first and they struggled to rearrange their order in the hole.

The mention of the other end of the hole re-kindled Raymond's worry about Mandy. The men on the trail must have come into contact with her on their way up and they had certainly shown no reluctance or hesitation to cause them harm. Astrid, probably reading his thoughts, squeezed his hand as she crawled over him. Determinedly, they set off down the tunnel on hands and knees.

The light rail, which had been used to extract the fill from the tunnel, was a good guide, but the ties it was laid on were hard on the knees. After a short way, they learned to measure their crawl so their knees went between them, into the more yielding clay. Still, the odd stone and continuous friction soon wore holes in the knees of their slacks.

At one point, a small cave-in had partially dammed the tunnel and water had built up behind it, slowly seeping through. The result was slimy ooze, which they had to slither through, squeezing up and over the pile. It was harder for Raymond as he had little light to see by, his only human contact being an occasional touch of Astrid's ankles when they slowed down ahead. He went by feel only and being the bulkiest of the three, he almost got jammed between the roof and the fallen clay. The tightness of their confines and the aftermath of the adrenaline rush above ground worked to build panic in him and he felt claustrophobia hurtling at him like a giant wave. He kicked in near terror when he felt the tunnel roof pushing down on him, and fortunately, he came free, sliding down the other side of the mud until he rammed his head into Astrid's bottom as she had waited for him to clear the obstacle.

"Raymond!"

"Sorry."

She heard his heightened breathing, understood his frenzied struggle behind her. "Come, Leibling, not far now."

In a few minutes, which seemed like eternity, they came to the mouth of the tunnel. It was immediately behind the equipment shop and could not be seen from above as it opened out into the gully. Streicher had turned off his light and gone ahead to check the situation out while Raymond and Astrid sat and tightly clasped hands. Their fears were too vivid to voice as they gazed at the light patch of night sky beyond the Stygian blackness of the tunnel.

Suddenly, the night sky with its single visible star was blocked off and Streicher's whisper came to their ears. "Come out." It was all in the voice. No inflection, just a flat statement. No enthusiasm for their condition. No briefing. They were caught. "Maybe pass the weapons out first."

Raymond hesitated. Mandy's fate was unknown and Astrid had been magnificent. Still, he would rather die here and maybe take out one or two of them, making them pay rather than go out the cheap way, the bullet in the back of the head, kneeling on the edge of a shallow pit. Still, there had been no hand grenade or burst of gunfire into the tunnel, so maybe there was hope.

"Mandy is safe." The statement disarmed Raymond completely and he proffered the weapons to the crouched figure. Streicher passed them to someone above him and they crawled out of the tunnel into the open.

Six men stood safely separated around them, weapons trained on them as they emerged. A couple more stepped forward and patted them down before leading them to the door of the equipment shop. The lights were on inside and they blinked at the brightness.

"Mr. Barton! I am very disappointed in you!" Raymond recognized the voice of the Israeli from Frankfurt. "You promised to return to Britain and look at the mess you are now in. Still, I did not expect you to heed my advice and it was very inconsiderate of you to get that car blown up, along with the tracking device we stowed on it. Anyway, you led us to Mr. Streicher, which has been fruitful, I think. Now, the outcome may not be so fortunate for you."

The threat in the words was reinforced by Raymond's glimpse of Mandy sitting against the wheel of a plough, holding a bloody field dressing to her head.

"Yes, she was narrowly prevented from killing one of my men. Combined with you shooting at us, we are not at all happy with you," the man turned and quickly gave orders in a language Raymond did not understand but which he took to be Hebrew. They were quickly and expertly frisked, with no respect for gender before being herded into a small parts room with two guards in the doorway.

"Are you all right, Mandy?" Astrid was quick to turn to her and offer assistance.

"Yeah, I'm fine, just a knock from a rifle butt. The bastard got me before I could pull the trigger. Sorry, Raymond."

"It's OK, Mandy. I think we were outmaneuvered right from the start. How a bunch of amateurs like us could expect to take on so many professionals and win is beyond me."

Streicher was slowly and reflectively bumping his head against the wall, furious, frustrated and mind working overtime.

The Israeli leader returned. "How many people in your party?"

"Five hundred."

There was the menacing cocking sound of an automatic and the man reached down, grasped Astrid by the hair and pulling just hard enough to extend her sitting body upwards, pushed the muzzle against her neck. "How many?"

"This is all of us," Streicher answered, "but there were four guards forming a perimeter, and you got to them before you fired at us."

"We found only two guards on the way up the road, and you were firing before we got here."

"What did you do to them?" Streicher felt responsible.

"They are handcuffed to some trees, near the road. Don't worry, they will be fine."

"Thank you for that. Your men came out of the east along the wire, took out our two other guards there and then opened fire when we drove out of the minefield."

"No. We came only up the road."

"Then who were the other men?" Streicher looked puzzled.

"We will find out."

Raymond and Streicher looked at each other nonplussed.

The answer came fifteen minutes later when the leader returned.

"We have some serious questions to be answered."

"Who were the other men?"

"They were British SAS Troopers, we think. Three are dead and the only survivor is badly wounded. He can stay behind and explain himself as best he can to the authorities. It seems you have killed some of Mr. Barton's countrymen, Frau Klemerer."

"But where did they come from?"

"I suspect they had been holed up in the woods for the past few days observing. Those people could hide in your backyard shrubbery for a week and you wouldn't know they were there."

"But surely the Israelis and the British work together?"

The man smiled knowingly, "On some things, yes. On other things we differ. I believe their orders were to kill you all, with no interest in retrieving the gold. Now, we came here for a purpose, to find three steel boxes, which were buried with the gold. Where are they?" He was met by silence.

"In about fifteen minutes, I expect police units here, attracted by the gunfire. Also certain other interested parties besides the British may be nearby. Time is therefore very short and I don't care if they find you alive or dead; the other group can take responsibility for that. If the police arrive before you have answered me, you certainly have to die. I must have those boxes."

"Why are they so important?" Streicher spoke for the first time.

"They contain vital information and are more important than all the gold, which is soon going to be loaded onto a helicopter."

"There never were any steel boxes buried there."

"How would you know?"

"I was on the Wehrmacht detail which buried the gold in nineteen forty-five. All the other men were murdered by the S.S. and are buried about ten metres away, behind the barn that used to cover the site."

"What is your name?"

"Wilhelm Streicher."

"Name some of the soldiers on your detail in nineteen forty-five."

"Unterscharführer Gottlieb Demsch, Georg Stowaski, Reinhold Beckmann. Also, Standartenführer Mannheimer, S.S. Manfred Dorffman and Rudi Kranzler."

The Israeli was obviously impressed, shook his head slowly and sighed. "There is much to be answered." Turning to one of the men he asked a question, listened, and then gave some rapid instructions. There was a bustle of activity outside and faintly in the distance, the sound of a helicopter approaching.

"You will all be coming with us. In a couple of minutes, you will be taken to a helicopter. Anyone causing problems of *any* kind will be instantly shot and dumped."

"Where are you taking us?"

The man turned to Astrid. "It is none of your business and any further questions will be considered a *problem.*"

"I have to have the computer," Mandy spoke for the first time and the gun was turned on her. "I believe I can lead you to the other people, the ones in Paraguay." Realizing she may be bargaining for their lives, she plunged on. "We got the computer from them and I think I can hack my way into their communication system and trace back to them."

"She is talking about the group who kidnapped her in London and took her to Frankfurt. You remember you acknowledged their existence? They are tied into this closer than either of us realized. These people are not British, nor Israeli, and we have traced their line of communication back to South America. Perhaps you need to know more about them?" Raymond put in, trying to sway the man.

"Did you say Paraguay?" The man's glance went from Mandy to Raymond, regarding them carefully. South America had been an acknowledged haven for Nazis for years and the connection was too much to disregard. There was too much happening right now to ignore any avenue of chasing success. Deliberations would have to wait for calmer times. He had not been briefed on all these possibilities. "Fetch the computer for her."

"The steel boxes are in a gully just to the right of the truck you shot up," Raymond spoke up, earning himself a glare of hatred from Streicher for exposing his lie.

"Go check!" The Israeli sent four men to the site.

The sound of the helicopter had grown louder. There was no place for it to land in the yard and it sounded like it was headed to land in the space cleared in the minefield. Under careful guard, they were led out of the shed and back up the trail towards the gap in the frontier wire. Passing Streicher's shot-up truck, they found six men lugging boxes of gold from it, back up to the landing area.

Raymond figured he had counted about a dozen in the party, all of them fit-looking and determined men, armed to the teeth. He recognized the demeanour of special forces soldiers. Passing the gap in the barbed wire, he saw a Bell Two-Oh-Five helicopter, squatting on the area of minefield they had cleared, its rotor spinning. Road flares burned, marking out the landing area.

To Streicher, it was dejà-vu, seeing men carrying the cases again. They had lain undisturbed for forty-five years and now, no sooner had he unearthed them, and they were being taken away from him. A stack of boxes, awaiting pick-up, evidenced the efforts of the Israelis. Quickly the four of them were pushed onto the helicopter and four boxes of gold and the three retrieved steel boxes were slung on for good measure.

The leader appeared at the door. "Mr. Barton. Thank you for the steel boxes," he waved a hand at them, as they lay on the floor, "you have done a great service to humanity, besides saving your own lives."

Two guards clutching Uzi sub-machine guns climbed in, sitting opposite them in the forward-facing rear bench seat. Suddenly, the machine was rocked by a blast of wind and a rattle of dirt as a second Two-Oh-Five landed close by. Men stepped up and rapidly threw boxes and sacks into the cabin of the second helicopter.

There was a yell from the Israeli leader outside and he began to gesticulate with his arms, telling the pilot to take off. Almost instantly, there was a winking flash from the trees as a concentrated burst of gunfire came at them. Men were hitting the ground behind the banks of earth piled the previous day, cocking and aiming their weapons at an invisible enemy. There was a series of plinking noises on the airframe and one of the Plexiglas side windows starred. The pilot was winding up the revolutions on the engine, the high whine and the accelerating tumult of the whirling rotors blotting out the external noise.

The pilot raised the collective abruptly and the big helicopter lurched from the ground. The two guards forgot their prisoners for the moment and standing, emptied a magazine each at the muzzle flashes amongst the trees. Hot cartridge cases clattered and bounced around the cabin. They were intending to give suppressing fire for their comrades on the ground, but the rapid ascent of the helicopter interrupted their aim. By the time they had inserted new magazines, the pilot had spun their craft, nosed it down severely in transition to level flight and headed west along the frontier clearing.

They were barely abeam the other Two Oh Five when a longer flash reflected back from the trees and almost instantaneously, that helicopter blew up. Hit by a rocket-propelled grenade, it disintegrated. In the initial explosion, the airframe seemed silhouetted, a black shadow partially blocking the growing sun within it. And then it all peeled back in a white-hot spasm and a yellow and orange fireball engulfed the whole area. Blazing jet fuel hosed out in fiery streaks. Molten titanium, at its flash point, rocketed out like a star burst of fireworks. Pieces of metal, men and gold bounced and danced over the ground.

A rattle of debris barely precluded the hot blast and their helicopter rolled dangerously to the right. The pilot cranked in full left rudder and exceeded all engine limits as he desperately fought for control. The engine howled as it sucked in the superheated air and all the gauges exceeded the red limits. The scorching blast rolled over them, melting Plexiglas and blistering paint on the outside of the machine. The helicopter rolled back the other way as the blast rolled by, its main rotor barely clearing the ground as the pilot fought to stabilize it after his initial over-correction.

He was flying by touch, screaming with pain because the light reflected back at him from the trees had overloaded the night optics goggles he wore. If the explosion had happened one second earlier, he would have been instantly blinded. Snatching the device off his helmet, he squinted ahead, the red glow of the burning chopper behind them giving him just enough light for his tormented eyes to see by. The glare of the explosion had lit them up like a searchlight and a half a dozen guns opened up on them. What was left of the Plexiglas was blown out and one of their guards gave a little cry and slumped down, toppling slowly out of the helicopter onto the ground below. There was a desperate cacophony of screaming and cursing going on in the cabin. Gradually, they recognized themselves as the cause as they escaped the overwhelming action behind them and were able to focus. The terror was quickly replaced by the dubious realization that while they were still alive, they were now hurtling through the darkness, barely under control.

Mandy's screams became distinguishable now. She screamed, not in terror, but in pain. A bullet or a red-hot piece of debris had grazed her upper left arm, wounding her. Astrid was rigid, totally out of air to enable her to scream any further. Raymond clutched a doorframe, convinced he had bent it with his panicked grip. Streicher was cursing, and, more driven than the rest of them, he turned suddenly and struck out at the remaining guard, catching him in the side of the head with a fist. The man lurched and yelled, off balance, but not subdued.

The helicopter skewed sideways and the pilot was screaming something at them. The Israeli was rebounding from the blow, rising from the seat he had fallen into and raising the Uzi. Raymond, realizing Streicher's intent, tried to get to his feet and block the man but the helicopter suddenly soared, gravity force pinning him into his seat. There was a horrible vibration growing around them and the helicopter was bucking like a wild animal. The lower frequency pitch and yawing flight movements were underscored by a rapid, shuddering vibration and the threnody of the engine. The pilot was still shrieking at them but his words were inaudible against the overwhelming clamour of the rotor blades.

Something coughed and banged and Raymond felt like he was inside some giant terminally sick animal getting ready to regurgitate him. The Israeli was still trying to raise himself in the forward facing rear seat and Raymond kicked out his leg, catching the man in the only knee he had under him, snapping him back into the seat. Inadvertently, the impact made him pull the trigger and half a dozen rounds from the machine gun zinged through the upper cabin, some ricocheting back around their cringing bodies.

For some reason, Astrid was climbing forward, hanging over the seat and leaning into the cockpit, screaming flight directions at the pilot. "Right!...Go right!... No!...left, too far!" She had recognized his blindness.

The down wash from the main rotor started directing choking smoke into the open door, adding to their misery. The engine was banging like an old tractor, compressor stalls following one upon the other and the pilot was still yelling. His voice trailed off into a long wail, and Raymond felt the deck tilt again beneath them as the pilot tried to trade forward speed into a hover. Then they hit. Because of the remaining forward speed and flat angle, the helicopter bounced and then slid forward. Propelled forward by the impact, their remaining guard almost crushed Astrid, crashing against the divider between the main cabin and the cockpit, and knocking himself out. The chopper hit again, the series of impacts seeming to go on forever as adrenaline-soaked brains took time passage down to a snail's pace.

The landing skids took out a trip wire in the minefield and four stake-mounted fragmentation mines exploded, spraying the area with a deadly cloud of metal. The front of the chopper took the brunt and was reduced to shreds. Thrown sprawling to the floor, the remaining passengers evaded almost all the deadly hail, although two more minor wounds were inflicted.

With a final spasm, the helicopter tilted and then slowly rolled onto its right side before stopping, rotors fracturing and spinning off into the darkness like deadly scimitars. Another group of mines went off, shrapnel bouncing off the airframe. For seconds, the brutal transition from flight to wreck created a pause. There was no sign of life from the dark interior. Hot metal began to ping as it cooled and smoke billowed from the turbine exhaust stack. The throat-choking smoke clouded the area, underpinned by the acrid stench of leaking jet fuel.

Mandy came swimming up first, spinning like a sycamore seed in reverse, conquering layer after layer of semi-consciousness until she could not ignore the tangle of limbs in which she found herself.

"Raymond! Raymond!" she cried. Recognizing the leg she grasped, she worked her way up to his face, cradling it desperately, "Raymond! Wake up!"

He came to with a dull moan, reluctant to reassert his right to life. Astrid was winded and could not find her breath. She was down in the area between her seat and the cockpit, the unconscious guard sprawled over her. Streicher became a self-starter, scrambling shakily to his knees before anyone tried to arouse him. He quickly grabbed the Uzi when his hand brushed it.

While the guard demonstrated life with laboured breathing, the front of the chopper, dark as it was, only dripped the lifeblood of the mangled pilot. Battered, bruised and wounded, only five of the original seven people had survived the helicopter's flight.

The drunken reaction to the terrifying onslaught came slowly. Like automatons, they pulled themselves from the wreckage, temporarily unconscious of the fact that they had come to rest thirty metres from the Western edge of the frontier. They were still in the minefield.

"Do not stray from the aircraft!" The warning came from Streicher, "We are still in the minefield!"

The reaction was one of stunned compliance, the full reality of their peril not immediately apparent in the general relief from the terrible danger they had just escaped. Streicher climbed out of the door, onto the side of the machine, glancing to the sky to find the Big Dipper and Polaris to affirm which way was north. Holding onto a main rotor stub, he planted a foot on the rotor assembly and began to scrutinize the ground between himself and the fence, invisible against the black wall of forest. Slowly he managed to discern objects, just as Raymond climbed up beside him.

"How the hell are we going to get out of here?" Raymond felt a trickle of blood run down his cheek from a scalp wound.

"Very quickly. We only have minutes before someone arrives," Streicher slid back down to the inside of the helicopter. Their guard was moaning, only semiconscious. "Grab the boxes, quickly!"

"At a time like this you only worry about the gold?" Raymond's protest was ignored as Streicher slid back into the cabin of the helicopter.

Mandy and Astrid were trying to sort themselves out and trying to comfort the guard who was totally dazed and incomprehensive. Setting the example, Streicher began to pitch the boxes out of the door in the direction they needed to head in. The grossly heavy boxes thumped solidly into the earth. At first, Raymond wondered why Streicher ducked every time he threw a box, and then he realized the man was trying to avoid the consequences of hitting a mine or a trip wire. He grabbed a steel box himself, and finding it amazingly light, tossed it out. It landed on one corner and rolled over and over, causing him to wince at an imminent explosion.

"This way," Streicher had the guard by the arm and was pulling him towards the outside.

"Streicher, you can't!..."

"Shut up!" Pushing and shoving the man, Streicher guided him out of the broken wreckage and sent him off. "You have to go that way. Hurry! The wreck will burst into flames any time."

"Streicher!"

The Israeli blundered and staggered, losing his balance and pitching flat on his face.

"Go on! Hurry! Your passengers need help!"

The man lurched back to an upright position, swayed precariously and then took a step forward. After a few steps, he pitched forward again, tripping over a tuft of grass. Everyone in the helicopter flinched and ducked down. Even Astrid, who had been first to define Streicher's horrible intent and made the first protest, was morbidly fascinated by the pantomime before them.

The man got to his feet again, only fifteen metres from the fence now and stepped forward with a little more sense of purpose. He was recovering from the blow to the head but had not yet realized where he was. At five metres from the fence which he could now see, everything came into focus for him. He stopped and turned around, mute appeal in his stance.

"Go on!" Streicher was implacable.

"Nein! Minen!"

"Go or I shoot!" Streicher loudly cycled the cocking mechanism on the Uzi. The man turned, hesitated and then turned again towards them. Both the women screamed as the machine gun opened up, firing five rounds near the man's feet. "Go or I shoot!"

With the hunched shoulders of the damned, the man again faced the fence. He paused, gathering his nerve and then took a first tentative step. The second was faster and by the time he took the third, he was in a full, panicked run at the fence. He leaped and threw himself onto the coils of barbed wire lining the ground and in the same instant, three sharp flashes erupted in the dark, accompanied by loud reports. The air hissed with terrible death and as the watchers ducked and clung to cover, the man, who had felt the trip-wire, screamed a shrill cry which went on and on even after the splatter of steel balls had turned the helicopter's aluminum body into a colander.

Before they could grasp the fact, Streicher was out of the machine and running over the intervening ground. A single shot rang out and the dreadful, agonized screams stopped. "Come!" Streicher returned to the crippled helicopter, seizing Astrid by the arm.

"Arschloch!...Pimmelkopf!...Speckiger!" Astrid was beating on him with her fists, letting fly a string of German invective. Yet, the fists beat with less force and more with the gathering acceptance of his ends.

He slapped her across the face, speaking in English, conscious of the need to also communicate with Mandy who was shaking with shocked rage. "Do you want to die? Do you realize he was to shoot you if need be? You can die, momentarily out in the minefield. Now! Or, they will be here in minutes, anxious to shoot without justification! You must live! You must come with me! Now!"

With brute force, Streicher dragged Astrid out of the helicopter and pushed her toward the safety of the fence. He paused only to reach down and hoist a box of gold to his shoulder. "Come! Grab a box!" Raymond followed without demur.

In minutes, they had made enough return trips to the helicopter to get all the boxes onboard safely into the forest where they were dumped into a clump of bushes, safe from sight.

0300 hrs. Friday, 13th July 1990. Eidelweissgasthaus, Near Plauen.

The meeting of the Three Musketeers took place on the rug of an isolated country hotel suite. Streicher had somehow found transportation and got them there. He now snored in one of the adjacent rooms.

"But Raymond, you were an operative in the British Army Intelligence Corps," anxious to have their situation explained, Astrid pressed him for an answer.

"Yes, but counting tanks, troop movements and lorries did not equip me in any way for this. I was not James Bond, working for "M", nor was I privy to the Secret Intelligence Service's operations. All I understand right now is that it is us against a whole bunch of people in a race for some gold which I don't want. Now we have the added puzzle of the three steel boxes that the Israelis want even more badly than the gold. You tell me the answer!"

"Perhaps we should open them and find out what it is all about!" Mandy cut to the chase. They turned and regarded the objects of the discussion. The boxes sat, smeared with dirt, cloaked in mystery, taunting them as to their purpose.

"The Israeli chap said *a great service to humanity*."

"Well, let's see!" Mandy was now insistent.

They chose a box for no better reason than it had, in faded numbers, '29' stencilled on it. The steel box had been liberally smeared with a tar-like substance to waterproof it, overlaid by strips of fabric bandages. Using a knife, Raymond patiently worked away at the ridge that marked the lid edge. The hasp was secured with a small padlock that he eventually levered off with the aid of an implement from the kitchen drawer.

Raising the lid, he was assailed by the strong odour of oilskin. Inside, half-filling the cavity was a number of bundles carefully wrapped and sealed in the sticky textured waterproofing material. Astrid stooped to help him and they counted twelve separate bundles onto the floor.

There were three layers of oilskin on the first bundle they elected to open. Within, a sheaf of paper headed by the heavy Gothic script favoured by the Nazis was further protected from damp by a sprinkling of silica powder. Time and the silica powder had dried the moisture out of the paper and it felt stiff and crinkled to their touch. Carefully flattening the rolled bundle, they found themselves confronted by a list of names and places.

"This must be part of the secret list of evacuated Nazis. It must be worth a fortune in the right hands! No wonder the Israelis wanted it," Raymond flipped the pages to check the content remained the same throughout, and then began to unwrap another bundle. Astrid was already ahead of him, bringing to the light of day another set of documents that had not been seen for forty-five years.

After a half-hour, they had unwrapped and sorted the papers into two classifications. The first was of little immediate value to them, comprising names and forwarding locations. The other was smaller, containing directives and planning policies. Their origin was the head office of the RSHA, domain of the evil Heinrich Himmler. Strangely, his signature was not present, most of the documents being signed by Ernst Kaltenbrunner and other senior S.S. officers.

Mandy had managed to hang onto the computer, and while she continued to explore its contents, Raymond and Astrid began to examine the second group of documents in more detail. It was Astrid who came across the first clue to their content. They had already found continuous reference to something called 'Höher Zwech', or 'Higher Purpose'. This appeared to be some kind of umbrella organization for the furthering of Nazis ambitions. Neither of them had heard of such a thing and it appeared to even be a secret from Hitler and his immediate cronies.

Now, Astrid suddenly dropped the document she was examining to the floor and abruptly stood up. "Oh no! No! No!" She walked to the window, stumbled and caught herself against the frame, gazing outside, shoulders hunched.

"What is it, Astrid?" Her head shook; refusing comment and Raymond could tell by the shaking of her torso that she was crying. He seized the two-page letter and scanned it quickly. The letterhead, dated September second, nineteen forty-three, showed it had originated at one of the death camps, Sachsenhausen, and was addressed to Oberführer Heinz Huehnlein of Amt IV 'A' (Nine) at the *Reichssicherheithauptamt* in Berlin. It was clearly marked as "Top Secret". Raymond looked up, squinting as he tried to retrieve in his memory the organizational chart of the RSHA. *Department IV,* out of the seven, he clearly remembered, was the *Geheimestaatspolizei*, the dreaded Gestapo. *Section 'A'* was '*enemies*' of the Reich but the *subsection 'Nine'* was a mystery to him. Oberführer Huehnlein he had never heard of. Why a full Brigadier would be in such a minor section was also a puzzle.

As he read, the blood drained from Raymond's face and he felt the chilled and bony fingers of the Devil encircle his spine. The letter contained a barely concealed thread of pride and achievement behind the terse report.

"I am happy to report success at the third stage of Project 'Ober alles'. *Ten subjects, under tight security, were successfully exposed to an airborne dosage of Agent Twenty-nine in a proportion of one microgram to the cubic metre. At the first sign of infection, they were moved into a dormitory with ten other subjects.*

Incubation periods and initial symptoms were classical in nature and an infection rate of ninety percent was achieved. Lack of total infection was thwarted by one subject who displayed all the symptoms but did not succumb for two days after the others died. Records showed this subject to have lived under unsanitary conditions that may have provided some natural, though imperfect immunity.

From initial infection to infectious exhalations by the victims takes from three to six hours. From infection to initial symptoms takes twelve hours. This guarantees that victims are infectious at least six hours before they show symptoms and might be effectively quarantined. Death ensues twenty-four hours after infection, following pneumonia-type symptoms and a high fever.

This is an almost perfect scenario, as you will see by the attached graph, showing that fifty-four hours after first ingestion, the virus is depleted to the point of no further propagation. We can infer from this that forty-eight hours after the virus is sprayed into the air, the risk to our invading forces would be minimal to negligible. This in turn allows a strategic advantage because the dispensing of the gas need only be planned two days in advance. This gives tremendous flexibility compared to conventional attack preparations which can take weeks of build up, become obvious to the enemy, and usually cannot be cancelled at such short notice.

The second group of ten subjects, specially trained to perform gross autopsies, was assigned to terminal care of the infected Jews. Postmortem, they removed necessary organs and tissue from the cadavers for our laboratories. After their introduction to the sealed dormitory, they in turn incurred a thirty per cent infection rate that proved fatal. A further thirty per cent survived secondary symptoms accompanied by temporary incapacitation. Of these, half were permanently afflicted with partial paralysis and transient seizures brought on by the high fevers accompanying the infection. The remainder showed virtually no effect, surviving exposure as predicted.

To conclude the experiment, ten more subjects were introduced twenty days after initial exposure. All ten exhibited no symptoms whatsoever, indicating the virus had, as predicted, become progressively non-viable over a period of approximately eighteen days. Laboratory tests on specimens from living and dead reinforced these findings.

We can deduce from this that third party infection rates are extremely low and fourth contacts over this time period will be negligible. It thus becomes clear that Agent Twenty-nine is the preferred vehicle for use against military formations where a ninety per cent fatality rate will be incurred before civilian populations are exposed. The subsequent falling infection rate as the Agent becomes progressively less viable ensures an intact population, which can easily be overrun by invasion forces without collateral infection risk.

As an example of the effectiveness of this weapon, we calculate that if this virus was efficiently sprayed along the south coast of England, our forces could land twenty-four hours later with little resistance from Army units. It would be necessary, for the next two days, to shoot any military and civilian survivors our forces came in contact with, thus avoiding their exhalations. It would, of course, be prudent to exterminate any person met for the first five days to avoid any possible contamination. Where this procedure is followed, we could guarantee a ninety nine percent success rate.

Once our results were positively established, the whole complex, along with all thirty subjects, was incinerated in place to secure against any outside contamination and to preserve security. The residue was buried.

Once again, I am happy to report these findings to you. As ordered, we shall now work at refining the strain and working towards improved methods of delivery. We are close to perfecting a crystallization process of the virus, which can then be stored indefinitely, to be reconstituted by the addition of water.

Heil Hitler!"

The letter was signed by *Obersturmbanführer-Doktor Otto Dietenweiler. Kommandant, S.S. Einsatzkommando Valkyrie Noyden.*

Stunned by the horror, Raymond could only watch through glazed eyes while Astrid shook and shuddered. He finally climbed to his feet and held her from behind, swaying her in a comforting embrace.

"Hey, you two, no fraternizing while the fiancée is in the room!" Mandy, buried in her work had not noticed the drama. Now, looking at them, she sensed the current of emotion in the air. "What is it? What have you found?"

"Bastards! Fucking rotten, evil devils in German bodies!" Astrid turned in Raymond's arms, eyes red and running. "How *could* human beings do such a thing?"

"Do what?" Mandy had rushed over, laying a hand on Raymond's shoulder, alarm on her face as she stared at Astrid.

Raymond was facing away from her but his voice, very small, seemed to be coming from a long distance off. "The bloody S.S. deliberately infected some prisoners at Sachsenhausen with some deadly disease, then put them in a room to see how many others would catch it. After they had watched them all suffer horribly and die, they sent in more to do autopsies and then watched as they too contracted the disease. Evidently, the disease got progressively less infectious, as they proved, by putting more people in. Once they established they had found the perfect bacteriological weapon, they killed and burned them all, every last one of the poor devils." Raymond's voice strangled with emotion as he thought of that charnel house with dismembered corpses, helpless and twitching surviving victims, watched over by fellow prisoners driven near to insanity by the horror of their surroundings. And all the while, the observers, safe behind their reinforced glass window, taking notes, recording the progress of their hideous experiments with the skills and terminology which had been established to save lives not to deliberately sacrifice them.

"Why do you say *bacteriological weapon*?"

"The letter makes it clear that if the disease were to be released primarily over military formations, almost all the soldiers would die while the outside civilian populations would be progressively less at risk on exposure."

"So?"

"With an enemy's armies infected, then an invasion force will surely conquer, meeting only feeble opposition from non-military defenders. The main populace would then be prostrate before them; have no choice but slavery."

"But, is this thing even possible, Raymond?"

"Well, during my time with Military Intelligence, we tried to watch for such things in chemical and bacteriological warfare. The mustard and chlorine gases in the First World War killed thousands, so we were aware of the potential in the hands of unscrupulous enemies. If they achieved what these letters claim, these researchers were maybe thirty years ahead of their time. There is no other record

I know of that even hints at such research being done, so it was carried out in the utmost secrecy. To have developed almost the perfect weapon, like this, they must have been on a research path we never knew about."

"These men were Germans, Raymond!" Astrid's voice choked between sobs. "They were born in my land, raised and grew up eating the same food and drinking the same water. How could they become such monsters?"

Mandy threw her arms around them both, "Thank God it was never used."

The upbeat atmosphere which had prevailed since they had reached the Gasthaus was now deflated. There was food in the kitchen, and Mandy prepared some. They opened a couple of bottles of Neirsteiner Piesporter to wash it down. Conversation was desultory, the food pushed around the plates with little enthusiasm.

Finally, Raymond left the table and tried to bury himself in the remaining documents. In so doing, he made the second horrible discovery, one that plunged them into fear and despair. It was a letter, with the familiar dramatic letterhead of the RSHA, this time from Oberführer Huehnlein, to the Obersturmbanführer at Sachsenhausen, dated February thirty-first, nineteen forty-four.

Dear Dietenweiler,

I must add my congratulations to those of our superiors for the magnificent achievement you and your staff have brought to the Fatherland.

Your creation will be added to the battery of Vergeltungswaffe, the miracle weapons which our beloved Führer has fostered and will use to bring about the ultimate victory of Nationalist Socialism.

Due to the political objections of the Oberkommando der Wehrmacht, Agent Twenty-nine will not be used in the immediate future. In order to circumvent these traitorous Generals, whom we trust the Führer will eventually bring to heel, Agent Twenty-nine will be administered exclusively by the Schutzstaffel. This decision is also influenced by the continued failure to find an adequate delivery system for the Agent.

You will, on your sacred S.S. oath, communicate only with me on any matters pertaining to 'Ober alles'. *Total secrecy must be maintained by you and your staff. You are authorized to take whatever steps necessary to preserve this secret, including liquidation of dubious staff members.*

Heil Hitler!

Raymond was aghast to see that such a terrible weapon had been placed in the hands of such an immoral, sick organization as the S.S. Still, as Mandy had said, the weapon had not been used. Breathing deep to expel the thought, he picked up the next document and was immediately plunged into an abyss of anxiety. This letter was written to Ernst Kaltenbrunner from an unsigned source but the style was familiar.

2nd April 1945

Thank you for the instructions concerning Operation 'Ober alles'. I agree that one day its time may come and it would be unwise to activate it now, as the outcome would be uncertain. I am pleased to hear that the preservation of Agent Twenty-nine and its mode of delivery have now been completed successfully.

Better that we keep this secret until its full potential can be reached to further our aims. I am dispatching vital information to our plans in three steel boxes tomorrow in the care of a trusted subordinate. They will be leaving Germany under the strictest secrecy, in company with a gold shipment earmarked for our use. The steel flasks will be in one of them.

Rest assured that whatever happens, our organization will remain faithful and true, ready to seize the eventual opportunity to bring victory.

Long live Nationalist Socialism!

"Shit!" Even though the box was empty, Raymond had to go and peer into it. The other two boxes sat close by. The content of this one was horrendous, yet mere words, describing an evil beyond imagination. One of the other two boxes, or both, contained the embodiment of the threat. He shuddered, not wanting to be in the same room as the horror it contained.

"More bad news?" Astrid was at his elbow while Mandy peered across the room.

"Yes. Agent Neunundzwanzig."

"Agent Twenty-nine. What about it?"

"According to this letter, it was to be shipped in one of the other two boxes like this one."

"You mean...?"

"Yes, you are in the presence of Agent Twenty-nine, with its potential to kill millions."

"So, where are we now?" Ever practical, Astrid wanted to move on. Raymond could not believe she was taking it so lightly.

"Well, we have numerous people chasing us for the gold. Other more knowledgeable and sinister people are chasing us for the information concerned with this "Höher Zwech" crowd, presumably to provide a cover-up to Allied-S.S. complicity, that is, if we believe the Israeli."

"But nobody is chasing us for Agent Twenty-nine?"

"Not yet. I doubt anyone but the mysterious "Höher Zwech" knows about it. Can you imagine the fury of the chase if it was common knowledge? Not only do we have the possible gold location, but also the secret inside information of how many Nazis got out of Germany and all the international ramifications attached to that. Now, we have in our possession some kind of biological weapon which many nations would kill us to possess."

"Why would they ship the goddamned stuff out of Germany if they didn't want to use it?" Mandy had joined them.

"Because the friggin' Nazis still believe they can launch World War Three and win with it. It would probably be worth billions sold as a military secret," Raymond was awed at the prospect.

"Can we use this as a bargaining chip with anyone?" Astrid was being her own shrewd self.

"Perhaps. But only as a last resort. Do you see the full implications of this?"

"Yes, a deadly virus in the hands of hidden madmen who will use it without compunction. They are unknown, biding their time, and an attack could come at anytime, out of nowhere. Except, for now, it is in our hands."

"No warnings or bargaining first, Astrid?"

"Probably, but I feel they might use it as a petulant child, trying to get revenge if they feel their security is breached."

"If it was shipped," Mandy gave them pause, "It may not even be in one of these boxes."

"Oh, I don't think we can afford to assume it *never* left Berlin. The people who entered the frontier zone in nineteen forty-seven and had a gunfight with the border guards may have had three, not just two pressing reasons to be there," Raymond said.

Mandy was puzzled, "Why *did* the Nazis not use this weapon during the war?"

"Combination of things. The letter tells us a lot. The delivery system was not perfected at first. The German High Command did not really want to use it. They all had bad experiences with mustard gas in the first war when the wind changed, including Hitler himself. They would want to be one hundred per cent sure of the means of seeding it. There was also some honour, some commitment to the Geneva Convention. Biological warfare was prohibited.

By the time they might have used it, the Allies were off the Normandy beaches and in too close proximity to make it a viable weapon. Even the German army would have become infected; so, even if they could have used it, it may well have backfired on them. Still, if they had been able to use it in nineteen forty, *Operation Sea Lion*, the invasion of Britain, would have been a walkover for them. The war would have been lost."

"Hitler clung to his notion that *super weapons* would win the war, right up to the end. Did he know about this?" Astrid asked.

"Probably, in a sketchy sense. His grasp of technical detail was poor and he showed no interest in the logistics of moving armies and virtually crippled the German Navy due to his ignorance. His so-called *genius* in the early years was a mixture of mule-headed determination in combination with fortuitous opportunity."

"Yet the S.S. would have used it," Astrid shuddered.

"Yeah. And still might!" Mandy put in.

"But there is no strategic opportunity today. They have no standing armies to invade and occupy any country. The international situation is basically stable and the Americans are surely too strong to fail in keeping world order."

Mandy looked determined. "They'll never use it if we stop them!"

"And how do we do that?" Raymond responded.

"Go to the British, or, the Americans?"

"They want to kill us for what we *already* know, why give them more reason?"

Astrid turned to Mandy. "So you are suggesting that we, the Three Musketeers take this cache of deadly Agent Twenty-nine and ensure it is never used?"

"Got a better idea?"

They headed off to a restless night's sleep.

At two in the morning, Streicher's cell phone rang. "Herr Streicher. I will not insult you by asking where you are, but I need your help."

"Who is this?"

"Well, you do not know me and do not need to. It was I who helped send Mannheimer on his mission, with your assistance, as you remember. Do you remember the night you met him in Berlin?" The voice was a little thin and reedy but had an authoritative tone to it.

Streicher's spine chilled as the authenticity of the caller sank in. "What do you want?"

"Specifically, I want three steel boxes that were buried with the others. One is lighter than the others and has a number on it. 'Neunundzwanzig'. Have you seen such a box, Herr Streicher?"

Immediately, Streicher sensed a business opportunity. He paused, thinking.

"Do not imagine that you can deceive me. You either have the boxes, in which case we can come to an arrangement, or, you do not and will lie to me, for personal gain. I do not recommend the latter, you understand. Now, do you have these boxes?"

"Yes, I believe I do."

There was a momentary pause. "I imagine that the activity in the Vogtland has raised a nest of hornets and you were unable to extract the rest of your due reward?" Streicher's extended silence confirmed the statement. "So! I am prepared to buy those boxes from you for ten million U.S. dollars, in gold."

"How can I trust you?"

"You cannot. You only have my word for the gold and that I will see no further interest in you once I have the boxes. Whatever gold you did retrieve you can now augment by a further ten million dollars."

"How?"

"At three this morning, in one hour, a man will be sitting at the crossroads three kilometres west of Zech. He will have the gold for you. You must allow him to inspect the contents of the boxes, which, incidentally, you would be foolish to look at. There is nothing of value to you in there, only trouble. Be alone, and I expect you will do no more than to take the necessary precautions to protect yourself. Anything more, such as getting greedy will have severe results. Do this for me and I promise you will not be bothered again in any way."

If it was worth ten, it was worth double. "Twenty million."

"Fifteen and any more will surely not allow me to forget you."

"Done!"

"Auf veidersehen, Herr Streicher."

0430 hrs. Friday, 13th July 1990.
Eidelweissgasthaus, near Plauen, Vogtland.

Raymond awoke. It had been a restless night, full of the scary images of Nazi concentration camps. Beside him, he knew, Mandy had fared no better but she lay on her back now, snoring in the soft comforting way he knew and loved. He needed a cup of tea.

Rolling off the bed, he pulled his pants on and scratching his chest, went into the kitchen area of the suite they had rented. Peering out the window into the darkness, he could see nothing. It was quiet as the grave out there. Turning to the sink, he filled a kettle and plugged it in. Walking to the lavatory, he pushed the door closed and relieved himself. He thought he heard a faint sound but it was non-specific.

Opening the door, he stepped out and was immediately tackled by two bodies. Before he could react, he was wrestled to the floor and felt the jab of something sharp in his arm. A hand covered his mouth as he tried to yell, and then the world spun into a black vortex from which he could not escape. Feeling his body go slack, the intruders turned their attention to the two bedrooms. The women there were helpless and in seconds, likewise subdued.

Opening the door, one of the men let in three others. While one man took the vital readings of the three bodies, the others fanned out, taking every scrap of clothing and belongings of the occupants. Three stretchers appeared and strapped onto them, the helpless Musketeers were taken away to a van outside. In less than two minutes, the suite was stripped of all evidence of their presence, the kettle unplugged and the door closed. The van pulled away from the gasthaus and headed west.

Thirty minutes later, the inert forms and their belongings were loaded onto a Gulfstream Three jet at an airport near Plauen. Two men got on with them and the jet quickly took off. Onboard, one of the men set up drip-feeds and catheters for each person and carefully inserted needles into veins. Then he opened a line containing a mild sedative. Strapped in and physically helpless, Raymond, Mandy and Astrid were kept in a semiconscious state while the jet soared to altitude. At forty thousand feet, it set course for Dakar, in West Africa, where it landed for a brief fuel stop.

Seven hours after leaving Germany, the plane again departed, continuing on almost the same course, winging its way over the South Atlantic as the flight crew warily set up flight for maximum range. It was to be almost four thousand nautical miles and another nine hours to their destination, with little fuel to spare for their next short leg. Landfall over Brazil took it high above the southern jungles as the afternoon wore on.

Finally, the navigation system prompted descent and the nose of the aircraft dipped as the power was reduced. Guided by the approach instructions on his clipboard, the pilot set up for what he understood to be a short landing.

1800 hrs. Friday, 13th July 1990.
Rio Pilcomayo, Gran Chaco, Paraguay.

Led downstairs blindfolded, Raymond, Mandy and Astrid had no idea where they were. The cells used for the *desaparecidos* were coming in handy. Wesler, aided by the bodyguards, saw they were each deposited in a cell, separate from the others. Exhausted by their ordeal, and still partially drugged, they each slept the fitful slumbers of the threatened.

0800 hrs. Saturday, 14th July 1990.
Rio Pilcomayo, Gran Chaco, Paraguay.

Although they could not know it, they were interrogated separately. Astrid heard the banging of the doors as first Raymond and then Mandy were led away and brought back some time later. Raymond called something encouraging out as he came back but his words were muffled by the walls and thick doors. A cry of pain followed, evidence of the guards' displeasure with him.

Then they came for Astrid. The low wattage light bulbs in the cellar gave no clue as to the time of day and she followed the shambling guard before her, being prodded by the other whenever she appeared to falter. They climbed the stairs, passing a landing where another set of stairs descended at a right angle to join it. She remembered turning on the way down, so now they were taking a different route upward. A heavy door at the top of the stairs was pushed open and, prodded from behind, Astrid emerged into a sunlit room.

It was a study, with bookshelves and expensive wooden panelling. Before her, a massive dark oak desk lay in a splash of sunlight. A man was bent over, seated behind it, studying some papers. His face was hidden, his thin white hair revealed a pink pate and he appeared scrawny. The faint mustiness of old age and decay permeated the room.

"You are Astrid Klemerer?" the German voice was low, without inflection, yet carried a menace beyond words. Until then, he had ignored her for several long seconds but now there was a focus. It took a moment for Astrid to even believe he had spoken.

"Yes."

The head rose with the slow confidence of the master predator and two rheumy blue eyes appeared. The face was skeletal, the skin taut over the bones between wrinkles and wattles. A slash down the right side of the face glowed a frigid white. There was a brief instant of neutrality and then it appeared like an electric charge ran through the man. The eyes became impossible points of blue sapphire and the face went rigid with shock. His mouth fell open and a claw-like hand grasped the desk edge for stability. Astrid felt the men either side of her stiffen into attack stances, fearing some threat.

The old man had lost what little colour he had. "You!" he pointed a bony finger at her. "You are Astrid Klemerer? What was your kinder name?"

"Von Heisler".

"Ja!" The man drew the word out long, nodding his head in agreement, "and your mother. What was her name?"

"Heidie Matilde von Heisler."

The man nodded again, reaching for a snifter of brandy beside him. He sipped at it, his piercing eyes running up and down her. Astrid felt like she was being eyed by a serpent, bent on coiling itself around her and then consuming her whole. The eyes returned to her face, satisfied with their bold and penetrating scrutiny of her body.

"I knew your mother," his words carried a propriety tone, possessive and secure in old lust.

Astrid wanted to answer, refute the horror and repugnance she felt, but something held her back. She was helpless here. A gesture of defiance would be only that, a futile response engendering reprisal perhaps against her friends as well as herself.

The man's eyes had not left hers, "Your father was a hero of the Fatherland, a Major in the Panzers. He fought in most of the campaigns."

"Until he was wounded in the Ardennes."

"Yes, he was lung-shot".

"You are well informed," Astrid was astonished at the man's information.

"I believe he died about eighteen years after the war, being frail all that time. And then, your mother married Hans Lankow." Unaccountably, the man's face now twisted in a sneer of contempt.

As if trying to defend her stepfather against this creature, Astrid continued. "Hans became a family friend, tending Varti during his frequent illnesses due to his wounds. When Varti died, he and my mother were already close and it was natural they should marry. I did not take his name though."

Again the man's face twisted in a gesture Astrid could not define.

"And your name?"

"In due course, Fraulein. You shall know me, I promise you." The double entendre of the words dripped a menace, not from any passion, but from the purely reptilian utterance. The man waved dismissively and returned to his reading.

"It is *Frau* Klemerer!" Something in the man's demeanour seemed to disregard Astrid's married status, but he ignored her outburst.

One of the guards grasped Astrid's arm and indicated it was time to leave. She hesitated a moment, determined to show resistance but the old man was paying no heed. It was as if she had already disappeared. Shuddering, she turned and headed for the opened door. As it closed behind her, she heard the hacking, tortured cough of the chronically ill. It sounded like the helpless muted barking of a dying dog being dragged tail first over cobblestones.

Raymond called out to her as she passed, but his voice was too muffled and soon she was incarcerated in her own cell. She could make neither head nor tail of the meeting she had just had. She might have expected to be roughly questioned, but nothing had come of that. The man had seemed shocked to see her and she could only suppose that it was the resemblance to her mother. Varti had often told her how much alike they were.

Back in the study, El Jefe replenished his constant brandy snifter. The woman he had just seen was gorgeous, the epitome of German Volksdamen. Just as her Mother had been, she would have been idolized by members of the NDSP. He felt a stirring in his groin, an advance on the powerful surge he had felt when he first saw her. With a rare smile, he reached for his internal telephone to give orders. *Frau Klemerer,* indeed! Well, having her for the night would allow him three distinct pleasures, including revenge.

It was later in the day before anyone opened Astrid's cell door. She was taken out and guided to a cell at the end of the corridor. Two Indian women were waiting for her. The room itself looked like a dressing room for a movie studio. Racks of clothes lined one side of the room and equipment normally found in a hairdressing salon occupied one corner.

Consulting a photograph, one of the women plucked some clothes hanging from a rack and handed them to Astrid, indicating she was to put them on. The stuff looked old, styled about fifty years before. Astrid shook her head. The woman waved the clothes angrily. Before she could know it, Astrid felt the muzzle of a pistol in her neck. The guard at the door had sneaked up on her. The meaning was clear. Shrugging, she stripped to her bra and panties and began to don the garments. She did not miss the intense interest shown by the man behind her.

The other woman bustled forward importantly and pinned and marked the clothes. Once she was done, Astrid was made to undress again. The first woman indicated she was to sit in the salon chair. Standing behind her, the woman again consulted the photograph and contemplated Astrid in the mirror, nodding her head. Seizing a pair of scissors, she began to trim the severed green mess Astrid had created in Hamburg. Astrid again made to resist but the guard stepped menacingly into view in the mirror, brandishing his pistol.

For the next ten minutes, the woman expertly cut and trimmed the hair while the whirring of her partner's sewing machine tailored the clothes. Eventually, the woman spun Astrid around and pushed her head back into the shampooing basin. When she saw her face again, Astrid saw a more familiar, if wet, colouring. She was back to her spun-gold blonde hair. The woman nudged her and indicated a shower cabinet, handing her a robe. Again, Astrid balked but the guard was ready. With a quick move, he severed her brassiere strap with a knife and then pointed the blade at her with a knowing leer.

"It is necessary that you shower, Fraulein."

She gave him a disdainful stare and then with the confidence of perfect beauty, peeled off her panties. Her reward was his quickened breath. Languidly, she walked to the glass door of the shower and went inside. The woman had already turned it on and she soaped herself down, wondering what the next big surprise was going to be. Coming out, she played more demurely, towelling herself with her back to the man, donning the robe before turning around again. All the same, she was conscious of his full attention. She carefully noted his weakness.

Seated in the chair again, she watched in the mirror as her hair was carefully coifed into a curly helmet of gold reminiscent of the nineteen thirties. Somehow the woman was able to make something out of the mess she and Mandy had created. Silk underwear of the same era was brought, including a garter belt and stockings. Lastly, the tailoring was done and the skirt, blouse and costume coat she had tried on were fitted perfectly to her body. Looking in the mirror, Astrid finally recognized herself. She was her Mother!

Before she was barely aware of her appearance and the implications, she was taken by the guard back up the stairs. This time they turned left up the adjoining stairs and exited the basement into a spacious hallway with a cool tiled floor. The lights were on and beyond a picture window she spied the last flushes of a Chaco sunset, long strands of dark scarlet suffusing high cirrus cloud.

They entered another room, the walls darkly panelled over the lower half and white-stucco above. Dark columns and beams supported a ceiling shadowed by the diffused light of a huge chandelier. Down the middle of the dining room stood a four metre-long wooden table, lined by elegantly carved chairs. Steadily burning candles dribbled wax down silver candelabras set at intervals down its length. The combined light barely illuminated expensive-looking paintings on the walls.

The table was set with two places only, one at the head and one to its immediate left. Expensive Dresden china and Czech cut glass goblets sat amidst heavy period cutlery and silver serving trays, gleaming opulent gourmet promise. The guard pushed Astrid towards the table and it was only then that she realized that the head chair, a massive and dark high-backed monstrosity, was occupied.

Lurching from the shadows, a frail but upright figure in black uniform suddenly stood erect to greet her. There was a loud click of jackboot heels and her host inclined his head stiffly. A high peaked black cap was held beneath his left arm and his right came out in greeting. Astrid quailed before the sight. Standing before her in full regalia was the uniformed figure of a senior Schutzstaffel Officer. Now that he had risen, the candlelight caught the Totenkopf badge on the hat, glittering on the S.S. runes on the collar and the medals clustered on the chest. A ceremonial dagger was strapped by a colourful belt around the waist.

"Welkommen, mein Fraulein," the figure nodded again and then handed Astrid to her seat which the guard set to the table for her. A hand appeared, and a bottle of Liebraumilch tilted on her right, the rush of white wine into the heavy cut glass goblet a splash of straw-tinted pleasure. She glimpsed the blue and yellow label of the bottle before it was withdrawn from view. "Kameraderen!" The other glass was held in a toast and Astrid slowly reached out and with an air bordering on insult, sipped the wine.

The old man was looking at her intently now, a black spider, happy to have the little fly into its web. He seemed unconscious of her demeanour, yet Astrid had a tremulous thought that her feelings had no significance here.

"I have brought you here so we may share a meal in the old way. Thank you for indulging an old man and dressing as you have. Your appearance brings back fond memories."

Astrid shuddered at the hypocrisy. Surely the old bastard knew the degrading pressure that had been exerted upon her.

"Where are my friends?"

"Both of them are here."

"Both? I have three friends."

"Yes." The man reflected and then looked up with a cold haughtiness. "Ah! You refer to Herr Streicher, I suppose. He was found to be expendable. I trust you will be cooperative and ensure the other two do not become expendable also."

Astrid went cold. She felt like a rat in a trap, but the old man continued his previous thought, unconcerned with her feelings.

"My memories are many. They particularly are filled with the Third Reich," the figure rose like a puppet, erect and raising a glass. "To Adolf Hitler, visionary, true patriot and leader of the German people! Der Führer!" he drank, oblivious to Astrid's non-compliance. He sat down again. "But, in essence, a precious memory," the voice had slid to a sibilant whisper, "in essence, my memories of your mother are much more precious and intimate."

Astrid felt the claws of a deadly, demonic beast trace her spine. Again, this old bastard had just hinted of intimacy between himself and Mutti. "And would Mutti remember you?" she almost blurted the words, conscious that they were almost confrontational.

The old figure was nodding his head, gazing off into the candlelight as if the flickering flame held some naked, pirouetting image of Heidie von Heisler.

"Then may I know your name?"

"Ah, pardon Fraulein..."

"Frau...It is Frau Klemerer."

"Indeed. Pardon. My name is Heinz Klaus von Huehnlein, Fourth Count of Stellenboch."

Astrid held his gaze and was rewarded with a faint flicker. Yes, she thought, just another Nazi thug claiming to be something he never was. At the same time, she realised she was looking at the monster who had been responsible for administrating the test of Agent Twenty-nine on helpless human subjects. She let it pass. No point in challenging this worthless piece of shit under these circumstances.

"Around here," he looked over his shoulder at the waiter and in a secretive gesture, whispered, "they call me *El Jefe*, which is Spanish for *The Chief*." He chuckled, Astrid failing to see the humour. "I knew your mother in the heady days of nineteen forty, when the Blitzkrieg knifed across Europe, carrying all in its path. Her husband was a hero, much decorated by Der Führer himself!"

"And then he was wounded!"

"Yes, gloriously in the cause of National Socialism!"

"Crap!" Astrid hid the remark by lifting her glass to her lips. She knew damned well from her mother that Oberst Otto von Heisler had given his life in a brave but futile gesture, lingering on for years suffering the consequences of his *glorious* act. His physical torture was nothing to his mental distress when he discovered the horrors his heroism had supported and he never forgave himself.

"I tried to comfort your mother, give her support after her husband was wounded, but she was independent, wanted to cope alone. I lost track of her soon after, but I always remembered her. You are so like her!" his cold handful of bony knuckles covered hers.

The situation gelled for Astrid quickly. She could see which way the evening was going. She was helpless here, a chattel in the game. The maudlin old bastard, who seemed to think she was her mother reincarnated, was going to bore her for as long as he chose and then would have her shipped to his room so he could try to have his way with her. She wondered how he would manage it. He was obviously frail so how could he be such a ram as to be even interested? With a shudder, sadism crossed her mind. The old fossil was certainly capable of the intent, if not the act.

The wine bottle came over her shoulder, appearing through the shadows and glistening in the candlelight. The golden liquid splashed into her glass, increasing her languid mood. Why was she languid? The bottle reappeared, correctly over the right arm of her table companion, tilted and expertly poured into his glass from the red and green-labelled bottle.

Red and green? Astrid tensed. Her mind went back to her wine being replenished and she saw blue and yellow labelling. The bastards were using two different bottles! Why? Of course, that was why! Her bottle was drugged to make her pliable. How else could the old fart cope?

Her mind darted around the possibilities. Already she felt woozy from the effects of whatever was in the bottle. Intuitively, she knew the drug would not be incapacitating. An incapacitated lover, however unwilling, was less than satisfactory. So, it must be a mild sedative that would allow the *Count* the upper hand in a sexual encounter. She decided to even the odds.

"What you have told me is entrancing. As a Deutsche-maiden, I am thrilled to learn of this. I wish you success. A toast!" she seized his glass and her own, proffering him hers and taking his to her lips. The old weasel paused. His face became a kaleidoscope of doubt, fear and repugnance. Astrid faced him down. He dared not refuse the toast and gingerly sipped on the contents of the glass.

"Nein, mein Herr! We drink to Adolf Hitler, Führer of the Deutschevolk and all the glory he and his men sought! Drink!"

Caught, knowing he had the final say in whatever happened, the old man drained the glass and issued a false smile.

"Tell me more!" Astrid was relentless.

El Jefe droned on for another ten minutes before Astrid took the initiative and signalled for more wine. The waiter stepped forward and replenished both glasses, again using different bottles. Casually, Astrid switched the glasses again, ensuring he drank from the drugged one. Next time the waiter came forward, he tried to whisper in the old man's ear but was quieted by a careless wave. Instead, the repulsive lecher leaned forward to Astrid, one hand on her knee.

"I must tell you, Fraulein - sorry, Frau Klemerer. Since you cannot leave, I am able to tell you. I have a plan, which cannot fail. You will be pleased to know that the sacrifices of your parents were not in vain. I have the means of performing a stroke of revenge in honour of the Third Reich," the putrid old bastard paused, breathing heavily with his vehemence, "I have dispatched my right-hand man, Wesler, to meet my associates from the Middle East and he will give them the means of destroying half of New York."

"No shit! How do you manage that?"

"Ah! I have a gas. It will kill thousands of Jews, destroy their cursed financial strangle hold on the world, and allow us to take over!"

Astrid swayed in her chair. The threat was real because she had read the concentration camp reports on tests and knew the gas actually existed. Yet the drugs were getting to her. She felt herself going in and out of focus. She frowned with concentration, willing herself to stay properly conscious and gather more information. "But how does this work? How can you release such a gas, even if you really have it?"

"Ah, but we *do* have such a gas and it was proven. We only have to release it on the wind in New York and we shall kill thousands of Jews."

"But, if you want to kill Jews, why New York? Why not Tel Aviv, or Jerusalem, for instance?"

"Because the gas is only the *beginning* of the plan! I have developed another *Endlösung,* a means of achieving world dominance! With the help of my other friends, success is assured."

Astrid shuddered. Endlösung had signalled the deliberately engineered, systematic extermination of Jews. If the old shit was using such a description, his plan must have serious consequences. "I don't see how you can do this, you must be crazy."

Two eyes turned to her, lizard-like, opening between folds of wrinkled flesh. The old man studied her, a flat gaze of cold calculation. Slowly, he nodded his head. "Ach so! You need to be made a believer. You are aware of the Agent Twenty-nine?"

Astrid shook her head, pretending not to know, soliciting more information but terrified of what it might mean.

"As you have discovered, we are able to use the portable computers to communicate. Wesler has left for Greece and will soon be in New York to supervise this plan. Come, I will show you!" Slightly unsteady, they both made their way to the study where Astrid had been interrogated days before.

On a side table, a computer console stood. The old man turned it on and sat in the chair. At the prompt, he typed in his access code. Astrid focussed hard. The old fool was making no secrets here, he was so confident of his security. She reflected she could knock him in the head right now and escape, but she knew Karl-Heinz was positioned outside the door. She remembered Mandy counting keystrokes and tried to count herself. The code was eight letters long and she managed to see it began with a 'v', an 'a' and an 'l', before his hands covered the keys. The last two letters were 'i' and 'e'. What word was that? She struggled, quickly repeating the letters, trying to imprint them on her brain while she could still focus.

"You see, here is Wesler's hotel reservation in New Jersey," his words interrupted Astrid's efforts, "He will be there in a few days and the gas has already been shipped."

A whole list of messages between the two men was strung across the screen.

"Wesler will do whatever I tell him. At my command, the gas will be released and directed at the New York financial district. That is where all the Jews are!"

"But what about all the other, innocent people? What is the rest of the plan?"

The old man looked at her and his eyes rolled upward. The drugged wine was getting to him. He caught himself, his head jerking like a person nodding off. He paused a moment and then she saw his eyes slide lasciviously towards her.

"Karl-Heinz!" In moments, the henchman appeared in the room. "It is time for us to retire. Lead the way!"

Seeing the state of his master, the younger man leered at Astrid, confident that she would soon be turned over to him. She gave him a slight pout to reinforce his desire and deliberately lurched, giving him a glimpse of ample cleavage. While he was concentrating on her body, he was going to be off guard, she reasoned. Following behind him, she lurched in the passageway, steadying herself with one hand on the wall. Behind her, she could hear El Jefe in similar circumstances, stumbling and cursing in low tones.

Escorting them along the passageway, the bodyguard opened a door to a spacious bedroom. Again, Astrid staggered deliberately to emphasize her incapacity and the eager Karl-Heinz gallantly assisted her to re-balance, one greedy hand clutching her left breast. She gave him a moue, her pursed lips evoking promise. He guided her to the bed, relinquishing his hold as she willingly slumped onto the mattress, stoking his desire.

"Very good, Karl-Heinz." El Jefe's words broke the spell the guard was in as he watched Astrid clutch her breast and slowly run her hand down to her thighs. Reluctantly, the man turned and left the room.

The ancient filth began to remove his clothes. He struggled for a moment getting off his tunic and then his shirt. His flesh looked grey and dead, ribs and drooping pectorals reflecting the bedside light. He dropped his pants to the floor, revealing a slack and small penis protruding from a sparse patch of white hair. His shanks were skinny and looked like dried-out chicken wings. Despite this, a gleam came to his eye as he looked at Astrid, sprawled on the bed.

He gestured, indicating she should undress. Since she had his full attention, Astrid complied. The man was too drugged to realize he was being led on. She rose to her knees and swayed in a coquettish fashion. She ran one hand through the blonde mass of her hair and then began unbuttoning the dress. His attention was rapt.

She inflated her lungs, stretching her ribs to good effect, proffering the prominence of her breasts. He gave a sigh and she noted with surprise that he seemed to be reacting. Dropping the top of the dress, she pulled the straps of the bodice off her shoulders. It was too slow for him. He stepped forward and pulled the garment down, revealing her nude upper body. He gasped and gave a little dry cough.

Hesitantly, he reached out and gently cupped one breast. Astrid's skin crawled. Creeping onto the bed, he tried to put his mouth to a nipple, but she fell back, dreading his touch. Encouraged, he climbed astride her legs, making it difficult for himself as he tried tugging off her lower garments. Glancing down, she was astonished to find he actually had an erection. His breath came raggedly and his eyes gleamed in the light. Astrid was working her way up towards the headboard, horrified by events, but he pinned her, one talon of a hand twined in her pubic hair. She felt herself falling, caught in the moment, the drugs playing with her mind. The head of his penis was pushed against her closed inner thighs and suddenly, everything became lucid.

She kneed upward, catching him in the groin. He squawked and curled up on top of her. Quickly, she reached out and seized him by the neck. With both thumbs in his throat, she threw him over and climbed on top of him. She didn't know what her next move should be but a glance to the floor gave her a clue. The scabbard with the ceremonial dagger lay with the uniform he had discarded. Releasing her grip on his throat, she clubbed him with a fist and rolled off him towards the floor.

He yelled, a partly choked cry for help. Almost instantly, Astrid heard the door rattle as Karl-Heinz, doubtless listening, began to enter. Quickly seizing the dagger, she returned to the bed as El Jefe rose to his knees. She grabbed him and dragged him from the bed, wrapping her left arm around his neck before thrusting the point of the weapon into the flesh of his throat. He gasped audibly at the threat and the pain.

Karl-Heinz was through the door, then froze at the sight.

"Tell him to throw his gun over here!" Astrid pushed harder with the blade and the old man squirmed. Karl-Heinz reached behind him and brought the pistol out. A smirk spread over his face and he began to level the weapon on them. With horror, Astrid realised that he was quite ready to shoot the old man too as a means to then having his way with her. Maybe she had overplayed her hand!

She shifted position of the dagger and forcibly dragged the point up the man's face. He screamed as the skin opened up and blood spurted onto the carpet. Karl-Heinz's face fell for a brief moment and then El Jefe began to shout and scream at him. Years of discipline began to take effect as the old man kept up a continuous flow of invective.

Reluctantly, the guard changed his grip on the pistol and then tossed it on the bed. He had gone rigid initially, but now relaxed. The pistol in his ankle holster was unknown to her and he would wait his chance. First he had to protect the old man, and then this bitch would be his!

Dragging the still struggling El Jefe, Astrid reached out and grabbed the gun. She saw it was an automatic Glock. Flourishing it, she waved Karl-Heinz away from the door. He moved to his left, closer to a solid, high-backed chair that might offer him protection.

"Now then, we are going downstairs to release my friends. You, Karl-Heinz! You go first! If you make the slightest wrong move, I will shoot this old bastard and then you, immediately. In case you don't know, I am an expert with firearms. You have keys?"

The man reacted sullenly. Before he knew what was happening, Astrid had snap-fired the Glock. The round took him through the upper right arm, breaking the bone. He cried out and clutched the injured limb, face wracked with pain.

"You have keys?"

He nodded grudgingly. With his useless arm, it would now be very difficult to draw the pistol on his right ankle with any kind of speed. She had unknowingly taken an advantage.

Stepping back from the old man, Astrid cold-cocked him with the pistol butt and he went down like a pole-axed steer. "Let's go!" Karl-Heinz now needed no second urging and wincing at the pain and clutching his arm, he led her downstairs. The release of Raymond and Mandy did not come too soon. By the time they were let out, she was seeing double from the drugs she had taken. Quickly she explained her condition to Raymond and passed him the gun. Raymond prodded Karl-Heinz into one of the cells, locking him inside and leaving him to care for himself.

"What now?"

"We have to get out of here. There is nobody around right now but by morning this place will be like an angry wasps' nest."

"Well, they boasted about a plane just a short walk away."

"Very well, get me into it, I'll start it up, climb to altitude, put on the auto pilot and then, let me sleep."

"Isn't that dangerous?"

"No more than staying here. It is only a mild sedative, so I can still function until I can sleep and it wears off."

"Where shall we go?"

"Somewhere up north; Brazil, Venezuela, Ecuador."

"Well, I can handle the navigating. Yet, would we not be better off in Paraguay or Argentina?" Raymond asked.

"No!" Astrid could not understand why she was so lucid when her eyes would not stay open. "We have to go north. We have to go to the United States. I will explain when I wake up. Besides, there are too many Nazi sympathizers in those other countries. Let's go!"

"And will you be getting dressed first?" Raymond's comment caused Astrid to look down. She was still naked as a jay.

"Shit! Find me some clothes!"

Mandy complied and while Astrid got dressed, went off quickly to the kitchen. The place was deserted and she threw into a cardboard box an assortment of drinks and snacks. When she came out, Raymond and Astrid were waiting.

"Just a minute. If we are travelling, we shall need passports. How the hell can we just enter countries without them?"

"They should be in the old bastard's office; they were on his desk when he interrogated me."

"Well, you won't find one for me, those bloody sods that lifted me out of London sure didn't bother about identification!"

Astrid waved a hand to silence Mandy. "We have to go back to the office. I know what the plan is for the virus. I know what is going to happen."

"What?"

"No time! Get me to the office." The world spun and Astrid clutched Raymond's arm for balance.

"Come on, then!"

They entered the study. "I'll find the passports." Raymond began tearing drawers out of the desk and dumping the contents on the floor.

Astrid and Mandy went to the computer. It was still turned on but the cursor was flashing, looking for a password to allow access.

"We need to be able to use this information, Mandy." Dimly, Astrid knew the computer connection was going to be important.

"I do not have the benefit of a super computer, Astrid, I need the password to gain access," Mandy was impatient.

"I have it! Or, at least part of it!"

"OK, what is it?"

"Umm, er, it ends with an 'i' and an 'e'."

"Good start!" despite her sarcasm, Mandy grabbed a note pad and scribbled the two letters. "How many keystrokes? Did you count them?"

"Yes. I learned that from you!" Astrid sought approval. "There were... Hmm... Eight."

"First letter?"

Silence.

"Astrid! Think!"

The insistent tone woke Astrid slightly. "The first letter was a 'v'."

"The second one?"

"A vowel."

"An 'a'? An 'e'?"

"'A'. It was an 'a'."

"And?"

"It was...It was an...'l'. Yes, it was an 'l'!" she said it with triumph.

"Fuck! I was never good at crosswords!"

"Valkyrie!" Raymond shouted it across the room, madly tearing drawers apart. "Ride of the Valkyries! Teutonic folklore! Wagnerian music to suit the Nazi moods! Ra-ta-ta-ta-ta! Ra-ta-ta-ta-ta! Ra-ta-ta-ta-ta, ra-ta-ta-ta! Winged spirits to carry the dead to Valhalla! Predictable bastards!" he snorted.

Turning, Mandy typed in the word. The screen rolled, revealing the messages Astrid had viewed only a while before. "Holy shit, I am in and on-line!"

"Let's get out of here!" Astrid insisted.

"Wait!"

"For what?"

"How can we get an advantage here?" Mandy was frowning at the screen. "We have to control Wesler."

"But he is on a mission of destruction. They are going to use the virus!" Astrid felt the room begin to spin despite her hyper state.

"Shit!" Raymond felt helpless on the side.

"I'll print the screen. Where is the computer we got in Germany?" Mandy's long fingers caressed the keyboard.

"It's here," Raymond reached out and scooped it from a shelf.

The printer began to churn pages into Mandy's waiting hands.

Raymond found an envelope in one of the drawers and grunted with satisfaction when his and Astrid's passports fell into his hand. "I have the passports! By the way, where is Streicher?"

"Dead."

There was a Land Rover parked outside with the keys in the ignition. No chance of auto theft in this remote place. Quickly they piled in and drove to the airstrip. In the lights of the small hangar, they looked at the sleek King Air.

"Are you sure you know how to fly this thing?"

"Oh yes. I fly a King Air Two Hundred for my husband from time to time and this is a One Hundred model, so almost the same."

"You are a woman of great accomplishments."

A radio control illuminated the airstrip for them and within minutes, the drone of engines faded as they took off and turned northwards.

El Jefe came up from unconsciousness like a black avenging angel of the great darkness. His last memory was of the dining room. Rolling over, he brought his knees up beneath him. The ornate footboard of the bed gave him purchase and he levered himself upright. He staggered to the door, bouncing off it before being restored to a shaky equilibrium. The knob slipped under unsteady hands before yielding, and then he was out in the passage. His head hurt. He called for assistance, but there was no response.

The dining room was empty but he recognized its character. Naked, he slumped into the head chair at the table, a rag-doll skeletal caricature of his former self. The table spun before him. Reinhard Heydrich raised a glass of schnapps, taunting him to drink a toast. Dear Reiny! He upended a bottle of brandy into a glass, the bottle rolling off his clumsy thumb, careening across the table and spilling fluid before finding an uncertain fate off the tabletop. He drank, responding to dear Reiny's challenge. Gott in Himmel! It was like the old days! Yet Reiny shrank, receding into the dark recesses of the upper reaches of the room, a phantom of the past.

He reached out, offering his hand. "Meine Ehre Heisst Treue" The face of the specter above him returned, changed to a death's head, mocking him. "Reiny!"

The quivering, wrinkled hand reached out, knuckles crackling with arthritic pain hardly noticed. "Rein-eeeee!" He fell across the table, upsetting a ten-kilogram silver candleholder, cast from metal gleaned from the concentration camps. Hot wax gushed over the table, and the wick ignited the brandy he had spilled. A decanter of schnapps, tilted by his fall, flooded over-proof alcohol into the flame. A spurt of yellow-blue ignition filled the room and a running wave of fire spread across the polished surface of the tabletop.

In seconds, the table legs were engulfed and the portraits on the wall came alive with the light of flames. The carefully waxed surfaces of the furniture readily gave up their secretions of flammable liquids as they boiled off the surfaces. The walls danced to the growing fire, and choking smoke oozed from every heated surface.

El Jefe breathed the fumes, an ancient, knowing memory prompting his thought processes. It was poison! That was it! Gases, poisoning his lungs, choking him to death. He recognized it; saw it for what it was. Poison gas administered to emaciated figures and then, oven-fire!

The heaps of dead, always, every time, a pyramid of would-be survivors, climbing atop the doomed, trying for the last oxygen in the chambers. Ah, now he understood! He crawled up onto the table as it began to suck oxygen like a living being, seeking to be consumed. The old wood ignited explosively, breaking into chemical decomposition. He drew a breath, exulting in the ancient Viking Valhalla of divine entry to the next world on a bier of fire.

But then came the crippling fear of death. Then came the realization of accomplishments left untended and unfinished. When he was gone, all would be lost! A parade of limp stick figures, starved in the camps, lurched to their long-dead feet. Slack and dead, they moved implacably towards him. Behind them, skeletal but temporary survivors dragged others to their final fate. All went to the ovens. Limbs dragging in the dirt, they were thrown onto griddles still reeking black sludge from the previous offerings.

El Jefe screamed, hiding his face behind hopeless forearms as the Jews finally came for him. Campies reached out, their only temporary reprieve being willingness to place him too on the hideous black griddle of the ovens before their own turn came. The room filled with smoke, stifling his last desperate screams.

The flames quickly went through the roof of the hacienda.

0615 hrs. Sunday, 15th July 1990. Brazil.

Porto Velho, on the Rio Madeira, is near the centre of Brazil, its airstrip a red clay slash alongside the dark muddy waters of the broad river. Dropping below the green canopy of the surrounding forest, the King Air flared and touched down. Astrid taxied the plane off the airstrip, cutting the engines in front of a raised tank showing a jet fuel symbol. The early morning sun was up and the temperature, descending the last thousand feet, had climbed substantially. She felt desperately tired. Mandy had woken her up a half-hour ago, with a proffered beer, it being the only drink available. Her head throbbed with the after effect of the drug. "Where are we?"

"Central Brazil. Porto Velho. Remember, we figured if we came to a little place like this, they might give us fuel and send us on our way more readily than a bigger place. The town is over that way." Shown by Astrid how to steer the aircraft using the autopilot coupled to a Global Positioning System, Raymond had managed the flight very well, allowing Astrid to sleep after she had levelled the King Air, and put it on course.

"Hmm." Astrid looked at the fuel tanks and saw they must have been airborne a little under three hours.

"Lookout! Somebody's coming!" Mandy was glued to the window.

A man had emerged from a shack close to the aircraft. He wore white cotton pants and a shirt, his face hidden under a straw hat. He scratched his behind absently as he strolled towards them.

"Anybody speak Portuguese?" Raymond went to the main door and opened it, lowering the air-stair door. A wave of heated and humid air invaded the cabin, carrying with it the smell of vegetation. "Buenos dios." He waved to the man, who sauntered on, oblivious to the greeting. It looked like he was about to fuel the aircraft without communicating with them in any way.

Behind the pilot seat was a briefcase with a padlock. Groping around in the pocket on the back of the seat, Raymond produced a tiny key. Sure enough, it fit the lock and he swung the lid open. Inside was a leather pouch with a zipper and several bulky envelopes.

"Bingo!" A handful of high value American currency and some documents, including passports were revealed. "There must be ten thousand dollars here. And look, passports for several nations: Argentina, Brazil, the U.S." There were three passports for the old man back at the hacienda and the same amount for a younger man, by features a European. The names and nationality were different on each. "I suppose these characters could go anywhere at a moment's notice and pretend to be almost anybody."

"Well the money will be useful."

"That's the man who was at my interrogation," Mandy looked over their shoulders.

"Who is he?"

"I don't know, but it seemed like he was the old Nazi's second in command to me."

"It must be Wesler. The old scab boasted about him to me. He is the man we are trying to track down. He has the cylinders containing the virus," Astrid countered.

"What are these?" Raymond held up some rolled paper with broad black stripes inside. He unwrapped one and revealed large black letters.

"They are decals, Raymond, and they solve a dilemma I was having."

"Which would be?"

"How to get into the United States. This aircraft has Paraguayan registry letters. I'll bet if we look, we can figure out how they were to be used to change nationality if these men had to run and hide."

They went to the back of the aircraft. In letters about eight inches high was 'ZP- ONF'. Holding up the pages of decals, Raymond and Astrid tried to figure out how they could modify the letters.

"Would this help?" Mandy was waving a handful of documents at them.

Reaching up, Astrid took them from her. "Ah! These are registration papers for the United States. See? This King Air, this serial number, is registered in the United States to the Kingsfield Organization of Dallas, Texas. The registration is 'N-ZPE'".

"So that's how these things fit!" Raymond was fumbling with the sheets, trying to hold them up against the fuselage in their appointed places. "We put on the 'N', then the 'dash', make the other 'dash' into an 'E', and remove the rest of the letters."

"Is that too convenient?" Mandy felt left out of the conversation.

"Not really! These bastards must have had it all worked out how to disappear any time they wanted to and putting American registration on the aircraft meant very few people would question it or threaten it. Pretty smart, really." Astrid looked over her shoulder to see how the fueller was doing.

"Yes, and the great thing is, we are trying to do exactly what they had planned in case of emergency; travel to the U.S.," Raymond nodded his head.

"I wonder what other goodies they have?"

The money was a huge windfall for them since their resources had disappeared.

"So, how do we get into the U.S.?" Mandy asked.

"Well, I believe we have to fly in with the King Air. After all, it belongs in Dallas," Astrid was figuring it out.

"So do we just go and land there?" Raymond inquired.

"Not exactly. We have to file a flight plan and advise Customs. Because of all the drug traffic from South America, the Americans are paranoid about planes filled with drugs arriving there. If we behave normally, we stand a better chance."

"Can we not just fly under their radar?" Mandy felt helpless.

"Possibly, but they watch for that and it would definitely look suspicious. We could easily be intercepted by one of their fighter aircraft and forced to land for interrogation, or even be shot down. The best way is to file a flight plan and try to look as legitimate as possible."

"So, how do we get to the United States from here?" Mandy did not know the geography.

"Well, from Brazil, our best choice is over Venezuela to, let me see..." Astrid pulled out a map. "Curaçao."

Mandy was lost. "Curaçao? Where the hell is that?"

"It is an island, off the Venezuelan coast, in the Caribbean. It is part of the Netherlands Antilles. I figure the sooner we deal with Europeans the better. If we try to go to Ecuador, or, especially, anywhere near Columbia, we could get shot down, or, if we land, locked up. Certainly, the Americans will focus on a flight like ours originating in Columbia because of the drug trade. Let's go to Curaçao, spend the night, get a plan together and enter the States tomorrow."

"And how do I enter this country without a passport?" Mandy asked.

"If we are only staying overnight and passing through, they might not care. Besides, what other choice do we have? We can't stay here. Curaçao is a great tourism place, so maybe we can play on that. Often Immigration is quite easy on pilots who are in transit through such countries."

"That chap has finished fuelling."

"Pay him cash and let's get out of here," Mandy was getting edgy.

"No, wait! Once he leaves, let's change the registration letters. I want to land in Curaçao as an American. It will mean less questions and I don't think anyone here will understand, or care, what we are doing," Astrid began to shuffle the decals.

By the time Raymond had paid the man, who still did little to acknowledge them, the girls had the decals ready. It took them a little over a half-hour to make the changes and then they departed. Astrid had consulted maps and decided where there might probably be radar along their route. She planned to be flying low enough to avoid it, since the whole flight across Brazil and Venezuela would be illegal, with no flight plan.

15th July 1990. Excerpt from Der Spiegel, West Germany.

'Authorities are now substantiating previous reports that a major find of treasure has been discovered in the process of de-mining an area of the old 'Iron Curtain'. A cache of boxes containing gold, excavated in the process of mine dismantling, has been trucked to an undisclosed destination for assessment. In Bonn, the Minister of the Interior has indicated that because of its source, the money has been earmarked for distribution to the victims of Nazi concentration camps and the promotion of peaceful societies everywhere.'

1600 hrs. Sunday, 15th July 1990. Hotel Otrobanda, Willemstad, Curaçao.

The flight had been anticlimactic, with huge sighs of relief as they crossed the Venezuelan coast undetected and passed over the straits to Curaçao. Astrid smooth-talked the air traffic controllers into permission to land, claiming their flight plan had indeed been filed but must have gotten lost, and they taxied into the general aviation ramp at the airport.

Within minutes, a Dutch immigration officer was on hand. Having scanned Raymond and Astrid's passports, he at first became a little stiff when Mandy had no identification. They had cooked up a story of Mandy's purse being stolen in Barcelona while they were on business there. With the girls working their best charms on him, the man unbent a little and suggested a solution to the dilemma. He would hold Raymond and Astrid's passports against the promise that all three of them would be departing the next morning.

He also made a phone call and made the condition they stay at the Otrobanda Hotel, down on Breedestraat for the night. He eventually became so helpful that he drove them down there and advised the desk clerk she did not need to hold their passports.

The hotel was a paradise after the places they had been in the past week or so. It was a light-mauve-blue colour, with red roofs and overlooked the pale tropical blue waters of the Willemstad harbour. After soaking the dirt out of themselves in deep relaxing baths, they gathered for drinks and to plan their next move.

Astrid had been studying the Jeppesen airways charts from the plane. "From here, I can file legitimate flight plans the rest of the way to the States. I think we should go to the Cayman Islands for fuel, then on into Brownsville, Texas, being the closest airport. That will also give us additional fuel should we need to divert for some reason. We should use the story we are returning to the company in Dallas. That route is largely over water, so we will not get involved with many countries' airspace."

"But we will be met by the authorities and I have no passport!" Mandy looked dismayed at the thought. "We got lucky here, but American Immigration won't be so easy."

"We will have to hide you somehow."

"In the *plane?*" she waved an arm, remembering the limited interior of the aircraft.

"Yes, well, it will be hard, but we have to find a way," Raymond trailed off dubiously.

"There is another way," Astrid looked up, thoughtful.

"How?"

"We land after dark and Mandy jumps out somewhere on the airport before we meet the Customs officer."

"Hmm."

"Then what do I do?"

"I don't know. We could try to hide you under suitcases in the baggage compartment, but if they want to inspect baggage, they will find you. I think you have to be off the aircraft before we stop which is why I suggest you jump off."

"Why don't you just parachute me in?"

Raymond turned, thoughtful. "Not such a bad idea. Have you ever jumped before?"

"No, stupid!"

"I like my idea best. You open the door for Mandy, she jumps off as we taxi slowly along and then she walks to some point where we can meet up again. My passport is still valid for the U.S. from when Rolf and I lived there. How about yours, Raymond?"

"I have an open two year visa under my journalism ties to visit, anytime."

"OK, so we are both acceptable, but not Mandy."

"Very well." Mandy shrugged resignedly. "I will jump off the fucking aeroplane and hike to some point where we can join up."

"Good. Now we only have to plan our arrival for night-time so nobody can see you do it."

They returned to the maps, concocting various viable stories should they be asked questions. The best route, as Astrid said, was first to Brownsville, deep in the south of Texas, then through to New York. She had filled Raymond and Mandy in on the overall plot which the incautious El Jefe had disclosed. They had a lot to plan. Already they had discussed and knew that warning the authorities was out of the question. They would be tracked down and arrested in the shortest possible time if they broke their silence. At the same time, they had not ruled that option out. Most likely, that would only happen once they got to New York and there was nothing more they could do to stop Wesler and the Arabs.

1800 hrs. Monday, 16th July 1990.
Laburnum Road, Tottenham, London.

George Jenkins walked down his street in the London suburb. His home was a semidetached, about halfway down the road. His neighbours knew him as a quiet person, unmarried, pleasant when spoken to, but reserved and private. He took the Underground to work, the Northern Line went right to the Thames and he was able to walk to work from there. Indeed, he preferred that to the traffic snarls. He had a small Triumph TR4 sports car garaged nearby if he had need of a vehicle. Usually, he only drove on outings into the country, accompanied by his friend, Tony.

Nearing his house, he thought about Ponsonby's actions. There was definitely something in the air and even though all his antennae were up, he had no sense of what it may be. Germany was involved, but then, Germany was the biggest news, the flavour of the season, with the Berlin Wall coming down, the Iron Curtain being neutralized and the two halves, separated at the end of the Second World War, seemingly coming together. He had served on the East German desk for four years but could dredge up no clue as to what was obviously concerning Ponsonby.

Regarding Tony, it was a casual relationship, neither one of them being particularly sexual, but one which his superiors would have seen as a security risk. They were discreet and rarely seen together around town. He thought of Tony now; they had a weekend trip to Derbyshire coming up and they would be free to enjoy the Peak District moorlands. He stroked his hand through his thinning sandy hair before opening the garden gate. He noticed with distaste that Mrs. Mullins' obese cat had visited his rose bed again. There was another fresh turd sticking out of the ground, rather like a rude finger gesture directed at him.

His front door was double-locked, as was the back. He was not particularly security conscious, but it was part of his existence and he had matured on the job during the Cold War. Opening the door, he found several pieces of mail had been thrust through his letterbox and inexplicably, some of them had traveled some distance along the polished parquet floor, beyond the archway to the lounge. He made a little sound of annoyance concerning Postal employees and bent down to retrieve them. Almost the instant the sense of a presence came upon him, a figure loomed over and blackjacked him to the floor.

Jenkins came up through layers of black with a feeling of impending doom. The feeling was realized when he tried to open his eyes and a flash of red agony surged through his head. He cringed and twisted, but his limbs were held fast. He was naked on his own bed, he knew the feel. Flat on his back and limbs spread, one tied to each bedpost.

Now, a figure slid into focus like mucus sliding down a windowpane. A man appeared above him. Dark, stubble, with craggy, Neanderthal features. The man peered down and grunted a signal, prompting a second face to appear. Dark also, greasy black hair tied back. A smile. A horrid, wicked, evil smile. Jenkins shuddered. He knew the type. Pitiless schoolyard bullies with psychotic burdens they never stopped unloading on the innocent.

"Mr. Jenkins, I presume?"

He gagged, terrified and mouth-dry.

"Give him some water, Tommy."

A wall of water hit Jenkins in the face, filling his nose, swamping his senses. He opened his mouth to breath, to scream, but a hard hand clamped over it.

"Tsk, tsk, tsk, *Mister* Jenkins. We must be quiet, don't you see?"

A rag was produced. Not a rag, but his silk shorts, known only to Tony. They were stuffed into his mouth while he spluttered desperately.

"Now then, I can talk without interruption," the voice was pure Cockney.

Jenkins recorded and analyzed every detail. He had been trained. They did the interrogation thing every few years at the school. Volunteer nothing. Know that you *will* break under torture. Give as little as you can, as slowly as you can. Hope for rescue. There was none. He was safe in his own home. Nobody would miss him until the morning.

"You have some information we need." The Neanderthal nodded in accord like a puppet in a Punch and Judy show. "Will you co-operate?"

Wildly, Jenkins' eyes flashed from one to the other, helplessly.

"Oh! I understand. You cannot speak because you are wearing your precious panties in the wrong place! Queer! What would lover-boy say?"

Oh, dear God! They knew about Tony!

"Tell you what, when you want to speak, you can nod your head. In the meantime, you know, I like sexy men too!" A calloused hand brushed his genitals, causing his testicles to retract in towards his body. "Can we have some fun?" Another hand grabbed him hard, squeezing his scrotum and inflicting deep, nauseating and horrible pain. He gagged.

"We need to know about a certain Mr. Raymond Barton. Where is he right now?"

Jenkins writhed.

"Oh, I see. No nodding head. So, if you don't want to talk, and seeing how I'm sure you don't need this..."

There was a horrible, sharp pain down below and a hand appeared, bearing a piece of meat dripping blood. A wet gush flowed between his spread legs.

"...Because you take it in the ass." The severed testicle was waved before his nose and then dropped onto his chest. "If you ever want to have children, Squire, you have one more refusal to talk."

Jenkins nodded, avidly.

"Ah! Suddenly you have information for us?"

Jenkins nodded again. Play for time, string them out.

"Now this is the truth?" The condescension in the tone made it even more horrible. "Because if it is not, you will be singing like a choirboy in about ten seconds!" A bloody knife blade was waved before his eyes.

Jenkins nodded again. He felt faint and there was no pain but he knew it was coming. He sought refuge in a safe place only he knew, striving to follow his lessons.

"Where is Mr. Barton?" The gag was removed from his mouth and he sucked air.

"I don't know," Jenkins squirmed, anticipating the pain, realizing for the first time in his life that his testicles meant something to him after all.

"Oh! I see! You need some more persuasion!"

Jenkins jerked wildly, shaking his head. "I really don't know where he is!"

"Best guess, then?"

He shook his head again.

"Well, let's see now. You like it in the ass, so let's see how you like this."

Jenkins arched on the mattress as the gag was re-inserted. A long cylinder was waved before his face, trailing a wire. He felt it drawn lasciviously down his body, past his dismembered genitals and pushed between his buttocks. He tried to clamp down, but the force was too great, the cylinder lubricated by some conductive cream. He screamed into the gag at the penetration.

A hand hove in view, bearing a crocodile clip and the pain burst anew as the clip was attached to his right nipple. And then the surge of electrical current overwhelmed his senses, plunged him into subservience.

2130 hrs. Monday, 16th July 1990. Highlander, New Jersey.

Abu el-Cetti was a tormented man. He stared at the television screen, the image of an overweight black woman haranguing her audience on some insignificant, puerile topic of life in America. His short association with the show had drained his patience. Now he sat in the painted concrete block room of a cheap Travelodge hotel, fraught with pain.

He had been told it was essential that his mission take place on a Tuesday, so now he was delayed another frustrating day. Every hour was torture to him, his mind soaring from rapture to despondency like a roller coaster.

The bathroom bathtub contained the mutilated remains of a black whore he had entertained the night before. He had made his mind up the day before that he really wanted to die. He wanted the virgins awaiting him in Paradise, but he had needed the earthly experience one more time, fortified by whisky.

He had picked her up on the street, paid her, penetrated her, felt her writhe beneath him, more from pain than pleasure as he forced his way into her. And then the knife! He had pushed it into her, blade up, carving back through belly tissue as she screamed into the hand over her mouth, spilling her intestines onto the bed. Yes, she had bitten him, bitten to the bone. Little good it had done her. He had dragged her into the bathroom, away from prying eyes, and hung the "do not disturb" sign on the suite door. Bundling up the bedclothes, throwing them in the bathroom and closing the door had done little to diminish the stench of her.

Yes, he was finally convinced he wanted to die. The previous morning, he had met the emissary of the man who had provided the destructive weapon. It had been the same man he had met in Athens. The Infidel had briefed him on his mission, with arrogance and a clear message that he was somehow superior to el-Cetti. Only the hand of Allah had protected him from retribution.

Early next morning el-Cetti was to board the eight five ferry from Sandy Hook Bay Marina, getting there by taxi. The deadly cylinder would be in his briefcase, part of his disguise as a trader on Wall Street. The suit clothes hung in his closet, fitted to his measurements. When he reached the Manhattan lower island, there would be a small service vehicle waiting in the car park for him.

A cell phone call would brief him on where he was to release the contents. First he had to open the cylinder. Then he would tip the contents into a tank with a screw top. A few minutes later, he would turn on a small compressor and direct a pipe out of the van. The contents of the cylinder would now be in liquid suspension. It would be piggybacked onto a carrier gas which would ensure it was dispersed on the wind without either rising into the sky or falling to the ground. Driven by what was forecast to be a light breeze, the deadly gas would permeate every building throughout the financial district of New York's Lower Manhattan. He had been assured that his mission would result in the death of thousands of Americans, whom he hated. More significantly, it would result in a higher-end annihilation of Jews in the financial business, whom he hated infinitely more.

This was not enough for el-Cetti. Ghosts that had once only occasionally plagued his dreams now walked openly through his waking hours. The images had grown recently, threatening a crescendo. It was time to escape them to the safe haven of Paradise, where he could not be sought. The only relief to his suffering was to be free, seek the eternal blessing of Allah.

Tomorrow he would die. He had made his choice. He would die in the service of Allah, carrying death to his enemies. What if the wind blew ill and did not carry the gas to its victims? He had been assured this would not be the case. But he doubted. No, there was only one way in his estimation that the gas could do total damage. He had to carry it to the maximum number of people and expose them to its deadly powers. By travelling up and down Wall Street and entering as many buildings as he could, he could maximize the effectiveness of the gas. None would be dispersed on the wind. All would find its way into a building, glorifying his sacrifice and contributing to the might of Allah! He would suffer the fate of his enemies, but it was naught to him now.

Yet he knew that this was not possible. He was trapped by duty, by the threat of el-Saeed's watchers and he knew he could not physically carry the cylinder and the other equipment. No, he was trapped by the plan and that furthered his frustration. But, nobody could stop him seeking his destiny. In the process, somehow, he would make the ultimate sacrifice. In'ch Allah!

In the meantime, he needed a crutch to help him through. He had grown to understand the weakness of el-Saaed. The strength of the Satan America was strong when it coiled around you, weakening your resolve. He went into the bathroom and turned on the bathtub cold water, seeking to drown the repugnance of the corpse. He grabbed a bandage from a pack he had bought and redressed his wounded hand. There was only pain and no response from the savaged fingers. The bitch had destroyed the tendons. Turning, he left the room, careful to lock it behind him. His crutch lay across the street, flashing the neon call *liquor, liquor.*

2145 hrs. Monday, 16th July 1990. Hotel, New Jersey.

The hotel was in some trees. Tasteful lighting splashed onto the ground in haphazard cunning to light the traveller's way. Upward beams picked out the ribs of trees supporting a green upper bonnet. The relief of a journey ended was redolent, even in the driveway. The lighting beckoned.

Joachim Wesler returned from his evening stroll, pensive. It was almost time for the operation to begin. He felt elated by it, the careful and intricate planning, which appealed to him, yet he wanted to play a bigger part. He felt he had been relegated to a courier role. Strolling through the shrub-filled lobby, he nodded to the desk clerk and went to his room. Entering, he walked to the table and chair, proclaimed by the management as a *mini-office* and sat down. The portable computer sat ready. He breathed deeply. Many thoughts were running through his head.

Fifteen minutes later, Wesler closed the lid of the portable computer with a gentleness, which belied his frustration. Pushing it to the side, he held both palms against his head and forcibly brushed them back through his scalp. He had tried several times to get through to the ranch in Paraguay. There was no answer.

He still remained terrified of El Jefe. His instructions were not to contact Paraguay. The operation was well planned and running as predicted. Yet he felt insecure, as if there was a threat out there he could not somehow identify. He felt the old man back in Paraguay was looking over his shoulder so put his own insecurity down to pure nerves. He had broken the order not to make contact unless absolutely necessary, but the silence in return he regarded as ominous. El Jefe, seemingly, was sticking to the silence whereas he was not and it made him feel inferior, vulnerable.

The fact that he could not, at the present time, communicate with El Jefe gave him grave misgivings. Either the old man was on the move, personally intending to supervise this supremely important operation, or, something untoward was happening. Partly out of fear, partly resolve, he decided to wait another twelve hours. Then he would phone Merguerita, his sister-in-law in Anunción. She could make internal phone calls on his behalf that would not be monitored.

2210 hrs. Monday, 16th July 1990. Highlander, New Jersey.

Albertina Bridget de Lacroisse had a multi-gene heritage. Her Spanish-American father had sired her with her Irish-Black-American mother. She in turn had given herself to a Cajun from New Orleans and given him three children, taking his surname in return, like it or not. She had worked at the hotel for four months, one of a string of jobs to support her children and lack-lustre mate. She moved her wide bottom in the cozy chair and reached for the bag of potato chips. Sometime soon she would go on a diet. At over two hundred pounds, her ample bosom and hips were not suited for many other kinds of work. It was a quiet night, one for viewing a little bit of soap opera television, which she loved.

Thus enthralled, it was a major annoyance to her when the first drip of water fell on her cheek. The second brought her to full awareness, attention taken away from the television screen. Looking up, she saw the dark stain of water on the office ceiling and the growing menace of another drip. She mouthed a curse which would have embarrassed her minister and headed for the door, ready to climb the stairs to the room above. It was not the first time she had seen an inconsiderate, drunk or stupid guest overflow some part of the plumbing. She had just reached the door when someone came in the other way. She did not recognize the slight, dark-skinned man before her as he had checked in on another clerk's shift. "Excuse me, sir, I have to go upstairs. Someone has overflowed upstairs."

El-Cetti recognized immediately that he had forgotten to fully turn off the cold bath tap. He blocked the woman's way, temporarily impeding her so he could think.

"Excuse me sir, please. I have to turn off the water upstairs, and then I can help you!"

It was the flourishing of the keys that did it. El-Cetti realized immediately that this woman was within seconds of running screaming from his room as a result of visiting his bathroom. The gun was an affront, a terrible departure from Albertina's day. The loud report stopped all life within her. She never knew another thing.

Dragging her heavy frame behind the desk, el-Cetti ran out of the office and up the stairs. Swiftly, he threw the clothes he had been given into his suitcase. He had sense enough to go along the upstairs balcony past the other rooms and down the stairs at the far end from the office, bound for another place to sleep for the night. Meantime, the security camera in the hotel office continued its footage.

Four blocks away, el-Cetti flagged down a taxi and directed it to another hotel. The driver made no comment about a man in shirtsleeves and carrying a suitcase, flagging him down on a street. Ten minutes after the shooting, el-Cetti was checking into another room. The shot had not gone unnoticed however. A nervous guest called it in and the police were there in ten minutes. They took several more minutes to look behind the check-in counter. The ceiling still dripped, but was not associated at first with the desk clerk's body. Three minutes later, however, they ascertained that the guest above, one Claudio Benares, was not answering his door. Using the manager's keys to gain access, they realized they had a major problem on their hands.

An all-points call went out and detectives at the scene were soon replaying the security camera recording. Within an hour of police response, a picture of the murderer was circulating the eastern seaboard.

0200 hrs. Tuesday, 17th July 1990. Brownsville, Texas.

"November Zulu Poppa Echo, turn right taxiway Bravo, ground one two one decimal nine."

Acknowledging the tower controller, Astrid rolled the King Air off the runway, onto the taxiway and requested taxi instructions from the ground controller.

"OK, Poppa Echo, the Customs area is down Bravo, left on Foxtrot and then off to your two o'clock. Watch for the red sign and park in the yellow circle. Your base refueller is about a hundred yards along the ramp, northbound. When you are finished with Customs, take it down the ramp at your discretion. G'night."

"Mandy! There is a shack up ahead on the left side. When you get off, go over to it and lie low so you are not seen. When you see us taxi to the refueller, wait until we are out of the plane and the guy is busy. Then walk over and join the group in the office like you belong. It is only about a fifty yard walk." Slowing the aircraft, Astrid nodded to Raymond.

He went back, gave Mandy a quick hug and opened the door. The sound of the engines grew loud as he lowered the air stair. Quickly, she stepped down into the slipstream from the engine, blasted by cold air and stinking exhaust. In a matter of a few steps she was on the grass, jogging to the shack about twenty yards away. She was halfway there when she realized they had not made a contingency plan in case Raymond and Astrid got arrested. Well, it was too late now. She sat with her back to the red and white painted shack, indistinguishable in the dark from her surroundings, facing towards the ramp as the King Air continued taxiing in.

Finding a large yellow circle with *Customs* painted on it, Astrid braked the plane to a halt and cut the engines. She had time to fret on the flight but the landing had focussed her concentration until now, when the whole impact of what they were attempting hit her. As the propellers slowed, she saw a small dark blue car with official emblems on the door pulling over towards them. A man dressed in Customs uniform unfolded his full six feet from the vehicle and hitched his pants. Reaching back in, he retrieved a clipboard and walked towards them.

"Good evening," Raymond decided on the bold approach.

"Evening. Y'all arriving from where?" The Texan twang from the long lean frame evoked a hundred cowboy movies from Raymond's past and he wondered how fast the man was on the draw.

"We're just in from the Cayman Islands."

"How long have you been out of the United States?"

"Actually, some time, we did not take the aircraft out, we are just ferrying it back for a friend."

The Customs officer pursed his lips. "Just the two of you onboard?"

"Yes."

"What are your nationalities?"

"Er, I'm British and Astrid is German."

A pair of pale blue eyes stared through Raymond. "Y'all have passports and visas to enter the United States?"

"Yes," they each proffered their documents. Astrid, of course, had a residency permit while Raymond's passport showed him as an accredited reporter, with right of entry. In the light from a flashlight, the officer carefully studied each and made some notes on a clipboard.

"Do you have anything to declare, any spirits, tobacco or other goods for sale you are bringing into the United States?"

"No, only a bottle of rum I bought in the Caymans, but it is opened and part gone."

"A'right but I'll have to take a look inside your aircraft."

"Sure," Raymond stood aside.

Slowly, the officer mounted the stairs. He sauntered up the aisle, ducking his head and peering under the seats and into the cockpit. "These your suitcases?" he was back again, by the rear cargo hatch.

"Yes."

"You mind if I take a look-see?"

"No."

Quickly the man sorted through the meager couple of bags they had.

"Okay, y'all short a couple of documents for entry, like the General Customs Declaration, but I'll show you how to fill them in. How long y'all planning on staying in the United States?"

"Oh, maybe a week. I have to get back to Britain by the twenty-third."

Five minutes later, Astrid had fired up one engine and taxied towards the refueling building. An officious-looking figure, with lighted batons held erect, marshaled her to a stop. "Hello, welcome to Brownsville," he was all enthusiasm as they opened the door.

"Fill it up, please," Astrid stared at the youthful man.

"Yes ma'am. There's coffee inside if y'all would like some," he strode off to a fuel truck nearby and started the engine. In a matter of two minutes, he was up a ladder, the nozzle of the fuel hose buried in the filler cap of the King Air. Behind him, out of view, a dark figure crossed the ramp and joined the others in the building.

Astrid quickly made use of the phone, obtaining weather for Teterboro, New Jersey, one of the airports she was familiar with around New York. She then filed an FAA flight plan to Dallas, in keeping with their plan. By the time the young man had finished fuelling the plane, they were ready to go.

0615 hrs. 17th July 1990. U.S. Customs Office, Brownsville, Texas.

Tom McKeness brooded in front of his fax machine. Reaching into his uniform shirt pocket past the row of pens, he fished out his cigarettes and shook one loose. The Zippo, engraved with the coloured rebel flag, flared as he lit the tobacco and dragged in a deep breath. Tossing the lighter onto the desk, he contemplated his map.

One of the papers he had made the King Air arrivals fill out had been the ultimate destination in the United States. Lots of people went to Dallas, and it was the airplane's home base. So what? There was nothing tangible about them to arouse suspicion. They had an aircraft they were returning for a friend. That was unusual, but not suspicious. What was it that gave him that feeling of suspicion, which, incidentally, had never failed him before?

He walked back in his mind through the aircraft again. There were only six seats, typically deep and comfortable recliners. There was a small bar cabinet at the rear, with a coffee dispenser, just forward of the baggage compartment. There was about the right amount of baggage for two people, nothing being almost as typical as a whole pile, in his experience. There were few clothes to suggest a long trip however and that was unusual. Then he saw it!

His eyes narrowed as he re-scanned the cabin in his mind's eye. The captain's cup holder in the cockpit had had an empty styrofoam cup in it. Likewise the co-pilot's. So, why was there another one next to one of the aft passenger seats? He reached for the phone.

"Brownsville Air Fuelling."

"Billy Joe, this is Tom McKeness."

"Oh! Hi Tom, how ya'll doin'?"

"Listen, that King Air a couple of hours ago..."

"Yeah, nice people."

"Listen-up! How many were there of those *nice people*?"

"Why there were three, Tom. Two women and one man."

"Did one get on there, waiting for them to arrive?"

"Well, no, they all arrived together, y'know, after seeing you, and I..." Billy Joe found himself talking to a dead phone.

The plane had departed almost four hours ago and it was now almost daybreak. While the plane was not in the registry list he had, it could be a newly registered one, and so he needed up-to-date information. Quickly checking with air traffic flight data, he knew the aircraft had filed a flight plan to Dallas before departure. With a sigh, he pushed the 'send' button on the fax machine and his request for an ownership search of King Air November Zulu Poppa Echo went out over the line to the Federal Aviation Agency.

The effect of the ownership search of the King Air entering the United States in Brownsville, Texas had a profound result. It is usually impossible to have an aircraft serial number registered in two countries simultaneously and the U.S. registry showed an anomaly. The subsequent inquiry as to the identity of the passengers was what really tore things loose. Tom McKeness was rousted from his bed by two FBI agents in the early afternoon. Flight records showed the aircraft in question had filed to Dallas but requested to be re-cleared to Pittsburgh en route, contrary to the destination given to McKeness. After that, the King Air had further requested Teterboro, New Jersey as a final destination. Since air traffic controllers are accustomed to such in-flight changes, the aircraft was re-cleared to the requested destinations without question. It was a clever ploy of the pilot to cover her intentions so authorities would focus on the wrong destination.

Confirming the identity of two of the people onboard, plus one illegal entrant, McKeness was then told the rest of the matter was none of his business, so quit asking. Five minutes after the Federal Agents left, his regional supervisor was on the phone, reaming him out because Washington was on *his* tail. McKeness responded that without his perceptiveness, nobody would know and besides, there was no obvious reason to detain neither the aircraft nor its passengers. Briefly cursing all spineless senior managers in the government, he rolled over and went back to sleep.

1000 hrs. Tuesday, July 17th 1990. New Jersey.

El-Cetti boarded the ferry at Sand Hook Bay Marina. He had seen the television news relating to the double homicide and the grainy picture of himself. Arranging to be chauffeured to the check-in area by a Mercedes limousine was, he thought, a stroke of genius. The uniformed police, strolling with anonymous conspicuity on the outside walk, were looking for a suspect of obviously bad appearance. Dismounting from the Mercedes, his smartly suited attire and nonchalant Spanish greeting to the Hispanic cop on the sidewalk had blown him right by their surveillance. As the boat cast off and powered up, he looked back, sneering at their pathetic efforts. Americans were so stupid.

Trailing its long wake, the sleek powerboat surged towards the indomitable skyline of Manhattan. The skyscrapers, dominated by the World Trade Center, loomed higher as the craft sped across the water at almost thirty-five knots. El-Cetti thought the buildings looked like the gigantic fangs of a monster, waiting to take him into its maw. He thought it a good analogy, since these teeth had devoured the poor of the world for generations. He thought how he had now come to wreak vengeance upon this monster, prostrate it and destroy it as it swallowed the contents of his mission.

The sky was blue, the wind only light. The trip took forty minutes and passing Staten Island and the Statue of Liberty; where a photographer would have seen a positive image, el-Cetti saw only death. After passing Brooklyn to starboard, and as the boat grew closer to the dock, his sense of outrage at this ostentatious display of casual wealth and power offended him more.

People in his experience died for less than the ferry fare he had just paid. They never knew that somewhere in this unequal world, it was the inalienable right of the average person to make this journey. He saw, in his mind's eye, the vision of his childhood friend, Ishmail, writhing on a Jerusalem street, victim of his own futile suicide bomb. He again saw the lifeblood gushing out, discharged worthlessly upon the arid dirt of the street. It was time for repayment!

Walking off the ferry, el-Cetti fastidiously avoided bodily contact with those around him. It picked him out from the usual jostling from such a crowd and the small anomaly drew a police officer's eye. He saw the brief stare and felt a trickle of cold sweat down his spine. He hated Americans! He wanted to pull out his gun and shoot them, one by one, gazing into their eyes as they died. But today, In'ch Allah, he would pay them dearly! Squaring his shoulders, he stepped forward resolutely.

The brown van he sought was fifty yards up the ramp from the Ferry terminal, the parking meter paid up for another half an hour. Using the key he had been given, he entered the vehicle. Quickly he leaned forward and looked back at the cop. The man was facing the other way. A cell phone lay on the passenger seat, as promised. Crouching over, he struggled into the coveralls provided. In seconds, he became a service technician. He reminded himself that by discarding them, he would become a well-dressed Wall Street trader again. Firing up the van, he drove away, headed for Wall Street. Only a block on, the cell phone rang.

"Drive to location five," the voice was precise and Arabic. To be so swift, the caller must have been watching el-Cetti walking from the ferry. So, now he knew that el-Saeed still watched. Well, so be it! In'ch Allah.

Ignoring the insolent car horns, el-Cetti drove carefully to the address he had been given. It was one of five possible sites for the gas discharge and he had been careful to study all of their locations on street maps the night before, memorizing the routing to each.

After taking a ticket at the barrier, el-Cetti drove the van up to the seventh floor of the chosen parking lot. There he found a green Chevy parked between two panel trucks. Climbing out of the van, he found the Chevy unlocked and the key in the ignition. Grunting with satisfaction, he backed the car out of the parking space. Contrary to the posted signs, el-Cetti then carefully backed his van into the space, leaving enough room behind to open the rear doors. On each side, he was now flanked by the two panel trucks, giving him complete privacy. So far, the plan was working. Sliding into the back of the van, he opened his briefcase first, retrieving a small machine gun. Nestled in a cardboard box under some rags, the deadly cylinder lay snug and ready for action.

In the back of the van, strapped down, a large gas cylinder was hooked up to a series of pipes and a manifold. A round steel tank with a screw-off lid was attached to the apparatus. Removing the finger-tight lid, he looked inside and grunted satisfaction when he saw it held the required ten gallons of water.

His next job was to unscrew the gas cylinder lid. He had been told the crystals contained should be tipped into the tank and dissolved. The contents of the tank would then be atomized and propelled by the big cylinder of gas, float on the air currents to the intakes of the air conditioning units, most of which were situated on the lower floors of the towering skyscrapers.

For a moment, he contemplated the act he was about to perform. He felt that the eyes of Allah were upon him, that he was about to play an important part in Holy Jihad. He had donned five pairs of under shorts to ensure his manhood was protected into Paradise. He wanted to be fully intact for the houris who awaited him there. Still, with a shudder, he realized he had assumed all along that the gas killed by ingestion. Perhaps it was a nerve gas, which would kill on skin contact? He shrugged. Allah would provide!

Opening a toolbox, he took a pair of plumber's pumps to the two wings welded to the threaded top. It was very tight. His injured hand hindered his efforts and he cursed the black whore who had bitten him. The pain was beginning to drive him over the edge. The hand was puffy and obviously infected. Red lines traced his veins as the poison crept up his arm. Still, he could not visit a doctor for treatment, as the bite was so obviously human that the police would probably be notified. Once this was over, if he survived by some miracle, once he had completed his holy task, maybe then he could risk it. His state of mind did not allow him to recognize the contradiction between seeking death and seeking healing.

Holding the cylinder between his knees, it took some effort to eventually move the lid. Removing it, he set it aside and inverting the container, shook about a kilo of small gray crystals into the water tank. His skin crawled, and with unseemly haste, he grabbed the top and reattached it before any of the hideous contents could escape. He flicked a switch and an electrical heater came on, hitched to the van's battery. It would bring the brew to the best temperature for solubility. A small motor began to churn the mix, stirring the contents to life.

After about three minutes, a thermostat triggered a small light, indicating readiness for distribution. Carefully, he opened the cock on the big compressed air propellant cylinder and a hissing noise came from the distribution line. This would suck the mixture into the gas stream, atomize it, and send it through the nozzle. Next he had to open the cock, which would gravity-feed the solution he had brewed into the distribution manifold.

His heart raced now, terror suffusing his limbs at the thought of the mass deaths he held in his hands. Getting out of the rear of the van, he took the distribution hose and nozzle and strung them over the parapet of the parking lot wall so the mix would be sent out. Reaching into the van bed, he tried to turn on the cock but could not quite reach it. He leaned further, and off balance, got the lever half turned before he toppled. Instinctively, he reached out with his injured hand, catching the corner of the welded frame of the apparatus. He cried out with the pain and fell, tumbling over the rear bumper onto the parking lot floor.

Something tangled in his legs just before he fell back, banging his head on the concrete wall. For a moment, he was stunned, despite the agony screaming from his hand and then he heard a sound that made his skin crawl with horror. Barely inches from his face, the manifold nozzle hissed and sprayed fine moisture straight at him. He had gotten caught up in it when he fell and it had flipped back into the parking stall. Terrified beyond belief, he whimpered at the sight, the fresh moisture on his skin telling him the horror was real. Suddenly galvanized, he seized the hose and flung it over the parapet.

Gasping for air, gasping for life itself, he stood up and hung over the wall, gazing at the New York skyline and waiting for the first hideous signs of death. The spray continued, a faint mist carried away on the breeze, fading as the tiny droplets disappeared, carrying death on the air across Manhattan.

His throat was too constricted to scream as the moments ticked by. His heart pounded so hard he thought it would leap out of his chest and he wondered if this was the first deadly symptom. He tried not to breathe, horrified at the same time that this may be some kind of nerve gas which could kill on contact, not ingestion.

After several minutes, an awareness of survival permeated through him. The gas must be no good. He had taken a good dosage and was still alive! A growing awareness of failure began to creep into him. Shedding the coveralls and grabbing his briefcase, el-Cetti left the van and headed down the sloping ramp. He decided not to drive away in the green Chevy, which had been left for him. Thirty feet behind him, parked on the inside row, a pair of eyes in a cream sedan watched him leave. El-Saeed had made no idle threat about observation.

El-Cetti reached critical mass. The gas had not killed him and a growing feeling of rage began. Probably, even certainly, it would not kill the New Yorkers. In the final play, he had been betrayed by el-Saeed and lied to about the lethal nature of the gas. The hedonistic Americans, the anti-faith had to die. Now, he too had to die! He trudged down the sloping ramp, past the Chevy. The briefcase, now clutched tightly to his chest contained the Remington mini machine gun, with six magazines of ammunition. He had been dishonoured too many times. Now, the will of Allah shall be done!

A door to the right was sign-posted as elevator egress to the street. He swung towards it, unconscious of the woman who closed on his left, headed the same way. He pushed the elevator call button, standing back again and staring at the lighted numbers above the elevator door, which showed its location. The woman stood back unobtrusively, an urban dweller reluctant to interact with another. While ignoring each other, they also ignored the pungent smell of urine in the elevator hallway, a relic of the homeless who sometimes dwelt there. A soft bell announced the arrival of the elevator car and the sliding doors opened.

They entered, the woman now studiously ignoring el-Cetti. Yet she could not because his lips quavered and soundlessly mouthed the Moslem prayer for the dead. Sweat had begun to bead on his forehead and a barely discernible quiver had suffused his frame. Attuned to possible rape and assault, her attention was inexorably drawn to him until she openly stared at his inattentive face. The briefcase was drawn tight to his chest and he seemed to be sinking into some kind of seizure.

"Are you all right?" the concern blurted from her fear-constricted throat. Yet it was a suicidal gesture, the sudden movement of helpless prey in the presence of a seeking predator. When the head swiveled and she saw the bottomless glaze of the dark eyes, she screamed, gnawing her knuckles.

El-Cetti took one hand from the briefcase and reached into his inner pocket. The huge flick knife blade snapped into place and in one quick movement, he plunged it into her neck. The scream stopped, replaced by a fluid gurgle as the woman watched her lifeblood spray up the wall of the elevator. She flopped to her knees and then toppled forward, propped in the corner like some desperate supplicant, praying in a church.

The elevator lurched as it hit the ground floor and the doors began to open. Reaching into the briefcase, el-Cetti grabbed the weapon within, stuck the spare magazines into his pocket and dropped the leather case to the floor. Striding out into the marbled foyer, he cocked the machine pistol and strode through the outer doors onto the street. Still he was not dead! What kind of poison was this that did not work? Catching sight of this bloodstained, gun-toting and wild-eyed apparition, people screamed and pushed out of his path. He strode above them like a colossus, like some avenging prophet, floating down the street in a haze of unreality.

Yet the screams had attracted attention. A New York beat cop, coming the other way, saw him marching along with the butt of the weapon on his hip, muzzle held aloft.

"Stop!" the cop fumbled for his weapon only as a secondary thought, unused to having to draw his pistol. Before he could free the thirty-two Special, five rounds took him through the upper body, tearing out his heart and lungs. He fell to the ground.

Now the sound of gunfire escalated the panic and people screamed and scattered instinctively. Pointing his gun down the sidewalk, el-Cetti sprayed the area with rounds, killing and wounding several people. Finally, he was bringing home to the Great Satan America the meaning of Jihad! Lacking targets, he ejected the magazine and slammed a new one into his firearm. Striding between two cars, he leveled the weapon at a taxicab in the first lane and killed all three occupants. Panic ensued as vehicles swerved and crunched into others to avoid his path. He walked down the street, alternatively spraying gunfire into every vehicle, left and right. Doors opened as people fled on foot, crouched down below window level.

Almost on instinct, he turned back and fired at a man who was standing up in a vehicle behind him, upper body out of the window, using a cell phone to report the carnage. The man flopped like a rag doll, hanging ridiculously out of the vehicle, pooling blood on the street. A group of people cowering behind the pillars of a ground floor restaurant shrieked and screamed as he opened fire on them, killing several. Another magazine went into the breach. A daring driver tried to run him over and paid with his life, blood smearing the inner windows in a spray.

Another cop down the street yelled frantically into his shoulder radio, summoning help. Blocks away, the rising wail of a police siren began to echo off the Manhattan streets. El-Cetti paid no heed. He was killing Americans in their own backyard. With each death, Paradise drew nearer.

Now the die was cast. Thirsting for the bullet which would end his torment, el-Cetti plugged in the next magazine and resumed firing, spraying around him with maniacal abandon. Store windows erupted into broken glass and errant rounds screamed off in ricochets as people sought cover. The kill ratio fell rapidly as the danger was acknowledged and victims became fewer. Screaming abuse, el-Cetti noted this and charged the sidewalk while loading the next magazine. Bystanders fell like mown wheat as he fired down the gap between cars and storefronts. A police officer, gun drawn, was coming the other way and loosed off two rounds, one catching the gunman in a foot.

Falling between two cars, el-Cetti screamed with pain and exultation. He erupted from cover with a fresh magazine and hosed rounds down the street. Ducking, the policeman fell into the gutter. Several cars away, an armed drug dealer fumbled for his automatic, terrified of going out in such a useless way, yet knowing he had to act. He fell out of the car on the opposite side to the gunman and draped over the hood, opened fire.

Ten blocks away, the members of a SWAT team sprang into their gear, erupting from the Precinct House like angry hornets from a nest. The radio net was swamped with calls but Captain Joseph Pirelli knew clearly where the action lay and ignored the spurious, panicky transmissions. Their van barreled down the wrong lanes, swerving across the street and accelerating into openings, the siren and flashing lights alerting most of the drivers. A delay at one intersection resulted in a chorus of curses and another ten deaths at el-Cetti's hands.

Finally pulling onto an open avenue, Pirelli could see the chaos. He had interpreted from the radio that he was dealing with one maniac walking down the street hosing ammunition at any target. When the van stopped at the end of the block, he pushed open his door and stood up on the sill, trying to see ahead. Vehicles were spread everywhere, some abandoned, most filled with cowering people. A rapid crackle of gunfire caught his attention and he saw a head bobbing through the stalled traffic. Quickly, he directed three of his men to the left of the street and three to the right. One other he sent up into a building as a spotter-sniper. There was a pause in the gunfire and he could see his men jogging resolutely down both sides of the street. He sent two more down the middle, giving himself the pincers movement. Another unit was moving in from the other side, so the madman could be isolated and trapped.

From a second-floor window, the sniper was already asking permission to open fire. Pirelli hesitated. Another burst of fire came from down the block and a couple of storefronts shattered into pieces on the sidewalk.

"Positive identity," the sniper was insistent in Pirelli's headset.

Now the team on the left called for permission to open fire. Instinctively, Pirelli knew there would be no takedown of this suspect and more people would die if he did not act. "Take him out, Green Team. Open fire! Sniper, you are cleared to fire."

Another burst of gunfire came echoing down between the buildings. El-Cetti ducked as a couple of vehicles beside him spewed glass shards and sprouted bullet holes. Spent rounds pinged off a car behind him. Moments later, a high powered round from the sniper took him through the upper arm. He screamed as the bone shattered and blood spurted across his face. Lurching and crouching low, he hopped awkwardly behind a truck and entered a fashion store. A dozen women screamed and scattered at the sight of him, hiding behind mannequins and counters.

He sprayed the place with gunfire, increasing the stampede. Putting the gun on a counter, he snatched at a mannequin, ripping off a scanty blouse. Using his teeth and injured hand, he fashioned a tourniquet above the wound and stuck the useless limb into his shirtfront. Pushing the weapon against the till, he released the spent magazine and fished awkwardly into his opposite pocket for the last one. Jamming it in, he lofted the weapon, finger curled around the trigger.

He contemplated taking a hostage but it seemed too much of an effort with only one arm and one leg. He flung his head back, foam spraying from his mouth. He felt faint from the pain of the wounds and wondered how much blood he had lost.

There must be a backdoor out of the place, but he did not want it. This was where he was to die! A shadow fell across the window and through the store-front display he saw uniformed men carrying arms. He growled like an animal and one-handed, pointed the gun at them, letting off half a magazine. He was rewarded by a scream of pain.

An arm threw an object into the store and a gas canister bounced and rolled under racks of clothes. A white smoke began to billow up, filling the space between the hangers. He caught a whiff and then a good lung full of the stuff and began to cough. He knew the direction from which they would come. Moving behind the counter, he laid the weapon flat, muzzle towards the door. He could hear the women behind him choking and screaming as he himself began to heave and cough. His body twisted and jerked as he tried to focus. Now! They would be coming now! He opened fire, moving the butt of the weapon left and right, setting up a spray of gunfire. There was another scream through the sound of rounds ricocheting off walls and fittings and then they fired back.

Three Heckler and Koch machine pistols with a combined firepower of eighteen hundred rounds per minute were directed at him and it was like the wooden counter was not there. Twenty rounds found their mark, along with deadly shards of wood driven out of the counter. Because they mostly hit him below the waist, he did not die instantly but, cut almost in half, he slumped backwards to the floor, driven by the impact. He stared up at bloody chunks of meat sliding down some dresses above him and realized they were part of him. The world began to blacken and he felt a great cold hand clutch at him. It was not how he had imagined the touch of his God. He was dead, gone to Paradise, before two police officers simultaneously covered him with their guns.

In the aftermath of the carnage, rescue teams summoned to the scene worked steadily to remove the wounded before tending to the dead. The ubiquitous television teams were everywhere, trying to film as much gore as they could while interviewing witnesses and bringing death into the homes of the nation in real time.

1145 hrs. Tuesday, 17th July 1990.
Eee-Zee-Park Parking Lot, Manhattan, New York City.

Achmed Bin Hassan had been living in the United States for six months. He had hated every minute of it, mostly because he had volunteered for Jihad but after being trained, had been sent to this den of sin and thieves and left to rot amongst them. He refused to acknowledge that he had freely enjoyed the bars, the freedom and the ability to get whatever his inner self had lusted after. He only acknowledged the torment of inactivity.

Now, he had been given a job, but it was a routine, second-rate task, with no glory to Allah attached to it. Driving from Philadelphia in a rental car, he had made rendezvous with two panel trucks, following them to one of the upper parking levels of this building. There, per the plan, they found a roped-off area with construction signs. Removing the signs, they had parked the two panel trucks with his rental car between them to preserve the parking stall. Leaving the key in the ignition, door unlocked, he and the two other drivers had walked to this cream sedan, a little further down the ramp. Giving him the key, the van drivers had left him to his vigil. He fretted at the triviality of his task, so mundane for a true soldier of Allah.

He was briefed that another man would arrive in a smaller van and after removing his rental car, park in the preserved stall. After a short while, the man would leave, taking the rental car and leaving the van behind. Bin Hassan had been given a cell phone with which to report these events, plus anything unusual.

His instructions were strictly to observe the van driver and report by phone when he left the car park. He was not to leave his vehicle under any circumstances, nor talk to the other man. A half hour after the van driver left, he was to drive out of the car park and when two blocks away, not before, place another phone call to a number written on the back of a business card. It was all very mysterious and frustrating that he was not allowed to be in on the plan.

After hours of sitting, his patience had worn thin. His coffee was all gone and he had to resort to urinating in a paper cup, the smell offending him. Everything had gone according to plan until the departing van driver had not taken the rental vehicle with him. This perturbed Bin Hassan who, despite his zeal, was intimidated by what he was doing. Twice he had opened the car door to go and check out what was happening at the van, even got a foot as far as the concrete before he chickened out, afraid of his supervisors.

Unknown to Bin Hassan, the second phone number was a trigger for two bombs, one either side of the van. Each of the panel trucks was lined with dynamite along the side nearest the van. The opposite side was lined with sandbags to ensure the blast from each truck was directed inwards, to vaporize the van when the devices were triggered.

He had watched el-Cetti arrive, dutifully remaining where he was and then phoning to report his departure, omitting the irregularity out of fear. When the faint sounds of gunfire came from the street, Bin Hassen began to become really concerned. As the intensity grew, he nervously consulted his watch. It was only ten minutes since the van driver had left the parking lot. As the number of emergency sirens grew in the streets, he began to panic. Something was wrong, and he did not want to get caught. It took another minute for him to lose his nerve.

Starting the car, he drove out of the space and down the ramp. The parking attendant scrutinized his ticket for an age while two police cruisers roared by, lights and sirens working overtime. "Sure is something going on down the block." In the name of the Prophet! Now the stupid bastard wants to make conversation! Bin Hassan was getting more nervous by the minute. "Fifteen dollars."

"Keep the change," Bin Hassan handed over a twenty and pulled away, cursing himself because now the man would remember him. Who gives five-dollar tips to a kiosk attendant on a fifteen-dollar charge?

A cop stepped out in front of him holding up a palm and Bin Hassan almost voided himself. Before he could react, the officer suddenly beckoned with his other arm, directing him to the left. It was the opposite direction from his instructions but he could see the street was blocked anyway. Traffic was dense and it looked clearer in the direction the officer was waving.

He pulled out, making slow but sure progress through an undetectable mist of vapor particles coming from the building behind him. Sweating, he turned up the fresh air fan, selected to *external.* His instructions now told him to drive to Philadelphia so soon he would be with his family there! In'ch Allah!

Two blocks on, he pulled out the cell phone and dialed the number he had been given. Seconds later, a colossal explosion came from behind. All he could see in the rear view mirror was a cloud of dust and smoke emerging from high on the building he had left. He knew instantly that he had to be the cause of it and it raised his panic to a new level.

As planned, the double explosion almost totally obliterated the van and the equipment it contained, masking its purpose. The blast then went upward, taking out a huge area of the floor above, causing it to jolt upwards and then collapse, tipping thirty vehicles into the void beneath. Half of them slid out into the street, falling seven stories into streets choked with vehicles and panicked people. More vehicles were projected into space by the force, falling into three separate streets. A major fire erupted from spilled gasoline and two floors were engulfed in no time. The building began to collapse. Other fires started in the street and dozens of people were killed or maimed by falling debris.

Tuning in to a radio station to learn more, Bin Hassan still felt panicky but a growing sense of pride grew in his chest as he realised the vital part he had played in striking so hard at America. The sense of accomplishment grew as the frenzy of the reporting exaggerated the situation.

Picking his way through Lower Manhattan, Bin Hassan took the Brooklyn-Battery Tunnel. It took a while due to the mayhem happening on Long Island, but he soon picked up Highway Two Seventy-eight. By the time he was paying his toll at the Verrazano Bridge, the radio was filled with on-site reporting about the destruction caused by the explosion and the crazed gunman only blocks away. Stories of terrorists were growing and he heaved a sigh of relief as he crossed the bridge. Only a few hours on the I-Ninety-five, and he would be home in Philadelphia, safe with his family.

Halfway home, he felt tightness in his chest. Afraid of a heart attack because of the strain, he paused at an off-highway drive-through to buy a coffee and rest for a few minutes. Back on the freeway, he felt slightly better, but by the time he got home, felt much worse.

1200 hrs. Tuesday, 17th July 1990.
Flamingo Hotel, Jersey City, New Jersey.

The Three Musketeers had taken two taxis and put some distance between themselves and the airport at Teterboro, knowing the authorities might track them down. The hotel was risky, but they were checked in under assumed names and hiding in a vast metropolitan area. It was the best they could do for now.

At the hotel, they had watched the television coverage of the parking lot explosion and the mad shooting spree on the street below. They subscribed to the popular belief that the shootings were the work of a drugged junkie.

"Well, if we don't find Wesler soon, we may wind up being victims here too, once the virus is released," Mandy shuddered.

"Astrid, did you not say that crazy old Nazi showed you a hotel reservation for Wesler?" Raymond asked.

"Yes, but I was drugged and it was only a glimpse. It is a miracle I remembered what state it was in."

"Maybe you should go through the *Yellow Pages* and see if you recognize a hotel name."

"That's a long shot, and we do not have a state-wide book."

"I just thought it may be a chain," he responded.

"Hmm. Even if we found the hotel, he is probably under an assumed name, so we'd have to stake the place out and hope to see him," Mandy looked at them both.

"Maybe he is using one of the aliases we found on the plane," Astrid was hopeful.

"Possible, but not likely," Raymond shook his head.

"We could flash the desk clerks one of the passports with his picture."

"And have the police on our ass in an hour. I don't think so, Astrid," Raymond again shook his head.

"It's too bad we cannot go to the police," Mandy shook her head too.

"Yeah, here we are, illegal entries, armed, dangerous, and hunted by half a dozen governments because of several hundred million in gold and secrets which will wreck modern history. By the time we get out from under explaining all of that, it will be the next century. Then, we still have to persuade them this deadly virus threat is believable. We need action now!" Raymond was trying to be realistic.

Astrid bristled. "For sure, if we do talk to *any* of them, we'd be lucky to survive."

"Right now, we only have our own story to tell. Without hard evidence, the police are unlikely to launch a major manhunt on those grounds alone. By the time they come around to our line of thinking, it will all be over," Mandy was backing Astrid.

Raymond homed in on the bottom line. "We need Wesler, singing like a canary, to spark any kind of interest."

"Our only hope then is to find Wesler," Mandy nodded.

Raymond spread his arms. "Where do we find him?"

Astrid became intense. "That's easy, make *him* find *us*!"

"Huh?"

"It's easy, we send him a message so he can find us and kill us."

"Astrid, have you gone crazy? I don't like that idea!"

"Yeah, but because *we* send the message, we can ambush him when he comes!"

Raymond and Mandy regarded Astrid with renewed respect. "Brilliant!"

After further discussion, they came to the conclusion that their only hope was indeed to find Wesler and he must be flushed out. They needed to tell him that they had escaped and used the King Air. They decided to make out like El Jefe had been forced to flee the hacienda by other means. As a means of authentication, to provide confusion and galvanize Wesler, they inserted the threat of treachery, blaming Karl-Heinz.

Astrid typed the message in German and it wound up reading: *Prisoners escaped. Hacienda attacked. I am in transit. Karl-Heinz betrayed us. Prisoners have information to destroy your mission. You are instructed to eliminate them immediately. Room 216, Flamingo Hotel, Jersey City, NJ. Do not make contact for twenty-four hours.* The last comment they added in case any recent communication would negate the message in any way. Wesler had to think this situation just came up and El Jefe was on the run for a while, out of touch. They recognized that if he were able to contact the old man after receiving their fake message, he would know it was bogus and then the trap they were setting would backfire on them.

With one last wary look at the other two, Mandy hit the *send* command on the keyboard.

"I wonder how often he checks for messages?"

"I can't think it will be more than twenty-four hours before he comes. If he comes. We need to sleep in shifts, with one person outside on guard duty," Raymond adopted a military style.

"What if he sends someone else?" Astrid always had counter-thoughts and both Raymond and Mandy gave her a sharp look.

"You mean like a contract killer?" Mandy now looked to Raymond, seeking an answer.

"Well, unless he is already set up with associates here, I don't see how he can arrange such a thing at short notice. We just have to assume it will be him."

"If it is someone else, maybe we can force them to lead us to Wesler."

They all exchanged glances of uncertainty.

0240 hrs. Wednesday, 18th July 1990.
Flamingo Hotel, Jersey City, New Jersey.

Dark clouds crept like cloaks across the full silver moon. The extensive lawns of the hotel were alternately darkly shadowed and then stark as the lunar light shone down. The dark patches of trees and shrubs stayed constant in the changing illumination as Astrid crouched beside the trunk of a tree, sheltered from view by shrubs. She was the sentry, armed with a pistol.

The illumination of the lower and upper walkways of the hotel endured, a warm yellow glow, tastefully subdued. As Raymond had laid it out for her, there was only one way to approach their room and that was along the upper balcony. The door numbers were too small to read without strong night glasses, so the rational thought was that the assailant would walk to the door before performing any attempt to kill them. He would need to identify the exact room. The actual killing could be done through the window, either with an automatic weapon for maximum effect, or an explosive device such as a hand grenade. Whether he would break through the door and gun them all down was open to question but would probably attract unwelcome attention. A silenced weapon was almost a guarantee.

The only other factor would be how the killer would approach. A stealthy approach to ensure egress and escape without being seen was an obvious tactic, but sometimes blatant openness would cause the assailant to blend in with the scenery. A person passing another guest carrying a suitcase, or a pizza delivery boy with a package, would attract no untoward attention.

Thus, Wesler could come either way. If he came at all.

Despite the doubt and uncertainty, Astrid had her money laid on the surreptitious approach and had already cocked her weapon, safety off, to avoid alerting him. She glanced at her watch. It was two-forty in the morning and she was beginning to feel the fatigue. Still, the lateness of the hour more or less guaranteed the surreptitious approach, so she kept her guard.

Off to her right, she suddenly heard a vehicle approach. It slowed and began to crawl to a stop. It purred for a moment, the faint light of headlights filtering through the trees. Moments later, calm and dark were restored as it was switched off. The faint sound of a door being carefully closed came to her ears. Most people closed car doors firmly. Only people who do not want to be heard do it so quietly. She keyed the mike on the walkie-talkie they had bought at an electronics store earlier in the day.

"I think we have company."

"Okay. Be careful."

Astrid almost cried out as the silhouette of a man suddenly appeared beside a tree only twenty feet away. His dark outline showed clearly in front of the hotel lights. He stood for a moment, surveying the scene before him and then, reaching under his raincoat produced what could only be a machine gun. Without taking his eyes off the hotel, he reached into a pocket and screwed a silencer onto the end of the weapon. Astrid clicked her mike twice, paused, clicked once, and then clicked once again. A single click came back to her. Raymond had acknowledged that he now knew that there was a confirmed attack, one person, and the first option, namely a firearm, was evident.

Astrid shrank back as the man glanced her way, fearful he had heard the tiny speaker against her ear. But he was only checking his surroundings. His head swiveled left and right, scanning the area. Satisfied, he stepped forward unhurriedly across the lawn. The short grass made no sound under his feet and no challenge rang out from nightly strollers. He gained the concrete walk around the hotel building perimeter and followed it to the staircase. The first flight went into a well against the building before turning outwards to the upper balcony. While he was ascending, Astrid sprinted to her right and curved back to the left to gain his trail. By the time she leaned up against the building, she could see his shoes steadily ascending the second flight through the gaps between the open steps.

When he turned at the top, she glided up the first flight. Gun held ready before her, she paused and clicked the radio twice more. A return click came back.

Keeping to the right side, avoiding squeaky treads and covering herself against the wall, she flitted to the top and placed her back to the wall. Around the corner, she heard the unmistakable click of a weapon being cocked. Having made this irrevocable step, the attacker would now, logically, look over his shoulder to ensure he was in the clear before making his move. She counted 'one, two, three', slowly and deliberately, and then stepped out, weapon leveled. She clicked the transmitter one more time and aimed at the man about twenty-five feet away, who was focussed intently on the hotel room door.

"Hande hoch, mein Herr!"

The man spun, startled, and at the same time, Raymond threw open the room door, a flood of light blinding the attacker. He saw only a large caliber pistol pointing at him at close range while his arms, already trying to point his weapon towards the woman's voice behind him had stopped halfway. He had no instantaneous target.

"One slip and you are dead! Put down your weapon!"

A second of time passed, as long as eternity, while three minds calculated the odds. Slowly, the shoulders of the man drooped, almost imperceptibly.

"Ve-ry steady!" Raymond sensed the man's resolve and cancelled it by raising the muzzle of his gun towards the man's head.

The intruder's right hand left the trigger and moved out sideways from his body. His left, clutching the forward handgrip, began to lower the weapon to the ground. He crouched slightly to accommodate the movement and the next second felt a gun muzzle in the side of his neck. The woman behind him had come up like a wraith and had him at her mercy.

"Good! Now you will kindly crawl on hands and knees into the room and once there, keep your head to the floor and put your hands behind your head!"

Astrid slipped into the room, gun trained on the man on the floor. Behind her, she felt Mandy closing the door. She glanced at Raymond, deferring to his leadership for the next move while she felt the adrenaline subsiding in her veins.

The man was dressed in dark clothing, his face buried in the carpet due to his uncomfortable position. Raymond nodded to Mandy who slipped a loop of rope over the toe of the man's shoes and then tightened it around both of his ankles. Knotting it securely, she stepped back.

"Hands behind your back!" Raymond gave the order and after a moment's hesitation, the man complied.

Mandy stepped forward with another loop of rope to secure his wrists. Just before she got there, the muzzle of a pistol was pushed into the man's lower back. His body tensed and then relaxed. With a gun in his back and Raymond covering him from six feet away, he was helpless and the compliance in his stance showed immediately.

In moments, he was trussed and secured. With a push of his foot, Raymond rolled the man onto his side. "Ah! Herr Wesler! *Welkommen* to New Jersey!"

Wesler's eyes swept the room, taking in all three of them with contempt and defiance. "You do not understand the trouble you are in! Others are on their way here!"

"Sure, and you just could not wait for them to arrive!" Mandy poked him with a toe.

"The reason we brought you here was to find out exactly what the plan is, so start talking," Astrid crouched down in front of him and waved the pistol in a careless gesture.

Wesler merely snorted derision and remained silent. His mind was whirling as to how he could escape. The plan was going forward even if he was taken out of the picture, so there was nothing these idiots could do to stop it. His comfort level was shredded by the next remark.

"That old bastard in Paraguay told me the whole story. We know that you are going to release some kind of poisonous gas in Manhattan. Your only chance of not going to the electric chair for this is to help us stop it now."

Wesler grinned at Astrid. "Then, if you know all that, go ahead and stop it yourself."

Astrid pushed the pistol between Wesler's eyes and pressed. He flinched at the threat, but kept his silence.

"Who else is involved? You can't be doing this alone," Raymond appealed to the man.

"I cannot stop the plan."

"So, there *are* others involved! Where is the gas going to be released, and how?"

"I cannot help you." Feeling on firmer ground, Wesler began to talk, confident they could get no more out of him.

"Gag him."

Standing ready with the roll of duct tape, Mandy tore off a length and wrapped it around Wesler's head, covering his mouth. They searched his pockets for other weapons or information, but found nothing, only a cheap wallet with some fake identity and a hundred dollars in bills. They adjourned to the bathroom, out of Wesler's hearing, with Raymond watching him from the door.

"So, what now? He doesn't want to tell us anything. If we hand him over to the police, we'll be arrested for kidnapping. Persuading them to interrogate him won't work," Raymond was in a quandary.

"Maybe we have to torture him," Astrid the action woman.

Raymond was scathing. "Right! Nobody in the hotel will hear his screams! The old cigarette-butt burns are out because none of us smoke."

"Yes, but this information is vital. Thousands of people are going to die!"

"Give me the plastic bag liner out of the waste can." Grimly, Raymond took the bag and walked back to Wesler. The man's eyes followed him, a slow dawning of the intent crossing his face.

"You can nod your head when you are ready to talk." Quickly, Raymond pulled the plastic over Wesler's head and pulled it tight around his neck. Helpless, the man drew in a huge breath, borne of fear. The bag collapsed like a pricked balloon, clinging to the contours of his face. For a minute, there was no movement and then the body grew more and more rigid. After two minutes, a puff of air inflated the bag partially and the body began to struggle.

Raymond removed the bag. "Ready to talk?"

There was no response other than heavy breathing and Raymond quickly applied the bag again. This time, after only a minute, there came helpless growling for help behind the gag. The head wagged and the bag was removed. Above the gag, Wesler's face was scarlet.

"Talk!" Raymond ripped off the duct tape.

The eyes bulged as the body gasped for air and the head turned in a negative gesture. Thrashing, helpless against his bonds, Wesler panted for oxygen.

Without bothering with the gag, Raymond slipped the bag back over the head. Brutally, he punched Wesler in the midriff, causing to him to expel air. The thrashing increased, accompanied by the horrible sound of lungs in spasm.

"Raymond, stop! You are going to kill him."

"How else?"

"His carbon dioxide level is down; pretty soon he will not be able to breathe, even if we let him."

With a look of disgust, Raymond pulled the plastic off Wesler's head. Wheezing, with paroxysms of breaths, the man struggled for air. His body shuddered and shook and beneath his buttocks, a spreading wet stain appeared. His face was almost purple and drool spilled from his mouth.

"Gag him again."

This time with more difficulty, Mandy wound more duct tape around Wesler's head. A high-pitched wheezing filled the room as his nostrils funneled air to his tortured lungs.

"What now?"

"You want to go buy some cigarettes?"

The two women looked at Raymond helplessly. None of them were truly up for this. They retreated to the bathroom again to confer.

"We have to call someone and ask for help," Mandy was insistent. "We cannot do this alone and the price of failure is too high."

Raymond and Astrid looked at each other and then nodded, glumly. There appeared to be no way out.

"So, who do we call?" Astrid asked.

Raymond summarized. "I get the impression that the British, the Russians, the Americans, have too much to hide. The Nazi gold is linked to too many things. There were too many cover-ups. Nazi medical research into human survivability aspects, their rocket program and other advanced weapons were too big a temptation for both the Allies and the Russian bloc to ignore. They all provided cover and deception for ex-Nazi scientists to further their individual ends. I say we trust the Israelis. They were not involved in that process and are only concerned with their survival. Their motives, I believe, are the most trustworthy from our standpoint."

"You have the Mossad's main phone line?" Mandy was sarcastic.

"Don't be facetious!"

"Sorry, but I think you know what I mean."

"Yeah, we can also be betrayed by any functionary of any of the bloody organizations!" Astrid chipped in.

"Uh-hu."

"Who stands to lose if this plan goes through?" Mandy wondered.

"The poor bastards on Wall Street."

"Yes, but they are mainly Jews, right? So therefore, again, the Israelis are our best bet," Raymond had made his choice.

"It is time to call Rolf," Astrid looked at them both. "We are running out of options, time, money and equipment. Either the legal authorities or one of the other parties hunting for us are only a step away. In their hands, we are without hope. The stakes are too high for us to expect to survive. To thwart the plan, we need outside help. Rolf is the only one we can turn to who has the resources to get us away to a safe place. We have done all we can here. From a safe place, we can expose the whole plan, maybe to the news media, and turn Wesler over to the FBI, or somebody."

Raymond regarded her gloomily. "I think you are right, we have gone as far as we can. Yes, Mandy?"

"Do you think it's likely he will help? Remember the news flash we saw about his last facility we visited? Our *friends* were not too far behind us there, either."

Raymond shook his head. "Well, we are screwed eventually, either way. I suggest we call Rolf and get what help we can. The net is closing in and without *somebody's* help it is only a matter of time before somebody out there gets their hands on us. Frankly, I have no idea whom I would prefer; they all seem to want us dead!"

"Pay phone?"

"Pay phone."

Conscious of it being the middle of the night, Astrid checked she had a telephone calling card with her, and summoned a taxi. Riding a few blocks away, she told the driver to stop at a twenty-four hour convenience store. Telling the driver to wait, she went to an outside phone booth and using the calling card, was through to Germany in a minute. While she talked, the driver eyed her speculatively. Doubtless, she was on the line to her pimp, getting the address of the next John. She was not dressed the part, but hey, if she was good, who cared what she looked like?

Conscious of the security angle, Astrid was as vague and innocuous as she could be. To Rolf's immediately voiced concern for her whereabouts and safety, she replied that she had been away for a few days visiting an old school friend. There was a long pause at the other end and then she realized he had caught on to the need for circumspection regarding the call. Carefully she outlined their location and asked to be picked up with her three friends for lunch.

"I will have a limousine there to pick you up at eleven in the morning. Gerd will arrange everything. I will travel immediately."

Eyes closed in silent thanks, Astrid hung up the telephone and bowed her head. Thinking she needed to justify her nocturnal trip, she went into the convenience store long enough to appear to buy something for her pocket and then got back in the cab.

"Tampons."

Reasonably tipped, the driver left her back at the hotel, shaking his head.

"Eleven this morning. He is sending a limousine and is getting on a flight right away," Astrid threw her coat on the bed.

"How long will that take?" Mandy asked.

"Eleven hours minimum if he can get a seat on a regular scheduled flight. Seven hours if he can get on a Concorde out of Paris or London," Raymond said.

"No. I know him. He will charter a private jet, especially if he is bringing help with him. Probably at least eight hours before the flight lands."

"Then what?" Mandy held little hope.

"Hopefully, the limo driver will take us to a safe place. He mentioned Gerd, one of his people here in New York. That I do not like, he is a man whom I have a poor feeling for."

"Very well." Raymond shrugged off that minor concern. "Now we only have to figure out how to get Wesler out of the room and into the vehicle."

All three of them turned to regard the object of their dilemma. They felt a sense of failure, yet not complete defeat in the fight. The relief of help being on the way was enormous.

0800 hrs. Wednesday, 18th July 1990.
Lubyanka. Headquarters, Committee for State Security,
Moscow, Russia.

The greatest weakness of every secret organization is the fear of penetration and betrayal. The usurping of their intent and reversal to an enemy's gain is their worst nightmare. Information is paramount. The only safeguard is security measures. And security measures, the *need-to-know* and the intrigue, the compartmentalizing of knowledge and control do not negate a continued fear of internal corruption. The result is a paranoid entity that will go to any length to preserve itself, even to turning on its own masters. When a 'mole' penetrates to the very heart of such an organization, the result is catastrophic and complete. The very structure is bent to the will of the enemy, from within.

Staring out of his darkening window at the statue of Felix Dzerzhinsky, General Kazimir Brokochenko smiled a wide smile at the information in his hand. The American National Security Agency, a secretive organization funded to the tune of billions of dollars annually, was working for *him*. As second-in-command of the KGB's First Chief Directorate for external intelligence, he had pulled off a major coup.

With *glasnost* sweeping the country, his future had been uncertain, but his part in this matter might well secure his place in new governments. He put the faxed paper on his desk, chuckling at the break he had been afforded. The Americans had procured for him the information he had sought so desperately. His ass was on the line and the spy he had in place had saved it for him.

Only moments before, he had briefed his deputy, ordering the dispatch of two *spetsnaz* paramilitary units to be sent to New York. Little did Brokochenko know that he in turn was penetrated and the data he had received was now being forwarded to yet another rival agency. The stakes were high and the players were emerging onto the field of conflict. Based on intelligence gathered from George Jenkins, a dozen commercial airline flights were soon bearing operatives of several nations towards New York.

A container had arrived on British Airways only the day before, shipped under diplomatic immunity to the British Embassy in Washington. Customs agents paid little attention to such shipments from America's staunchest ally and the shipment was released to a trucking company, which failed to complete the delivery to the nation's capital.

Travelling separately, several Britons arrived in Toronto and brandishing fake passports, crossed the border into the United States. They rendezvoused with the container at a predetermined warehouse and unpacked it, checking the weapons and ammunition it contained. The SAS, the Special Air Service, had arrived in New York City.

1045 hrs. Wednesday, 18th July 1990.
Flamingo Hotel, Jersey City, New Jersey.

Shortly before eleven, Astrid took up position in the hotel lobby. Mandy was out front, strolling on the sidewalk, acting as a back-up. Raymond had Wesler ready in the room, his legs untied. There was a back egress to a carport behind the hotel, just below the stairs, and they planned to get him into the limousine there.

Two minutes before the appointed time, Mandy was on the radio, announcing a limousine coming down the street. She moved down the street so she had a clear view of the walkway outside the room and could let Raymond know when it was clear.

Parking under the reception portico, the driver got out and opened the passenger door of the long vehicle. A heavy-set man with thinning grey hair and a craggy, pockmarked face stepped out and after glancing around the area, walked into the lobby.

"Frau Klemerer, gutten tag."

"Gerd," Astrid recognized the man and gave a small shudder, wishing Rolf had sent someone she was more comfortable with. Indicating her bags, she had him pick them up and they went outside. In the time it took for Gerd to give the bags to the driver at the rear of the vehicle, she was able to open the door and ascertain the vehicle was empty. She gave two clicks of the radio in her pocket. Faintly, she heard Mandy give Raymond the all clear.

"Where are your friends?" Gerd was getting into the side seat of the car, his weight shifting the suspension.

"Around the back. Please drive around the back." The driver nodded to Astrid and they pulled away.

"Right here." The vehicle stopped and Raymond appeared, propelling Wesler in front of him. "This man is in our custody. He is very dangerous and must be guarded carefully."

Gerd nodded, showing little surprise. Astrid shot him a curious look. They pulled away.

"Take a left and go back around the front of the hotel." Astrid keyed the mike of the radio and Mandy responded, assuring them the street was clear of suspicious traffic. Seconds later, the limousine stopped long enough to pick up the rather good-looking woman who had been strolling the street, and accelerated away.

"Where are we going?" Mandy was almost shaking with fear.

"We are going to a place in Westhampton. It is fairly private and you will be safe there." The man spoke with no accent. "My name is Gerd. Please, relax and try to feel comfortable. Mr. Klemerer has briefed me on the situation and Richard, who is our driver, and I are both armed for your protection. It will be a little over one hour to complete the trip. There is alcohol in the bar, if you would like a drink."

"What did Rolf tell you about us?" Astrid asked.

Gerd paused as if seeking a tactful reply. "Only that you have a *situation* and need a safe haven until he gets here."

"What time can we expect him?"

"Probably about four this afternoon. His flight will be arriving at

Westhampton Beach Airport. I believe they have Customs service there. He told me to tell you he will personally take charge of the situation."

"And what is our *situation*?" Raymond pitched in.

"I really do not know, sir. I am responsible for security for the company here in North America and I merely follow Mr. Klemerer's orders."

"Are we going to the old house?"

"Yes Ma'am."

"So Rolf did not sell it when we returned to Germany?"

"I believe not, Ma'am. It is company property."

"We had the King Air here while we stayed in the States. I got my American pilot licence and flew out of Westhampton lots of times," Astrid explained to Raymond, reflecting on better times.

Satisfied that security was being maintained, Raymond sat back, reaching for Mandy's hand.

The place they arrived at stood on a small estate, enclosed by ivy-covered stonework. An electrically operated gate opened after the driver announced them and they took a short curved driveway to the front door. The place was fronted with fieldstone and mellow-toned heavy timbered windows and doors, with leaded windowpanes. A balding man wearing a dark blue smock met them and ushered them inside. The floor was stone tile and a dark oak staircase wound up to the upper story, lined with oil paintings.

"Welcome." Hard deep-set black eyes scrutinized each one of them, almost robbing the greeting of sincerity. "My name is Josef. I have the honour of being instructed to attend to your every need." The accent was mid-European and the syntax slightly stilted and old-fashioned formal. The remaining black hair was sleeked back and tight to the man's scalp and his cadaverous features evoked images in Mandy's mind. She thought that, had he been taller, he could be Christopher Lee playing Dracula. But then, maybe it was just the castle-like surroundings sparking her imagination.

Gerd and Richard came in, each carrying a holdall.

"Let me show you to your rooms and then we can serve a light lunch...Shall we say in fifteen minutes?" Josef extended an arm towards the staircase to indicate the way. It was done with such a theatrical style that Mandy expected Peter Cushing, as Dr. Van Helsing, to run into the room, desperately trying to prevent them going to their eternal doom.

"We need this man locked up and guarded," Raymond indicated the hapless Wesler, looking the worse for wear.

"Yes sir, please bring him this way. We can lodge him in the cellar, there is a strong lock on the pantry door." The man gave no hint of curiosity regarding this unusual request.

Leading Raymond downstairs, Josef indicated the room. He searched an adjacent closet and produced a short length of chain and a padlock. Stringing the chain round Wesler's neck, they secured him to a stout iron pipe and locked the door. It never even occurred to Raymond to explain to this total stranger why they had the need to keep him prisoner. Nor did it occur to him why the stranger did not elicit an explanation.

The three rooms they were shown to proved comfortable, furnished with excellent taste and each with an en-suite bathroom. Astrid moved into her old bedroom but they congregated in Raymond's room, since Mandy had already moved in there.

"What do you think?" Raymond asked.

"Well, I guess we are safe for a little while. It is comforting that Rolf is coming; he is a take-charge kind of person. What about this Josef?"

"Good a-evening everybody. I would like to suck-a your neck!" Raymond gave his best Dracula impression.

"You think so too, eh?"

When they went back downstairs, the two bodyguards were missing, but Raymond thought he saw one of them patrolling the grounds. A chubby little woman with a garrulous New York accent fussed over a table loaded with pastries, cocktail sausages, sandwiches and chilled wines. Her name was Rosalie and she excitedly regaled them with details of her grandson's bar mitzvah which was happening next week.

She was eventually waved off by Josef and disappeared into the rear of the house after reassuring herself with them that beef stroganoff and chicken Kiev would be suitable for dinner after the master arrived.

The limousine had left for the airport and it was about four thirty when Rolf called to say he had arrived and would be with them in about fifteen minutes. They were sitting watching CNN. The media were still on about the nasty explosion the day before. Initially, they had focussed on a vehicle propane tank explosion but since several floors of the building had collapsed, the blast was now being described as a deliberate detonation. Dozens of people had been killed by debris falling into the streets below. The quest for an explanation was offset by images shot in the streets of the deranged gunman who, in the same locality, had killed another thirty-one people in a shooting frenzy.

The talking heads were having a field day; nothing like catastrophes to brighten up their day. One reporter avowed how the mayhem looked like a street in Jerusalem after a terrorist attack. Signing off the news item, the anchorwoman remarked casually that so far, the police were not linking the two events.

"On a different front, hospitals have been inundated with people reporting flu-like symptoms and for some, the effects have been deadly. Tom Barrett is on the scene...Tom."

The screen shifted focus to a young reporter, with a crowded hospital emergency room in the background. "Medical authorities," he stated, "were puzzled by this early outbreak of the flu and recommended that the young and elderly seek inoculations. We have reports of some deaths, but at this time they are unconfirmed."

At four-forty, there was a stirring in the house and Josef opened the front door to Rolf. He looked tired after the rushed trip and entered the house with two other men. He embraced Astrid briefly, and then turned to be introduced to Raymond and Mandy.

Raymond felt awkward meeting this man for the first time. After all, he had intimate knowledge of the most extreme kind of his wife and still, admittedly, harboured deep feelings for her. If Rolf knew anything, it was not manifest in his greeting, although Raymond saw him as a little cold.

He was tall and athletic, just as in his photographs, a long face with blue eyes topped by short-cropped hair the colour of a ripened wheat field. He had a commanding presence and Raymond could see why Astrid would be attracted to him, but the eyes were a little too icy. He thought he discerned a calculating look to them. Still, he had come to save them and that was all that mattered.

After shaking hands in turn with Mandy, Rolf introduced the other new arrivals. Tomas Halpern and Helmut Stein were introduced as management representatives in the United States who had come along to consult on how things could be managed. Raymond thought this comment a little strange, given that they were trying to hide from the authorities. However, he was used to the rather over-managed style of the Germans and shrugged it off.

A half hour later, they were sitting down to dinner. The table had been laid in an observatory type of room at the back of the house, with large windows overlooking a well-maintained lawn. The Three Musketeers were joined by Rolf, Tomas, Helmut and Gerd. Josef assisted Rosalie until he dismissed her for the day. Once she was gone, it was a signal to get down to business.

They told their story, having decided it was the only way to deal with Rolf. Raymond described how he had gone to Germany, the deaths that followed him and the removal of the gold and steel boxes from the frontier area. They told how they had been abducted to Paraguay and had escaped from El Jefe. Rolf seemed particularly interested in the remote ranchero and occasionally, Tomas and Helmut interjected questions. Astrid related what El Jefe had told her about a plan to release a poisonous gas in New York, and some undisclosed threat attached to it.

At the end of the story, Rolf sat back and gently swirled the brandy glass he held. His gaze was down into the amber liquor and he spoke softly. "And so. Where are the steel boxes and gold now?" he looked up then, eyes sweeping over all of them.

Raymond answered first. "Everything that we were able to keep is safely hidden."

"Very well, that is not the most pressing thing. We need to know what you have done to help the authorities to stop this supposed attack on New York."

"Well, precious little, actually. We are fugitives from about four of the major nations, plus these shadowy Nazi bastards. If we land in the hands of anybody, even the police, we will spend too much time explaining everything before they will take any action. We have precious little proof, especially without the steel box containing Nazi records in our hands."

"Hmm. You will have to tell me where that is. It may, as you say, be the means of convincing the authorities about your story. However, perhaps we should sleep on it and formulate a plan tomorrow."

Josef interrupted, indicating the television set, which stood in the corner, still tuned to the local news channel. A flashing emergency slogan was running across the bottom of the screen, demanding attention. The reporter they had seen earlier now stood outside the hospital entrance, a mask over his face. The man looked jittery. "We have just learned that there have indeed been deaths attributed to the influenza outbreak here. So far, medical authorities are advising it is only a few dozen, but First Channel News has learned in the last few minutes that medical facilities throughout New York are crowded with cases and there may be hundreds of deaths.

The source of this deadly disease and its means of transmission are as yet unknown, but, pending further information from the State Department of Health, we are urging viewers to avoid unnecessary contact with other people." At this point, conscious he had only just been in a room with dozens of sick people, the reporter could not help turning his head towards the building behind him.

As if to underline the man's words, two men appeared in the door behind him wearing bio-suits. They began to string plastic sheeting across doorways, while another two men erected a huge air extraction fan. Three security guards wearing surgical masks appeared, their obvious intent being crowd control.

The anchorwoman turned the scene over to a reporter in Philadelphia. There had been an outbreak there too. A family, Arabic by their names, had been stricken, the father dead and the others dangerously ill and in quarantine. Even as they watched, the news scrolling along the bottom of the screen showed a thousand people confirmed dead and another five thousand were being installed in hastily contrived isolation centres.

Suddenly, eyes turned from the television at a crash of crockery. White and nerveless, Astrid had dropped her wineglass onto her plate.

"Astrid?"

Tears flowed, her face framed by long hands pinned to her cheeks in shock. Her eyes were wide, horrified. Choking on the words, she told them. "The flu! The hospitals! Don't you see? It has started! It is not the flu, it is Agent Twenty-nine!"

"Oh, my God!"

Astrid turned to Rolf. "We must advise the authorities at once. They do not know what they are dealing with."

"If we talk to them, it will give away where you are. I have come all this way to protect you from the authorities, who you say want to kill you. Why would you surrender to them now?"

"But there must be a way! People are dying already and thousands more will contract the disease. We know how this agent works, telling the authorities will assist them in dealing with it!"

"We need to talk to this Mr. Wesler first. We do not know what the overall plan is," Rolf was galvanized into action, taking charge, "Josef! Where is he?"

"In the basement, sir."

"I'll come with you," Raymond started up.

"No, I think it is better that Gerd and I question him. Please stay here and look after the ladies. Helmut, Tomas! See what information you can find out about what is happening in New York." He glanced at each of them in turn. "Please, stay here in the dining room and no phone calls to anyone about this until I return." A hard glance passed between him and Helmut. Quickly, Rolf left the room with Gerd and Josef in tow.

In the basement, Josef let them into the locked pantry. Wesler was sitting on the floor, still attached to the water pipe.

"Joachim!"

Wesler started at the mention of his Christian name and looked up. "Herr Klemerer! Ach! It is so good to see you. Thank you for rescuing me!" He started to his feet but was met by a blow to the face, and fell back to the floor, stunned by the attack.

"Pimmelkopf!... What have you and that old fool Huehnlein done?"

"I do not understand!"

"You have launched an attack on New York with poisonous gas; endangered the existence of Höher Zwech."

"No, Sir! It is all part of a plan by the organization. El Jefe briefed me on it."

The reaction was so genuine that Rolf immediately saw that Wesler had been used. With growing trepidation, Rolf saw him as only a pawn in the works.

"Where is that old fool and tell me what you know!"

Sensing that he was caught between two irresistible forces, Wesler told the whole story. He explained how El Jefe had planned one last act of revenge for the Nationalsozialistische Deutsche Arbeitpartei. The recovery of the gas canisters in Germany had been too good an opportunity to pass up and the old man had dreamed up their use against, primarily, Wesler thought, Jewish New Yorkers.

Using the gas as a diversionary tactic, the next step in the scheme was a brilliant plan to usurp righteous ownership of the major American corporations. As he told it, it was virtually world conquest without a declaration of war, or major conflict. Wars, as El Jefe had explained to him, had always been fought because of the greed of the Zionist bankers who financed both sides in a conflict. The blood of the masses was sacrificed for profit, for reasons of finance. And now, this war would be fought right where it originated, right in the stock exchange itself. He finished by pointing out how eloquent, how neatly tailored, the plan was. One of the assured fall-outs of the takeover of the American commercial giants was the ability to control the American economy and engineer the demise of Israel.

"This is nonsense. It is a grandiose scheme that cannot succeed."

"But, El Jefe has carefully arranged this plan. The biological agent was released on Tuesday morning. The ensuing deaths and panic concerning them will last as long as it takes to complete the mission. It is intended that the stock take-over will be accomplished on Friday, so that there will be a weekend of delay to cover the changes. A group of men has been recruited who will re-program the computers on Friday to show legitimate and wholesale purchase of shares in American corporations. In that period, many decisions can be made to sabotage the American economy, in legal ways, since the new owners have that right. We are on the brink of world domination by taking over the American economy and bending it to our own purposes."

Rolf listened in dismay to the rambling dissertation. The eventual dominance of Nationalsozialistische Deutsche Arbeitpartei was endemic to his own agenda, so they had a shared objective. This radical, audacious plan made that possible but he was unwilling to accept it because it was almost too huge, too ridiculous, to grasp. Additionally, since it was not *his* plan, he found little accord with it and feared any faults which may be built into it.

"How do we stop this?" Rolf could only see disaster.

Wesler felt a triumphant response building inside him, but he had begun to seriously feel the censure of his inquisitor. He answered cautiously instead. "There is no way. The gas has been delivered already. I was merely a courier. El Jefe dealt with other people on the rest of the plan. They were to develop the computer program necessary to break into the New York Stock Exchange system of recording stock sells and buys. I only know they are Arabs, old acquaintances of El Jefe. I met their representative in Athens a few weeks ago. I do not know who these people are."

"Anything else you have not told me?"

"No, sir." Wesler felt a tremendous sinking in his stomach. El Jefe had betrayed him, used him for purposes not approved by Höher Zwech. The message about him fleeing the ranch and Karl-Heinz's betrayal had been bogus. So, how did Barton and the women escape? He wondered for the hundredth time since his capture. His thoughts were interrupted by Rolf.

"Are you able to contact these people?"

"Yes, but they are not obliged to respond since the execute order has long-since been given."

"There were some metal boxes recovered in Germany. Where are they?"

"They were sent to Paraguay."

"Where are they now?"

"I have not seen them since Frau Klemerer and the others arrived at the ranch. El Jefe took possession of them, only giving me the two gas cylinders from one of them."

"Both of these cylinders were used in New York?"

"No, there is one more cylinder."

"Where is it?"

"It is in a half-ton truck, in the long-term parking lot at Kennedy airport."

Wesler produced a key and a description of the vehicle. Leaving the man, Rolf was inclined to liquidate Wesler, but he may yet have some use. Quickly, he had a man sent to pick up the vehicle, a dark green Dodge Dakota. The man was to call in when he retrieved the vehicle.

Going to a ground floor study, he poured himself a brandy. Summoning Helmut and Tomas, he filled them in on what Wesler had told him. Then, staring at the wall, he tried to assimilate what was happening. He had come to America to detain Astrid, Barton and his bitch. His people had been trying to apprehend them ever since Höher Zwech members in the Kriminalpolizei had revealed that the three of them had knowledge of a vast horde of gold and the steel boxes, critical to the survival of Höher Zwech.

Then, Huehnlein, that stupid old criminal, had evidently kidnapped them from under his nose, causing them to disappear. How he wished he had yielded to the opinion of the other members and disposed of the over-opinionated old fool months ago! When Astrid had called from New York, it had been a huge relief to him. Now that he had them in his grasp, he could have them killed and disposed of. Still, he was reluctant. There were too many loose ends and he needed them interrogated to ensure the security of Höher Zwech was intact. What had initially been a relatively simple solution to a security problem had now landed in his lap as a monstrous plot with worldwide ramifications.

Helmut and Tomas stood attentively as he sipped the brandy and then, impulsively, drained it in one gulp.

"Well?"

Tomas stepped forward. "If it seems we cannot stop this, then we must join it. It is a masterfully conceived plan," he stopped momentarily, arrested by a glare from Rolf, "If the plan works, we must be ready to take advantage."

"And, do you think Höher Zwech will remain a secret?"

"I see no reason why not. We can profit from this without exposure, especially since the work is being done by a second party who can take the blame, if found out."

"Oh, they will be found out. Can't you imagine what the Americans will do when this is revealed? And, what kind of a plan is it anyway? The Americans can simply declare all the transactions null and void."

Helmut spoke up. An accountant, his mind had raced at the concept. "Actually, it is not that simple. At minimum, trading will be halted for days, weeks even months, while the mess of *'who owns what?'* is sorted out. The American economy will be thrown into chaos and the ramifications will spread worldwide. More likely, even with American efforts to roll-back trading, the economy will be frozen globally because the first banks to honour massive payments will likely go bankrupt immediately. It will be like a house of cards. The dollar dictates use of the gun in warfare and rules here, also. Any kind of victory here would equate to a successful armed invasion of America, without a shot being fired." He paused, thinking quickly.

"I believe this plan, if nothing else, may trigger another world depression. This would provide fertile ground for a new political order throughout the world, such as the Nationalsozialistische Deutsche Arbeitpartei. You could become the new Führer. So, I recommend we quickly take over this operation, and improve on it."

"I doubt there is time, but we do know where they intend to strike whereas nobody else does." Rolf poured another brandy, the grandiose swell of impending success rolling over his psyche. "Find out where the computers are located for the Exchange. That is where these people will have to be. Also, set up a downtown control centre for us, complete with self-contained accommodation and food. I want a dozen men there today, fully armed. Find people from out of town, we cannot risk infection. Use the warehouse down in Brooklyn."

Back at the dinner table, Rolf took his seat. "Wesler has told me the whole thing."

"Just like that?"

Rolf glanced at Gerd. "Gerd can be very persuasive."

"So, what can we do?"

"Nothing."

"Nothing?"

"There is a second part to this plan in effect, launched from Paraguay, as Astrid alluded to. We cannot stop that and we may be at risk to our health if we stay."

"We are leaving?" Raymond asked.

"No, there is more to do."

"I don't understand. What is the second part of the plan?"

Rolf turned to Raymond and his features took on a hard look. "I need to know where all of those steel boxes are which you have hidden."

"Astrid?" Raymond looked from Rolf, to Astrid, to Mandy.

"Why do you need to know, Leibling?" Astrid had been mildly attentive to Rolf throughout the meal and now reached out to lay her hand on his arm.

He shook her away and leaned forward, staring intently at Raymond. "I want to know where the stuff is!"

"But why? It is dangerous to know, look how we have been hunted!"

Something seemed to snap in Rolf. "I want to know because the boxes and the gold belong to *us!*"

Several chairs scraped back and Raymond felt an icy chill flow through his spine and settle in his guts. "Oh my God!" But it was too late. Behind him, he felt Josef close to his chair. There came the snick-snick of an automatic weapon being cocked and he felt the cold muzzle against his neck. Shit! They had been discussing such great secrets in front of a servant and he had not tumbled to the fact the man was a confidante of Rolf's. He looked at Mandy and saw her white-knuckled hands held to her mouth. Astrid was agape, staring at her husband.

"Höher Zwech! You are part of Höher Zwech?"

"I am the new leader."

"Arschloch!" Astrid leapt at him, one hand's nails clawing at his face while the other beat the side of his head. Rolf rose and drove her full in the face with his fist. She went over backwards with a scream, crashing to the floor. Gerd had a weapon now also and stood on the other side of the table, covering Raymond and Mandy.

Helmut went to Astrid and dragging her to her feet, dumped her back in her chair. Blood flowed from her nose. She alternately whimpered in pain and cursed solidly.

Raymond stared, horrified and numbed by this new turn of events. Lots of things barely suspected began to fall into place. They had been duped and now they were in the hands of probably the most unscrupulous of all the groups hunting them.

"Where are they?" Rolf interrupted Raymond's thoughts.

He shook his head, biding for time, unable to fully assemble his thoughts. Rolf's response was to step to Astrid and slap her furiously. Her head snapped back and forth, spittle and blood spraying from her mouth.

"We have little time and less patience. I want to know. I want to know right now!"

"You animal, you horrible fucking animal," Astrid sobbed between words, "There are thousands out there dead and more dying. Because of you!"

"I had nothing to do with the release of gas. You just got through telling us it was Huehnlein's idea."

"But you are still one of those beasts, those inhuman Nazi monsters who created it, who killed millions for your stupid, misguided and self-centred ends! How did you get into this abomination?"

"Why, through your step-father of course."

"Varti...?"

"Yes, he is a very dedicated member of the Nationalsozialistische Deutsche Arbeitpartei. He was an early party member and reached the rank of Oberführer."

"And Mutti?"

"Ah! She was always a problem, wasn't she? But for the fact your real father was a hero and Hans Lankow defended her, her criticism of the Party would have put her in a concentration camp."

Across the table, Raymond's skin crawled. He had almost married into this family. But for Lankow being a secret Nazi and therefore hating the English, he would have. Now he understood the ramrod Aryan attitude a little better. His heart went out to Astrid at the thought of such betrayal. She had her head down on the table and was sobbing.

"I am not interested in the gas. I want the steel boxes. The contents are more important than any gas. You are too stupid to understand what is at stake here."

"National Socialism?" Astrid looked up and sneered at him and was rewarded with another slap.

"I can't believe you and I were raised on the same water. I can't believe I loved you, shared your bed, you contemptible piece of pond slime."

Rolf kicked out at Astrid's chair, propelling her against the wall. She jerked like a puppet and at a nod from him and before she could react, Helmut had a pistol muzzle grinding into her throat.

"Now!" Rolf swung around to Raymond. "You have ten seconds and then she dies."

Horrified, Raymond looked at Mandy but she was weeping, head lowered, not focussed on him. He turned and looked at Astrid and her eyes rolled at him, refusing to give up. Raymond knew he had to play for time. Last time he had seen the boxes was in Germany, before they were abducted. If he told Rolf that, they would have no cards to play. They would probably be dead.

"I know only a little about the steel boxes. One contained the poisonous gas, virus, whatever the hell it is. Another was filled with patents. The one you are probably interested in contained lists of Nazi party officials, where they escaped to at the end of the War, and which government they were assisted by." Encouraged by Rolf's apparent interest, Raymond pressed on. "That last box is in Brazil, we left it there on the way north. I guess we could..."

He was interrupted by a slow rhythmic tapping of a spoon on the tabletop. "Six...Five...Four..." Rolf quietly tapped out the last seconds remaining in Astrid's life.

"For God's sake, man! I...I will give you the damned boxes. Just hold on!"

Rolf turned and stared at Helmut. The man still held the gun muzzle to Astrid's throat and she was choking at the pressure. Helmut's free hand moved, palm out above the barrel, ready to shield himself from the imminent splatter of blood and brains. With a flutter of eyelids, Rolf indicated he should not pull the trigger. Raymond felt a huge sense of relief but knew he could not show it.

Outside in the garden, Richard was making another circuit. His life ended with the impact of the first silenced round, the second expertly fired shot targeting a dead man. A group of figures dropped over the boundary wall and loped towards the house. The security of Rolf's choice of a hideaway had been easily breached by determined people checking his past. Almost immediately, the intruders triggered a sensor beam and an alarm sounded in the house.

Gerd heard the beeping sound and grabbed a radio from his belt. "Richard." There was no response. "Richard!" He turned to Rolf. "We have company!" He stood, awaiting instructions.

The sound of breaking glass and a blare of alarm bells galvanized Rolf. "Get everyone upstairs." A blast of gunfire assisted in getting everyone to comply and very quickly, the Musketeers and their captors fled upstairs. Gerd followed last and turning at the top of the stairs fired down on a dark-garbed figure, which had appeared below. There was a scream of agony and then a burst of return fire from below. Fragments flew off the walls and pictures disintegrated.

There was a thud on the landing behind them followed by the skittering sound of a heavy object on the floor. "Grenade!" Someone screamed, and then it went off. A flash of flame and concussion followed, their temporary deafness penetrated by someone new screaming in pain. Hustled along, the whole party found itself in a room at the end of the hallway.

Gunfire erupted at the head of the stairs, the muzzle flashes flickering on the walls. Return fire came from below and someone nearby made a retching noise and there was the sound of a body hitting the floor. The rounds were coming through the floor, tearing out huge slivers of wood and making the carpets dance. The room they were in was set up as a meeting room, with chairs and overhead projectors. Josef led them to a corner and pulling aside a large easel, revealed a hidden door. A flight of stairs beyond took them quickly down to the garage. There were four vehicles parked there, a mini-van, a half-ton truck, a Jaguar XKE and a Lincoln.

Quickly, Rolf delegated people to each vehicle. Helmut and Josef would take the half-ton and run point, directing fire at their attackers while the Lincoln departed with himself covering the three Musketeers, while Gerd drove. They piled into the vehicles and started them up. Automatic garage door openers triggered two of the doors and with a wailing shriek of tires, they popped out of the building onto the gravel driveway. Both vehicles swerved and fishtailed, erupting fire towards the house. A figure on the door stoop yelled and leveled a weapon at them, the winking of the gun he held stopping abruptly as he was caught by overwhelming fire from the truck.

Other guns opened up and holes dimpled the side of the truck. A couple of rounds went through the rear window of the Lincoln, causing them all to duck. Raymond was looking for an opportunity to tackle Rolf, but he was being too smart, out of his reach and with his pistol held to Astrid's neck.

The truck, to their left, suddenly veered towards them and began to steer erratically. More rounds dimpled the doors and suddenly, the truck hooked hard left and ran full force into a tree. The passenger door burst open and Josef fell out, but he was already lifeless. Gunning the motor, Gerd went full speed down the driveway, swept between the gate columns and floored the accelerator. The car sped down the country road, the trees whipping by on either side.

1730 hrs. Wednesday, 18th July 1990.
Situation Room, White House, Washington D.C.

The President of the United States sank into his chair as the icy grip of fear seized his vitals. With the collapse of Communism happening, his security advisors had warned him of the possibility of rogue parties getting their hands on nuclear or biological weapons. It had seemed unlikely and other than ensuring that the Central Intelligence Agency was keeping a watchful eye on events, no clear policy had been put in place.

Now, it was upon them. The news had come with terrible force. Thousands of people were sick in New York City and, already, thousands more were dead. His National Security Advisor sat with him as they faced several television screens showing personnel assisting with the situation.

Major General Richard F. Kaminski, Commandant of Fort Detrick in Maryland was on one screen. As the boss of the U.S. Army Medical Research and Materiel Command that dealt with biological and chemical warfare, he was on the hot seat for an answer to the problem. Now, conscious of the seriousness of the situation and charged with the responsibility to quickly resolve it, Kaminski spoke up."Mr. President. The speed and deadly nature of this outbreak strongly suggests a biological agent. Pathologically, there is nothing occurring naturally, other than Ebola Fever, which can equate to it."

"Is it like Ebola?"

"No, Sir. This affliction is more like a pneumonic plague, which has a ninety-five percent plus mortality rate. There is a rapid onset of symptoms, including tightness in the chest, followed by edema in the lung bronchioles and escalating temperatures of over one hundred and three degrees, leading to seizures. Initial conclusions are that it is airborne, has a brief incubation period, during which time the person is highly contagious. The agent is so virulent that it does not discriminate between the elderly, the sick or the fit. Everyone is equally at risk upon exposure."

"When will you know what it is and recommend an antidote?"

"We are preparing cultures as we speak under Level Four security protocol. We hope to have them available for examination in the next four hours."

"What about the World Health Organization and the Centre for Disease Control in Atlanta?"

"We have talked to them, Mr. President. They know no more than we do, but have recommended the strictest of quarantine measures. Incidentally, my duty is to inform you that New York and any other infected areas which are identified should be isolated, with prejudice."

"What are you saying, man? Cause a national panic?"

"Mr. President." General Kaminski gathered himself in and paused to find the words. "Mr. President. It is the considered opinion of this Command that the United States has been attacked by a biological weapon, as yet unidentified. The highly virulent nature of this agent is such that we may incur casualties in the millions if we do not take radical steps."

The silence went on like an expanding vacuum, sucking the life out of the men in the room while faces on the other screens, all in conference to the call, appeared incredulous.

The Governor of New York State, Alberto Tomaltino, spoke first. "You are suggesting we shut down New York City and isolate it from the world?" The words were accusatory, as if Kaminski had committed some kind of heresy.

"Every train, plane, highway, ship, car, bus, bridge, pedestrian, tunnel, waterway. The police, the Army, Navy and the Air Force have to interdict any kind of movement of people to prevent the spread of this disease. Everyone has to be quarantined in their homes for the duration. It may even be already too late to save millions."

The last words took a deep toll on the listeners.

"General Eichenhorn." The President spoke to the Chairman of the Joint Chiefs of Staff. "Call out whatever units you require to isolate New York, its environs, and any other outbreak areas which may be identified. I am declaring a state of National Emergency immediately. Everything possible must be done to prevent the spread of this disease. All inbound and outbound means of transportation must be diverted and sealed off. I will go on television in five minutes to advise the Nation. Please advise me in one hour of the means you have taken to ensure that these orders are carried out. I am immediately elevating our security level to Def-Con Two. Mister Secretary." The President turned to the screen showing Defence Secretary Robert Vandermeer. "Please advise NATO and the Soviets of our reasons for this. We sure as hell don't want an escalation of nuclear tension right now. Ask the Russians if any of their biological warfare stocks have been stolen. Don't take any bullshit about them not having any, this is a problem they may be unfortunate enough to share with us, whether they have responsibility or not. Tell everyone, frankly, the problem. They could all be in trouble with this too."

Three minutes later, across the United States, newscasters broke into regular television programs to warn people that the President was coming on the air to announce a matter of national importance.

"My fellow Americans. I come to speak to you under the gravest of circumstances. An outbreak of illness in New York City has been tentatively identified as a possible biological attack upon our great nation. As a means to contain this outbreak, I am ordering martial law in the States of New York and New Jersey. All highways, bridges, ferries, trains, flights, vehicular traffic in and out of New York City and the Jersey shores is prohibited and this prohibition will be enforced by police agencies and military units.

I ask you all not to panic or despair. All resources are being brought to bear to resolve this situation. Please, stop whatever you are doing at this moment and go to your homes. Stay there, and avoid contact with others as much as possible. Pay attention to your local radio and television stations for future guidance.

Anyone who has travelled out of New York in the last two days should avoid contact with other people for at least twenty-four hours. I ask you, please, voluntarily quarantine yourself from others to stop the possible spread of infection. The fate of many Americans rests in the hands of each and every one of us. Everyone must assist in complying with these requirements.

I assure you that everything possible is being done. Antidotes should be available soon. I promise you that the perpetrators of this infamous deed will be hunted down by all our means and brought to justice. God bless America!"

The haggard face of the President faded from millions of screens, replaced by the now trite soap operas. These lasted only seconds before bewildered junior newscasters, the only ones immediately available, took over, stumbling their way through conjecture and vague interview contacts hurriedly put together.

The national electrical grid went to the limits of capacity as millions of telephone calls were made and the communications system was swamped. In buildings throughout New York, people looked at each other and shrank away, fearing contagious contact. In short time, throughout the nation, supermarkets were inundated by people stockpiling food.

Within fifteen minutes, New York police units and Port Authority personnel were dispatched to close bridges, tunnels and subways. Traffic, swollen by people determined to escape, backed up immediately. The streets began to fill with people walking. Dozens had already been injured in the press of personnel exiting buildings. Panic began to set in as many realized they could not get home across the bridges and had no place to stay.

The FAA closed airports and air traffic control diverted inbound flights and grounded anything going out. Inbound Transatlantic flights were diverted to Canada, well away from the problem. Inbound ships were intercepted and told to anchor in the approaches to the New York harbours. The QE2, loaded with passengers and ready to sail, was quarantined at the dock.

Within two hours, military units arrived at vital points, controlling the docks, airports and bridges. Helicopters flew around the clock to prevent small boats crossing the various waterways. The National Guard cut off highways twenty miles out of the metropolis, turning back traffic. Yet still some people escaped, terrified of the consequences of staying in New York. Looting began almost immediately.

Seven hours after the Presidential address, a strange phenomenon fell upon New York. The streets became deserted. Parks were empty. Commercial buildings and stores sat mostly deserted, except for people who had decided to hole up in them. Safe in their homes or ensconced in hotel rooms, people stayed glued to the electronic media.

Morning. Thursday, 19th July 1990. New York City.

The sun had risen this day on a sight alien to New Yorkers; a deserted city. One of the great metropolises of the world, New York normally buzzes perpetually, twenty-four hours of the day. Now, for a day, the streets had been virtually deserted. The famous buildings towered in relief but silence, the atmosphere clearer than usual because of the lack of traffic-generated smog.

The total curfew announced by the authorities worked because the media had pumped the deadly consequences of disobedience into everyone's minds. The risks of venturing out were documented and deadly. Within the city, the police had little need to patrol in any force. They responded to a fairly steady stream of emergency calls created by the perennial wrongdoers who, because of lack of caring, habitual criminal behaviour, drugged nonchalance or sheer stupidity, continued their way of life.

Most were rounded up quickly and easily, response times being the epitome of efficiency in the face of zero traffic delays. Nonetheless, it was terrifying for these criminal elements to be apprehended by bug-eyed masked officers dressed like extra-terrestrials who seemed to have no desire to come within six feet and generally herded their prisoners into vans at gunpoint. They were incarcerated in large pens pending processing later. Because the huge numbers quickly had overpopulated normal jail facilities, little regard was shown for potential infection between these people. Demands for lawyers were laughed at by the police. Despite the desperate nature of the situation, it was novel for the officers to apprehend criminals and throw them behind bars without a lawyer's interference.

Otherwise, backed by military units, the police only had to set up checkpoints, which were mainly on the bridges and tunnels, to control traffic in and out of the downtown. More stringent measures coped with attempted movement by people to the northwest. Thousands had been turned back and ordered to remain in their homes, listening to newscasts to stay informed. Many people shared hotel rooms, thrown open by Presidential order, as it was the only place they could stay in New York City. Thousands of people sweltered in such isolation, with the air conditioning turned off to prevent the airborne menace spreading. One radio and one television channel broadcast the *official* line of the authorities, while news networks produced their own agenda to raise the hype.

Huge trucks roamed the streets escorted by police vehicles and residents needing groceries could shop from them for staples. Canned goods and loaves of bread were thrown from the tailgate while the vehicles cruised slowly down the streets. It was all relatively orderly.

Emergency services only were officially allowed on the streets, although there were still many brave or task-driven souls who ventured out. Although the police were supposed to stop and apprehend curfew-breakers, it was too big a task and they basically ignored it where they happened across it. Besides, they saw no need to hazard their own health by unnecessary exposure to other people. Often, such people were only going to look in on and care for shut-ins who would perish without care and create another health problem. Hospitals were basically shut down, dealing only with extreme cases, and then only at the instigation of brave and dedicated medical personnel.

Looting had been declared a capital offence under martial law and the televised image of a dozen perpetrators being summarily shot dead at such a scene had discouraged further acts. The effectiveness of such brutal enforcement by the authorities had, mostly, the required effect. In the aftermath, the twenty-twenty vision of legal scrutiny by bleeding-heart liberals as to these looters' rights was defused, thanks to the foresight of a mayoral assistant who had faked the whole thing in true Hollywood style with a film company. Linked to the real-life televised shootings of el-Cetti, watchers were further convinced of the dangers outside their doors.

And so, movement around New York was restricted, especially crossing the rivers. Throughout America now, air travel was suspended. Several aircraft had tried to flee the Continental U.S., but had been turned back by aggressive intercepts by Air Force fighter planes. The ultimatum of being shot down or returning was persuasive. Inter-state driving was forbidden and the thousands of miles of highway ribbon were eerily deserted.

Dozens of ships were anchored offshore awaiting berths while outbound sailings remained moored to the docks. The authorities had quickly discerned that the outbreak was mostly confined to New York City, with a dozen or so related occurrences elsewhere. It seemed that while there was a concentration in the New York area, second and third contacts were weak. Authorities suspected that some unknown suppressant of the disease had limited its ability to propagate. A worldwide alert had gone out and though there had been some overseas deaths, most of the cases reported were people who were only getting severely sick.

The most gruesome task was the gathering of the dead. Unable to deal with each of the victims individually, the care system was totally overwhelmed and the true horror of biological warfare was brought home. The television gave instructions on home care for the afflicted, but there was minimal aid to provide cure or care. Families and friends were instructed to stay in touch, to check on each other and where one member died, a telephone number was provided for teams to pick up the dead. Contagion, typhoid and other natural diseases associated with decomposing bodies threatened to worsen the situation if not dealt with.

Large trucks roamed the streets, manned by troops dressed in biological warfare equipment. They would reach an address, deliver a body bag and wait while relatives shrouded the deceased in it. The body was then taken away and stored in one of many huge morgues where it was stacked like cordwood with others, pending disposal. Sadly, there were repeat visits to some addresses until nobody was left.

It was inevitable yet still macabre that the media would relate this to the mediaeval plague, the Black Death, which had decimated European populations. The modern counterparts of the fourteenth century men roaming the streets with handcarts, sonorously calling out '*Bring out your dead*' was, perhaps, impossible to ignore.

To the various protagonists seeking free movement for the end game, there was very little to offer. In their urgent quest to find Raymond and the girls and thus the Nazi treasure and documents, undercover teams resorted to various means. Obviously, impersonating authorized personnel such as police officers gave them relative ease of movement, with minimal risk of challenge.

Parked on a street four blocks off the Brooklyn Bridge, panel trucks and telephone company vehicles concealed fifty FBI agents, armed to the teeth. Not far away, cloistered in a vehicle parking lot, a hundred Rangers sat ready for action. Navy SEALS were safely ensconced on a Coast Guard vessel anchored in the Hudson River. On the Jersey shore, seeking out possible targets, were half a dozen Russian embassy staff, SPETSNAZ commandos by trade, who had caught a stale scent of el-Cetti. Two groups of Israelis roamed, passing out food from trucks, their weapons hidden behind cases of rations.

The SAS were boldly driving around in an Army National Guard unit truck. Outdoing them all, an ingenious German group had given itself free access anywhere by posing as a body-removal unit. Completely disguised by the biohazard suits, secure in their marked vehicle, they risked little challenge from American security units who shuddered at the very sight of them.

Radio scanners betrayed every transmission to the intruders who awaited only one key piece of information before committing themselves to deadly action. Their quest was in full swing.

1000 hrs. Thursday 19th July 1990. Queens, New York City.

Dennis Piercy had worked for the NYSE for five years as a computer programmer. He was an expert on the software used to track the millions of shares traded each day. When the disease outbreak occurred, he obeyed the instructions of the authorities and retreated to his home in Queens. His wife, Ellie, blew a bunch of their savings stockpiling groceries and bottled water at the local supermarket and they and their two young children hid away in their house. They tuned in to CNN and settled to wait out the horror beyond their front door.

After one day, the children were a nuisance; they did not understand why they could not play with their friends. They were so psyched; young Joshua even wanted to go back to school. Now, a knock on their door revealed two strangers on their doorstep, wearing gas masks.

Flashing official badges, the men insisted that Dennis had to come with them to his workplace as a matter of national urgency. Dennis was unwilling but they became insistent without totally revealing what the matter concerned. They pointed out that he would be able to call his wife at any time, his safety was guaranteed, and indicated a van parked on the street which they said contained other agents who would ensure the safety of his family. When Dennis became more wary of their intent, and suggested his supervisor be called for corroboration, they became forcefully aggressive, quoting Presidential order and possible prosecution for non-compliance and obstructing Federal agents. They insisted it was a National security emergency, empowering them to arrest him if necessary. Ellie became frightened and hanging on the promise he could phone her any time, urged him to go with the men.

Quickly packing an overnight bag, Dennis kissed his wife and children and departed, donning a mask proffered by the men. El-Saeed had secured his inside computer expert. Plus he also now had hostages, isolated by courtesy of the United States government from relatives and friends. Until it represented a threat, the telephone line to the house would represent a calming influence.

When Dennis Piercy reached his office building, there were some unfamiliar security people on the front desk. The office building was fairly nondescript from the outside, but there were two administrative floors above a large secure basement that more closely resembled a bank vault. An innocuous looking down elevator deposited visitors into a concrete basement hallway off which a huge iron door blocked further passage with elaborate security systems.

The main street entrance was dominated by an *Information Desk*. This was a sorting point, where casual or dubious visitors were referred to one doorway where they were processed or turned away, and another that led to the choice of separate elevators serving the basement or the upper floors.

The glass panes fronting the street were covered by plywood and when Dennis enquired as to what had happened, one of the men told him that a car, driven by an incompetent elderly woman, had reversed at full speed into them. The familiar reception desk had been removed and replaced by a temporary collapsible trestle table. In some ways, the damage raised Dennis' suspicions, yet at the same time accorded him some reassurance that some events had taken place that required intervention by the authorities. An NYPD uniformed officer strolled through the lobby, nodding to them as he went by, further reassuring Dennis.

His escorts did not tell Dennis that it was a reinforced van that had backed at full speed through the windows, spraying the place with gunfire. They did not acquaint him with the fact the desk and the two security people behind it had been destroyed by the assault and that an hour had been spent swabbing blood from the marble floor.

Quickly, they marched to the elevator past the two guards on duty. One of them, a black man, matched Dennis to a picture in his hand and accorded him a friendly "Hi! Mr. Piercy, nice to see you are okay!" Encouraged by the familiarity, Dennis reached into his wallet and extracted the plastic identity card which would grant him access to the basement elevator. He did not even think to challenge his escorts' right to be with him; he merely swiped the card and waited for the elevator to arrive.

Together, they descended to the basement. When the doors opened, he stepped out, the two men in trail. The basement was environmentally conditioned for mainframe computer operation. A glass-walled cubicle separated the elevator passageway from a large work area filled with metal cabinets housing computer components and slowly revolving magnetic tapes. Several offices opened off the large area and two men, heads bent, could be seen, busy at workstations.

Only one glass door now separated Dennis from his fellow employees. He reached for a telephone mounted on the wall and pressed a button. One of the men interrupted his task and picked up at his end.

"Hi, Sandy, this is Dennis. Beam me in," it was a standing joke, *'beam me in'*. The man looked up, obviously ready to comply until he saw the other visitors.

"Who are those guys with you?"

"Federal agents."

"Agents?" The man's whole posture became one of caution.

The man to Dennis' left stirred.

"Dennis, you know that without proper authorization, we cannot let visitors in here!" Sandor Kovacs' eyes were shifting, ranging over them all in open mistrust.

The man who had stirred reached in his pocket and smacked some kind of putty against the lock of the access door. Before he could react, Dennis found himself buried in the corner beneath four hundred pounds of beefy guys. A second later, there was a loud explosion that made his head ring. He felt like he was floating, but in reality, the weight on him was lifted as the two men turned and charged through the breached security door. Shots rang out, reverberating through the basement and his head seemed to depart from reality.

A strong hand grasped him by the shoulder and dragged him twenty feet through the door. Dumped to the floor unceremoniously, he found himself gaping at close range into the dulling eyes of Sandy Kovacs. Beneath the eyes, the rest of Sandy's face was a loose red splash of tissue, a spreading pool of blood around his head announcing his violent death. Dennis turned his head and threw up, his brain trying to acknowledge that he had somehow been responsible by coming here with these men. He shuddered as he saw a pair of feet sticking out from behind a desk. Poor Ed Betkowski had shared Sandy's fate.

He was dragged to a chair and pushed into it. He tried to speak, to protest, but a weapon was waved in his face with the unmistakable signal to be quiet. He now knew the reason for bringing him here was bogus, but what could these men want? Dennis Piercy was a mild man, perhaps the epitome of a computer geek. The most violent thing he had done in his life was to once play football, but the inherent disregard for others in the game repelled him and he never played again.

The elevator arrived and two men entered through the shattered door. One held a gun and was obviously a bodyguard. The older one spoke good, though slightly guttural, English. He placed a package on the desk and leaned up against the wall. "Mr. Piercy, I need your assistance in accessing the data relating to the purchase of stock on the New York Stock Exchange."

Piercy shook his head. Now he began to perceive the nature of the crime at work here. The very notion of penetrating the pristine sterility of the system was abhorrent to him. He would not be a party to theft.

"You will not co-operate?"

"You cannot steal stock. It has to be properly purchased and accounted for."

"Yes, you are correct. It is however possible, and you *are* going to help me do it."

"I cannot, it is not possible with this system. It is duplicated, but created in an electronically segregated state. Change, on the other side of the water, in Manhattan, or here, cannot be done independently. Besides, I will not be party to it."

The man stared at him, an empty contemplative mask. Without another word, he consulted a notepad, reached for the phone and dialled a number. He handed Piercy the instrument. With a sudden feeling of dread, Piercy knew what was about to happen. The phone was still ringing but then it was answered. "Hello?" The voice quavered with fear but he knew it well. His throat went tight and he thought he was about to void himself.

"Ellie!" his voice was a croak.

She cut him off. "Dennis, they are here! In the house! In the room!"

Panicked, her voice gave staccato details, trite, yet totally revealing to the situation. "They..."

Her voice was cut off at the sound of a child screaming in pain in the background. The phone went dead. "Ellie! Ellie!" He kept calling into the phone as if by force of will he could transmit his voice. Gently, a hand relieved him of the phone and put it back on the cradle.

Piercy shuddered and tears streamed down his face. The man said nothing, waiting like some predatory animal. "Wha...What do you want?"

"I want your full co-operation in ensuring my work here gets done. We are going to conduct a full scale transferring of major shares to principals of mine."

"But I have told you it cannot be done!" The irrefutable fact brought Dennis back from the brink of despair and defiance rose within him. "And I will absolutely not help you unless you guarantee the safety of my family!"

"Mr. Piercy," the voice was quiet as the man leaned forward into his face, "I don't care one tiny little bit about you, or your family. To order the killing of you all is entirely within my power, at any time. However, right now, that small expenditure of effort would detract from my concentration on my task at hand. Believe me, your family is totally insignificant to me. They will remain that way unless you influence me negatively towards them by lack of co-operation with us." The icy cold dismissal, the sheer ruthlessness, was overwhelming.

"Show me what you want."

"First, we want access into the security of the system. How do we accomplish that?" Another man stepped forward. Piercy noted the accent and skin colouring and finally guessed the man to be an Arab.

"The security of the system rests in a continuous challenge and response between the two facilities. Obviously, the cable connection between them is not immune from interference, such as tapping in. This is actually covered by sending signals down the line and ensuring the resistivity of the line remains the same. Reflections would be caused by any change in line impedance due to tapping. The challenge and response are encoded pulses sent from both ends. The encoding itself is randomly generated by a computer but the response is prearranged. It is a little like sending a *three* down the line and getting a *six* back, the factor being a predetermined *two*," Piercy spoke with a little propriety pride at the cleverness of the system, "Of course, it is not entirely that simplistic but if any security anomaly is identified, it will result in suspension of information transfer until it is resolved. In short, any trading taking place during such a break would not be confirmed."

"So it could happen that the master end could have a pile of information awaiting transfer?" the man already knew this but needed corroboration.

"Yes and the transaction of any sales or buys might not be honoured, or recognized until the system is in normal operation."

"So, human observers could be aware of this and expect a huge transfer of information when security is re-established?"

"Yes."

"How often does this happen?"

"It has only happened once in my time here. That was due to a fire in a cable vault over in New York."

"So, we have to interrupt the security and sign-in somehow. Can you do that?"

"I think so."

"You had better! It's your family!" the man punched a line Dennis recognized as direct to the NYSE and spoke rapidly in Arabic.

1200 hrs. Thursday, 19th July 1990.
Reuters News Service, Worldwide.

'The U.S. State Department has issued a global warning to all countries concerning suspected deployment of paramilitary teams in the United States, especially New York City. By Presidential order, any such teams found operating within the U.S. shall be regarded as committing an act of war and will be destroyed by any means required.'

Personal telephone calls from the President to his principal allies, and the Russians, underscored the seriousness with which his government regarded the matter.

1843 hrs. Thursday, 19th July 1990. Westhampton house.

Captain Julian Bartholomew de Beauville had a recorded lineage dating back to the thirteenth century. A graduate of a favoured boys' school and Cambridge University, he lacked the aloof elitism of his ancestors. He enjoyed a few pints of bitter with interesting men of his own timbre and as a result, was beloved of his men. As a paratrooper, he had become notorious from an incident where he bailed out of an aircraft without a parachute, linking up in mid-air with an unsuspecting trooper to make a safe descent. He now served in the British Special Air Service Twenty-second Regiment and led one of the teams dispatched to America in pursuit of Raymond Barton. He operated under authority of a code name, *Search One*.

Now, he stared with surprise at this man shackled to a water pipe in a Long Island house basement. His Sergeant Major, a man renowned for difficult mountain ascents and undercover work against the IRA in Northern Ireland, had alerted him to the man's presence. Wesler now regarded him with open contempt following his initial question.

The rattle of the cocking mechanism partly unnerved Wesler as the machine gun was placed on single shot and pointed at his head. "Wait!" he croaked.

"You have something to offer us?" De Beauville's tone was too casual and disinterested for Wesler's comfort. He realized he had to offer something. After all, he was tied to this water pipe and was helpless without help from someone.

"I am part of a plan," the words floated in the air, like errant butterflies, seeking a place to alight.

"You see, S'arnt Major? This man is part of a *plan*."

"Personally, I think you should just tell me again to shoot the fucker, Sir," the weapon came up; close, nasty, and personal.

"Wait!" in his now panic, Wesler realized he was repeating himself. "There is a plan which involves a bacteriological attack on New York. It has already been set in motion. But I was not a part of it, except for being a messenger!" Hurriedly, he tried to distance himself from implication and responsibility.

"Tell me."

"The biological weapon is only effective for about two days. After that, it wears off and becomes ineffective."

"So, what is the point?"

Wesler recognized the separation point between the first phase of the plan and the second, which he was not about to divulge. "I don't know. I was only the contact man." The slight hesitation of the soldier gave Wesler the sense he had won at least a reprieve.

De Beauville strode from the basement and grabbed the satellite phone proffered by one of his men. The situation and the information coming to light were too much for his level of responsibility. He called London.

2200 hrs. Thursday, 19th July 1990.
Holiday Inn, Buffalo, N.Y. State.

The plan that el-Saeed had put together, within the bounds of the outline from El Jefe, was executed very carefully. The idea of taking over the New York Stock Exchange long enough to raid ownership of shares traded there had thoroughly appealed to el-Saeed. To steal America out from under the Americans using their own technology had a definite elegance. Now, he thought back retrospectively to the meeting he had had with Yussef Bin-Yussef, on the fourth of July, in Tunis.

He had had to employ a considerable level of knowledge and skills, but managed to organize it all. Initially, his mind had raced with the various scenarios that might ensue. Pure larceny, he knew, would not prevail. The electronic theft of shares, even if successful, would be revealed and cancelled. Legitimate purchases, with proof of money transfers would have to be honoured, but that was a route open to any buyer at any time. The wealth of oil-rich sheikhdoms might be assembled to buy shares, but they could not overwhelmingly purchase American companies away from Americans. He knew enough about the system to know that a buying spree would automatically halt trading on any stock. It was one of the protections of the system to guard against dishonest trading.

Yet, El Jefe had found an audacious way to distract and prevent the Americans from halting any suspicious trading. You simply removed the Americans. All that remained was to ensure the computers would allow the transfers and not prevent trading. And, computers could be manipulated, programmed on how to act. Acknowledging his lack of expertise on the subject, he had known how to get advice.

That was why he had risked the journey from Libya to Tunisia, to meet Bin-Yussef, who was a professor of economics and computer technology at Alexandria University, in Egypt. Although this friend owed his sinecure to the existence of world commerce, he hated the Americans and their dominance. Needing his expertise, El-Saeed had placed a call and met him. Yussef Bin-Yussef was intrigued by the challenge, tempted by the three million dollars negotiated offer, and naive concerning the fact that his choice of non-involvement carried the death penalty.

Having heard the plan, he had arrogantly mused over after-dinner coffee, "Buying shares is not usually a problem. Buying massive amounts late in the day may reduce the chance of the stock being halted, but you likely could not buy enough shares in such a short period to gain control of a company. That is done by take-overs, but still may take weeks. It may even be possible to break into the security of the trading computers and falsify sales. However, there is one major hurdle. There is, in New Jersey, a duplicate set of computers recording sales and buys. The Exchange set this system up as a parallel, a *carbon copy* of the accounting to ensure that the records would not be lost in case the Exchange record was lost or somehow destroyed and it also acts as a security measure. In order to *legitimize* any trade, the information would have to be recorded in New Jersey also.

I cannot see how Exchange personnel could overlook such a binge of buying without suspending trading. The computers are set up to alert them to such eventualities. It would be bad enough if they saw binge buying of one corporation, but the whole market? Such an event would sound all the alarm bells."

"We think we have a way of overcoming the human aspect. I just need you to write some programs for the computers so they do not issue an alert to abnormal trading," El-Saeed had seen no reason to enlighten Bin-Yussef as to the rest of the plan.

"Can you get me information on the language the computers are programmed with?"

"Yes. Money talks."

"Inch Allah!"

El-Saeed had then seen that an enormous amount of information and expertise would be required to crack the access codes of the Exchange and since a trial run was out of the question, success was not assured. There was however one avenue that had come easily to his terrorist mind and that was the subjugation and forced co-operation of people who knew the system best, namely the employees at both sites. With preprogrammed software plugged into a compromised system, the American economy would be at his mercy. The biological weapon would create the kind of hysteria in New York that would mask his actions. Thus, in preparation, he had promised the information for his friend. He had carefully noted and executed the need to invade the duplicate Exchange facility on the New Jersey side of the river.

"I will have the information for you in a couple of days. You will have to go to New York and supervise the programming, be ready to intervene if adjustments need to be made."

Bin-Yussef had nodded, indicating his willingness and el-Saeed again had seen no reason to brief him on the biological weapon. If the Professor contracted the disease, it would just mean one less security leak after the event. In fact, el-Saeed had noted, the Professor's demise should be made part of the plan, once the raid on shares was completed. Besides, the bearded Egyptian had had the effrontery to demand more than el-Saeed had initially offered! He had made phone calls.

The group el-Saeed had put together included quite a few Arabs, some of whom were computer experts like Bin-Yussef, or soldiers like el-Cetti. Many of the others were mercenaries with skills he needed, recruited easily with the lure of a million dollars reward.

Within days of the Tunis meeting, they had met in a New York warehouse, packed with arms, electronic equipment and mock training spaces modelled on plans of the two establishments they were going to hit. The full details of the plan were kept secret; the only knowledge the men had was of the taking of the facilities and keeping them secure for as long as it would take. Their own security had been tight, the windows blanked over. The men were transferred in and out blindfolded and kept unaware of the location. Once there, twenty rooms served as dormitories.

The only part of the training that might have been essential was kept from them and that was the wearing of masks to avoid being contaminated by the bio weapon. El-Saeed had decided that since the effects took enough time to show, they would accomplish their side of the bargain before getting sick and the more of them that succumbed to it, the less of them there were to either pay off or eliminate in some other fashion. To brief them sufficiently to accomplish the plan, the men had to be told of the diversionary nature of the *poison gas* which would disable most of New Yorkers, but were unaware that it had highly contagious effects.

The sheer importance of the project and the need for security had demanded that el-Saeed himself be present and in direct control. At enormous risk, he had travelled to the United States under a false passport. With plans completed and the mission on countdown, he had left New York hours before the gas was released. He sat now following events on television, safe in Buffalo, the Canadian border a close option for escape, if necessary.

He had witnessed the bombing of the parking lot creating uproar in New York. The television channels were still re-running it, speculating and stirring up more panic. He noted with satisfaction the death of el-Cetti. For two days, the police and the FBI were in a frenzy to discover the bombing culprits but found no immediate clues. Late on the Tuesday night, the news media was reporting an influenza breakout. Since early Wednesday had brought deaths, there was a huge public reaction. The President had made his national address and in a matter of hours, CNN was reporting dozens of people dead at hospitals throughout the region and hundreds of confirmed cases. Doctors were helpless and when they themselves and nursing staff began to come down with the symptoms, the system collapsed.

El-Saeed sat and gloated. Bin Hassan and his family had died in Philadelphia, preserving security. Even as he watched CNN, stock quotes were displayed on a moving ribbon at the bottom of the television screen. Because the need for commerce transcends human suffering, the New York Stock Exchange was continuing its activities. Hundreds of people had died or were dangerously sick, but a skeleton staff manned their posts and kept the organization functioning, albeit at a slow pace. An emergency telephone conference meeting, held between the Exchange President and his managers, had resulted in a decision to keep things running. They wanted to show the solid nature of the NYSE; that it could function, even in the face of a crisis. The skeleton staff remained at the Exchange Building, safe inside from the disease outside. America was still in business.

As a result, they were playing into the hands of the perpetrators. El-Saeed reflected that the plan was working almost better than they had anticipated! Late on Friday, the stock buy would be accomplished. With trading stopped for the weekend, it would be three days before the Americans realised that they had been sold.

Meanwhile, people still tried leaving the city in droves, despite the Presidential order. Yet, the total curfew had been established by the police and armed forces. It mattered not to el-Saeed at this point. The plan was working. It amused him to think that American soldiers were firing on American civilians.

0813 hrs. Friday, 20th July 1990. Long Island N.Y.

Rolf had been busy. Driving in from Westhampton earlier in the morning, his men had approached a New York police van. The two luckless officers inside had been forced to strip and then were shot with silenced handguns. Dumped in a disused lot, their identities were then assumed. Acting as an escort, the van led the group in the Lincoln to a warehouse on the Lower East Side. The trip went smoothly since they were recognized as an *official* party by the few cop cars that saw them. Inside the warehouse, they joined a dozen men who had arrived under the cover of darkness. A heavily armed operations centre was set up.

Raymond and the girls were incarcerated up on the fourth floor, in a brick-walled room. Rolf was out in another room, busy on cell-phones and radios, coordinating his operation. Several armed men guarded them, and the opportunity to escape seemed zero.

0950 hrs. Basement, New York Stock Exchange.

The air at the NYSE computer facility was charged. For some reason, the information given by Piercy could not force the access Bin-Yussef required. He knew that Piercy was not holding out on him, his accomplice in New Jersey assured him the sweat on the man's brow was not contrived. Ellie Piercy had been tortured on the phone, her screams ensuring Piercy was encouraged to make progress. Since they could bide their time once they gained access, they had allowed time for problem solving. Now, that cushion was almost expired. Finally, Bin-Yussef had to admit he was stuck for an answer and he was now on the phone to el-Saeed, not knowing where he was. "I am convinced the problem is in the algorithms and if we are going to complete this in time, I need some help."

Awakened, el-Saeed reached to his bedside table and poured himself two fingers of Scotch. "What kind of help?"

"Someone who is an expert in computer programming. I can do this, but it will take me too long."

"How am I supposed to find such a person right now? You are supposed to know all of this! You are threatening the success of the plan!" el Saeed screeched his discontent.

Bin-Yussef was silent, shamed by the accusation, yet stolid in his need for help.

El-Saeed thought a moment. Someone working for Herr Blücher had also been trying to reach him on the phone. It could only be the man who had met el-Cetti in Athens. He was the contact, the cut-off man. He had been reluctant to return the call, but now he needed help himself. The six sense, the strange prickle of alarm that had kept him alive all these years twitched and tingled. "I will get back to you in a while. Keep trying, time is running out!" Draining his Scotch, el-Saeed consulted his notebook and dialled the number he needed.

"Hello?" The voice was cautious.

"This is *Asunción*," he used the agreed identifying code name.

"Yes, I have been trying to reach you."

Alarmed at the lack of coded response, el-Saeed almost hung up but his desperation kept him on the line. "Herr Blücher?" he used the only name the German had ever offered.

"No, this is his superior. I am aware of what you are doing. We need to meet in the city immediately."

"No, that is impossible." El-Saeed felt a sweat break out at the prospect of going back to New York, unwilling to admit his location.

"If you do not co-operate, I will ensure the operation is terminated. You will be caught by the authorities."

"No! You cannot!"

"I can and I know how. This thing must be done my way. I am taking personal charge as of now. Where are you?"

"It may be doomed anyway," now el-Saeed thought of flight. If the operation was going sour, he wanted away, safe from the wrath of the man on the line. He knew well the reach of such power.

"What is wrong?"

"We are hung up and need an expert programmer to solve the final problem."

Rolf scowled at the news. "What is the solution?"

"We need someone who can write a quick program to solve the problem."

"You cannot do it?"

"No, it is beyond our expertise."

Sitting in the warehouse in New York, Rolf chewed on his lip. Now that he was committed to making the plan work, he was getting dragged in deeper. Still, if he could find such a person, delivering them to the computer facility would give them a means of getting in and taking direct control. Now he wished Werner Kallembach was still alive.

He slammed his fist into his leg in frustration. Where on earth...? But there was such a person! Only yards away from him, and under his control! Someone who had previously been clever enough to use his computer facility in Germany with Werner!

"Franz, get Fraulein Smythe in here," he turned to the phone again, "Asunción, I have an expert for you. They will be there in less than an hour. Three of my men will be along."

"...But!..."

He cut off the protest, "You will allow my men in or there will be an armed assault to stop this!"

El-Saeed's silence on the far end signalled acquiescence.

"Phone your people and let them know!" Rolf threw the phone down and checked his watch.

1235 hrs. Basement, New York Stock Exchange.

Mandy sat, completely puzzled. Fatigue chewed at the edge of her consciousness like a somnolent dog worrying a bone. She had been removed from Raymond and Astrid at gunpoint hours before and bundled into a police car for the journey here, deep under some Manhattan building. Only signs on the walls acquainted her with the fact she was in the New York Stock Exchange. Three tough-looking men, armed to the teeth, had accompanied her and now were stationed at strategic places in the facility, as if they had taken over.

A bearded Arab, skilled with computer technology but stuck with a problem, had finally laid out the scheme to her. She was astonished at the scope of what they were trying to do, but her hacker instincts kicked in the moment she understood. What really appealed to her however was the fact that she could exercise her instincts, but then had to find a secret way to scuttle both her own efforts, and their plan. The adrenaline rush of the challenge had worn off hours ago under the serious circumstances and the frustrations she was fighting to actually break into the Exchange's system.

The screen before her blurred and slid around. She had thought herself within an ace of carrying off the connection to the New Jersey facility but there was one last frustrating and encoded hurdle. The computer program was a radically modified COBOL language and she was having difficulty trying to get acquainted with it. One of the Arab guards was coughing again. It was so distracting and annoying and he had been doing it since she arrived.

1302 hrs. New York Dockland.

Two men arrived and took Raymond away. It was hours since Mandy had been removed and he and Astrid were worried sick about her. There was no indication that she was even alive. Rolf was sitting at a long table covered with communication equipment and pads of paper covered with notes. Three other men were working, directing action, while a fourth stood ready with a Remington machine pistol.

"Things are not going well. Your girlfriend needs some persuasion to move along and get things going. I want you to talk to her and ensure she is successful."

"What is she doing?" Raymond tried for information, but Rolf cut him off.

"None of your business!" he jerked a finger at Raymond who suddenly found himself seized from each side. A knife appeared, held to his throat. Rolf punched numbers on a nearby phone and hit the speaker button.

"Yes?" It was Mandy's voice.

"You are not cooperating, Miss Smythe."

"I am doing the best I can. It's not my fucking fault you ignorant bastards have this so screwed up."

"Failure is not an option. Raymond is here and has a knife to his throat. He wants to tell you to hurry."

"You lousy bastard!"

Rolf let the insult roll off him without reaction. "You have fifteen minutes to prove some progress and then we shall start removing Mr. Barton's fingers, one by one, as each five minutes elapse. The clock is ticking. We will phone back in fifteen minutes and if my men cannot report progress, you shall hear the first finger being removed."

"Raymond, are you there?...Is it true?"

"Yes."

"Hold on, darling, I'm trying."

Rolf broke the connection, looked at his watch significantly, and then stared at Raymond. Raymond felt a trickle of cold sweat run down his spine.

1304 hrs. Basement, New York Stock Exchange.

"Hey! I need some help here."

The tall Arab with the automatic pistol stuck in his waistband walked over.

"I need to talk to whoever is on the other end of this system; otherwise I cannot go any further."

The man studied her inscrutably, his dark eyes fathomless. Without taking his gaze off her, he reached out for a nearby telephone and dialled a number. He spoke a few incomprehensible words and then proffered the instrument.

"Hello?"

"Yes," the man on the other end sounded cautious.

"Are you working the consoles over there?"

"Yes."

"What's your name?"

"Dennis."

"Very well, I am Mandy. I need the protocol for access to file seventy five, giving me the gate."

There was a pause. "The code is zero bravo eight Yankee four five," the man seemed reluctant to divulge the information.

"Then what?"

"I will pass you the next step on-screen," Dennis Piercy thought the woman sounded a little less threatening than the others he was dealing with and decided to take a chance, "Just give me a minute to input."

Mandy punched in the code and waited. The screen soon dissolved and came back up with groups of numbers. She began to type them in, but suddenly stopped. There was a familiarity to the number sets. Conscious of the Arab guard watching her, she idly tapped the *space* key to simulate activity. She scrutinized the numbers, certain she had seen the pattern before. Seizing a pencil, she scribbled on a pad, offering the telephone handset back to the Arab. As she intended, he took it as a dismissal and after hanging up, he moved away. As he did, he coughed, a non-productive hack, without using a hand in front of his face.

Mandy studied the numbers. What she had was '0114 0218 049 043 084 0104 0101 077'. The repetitive zeroes had caught her attention. It was not logical for use in a discrete code because, in encryption, repetitive symbols compromised the whole thing, making it easy to break.

Damn - what *was* this?

It made no sense. Going back to her pad, she traced the groups of numbers with her pencil and suddenly saw the rhythm of the whole thing. It was ASCII code, the protocol for changing symbols on a standard keyboard!

She went into a *Word* program and through *Insert*, brought up the character sets. By substituting, she came up with 'r Ú 1 + T h e M'. For a short eternity, it made no sense until she said it in her head. *'Are you one plus them'... 'Are you one of them?'* That was the message!

Grabbing the pencil, she assembled a message in return. "No /duress."

"Me2 I - 2 help W+kids."

'Me 2.' Mandy decided a small fib was justified. Pursing her lips, she blew out a long breath of air. She had an ally at the other end of the line who did not want to help but had a family to protect, but how could she make use of that? The bearded Arab was circulating back in her direction. Erasing the screen, she disguised her purpose by typing in numbers, peering intently as if in high concentration. The tension made her feel hot and short of breath. Come to think of it, it seemed to be getting very warm and close in the building. That seemed strange for the climate-controlled nature of a computer centre.

The man drifted away again, torn between curiosity and being accused of holding her up. Out of the corner of her eye, she saw him sit and become busy on another console, deep in concentration. Suddenly, he stopped and hacked into his hand, mopping his brow with the back of his forearm. These men should sure give up smoking, she thought.

Carefully, Mandy analyzed the situation. If they did not get the system running as the Arabs wanted, they would all die. Raymond, Astrid, and her new friend's family would also be sacrificed. Rolf had made that clear when he pushed her into this. At the same time, she needed to thwart the operation.

Just suppose there was a way of making it look like it was working and then it would self-cancel later?

Coding a message to Dennis, she made the suggestion.

He came back. 'E c e x d a t e'...'*Easy. Execute date.*'

Why were all the good solutions simple ones? Mandy saw it immediately. By burying a false execute date in the program, the data exchange could be made to revert to its values on that particular day. For instance two days ago! All the transactions would go ahead for today, but then, at an executive time command, revert to where they were. Then she saw a better way of doing it. It was elegant in its total simplicity. There was an element of risk, but they were already in a state of huge risk! For her plan to be successful, the bearded Arab would have to miss seeing what she had done. With an apparent success on his hands, why would he look for such a perfectly simple way of it all being sabotaged?

Excited now, she went into the computer settings and found the control panel. Sure enough, she found that it was possible to change the date in this computer. Her fingers blurred on the keyboard, striving to keep up with her racing mind.

'Maybe use computer control panel date setting for year 1990?' She sent to Dennis.

'R' came back. '*Roger!*' The international acknowledgement! She felt his enthusiasm and it sparked her determination to try it.

Mandy turned in her seat, calling to Bin-Yussef. "I think I have solved it! Get me that phone number again."

The Arab came over himself, and dialling the number, handed her the handset. Obviously excited, he hovered over her, watching every move. The tall guard stood behind him.

"Hello, I am ready for the execute file now, please send it to me."

Five minutes later, the buying and selling of America's major companies flooded across the screens. In a matter of seconds, Exxon was sold to foreign interests. Boeing fell into the hands of a buyer from Lebanon by massive buying. General Motors went the same way, followed rapidly by four hundred companies listed on Fortune Five Hundred.

Trades, buys and sells were all accommodated by the program set loose on the New York Stock Exchange. In fifteen minutes, it was done. Fortunes had been lost, transferred to other interests. Trillions of dollars had been injected into the markets to perform *legitimate* sales. Money transfers had crisscrossed the continents, ensuring that total confusion as to their allocations would result. The trillions had eventually reverted to the source, along with the accumulated value of the market. Not a single bank or corporation would now make a payment because once the gridlock was released and money began to flow, the monetary system and the markets would collapse. Defensive greed would ensure that nobody would want to be the first to go bankrupt by making a payment.

Such abnormal activity on the NYSE would automatically close the market, pending investigation, but there were only a handful of people in attendance and they knew nothing about the computer infiltration. Bin-Yussef's program had defused alarms concerning such a run on the market, so it was invisible to them. Besides, in the abnormal confusion of the place, they were not looking for any more problems than they had already.

Now, in fifteen minutes, America had been sold.

Mandy was elated that, outwardly, she had achieved the objective of the terrorists, as she now recognized them, but had perhaps, managed to thwart their plan in the long term. She wondered what would happen next, how she could effect some kind of escape plan. Before she could make any progress with that thought, there was a sudden clatter nearby. The Arab who had been coughing so much had fallen to the floor, dropping his weapon.

Two men rushed over to him, finding him shaking and jerking in some kind of seizure. The room was filled with the sound of several people coughing and suddenly, with a chill that doused her elevated temperature, Mandy realized what she had been listening to for the past several hours. These people were succumbing to Agent Twenty-nine! Her mouth fell open in shock and dismay, even as a cough began to well up from her own lungs.

"It's the disease! Don't you see? It's what has shut down New York! He has the disease! We *all* have it!" she screamed the words and the men all turned at once. One by one she saw the horror creep over their faces as they acknowledged the fact. Two more of them began to cough and it was almost like a signal.

From the paralysis of realization, there came panicked reaction. One of the Arabs began to head for the door, intent on fleeing. There was an immediate clatter of weapons being cocked and the three men who had accompanied Mandy levelled their guns, intent on keeping him in the room. Immediately, two of the Arabs turned their sub-machine guns on them and opened fire.

The sound of gunfire in the room was overwhelming. In the first exchange, two Arabs and one of Rolf's henchmen went down in bloodied heaps, falling over desks and leaving red smears down the walls. Everyone else went to ground behind protective furniture. Bin-Yussef was screaming for them to cease fire, afraid the bullets ricocheting around the room would destroy computer equipment and affect the outcome of the mission.

A burst of gunfire was his reward, the rounds taking him through the chest and head. He staggered back; embracing a computer screen for support before sliding to the floor, dragging the whole assembly with him in an explosion of sparks and smoke.

Mandy was under her desk, cringing against the metal wall of a filing cabinet. Someone nearby was screaming, horrible tortured screams of agony. In another round of fire, something made a heavy thud into the desk and she curled up in the fetal position, vainly seeking protection. There had been about eleven men in the place before they started fighting. She tried to play back in her mind how many were left and where they were. Three had gone down in the initial exchange. Bearded man was next and obviously, another was wounded but maybe still armed, plus the man who had keeled over. That left five active fighters.

The remainder of Rolf's men were closer to the door, over to her right while the three Arabs were over to the left. Just as she figured this out, the Arabs made their move for the door. Laying down a curtain of gunfire, they stormed forward, to be met by an equally daunting exchange of bullets. One of them went down while the two others went to ground again, having gained several yards.

Mandy knew she had to escape. Everyone in this room was doomed by Agent Twenty-nine, but they would all be killed in this madness first. Figuring they were too busy concentrating on each other, she began to crawl across the floor. After a minute or two, flinching from the occasional flight of errant rounds, she found herself behind the reception desk, at right angles to the door itself.

She would have to go around the desk, open the door and get through it before anyone could shoot her. It would take about four seconds, assuming the door was not locked. Not far away, she knew one of Rolf's men was holed up with a clear shot at the door. Casting around, she found a three-tier filing tray on the desktop. Hefting it, she took two deep breaths and then tossed it clear across the room.

As soon as the clatter of the tray hitting something sounded, both groups of men opened fire at the source. In a half-crouch, Mandy tore around the desk, bumping into the metal of the door. Expecting to feel the impact of rounds in her back at any instant, she seized the doorknob but it slipped under her sweaty grasp. Frantically, she grabbed with both hands and twisted. The door opened inwards and just as she pulled and swung it open, someone yelled.

Diving to the floor outside, allowing the door to swing shut behind her, she heard someone open fire on her, the rounds whipping over her and singing off the concrete passageway outside. Another burst of counter-fire came from inside and the shooting stopped. Rolling over on the linoleum floor, she sat up against the wall, protected by the angle of the wall near the door.

She had to get away before somebody pursued her, but there maybe a minute or two of grace, given the standoff situation inside. Dimly, she became aware of a voice calling. There were stairs further down the passageway, coming down from one side and somewhere above, someone was calling out, anxiously questioning what was going on down below. She did not recognize the language, but thought it must be Arabic. That meant there was no way out and sooner or later, the man above would come down to investigate.

Carefully staying against the wall, Mandy opened the first door on the right. It was a janitor's room, stacked with boxes, mops and pails. There were only two more doors before the stairs. The next was locked. More sound of gunfire came from the computer centre as she tried the next door.

The light was out in the room but she groped and found a light switch. It turned out to be a utility room, with an open area to one side about twelve feet square. There was almost nowhere to hide, especially from a determined search. About a quarter of the space was covered by a series of long black bags and she went over to investigate. At the last moment, with repugnance, she recognized them as body bags. She was ensconced in the room with about a dozen corpses!

At first she wondered what they were doing here, then remembered from the television instructions that the authorities had been handing out such things for families to bag their dead, awaiting removal. The Exchange must have had some deaths and put these poor people down here to be removed later. She coughed, almost feeling the telltale symptom of fluid in her lungs, growing by the second, eating up her life. Her skin felt flushed and she knew she was already running a temperature. She wondered for a moment about Raymond and Astrid.

Outside, she now heard two men calling, closer by, in the passageway. Stooping, she grasped the tab and opened the zipper on the nearest body bag. A foul stench met her, feces and urine released by the nerveless orifices of the cadaver within. Momentarily, she paused and then, opening the zipper fully, rolled the body out. It was a middle-aged man, dressed in a once-expensive suit, now ruined by unmentionable stains. Half of his face was shot away and she realized that some of the dead were probably victims of the forced entry by the Arabs, taking over the computer centre.

Seizing the empty bag, she dragged it across the floor closer to the wall and taking a deep breath, slid into it. Reaching down, her bottom soaking in a cold reeking wetness, she pulled up the zipper to her forehead and rolled over. Moments later, the door opened.

There came a sharp command and one of the men entered the room. He immediately made a strangled protest, obviously assailed by the stench. It was followed by a low exclamation of horror, and then by obvious praying. The first voice gave another command and the man in the room made another protest. At more vocal insistence, he came further in and Mandy heard a steady thumping noise. At first she was puzzled what he was doing, then realized he was kicking the corpses, ensuring they were indeed dead. She desperately needed to cough, a steadily growing rigidity and swelling of her chest and throat threatening to betray her.

Desperately, she willed herself to relax, hoping the shock of the kick would not release the paroxysm of expectoration her body demanded. She heard the dull thud of the kick at the nearest body bag and steeled herself for her turn. Barely heard in her confined space, a new burst of gunfire sounded and the man in the doorway issued a quick order. With a grunt of relief, the man lowered his foot from the bag he was about to kick and headed quickly for the door.

It was horrendously hot in the bag, made worse by her rising temperature. Mandy could feel herself drifting in and out of consciousness as the fever took hold. A sudden chill made her begin to shiver, no longer in control, hoping the men would not come back. She reasoned they were not searching for her specifically, at least for now. They had turned the light out on leaving and she was in total blackness. It was desperately hot inside the bag. Reaching down, she unzipped it, no longer caring if the men did return. Despite the horror she lay in and the other horrors around her, she felt relatively calm, caught in the aftermath of adrenaline overdose.

She had a brief moment of lucid thought and felt elated that the bearded Arab had died before he could discover the anomaly she had injected into the computer program. She had achieved her purpose, and Raymond would be proud. She tried to picture his face, hoped he was okay. It was her last conscious thought. Exhausted, dehydrated and oxygen-deprived, she sank into torpor. Passing one hundred and three degrees, her body began to shut down functions unnecessary to life. She entered a world of descending darkness and drifted away, downwards past phantoms that could no longer threaten her.

1310 hrs. Warehouse, New York Dockland.

Raymond was sent back to Astrid. When the door closed, he quickly filled her in on events. She pointed silently up and he followed her gaze. Ten feet above them, high on the wall above a rickety chair, an air register screen had been loosened from its mountings. It was a narrow rectangle, about twenty by fourteen inches. Silently, Astrid tapped her chest and pointed up. It looked hopeless, but probably their only chance. Quickly, Raymond nodded and moved with his back to the wall. Astrid put her foot in the stirrups he made with his hands. Just as she went to hoist herself up, she stooped and gave him a quick kiss. One knee went on his shoulder and for a moment, he was treated to her belly shoved in his face before she stood fully on his shoulders.

There was a considerable amount of wriggling and she whispered down for him to step away from the wall. Taking the soles of her shoes in his hands, he helped her up. Moments later she was in the ductwork. He listened for noise but after a brief sibilant series of metallic scrapings, there was silence. Astrid was gone.

Inside the ductwork, Astrid fought down a brief moment of claustrophobic panic. Her arms were out ahead of her and the only way she could move was to grab the joints in the metal which occurred every four feet and pull herself along. Her legs were useless as there was no room to move them and her hips almost filled the space. She could feel her nails breaking and the skin coming off her fingertips as she reached and pulled, reached and pulled. There was almost total darkness and she had to go by feel. After what seemed like forever, her frantic hands reached out into nothingness. Feeling around, she discovered her branch of the ventilating system had opened out into a larger supply line that was circular and almost three feet across.

The system was not working, so lack of airflow did not tell her which way to turn. Desperately, she tried to figure a logical direction to go in. There seemed to be a slope and deciding that the hot air source would be downwards, she set off in that direction on her hands and knees. A very faint light filtered in through holes and from tributary ducts like the one she had entered. A tingling in her nostrils told her of the dust collected in the bottom of the duct which she now stirred up. In moments, her body stiffened with the need to sneeze. Seizing her nose, she had to give in to the involuntary reaction. There! Once, twice, three times! Stifling the paroxysms shook her whole being and she felt a faint vibration through the duct from the rigid contractions of her body. She froze, fearing a swarm of bullets like angry bees hunting her body, but none came and no cry of alarm betrayed her.

As quickly as possible, she moved on. A growing light ahead suggested an opening. At a bend, she found another wider grille. Focused on that, she missed the vertical shaft yawning below her and pitched in headfirst. She loosed an involuntary little cry before spreading herself out like a giant spider. Her legs and arms made friction against the sides of the duct and by twisting her body, her hips and shoulders arrested her fall. Hands and forearms screamed with lacerations against sharp metal. The ductwork rattled and pinged, amplifying the sound of her struggles like some vast communication network determined to advertise her presence.

She listened, but again, no alarm came. Encouraged, she reached back between her legs and grasped the lip of the tunnel she had fallen into. Taking her weight with her left arm, she shrunk her body and pulled, expanding herself again to lodge her body in the shaft. Inch by inch she pulled herself up until she lay across the vertical drop. The grille opening was on her right and she twisted to push on it. There was no give to it. Angling herself around, she placed the flat of her feet against it and pushed. It bent but would not come loose. With no other option, and there being no attention paid to the row she had been making, she kicked it hard once and was rewarded by one corner separating. Again, the ductwork announced her efforts with a fanfare of sound. Her body seemed to shrivel with the expectancy of discovery.

Now she was able to open the gap by steady pressure, bending the grille, hearing the tearing of screws out of their metal beds. Carefully, she bent the grille back out of her way, supported by one screw so it would not crash to the floor below. Wriggling around, she let her legs out and slid until she hung down the wall. At the last moment, her hands failed to grip as they slithered on some wetness and she crashed unprepared to the floor.

She wound up sitting against the wall, the breath knocked out of her. Holding her hands before her face, she found them bleeding profusely from the metal snags they had encountered in the ductwork. No wonder she could not hold on! Recovering, knowing time was limited, she discovered she was in another large room. Pieces of equipment lay around, dusty and discarded. As a weapon, she chose a piece of metal pipe about two feet long. Praying the door was not locked, she moved to it and tried the handle. It turned easily and with a sigh of relief, she cautiously opened it a crack. Outside was a landing, with stairs descending to the left. Seeing no other sign of life, she opened the door wider and slid out. Almost immediately, she was assailed by the smell of cigarette smoke and froze.

Inching towards the railings, Astrid cautiously peered down the stairwell. Ten feet below her, on the next flight of stairs, a man sat smoking. He was on the fourth step up, facing down, a machine pistol laying on the step beside him. Taking a deep breath, Astrid inched over to the left side of the stairs, away from him and crouching down, began to sidle her way downward. At any moment he could look up and see her and she would be totally helpless. She figured she could flee back the way she had come in the time he could grab his weapon, cock it and open fire, but it would be a close thing. Once she reached the reverse landing, she would be more behind him, but more committed. In the event he became aware of her, she would have to rush her attack and get him before he could react.

Praying the stairs would not creak, she eased her weight onto each tread with elaborate care. Reaching the landing, she kept to the side. Pausing momentarily, her pulse beating in her head like a thunderous drum, she started down again. There were four steps before she would be in range of him with the steel pipe. On the third, the wood creaked, almost the same moment that he became aware of a presence behind him. He turned to his right, away from her and it gave her the split second she needed. Darting down the last step, she swung the pipe as hard as she could, catching him square across the top of the head. Astrid felt a jarring in her wrists and shoulders as the pipe connected with a horrible thud, accompanied by a crack as the man's skull caved in. He went down without a sound, slithering to the landing below in a lifeless heap.

Seizing his weapon, Astrid stepped over the body and went to the door off the landing. A sign on the door told her she was now two floors below the one Raymond was being held on. Cracking the door, she spied a corridor beyond. A window at the near end looked out over a fire escape. The stairway they had climbed on arrival had been a mangy beige colour whereas the one she had just exited was white. Did she now choose the white or the beige one to effect a surprise entry? Did the white one provide access to Raymond's floor? Going back into the stairwell, she found a two-way radio next to the man she had clubbed.

She thought she could use the radio to create the diversion she needed to get onto the upper floor. A red fire alarm pull on the wall reminded her of the method they had used to get Mandy out of the hotel in Frankfurt. This one was probably disconnected though. Since the man at her feet had been guarding these stairs, it made sense that someone else would be guarding the others and she would never get by them with any element of surprise.

Making her choice, she went quickly up two floors and paused at the door to the fourth story. Cracking it open, she peered along the corridor. Nobody was in sight. The double doors they had entered earlier off the corridor opened to the right, about halfway along. At least she had found her way back. Checking the magazine and cocking the weapon, she stepped into the corridor.

Back against the wall, she peered around the corner into the suite of offices in which Rolf and Raymond were. She could see two men sitting at a table inside, armed to the teeth but looking quite relaxed. They would have to be taken out first. At the first shot, everyone would be alerted and she did not know how many men guarding the lower floors would come up behind her. As if in answer to her thought, she suddenly heard voices behind the door at the far end of the corridor and the door began to open. Another second and the persons arriving would spot her and the game was up. Kneeling, she aimed and made ready.

Two men stepped through the doorway, the first looking back at the other as he gesticulated to make a point. It was the second man who saw Astrid first and he made to yell and draw a pistol. The weapon bucked in her hands as she opened fire, two quick bursts that took the two men reeling and tumbling to the floor. Without pause, she triggered the weapon again, stepping around the doorpost to kill the men at the table. They both went backwards out of their chairs, arms, legs and equipment flying.

With lightning swiftness, Astrid pounced on another machine pistol on the table, cocking it and swiveling towards the next room. She caught a third occupant in the doorway, gunning him down as he opened fire. She screamed and ducked as bullets deflected off the walls. With her free hand she grabbed an automatic from the floor and shifting grips, cocked it so she had a gun in each hand. Furniture crashed over in the next room and there was a heavy pounding of feet. Two guns opened up, spraying her area with rounds. Next moment, two more men darted into the room.

Crouching, Astrid caught one with a round from the automatic, simultaneously opening up on the other with the machine pistol without aiming. Before she knew it, the second was on her, kicking the weapon from her grasp. For some reason, her left arm would not move and she was helpless as he raised his own barrel, a look of triumph on his face. Next instant, his face blossomed red as a fusillade of fire came from behind him. His partner, blinded by blood, had opened fire and cut him down.

Rolling away, Astrid grabbed her weapon again and finished the second man with a couple of rounds. Behind her she heard a ruckus as other guards pounded onto the floor in answer to the gunfire. She needed help. Grabbing a couple more guns, she darted into the anteroom and found the door where Raymond was. Quickly she unbolted the door and swung it open. Another door slammed close by and she heard feet pounding away. Rolf escaping!

"Watch the door!" Raymond's anxious face appeared and she thrust the weapons into his hands. Almost immediately, he opened fire and someone outside yelled. Frantically, Astrid went to the window of the outer office and peered out. An iron fire escape ran beneath the window and disappeared around the building corner to meet the escape stairs she had seen earlier.

"Raymond!" She smashed the glass with the butt of her gun and started to climb out. Taking in her intent, Raymond slammed the door to the room and one-handed a filing cabinet behind it. Sprinting across the room, he straddled the sill and pumped off a few rounds through the door to discourage pursuit.

They made it around the corner a split second before bullets howled off the stone trimmed wall. Reaching the escape steps, Astrid, without looking, pressed the muzzle of her weapon against the window at the end of the corridor and opened fire, hosing the passageway beyond. Screams from nearby saluted her action and they pounded down the steps. Someone tried to draw a bead on them from above and bullets ricocheted off the ironwork. In seconds, they were down. A metal canopy running along the building gave them cover from gunfire from above and they sprinted around the corner.

A small fenced-off staff parking area stood to one side of the main entrance. Just as they arrived, a dark green truck pulled in and braked hard to a stop. Flinging open the driver door, a man got out and ran head-down away from the vehicle, groping inside his jacket while watching them both. Without thinking, Astrid fired at him and he staggered and fell. Running over, she kicked the drawn handgun away from the man.

"Here!" She jumped into the driver's seat of the pickup and twisted the key in the ignition. Blue smoke billowed around the tires as she gunned the truck backward out of its parking stall. Raymond bailed into the back bed and she took off, flinging gravel. Blowing by the entrance to the warehouse, Raymond leveled his weapon and emptied it at some movement and the next moment, they were gone, the truck rocking as Astrid straightened it out on the street and floored the gas pedal.

After a few blocks, Astrid slowed down on a quiet street and Raymond nimbly climbed into the front seat. "Phew, that was close!" Astrid grinned at him.

"Yeah, but now we have another problem."

"Like what?"

Raymond tapped an object on the floor with his foot. Glancing down, Astrid was horrified to see one of the Agent Twenty-nine cylinders lying on the floor.

"The biological stuff?"

"How come we can't get away from it?"

1334 hrs. North Brooklyn, New York City.

"Shit! They are after us!" Looking back, Raymond could see the Lincoln coming around the last corner. There was a winking of light as one of the men leaned out of the window and opened fire. The rounds went high, more intimidation than threat.

"What shall I do?" Astrid fought the wheel, careening around another corner of the deserted streets, the accelerator to the floor.

"What street are we on?"

"What difference does it make?" A couple of rounds fired from the Lincoln howled off the roof and Astrid ducked.

"Division Avenue," Raymond answered his own question, "Turn left at the next!" The patient progress of red traffic lights hanging over empty streets was superfluous as the Dakota's tires shrieked around the intersection. Desperately, Raymond tried to visualize a map of New York in his mind.

"What street?"

"Missed it!"

"Oh fuck!" The Lincoln was gaining and their rear windshield disintegrated. They were coming up fast on an overhead freeway. There were traffic lights under the arch and a sign that pointed left for *Manhattan. Williamsburg Bridge.*

"Go left, Astrid!"

Swerving over to the left lane, Astrid cranked the wheel hard. They shot under the overpass, skidding onto an access road. "Oh-oh!" Directly ahead, the approaches to the Williamsburg Bridge gave them no more opportunity to turn off. The freeway was ramped upwards, the huge steel-girder and cable structure of the bridge looming ahead.

The Lincoln was only a quarter block behind now, closing fast. Another rattle of gunfire came from it but Astrid was weaving, throwing off the aim of the gunmen.

"Shit! Goddamn!" Flashing lights showed a police roadblock directly ahead. There was no point in stopping; the occupants of the Lincoln would finish them off before the police could intervene. Three cars were parked across the roadway, with wooden barricades stretched out in front of them. Already, Astrid could see officers taking position, alerted by the sound of gunfire coming their way.

There was one small chance, in the left of the roadway. She swerved left, lining up the narrow gap between the rear of the cop car and the bridge divider. Seeing the roadblock, the Lincoln gunmen opened up on it, spraying rounds into the police cars. Glass and debris flew under the assault and one police officer went down as bullets went right through the vehicle he was hiding behind. Recognizing the major threat, since no attack was coming from the green Dakota, most of the officers turned their weapons on the Lincoln.

Astrid straightened the wheel again and floored the gas. She ducked as the wooden barrier disintegrated over the hood, starring the windshield and littering the area with shattered wood. In seconds, the right fender of the truck contacted the right rear of the police cruiser. There was a thunderous crash and they were thrown against their seat belts. The cruiser, as Astrid had planned, was jammed around, making a wider gap, while the Dakota was hurled to the left. It bounced off the road divider, back into the cleared path. A courageous policeman straightened up as they went by and discharged a shotgun through their right rear tire. Then they were by.

Following close in their path, the Lincoln did not fare so well. Swerving to make the hole Astrid had prepared, the driver threw off the aim of the three gunmen inside. The police had been augmented by three National Guardsmen who bravely stood up and emptied their M-16 automatic rifles at the speeding car.

The driver died before the Lincoln hit the divider and with its engine block shot through, only the sheer momentum of the big car kept it going. It too bounced off the divider and lurching right ninety degrees, headed for the parapet of the bridge approach, now inside the police barrier. Two more of the officers emptied magazines into the stricken vehicle before it ploughed into the parapet, still travelling at fifty miles per hour. It stood on its nose, displaying its underside for a vital second before slowly toppling forward out of sight over the rail. There was a crash from below and a column of flame shot up.

Seeing the Dakota getting out of immediate range, one of the officers got on the radio to the roadblock on the other end of the bridge. Half the roadblock force sprinted to standby vehicles and set off in pursuit.

1343 hrs. Williamsburg Bridge.

The Dakota was labouring. The front end was entirely smashed, the fenders rubbing on the tires. Steam from the shattered radiator further obliterated Astrid's view through the starred windshield. A deep gash on her forehead flowed blood into her left eye. She had the wheel hard over to the left to try and keep straight since the right rear was now just a rim. Her lacerated hands screamed at her, flowing blood over the steering wheel and making steering difficult.

Raymond was leaning against the door, nursing some wound she could only suppose at. She yelled at him, rewarded only by an anguished shaking of his head. The radiator steam became a total fog and she could hear the scream of tortured metal. The truck lurched, swung out of control to the right and ran into the bridge railing, forty-five degrees to the road. Leaping out, terrified of fire, Astrid ran around the rear to the other door and yanked it open. Raymond half fell out.

"Come on, we have to get clear!" she pulled at him, sensing his body resisting, "Raymond! Let's go!"

He was mumbling something at her, reaching back into the truck. "Have to finish it."

She hesitated, and then suddenly understood as he emerged, the cylinder of Agent Twenty-nine cradled in his arm. Staggering, Raymond went to the bridge parapet. He looked at the water. From between the huge girders, he could see that the East River was choppy under a brisk wind out of the west. The high vantage point showed the tall buildings either side of the river, silent under the sunny day, still under curfew. He heard the distant hoot of sirens as their pursuers came upon them from both directions and he knew they were too exhausted to evade them any longer. He looked down at the cylinder of gas.

"This cannot fall into the hands of anyone."

Astrid raised her head, her face gray with fatigue, "So what?"

"The gold. The names. The history. All of that is perhaps just and I acknowledge that. However, this stuff is too horrendous to contemplate and I do not want it in anyone else's hands; it does not matter who they are!"

"Throw it in the river," Astrid's voice was dull.

"But it is so dangerous!"

"The ocean has always been the great dumping ground for poisons. The wind is going off shore and the tide is going out. Surely there are no drinking water uptakes for New York downstream from here. It should be safe. Open the lid and throw it in the water."

The sirens became louder, insistent and threatening.

Raymond took the cylinder and with one more glance around, held it over the water on the side of the bridge. Grasping it at arm's length, he took a deep breath and held it. He tried to turn the screw top on the cylinder but it resisted his efforts. The sirens were getting closer, the cars almost on top of them now. He brought the cylinder back and studied the end closely. There were a couple of raised dogs on top that were probably designed to be engaged by an opening tool. Shifting his grip on it, Raymond rapped the top smartly a couple of times on the bridge railing, trying to catch the raised dogs at an angle that would jolt the threads.

Hunched over, the cylinder jammed between his thighs, he clenched the top in a vice-like hold, locked his arms and used his upper body to rotate the lid. He did not know what the contents consisted of but he was terrified of being exposed to them. Conscious that he was only inches away from a certain and horrible death, he strained as hard as he could. The old screw top resisted at first, but then gave way to his force. Someone nearby was shouting loud demands at him.

He felt Astrid step between him and the loud voices, shielding him. Bravely, she faced the armed men, hands raised, reassuring their fears and giving Raymond time. Finally, spinning the top off, he dropped it and inverted the cylinder over the drop below. Momentarily, he saw a shower of gray crystals pour from the opening before he dropped the whole assembly. It quickly disappeared from sight, its path into the water marked by a faint splash far below, seconds later. Then it was gone.

Turning, Raymond found a dozen police officers and National Guardsmen pointing guns at him and Astrid. With a sense of relief, he recognized that the running was over.

1359 hrs. 1000 feet above New York.

Captain Lee de Silva of the United States Army looked down from his AH64A Apache helicopter gun-ship at the expanse of New York below. It was a clear day, with none of the usual smog. He shuddered to think of the death abroad in the otherwise peaceful scene. The helicopter was on patrol, powered back to conserve fuel and extend his patrol time. It had been a boring assignment for the past few days, but they had been briefed that there were armed and dangerous elements operating in the city that they may be called upon to engage at any time.

The only excitement de Silva and his crewman, Lieutenant James 'Liquor' Galliano had encountered so far was to pursue vehicles on the freeways that had somehow eluded roadblocks. The nightmarish sight of an attack gun-ship hovering ten feet above the road, nose-on to a speeding vehicle had a very persuasive effect. For the umpteenth time, he stifled a yawn and then bugged Galliano about the lifelessness of his native city. Before Galliano could find words, their radio burst to life.

"Stand-off Two Six, expedite to Sector Alpha One Niner for possible interdiction. Coordinates follow."

"Stand-off Two Six." De Silva increased power as he swung the big helicopter on course, nosing it down to speed up. Galliano punched numbers into the Global Positioning Navigation system, giving him a track to their destination.

"Stand-off Two Six, switch Two Two Three point Five for further."

On the new frequency, de Silva checked in.

"Roger, Two Six, this is Curfew One Five. We have a New York police van which has shot-up two patrol cars and is proceeding northbound. One of our cars is following at a safe distance. Occupants are not, repeat, not police officers. Considered heavily armed and dangerous."

"Sounds just like us. Coordinates?" The radio responded with a series of numbers that de Silva ignored, knowing Galliano would be punching them into the navigation system.

"Let us know when you spot it. A roadblock is being set up and it should be there in about three minutes."

"Wadd'ya think, 'Liquor'?" De Silva spoke to his weapons officer.

"I think I am doing a weapons test. Heading to target is on your gyro." Quickly and efficiently, the two airmen ran through their checklists as the pilot swung onto the assigned heading. De Silva threw a switch and an enunciator light told him that the chain gun in the nose would now point wherever he looked. He only had to depress the firing button on his control stick to shoot anything he looked at. Radar and the infrared tracking were selected to standby. The two point seven-five inch rockets were probably overkill, but they too were checked for status. The specified stretch of road appeared ahead and de Silva eased the Apache down to five hundred feet above ground.

"Curfew, this is Stand-off Two Six. Target vehicle in sight. Northbound, speed about sixty. I see your following squad car."

The highway below was starting to run through more rural scenery, with fields and woodland at the roadside.

"Roger Two Six, if he does not stop at the roadblock, your assistance may be required."

1403 hrs.

In the van, Rolf and four of his men were headed for Westchester. Rolf was hoping to escape in his aircraft but a nosey pair of cops had tried to pull them over. The two luckless officers had taken on more than they could handle and been gunned down. Two police cruisers had found the van soon afterward and when one of them had gotten too close, the rear door of the van had been thrown open. The combined firepower of two assault rifles had taken out the front of the car behind, killing the driver. The vehicle veered out of control, hit a barrier and flipped into a car lot.

"Roadblock up ahead!" the van driver called out, "I think I can go around it through the ditch!"

One man took position behind the driver and one on the passenger side. Each held an assault rifle. Coming up on the three police cruisers parked across the road, they leaned out of the open windows and commenced firing. Officers dived for cover under the overwhelming firepower. Swerving to the right and gauging his speed carefully against the slope of the ditch, the driver expertly took the van around the police cars.

Rolf kicked the rear door open and opened fire on the policemen. At the same time, dust and debris flew off the van as the officers returned fire. Holes dimpled the sides and the man behind the driver slumped over him, blood spraying the windshield. Desperately holding him off with one arm while wrestling the steering wheel, the driver hit the gas pedal and the van fishtailed onto the tarmac again.

1404 hrs.

"Two Six, this is Sheriff Beatty," the man was yelling into the mike and must have been at the roadblock, "You are authorized to use full force to stop that van. Kill those mother-fuckers!"

"Roger, Sheriff. Consider it done," de Silva pitched the nose of the helicopter down. He had witnessed what had happened and now went into the deliberate, cold-blooded and methodical state that had earned him top awards in training.

1405 hrs.

In the back of the van, Rolf finished jamming another magazine into the Kalashnikov he held. The door had swung half closed and he kicked it open, ready to fire on the roadblock, now receding fast behind him. What he saw froze his blood.

De Silva had leveled the Apache, nose angled down, twenty feet above the road, only about fifty yards behind the speeding van, and matching its speed. He saw the rear door fly open and a man trying to bring a weapon to bear on him before he depressed the firing button. The Boeing M230 chain-gun fires thirty-millimetre explosive shells at a rate of six hundred and twenty-five rounds per minute. Guided by de Silva's eyes, the two-second burst put fifteen rounds into the van.

The occupants were reduced to bloody shreds. The walls of the van burst like a tin can and the front end simply disappeared. Only the axles made it to the ditch. Pulling the Apache around in a tight climbing turn to avoid debris, de Silva returned and hovered close by until several police cars arrived.

New York, the aftermath.

In the days following, thousands of fish were washed up on the shores of the Hudson. The authorities broadcast warnings to people not to touch or eat the dead fish and dispatched crews to clean up. They did not know the cause, but regarded it as some possible industrial contaminant.

After two weeks, with no further cases of the respiratory virus, the scare was over and life began to return to normal. Meantime, unable to identify themselves as Americans, Raymond and Astrid had been interrogated at a local office. In a matter of hours, they were in the joint hands of the Central Intelligence Agency and the Federal Bureau of Investigation.They were flown to Langley, separated, and when their identities were admitted, the evidence already compiled ensured their stories were listened to and treated as true.

August 1990. Fallout.

Sixty three thousand New Yorkers had died as a result of the biological attack and a further eighty thousand had survived symptoms of the sickness. Recalling the SS letter describing the nature of the illness, Raymond and Astrid were able to guide the authorities in coping with the progress of the disease. Despite that, a worldwide epidemic was narrowly averted by the prompt action of the U.S. Government. Nationwide, a further seventeen thousand people had died and there were isolated deaths throughout the world amounting to a further five thousand.

Putting the pieces together took some time, especially in view of the chaos and scarcity of people working. Someone had called the police when gunfire and explosions had erupted in the basement computer centre at the NYSE. The place was wrecked by bullets and someone had tossed a hand grenade, killing all present.

The mystery deepened when the New Jersey facility of the NYSE was visited and similar mayhem was found. All the occupants had been shot dead, although the equipment was intact and functioning. It was not until Monday morning that the significance of activity at both places became apparent.

Initially stupefied by the immensity of having America's businesses sold off, the Government went into rapid action. All transactions made on the Friday were declared null and void by Presidential order. The President also made another appearance on television and openly declared war on any party who made any act relating to ownership or was found to illegally hold shares.

The world money market ground to a halt, with money transfers frozen. Banks were ordered closed. The media blared that it would take months, even years, to resolve the situation. The authorities had not yet discovered the anomaly that Mandy and Dennis Piercy had put in place.

Raymond and Astrid had done all they could to assist. They told the story from beginning to end, exposing Streicher, El Jefe, Wesler, Rolf, and the international teams that had pursued them. It all sounded like fiction, but it was backed by events they could not otherwise have invented. They each tried, desperately, to get the authorities to find Mandy but in the chaotic aftermath, there appeared to be no trace of her. Raymond was desperate. He did not know where Rolf had sent her, only that she had been forced to do something under threat of harm to him.

Days after the biological hazard was declared over, Raymond and Astrid still fought for information on Mandy. They had been interrogated relentlessly by teams of people from a multitude of government agencies, anxious to resolve events. They told the truth, independently corroborating each other's stories until even the staunchest of investigators suspecting connivance agreed that they had reached the ground zero of truth.

Each of them tried swapping information on Mandy for information on their story, but it resulted in nothing. Either the authorities knew nothing, or they were holding out.

Finally, one week after their capture on the bridge, they were told that no trace of Mandy had been found. The bombing of the underground computer control room at the New York Stock Exchange had resulted in fires and almost total destruction of any human remains within. Since it was the place most likely for her to have been sent, they had to concede that to all intents and purposes, Mandy was lost. There was the added grim reality of corpses there which had succumbed to the virus.

Given some time alone together at the end of their interrogations, Raymond and Astrid were inconsolable. She had lost a husband through a betrayal beyond countenance but whether he was dead or alive was unknown. The effect was the same. Raymond had definitely lost Mandy. The fact that she had not surfaced in the last week spoke legions to their concerns.

Raymond cried in Astrid's arms, and she in his. She cried for her loss, the treachery, the deceit, while he cried for love lost. They had been comfortable together as lovers, now they mourned with the same degree of loss. It was strange that they could each bemoan their loss, yet find little comfort with each other, so great was the torment.

Ten days later, Astrid received confirmation of Rolf's death. This had been achieved by dental records and DNA. Although they told her the facts surrounding his death, they said a different official story would be issued, one she would have to accept.

Captain de Beauville's message to his superiors was flashed to Ponsonby. With the knowledge they had a major conspirator in their hands and conscious of the U.S. President's threat concerning foreign forces on U.S. soil, he decided to preserve this asset. He ordered the SAS troopers to go underground and interrogate Wesler fully.

The revelation that the apparent biological attack had a limited time period was a huge relief. He quickly briefed the Prime Minister, who cautiously relayed some of the information to the U.S. President. Since this corroborated what Raymond and Astrid were telling them, the authorities were able to formulate a plan. At this point in time, the British refused to reveal their source.

Once started, Wesler sang like a canary. The interrogators showed him news footage that showed irrefutably that the plot had failed. He confirmed the steel boxes containing Höher Zwech information had been sent to the estanzia in Paraguay. He told of El Jefe, the gold buried in the Vogtland and revealed his limited knowledge of the New York attack. The British quickly visited the ranch in the Chaco. When they found the charred remains of the house and heard the story from the servants, they were able to conclude, somewhat guardedly, that the documents had been destroyed.

After breathing several sighs of relief and rocking his chair to within a millimetre of total destabilization, Ponsonby decided to pass the information along to the Israelis. Mordecai bar Havalah did his own investigation and while not entirely trusting the British, was forced to the same conclusion. One man hoped the documents were destroyed and the other wished they had survived the fire. The likelihood seemed to be that they were lost. A few weeks later, the Israelis were given Wesler to interrogate, with the stipulation that the British did not expect to get him back. Information on numerous Höher Zwech identities worldwide was retrieved, much of it based on Wesler's revelations.

Gazing up near-vertically at his ceiling, Ponsonby reflected that it was a very neat move on his part to launch the Israelis on a track of vengeance against mutual enemies. Because Höher Zwech had been such a deep and well-kept secret, the conditions of Operation Sandbag were more easily met. The Arab extremists were blamed for the whole biological attack and assault on America's businesses. The Americans meanwhile went on the most massive manhunt in history for the culprits. While Ponsonby regretted the loss of George Jenkins, he counted his death as an expense to the total end.

Eventually, the disappearance of Rolf Klemerer in the U.S. was attributed to his contracting the disease and his death and final disposition of his remains was listed amongst thousands of other unknowns. His family, friends, employees, and his wife accepted this explanation.

Only days later, an eighty five year old man whom local Phoenix kids called *Grandpa Gustav* died of a pulmonary embolism after disappearing for several days. Because of his age, the coroner department's cursory postmortem examination missed the anal needle puncture. He had no next-of-kin and lawyers found no history of him before he immigrated to the United States in the late nineteen forties.

He was followed by one hundred and fifty other elderly persons of Germanic origin spread throughout the world, many in the new, united Deutschland. There were too many liberal attitudes in the world to oppose the showcase trials and successful executions such as had been staged for Adolf Eichmann. Quick and positive results were authorized. Three Swiss banks in Geneva were bombed and information found its way into newspapers disclosing account numbers and quantities of gold which had been deposited in them by fleeing Nazis. The banks went out of business.

A series of attacks were made on real and suspected terrorist training camps throughout the world. A multinational committee sat in constant session to approve authorization. The world was angry enough that little justification was required. Beyond the knowledge of the committee, many nations exercised their own covert sanctions against terrorists.

Hans Lankow, a prominent West German surgeon, was found dead on his wooded estate, victim of an apparent self-inflicted shooting accident. Wilhelm Streicher had disappeared. His Hamburg company had been sold off and most of his assets had been transferred to offshore banks. The German authorities managed to seize over five million Deutschmarks before running out of clues as to his whereabouts. Since he was not part of the American conspiracy and had no reason to know about anything else but the gold, there was no apparent reason to pursue him further. Raymond and Astrid were able to corroborate his interest was in the gold alone. Astrid further added that El Jefe claimed to have had Streicher killed. In view of the embarrassing ramifications of exposure, the German government decided to bury Streicher's involvement.

10th August. New York City.

Two weeks after the official termination of New York's curfew, the hospitals began to get back to normal. Their first priority was to discharge as many patients as they could. There were many people lingering with symptoms of the epidemic and many would never recover fully. Permanent but partial paralysis, for many, was a cheap price to the alternative. Records of victims were chaotic. Newspapers listed the dead who had been identified and each hospital posted long printed lists in their lobbies. Once the fear of mingling in public was over, these institutions were crowded with desperate relatives, seeking the missing.

2100 hrs. 11th August 1990. Wadi al Kebec el-Zendre, Libya.

El-Saeed had learned of the devastating attacks on friends and allies. He had fled through Canada to his Libyan refuge, haunted by the apparent failure, fearing reprisal. It was dark outside now and secure in his bedding, naked and comfortable after a half bottle of Glenfiddich whiskey, he pulled back the covers and grunted at the woman, waving at his slack manhood. She hesitated, receiving a slap for her apparent resistance. Throwing back the shoulder of her robe, she bent over him, feigning compliance. She hoped in her deepest heart that the risk she had taken in getting on the satellite phone and passing co-ordinates may pay off, but could not know. Just as her face hovered over his fat hairy belly, there came the faintest whisper of sound high over the desert.

Already three miles downrange, the F-117 Stealth fighter-bomber kept its laser guidance system focussed on the Wadi, guiding a five hundred pound JDAM multipurpose bomb onto its target. The bomblets and flechettes it contained would kill every living thing within sixty metres of the air burst.

1530 hrs. 18th August 1990. Auxiliary hospital facility, New York City.

A young woman was examined and found fit for discharge. Bureaucracy had caught up with essential need and she was found to have no record of medical insurance, no ability to pay, nor other means, even basic identification. Originally known as Thirty-five, July Twenty, Sixteen Hundred, because of the place and date-time she had been admitted, she had later volunteered her name as Wanda Smith. Heavily drugged to counter the spasmodic seizures and paralysis of her left limbs, her apparent state of amnesia regarding her origin and relatives went without remark in the chaos. She was, by her accent, British, so when the hospital went to discharge her, she was interviewed by a female U.S. Immigration officer.

The ex-patient's dilemma was in not wanting to reveal her true identity for fear of immediate arrest. Not knowing the fate of her friends, she was loath to open any avenue of inquiry. The problem for the Immigration officer was in establishing her point of entry, and, the officer suspected intuitively, learning her true identity. The solution was not hard.

"Wantage four one six two," the voice was familiar and old, the archaic British form of answering the telephone somehow comforting.

"Hello, Mummy, it's me."

At the other end of the line, Mandy's mother collapsed to the floor.

There came muffled responses and rattles, and then another voice came on the line. "Hello...Who *is* this?"

"Raymond, you fucking arsehole! What are you doing over *there*?"

They both cried.

0800 hrs. 19th August 1990. London, England.

Wishing to ensure immunity from any further action, Raymond had previously made contact with the British Secret Intelligence Service, using some old contacts. In exchange for full disclosure of his knowledge of events, he had extracted a promise of an interview with the top person at Century House.

The interview had actually been held in a Soho restaurant, with two men. The younger one of the two had been the spokesman, the other, a hugely fat and apparently innocuous assistant making only occasional input. At the end, the younger one had declared *in official terms* that Raymond and Astrid were off the hook concerning any kind of prosecution, or other clandestine attention. Raymond had also enlisted their aid in tracing the fate of Mandy, but held little faith.

Now, he phoned the number they had given him. Never having been fooled by the restaurant charade, Raymond immediately recognized the voice of the fat, older man on the other end. Quickly, he outlined the situation. Within an hour, a British Embassy official arrived at the New York hospital, guaranteeing to the U.S. Immigration Officer that *Miss Smith* would be returned to the United Kingdom immediately, courtesy Her Majesty's Government.

Mandy's information concerning how the computers at the NYSE had been fooled by resetting the execute date was invaluable in re-establishing normal business throughout the world. She in turn was dismayed that Dennis Piercy had been one of the victims and was quick to relate his heroism to the U.S. authorities.

1400 hrs. 21st September, 1990. Far away.

High above the still waters of Okanagan Lake in Canada, Gerhardt Demmler reached for the glass of chilled white wine beside his lounger. It was the best they had produced yet in his vineyard since he had purchased it in the late nineteen sixties.

The hot sun and dry climate was perfect to prevent the dull ache of his left arm and he felt happy and relaxed here. It was certainly better than the North Sea air he had lived with in Europe. The winery was extremely profitable and if he needed any more money, then he merely had to go and dig up some more of the gold that he had buried nearby. The lumber mill, trucking-line and his other investments were all flourishing and he looked forward to relaxing for his final years.

A little over seventy years old, he was still physically active and enjoying good sex. Over the years, he had favoured liaisons with buxom blondes and now was no different, although more permanent. He glanced over at the woman nearby, lounging in a tiny yellow bikini, her large breasts barely restrained by the fabric. His wife was very beautiful and very smart, he reflected.

The physical bruises were all gone and she was finally learning to cope with the mental stresses of her ordeal. Mutual secrets initiated their bond, but mutual affection had cemented it. He had tracked her down soon after she left New York and he had carefully avoided any reference to his complicity in her kidnapping by El Jefe. Despite his love for her, he knew he could never disclose the true facts. It had been suffice to explain his own fortuitous escape from death. Since she had reported him as dead, it ensured that the authorities, or anyone else, would not be looking for him.

Her hair was growing back to the full mane of white-blonde he so treasured. Like him, she had escaped most of the publicity concerning their adventures, largely because of media suppression by various governments. Part of her price of being here had been to cut in two friends of theirs into the gold he had buried but he did not begrudge that, after all, there was plenty for each and they had, after all, helped return it into his hands.

So finally, life was good.

Golden Quest is John Warner's second published novel.
He is a history buff who enjoys writing thought-provoking novels.
He lives in Airdrie, Alberta with his wife, Laura.
ilthyn@shaw.ca